# THREE LESSONS IN SEDUCTION

## SOFIE DARLING

SOUL MATE PUBLISHING

New York

THREE LESSONS IN SEDUCTION

Copyright©2017

SOFIE DARLING

Cover Design by Anna Lena-Spies

Published in the United States of America by
Soul Mate Publishing
P.O. Box 24
Macedon, New York, 14502

ISBN: 978-1-68291-532-5

ebook ISBN: 978-1-68291-512-7

www.SoulMatePublishing.com

The publisher does not have any control over and does not assume any responsibility for author or third-party websites or their content.

*To Eric, my love.*

# Acknowledgements

This book is a dream made reality with the help of some very special people.

Thank you to the wonderful people at Soul Mate Publishing. For giving me the opportunity. For guiding me every step of the way.

Thank you to Caroline Tolley. For believing in my work. For your insight and thoroughness.

Thank you to Elizabeth Harris, Sandra Spicher, Dunya Bean, Elizabeth Schultz, Karen Davidson, Julia Lee, Katie Graykowski, Brooke Salesky, and Kate Ramirez. For your wisdom, inspiration, and talent.

Thank you to Pam Halter, Debi Phillpott, Robin Selman, and Diane Guccione. For your unwavering friendship and support.

Thank you to Liana Lefey and Sherry Thomas. For your good advice.

Thank you to Bosco. For your loyalty, laziness, and companionship.

Thank you to Max and Nate. For your love and light. For being you.

Thank you, Eric. It all begins and ends with you.

# Chapter 1

*Married: Persons chained or handcuffed together, in order to be conveyed to gaol, or on board the lighters for transportation, are in the cant language said to be married together.*

*A Classical Dictionary of the Vulgar Tongue*
Francis Grose

*Paris*
*12 September 1824*

Nick spotted her across the cavernous expanse of La Grande Salle, and the breath froze in his chest. There would be trouble.

From his shadowed position inside the opera box opposite hers, he could easily pretend she was just another sophisticated Parisienne. After all, he couldn't see her face as she made conversation to her right.

Except he didn't need to see her face. Her profile, limned in the soft glow of gas lamps, was enough for the heavy thrum of recognition to flood him with both a dread and a thrill that had excited him from the first moment he'd laid eyes on her more than a decade ago.

Why was she in Paris?

As if in response to his unspoken question, she canted her head to the side and froze as if she sensed something unusual, or was it someone unusual? He stepped deeper into shadow. Her gaze shifted sideways and unerringly found the exact spot he'd occupied no more than a trio of seconds ago.

He resisted the urge to run frustrated hands through newly shorn hair. She might have caught a flash of him. He couldn't be sure.

*Blast.* Why was she here?

She was here for him. The thought sank in, and horror unfolded within him. Deep down, he'd known this day would come—the day she would enter his shadowy world.

For one thing, he was missing, or was he dead? Or maybe he was on a trip to Italy. No one could say with certainty. And he preferred it that way until he discovered who had sent two men to attack him in his hotel suite a fortnight ago.

The woman was more than trouble. She was a threat to half-formed plans that were barely treading water as it was. Ignoring her presence in Paris wasn't an option. If she was here for him—and she was without a doubt—she would find him. She was that sort of woman. She didn't fade into the background when it was convenient for others that she do so. In fact, she only responded by foregrounding herself further.

He must find a way to seize control of the situation before it spiraled away from him, as situations tended to do around her. If she'd caught a glimpse of him, perhaps he could use to his advantage the curiosity such a sighting would stir within her.

She must be handled, and this ran him square into the second reason there would be trouble: she was his wife. If one person in Paris could best him, it was Mariana.

~ ~ ~

"*Ma chérie,*" Mariana heard this as if from a great distance. "To sit in La Grande Salle is a privilege and a joy. Settle and experience it. You have *les fourmis.*"

"*Les fourmis?*" Mariana's French didn't extend beyond the schoolroom basics of *bonjours* and *adieus.*

"Zee ants. You sit like ants are crawling against your skin," explained Helene de Vivonne, her mother's dearest childhood friend. "I lived in London during *la Terreur*. Have you forgotten? Everything is rush-rush. Tick one item off your list, so you can complete the next. Posthaste, you English say. This is not the French way." The older woman pulled Mariana close. "Savor the night, *ma chérie*. London has nothing on Paris."

Possessed with the attention span of a butterfly, Helene released her hold on Mariana and turned to her other neighbor, leaving Mariana alone to take in the crowded room.

From the ornate ceiling frescoes illuminated by a magnificent cut-glass, ormolu chandelier, and the parquet floor cushioned by dense Persian carpets, to Society's glittering *monsieurs*, *madames*, and *mademoiselles* in between, La Grande Salle was nothing short of sumptuous, the sparkling epicenter of Parisian Society. Inside this spectacularly gilded room, one could forget Paris had been in shambles not so long ago. This room could tempt one into pretending that the Revolution had never happened, and that it was only a wicked night terror revealed to be without substance in the warm glow of morning sunshine.

It was within this world that her husband had spent the better part of the last decade. Oh, Nick . . .

She slipped the note from her reticule and fingered its newly worn edges. She'd looked at it so often these last three days, she could quote its contents from memory:

*9 September 1824*
*To the most esteemed Lady Nicholas Asquith:*
*It is with great and solemn regret that we inform you that your husband, Lord Nicholas Asquith, younger son of the Marquess of Clare, is missing, presumed dead in the service of his King and Country. He was last seen in Paris on 30 August. Please accept our most profound and sincere condolences to you and your family.*

Unable to comprehend the subtleties contained within the note at once, Mariana had sprung into a course of action regarding its more concrete elements. Namely, she would hasten to Paris and find her estranged husband—either dead or alive.

First, she'd seen to the care of the twins. Her sister, Olivia, took Lavinia with few questions asked, and Geoffrey would remain at school in Westminster.

She couldn't get Geoffrey's solemn, intelligent, ten-year-old eyes out of her mind. He'd known that something was wrong. "Tell me again why you're leaving in such a hurry?" he asked as if she hadn't already explained herself twice.

"I'm visiting your father in Paris. It will be a holiday."

"You never visit Father in Paris." His head had cocked to the side. "Or take holidays, for that matter."

"There's a first time for everything," she'd said, bright and shrill.

Geoffrey's eyes had only narrowed.

Even so, he, like Lavinia, had agreed to post an express letter to Helene's Paris address every single day. With the possibility their world had been irrevocably turned upside-down looming over their heads, Mariana needed to know her children were safe while she searched for their father—their missing, presumed dead father.

Next, she'd rushed from London to Margate. There she'd used a combination of desperation and gold to convince a reluctant Captain Nylander to transport her across the Channel in his East Indiaman. He was set to sail to East Asia within hours, and a quick side trip to Calais would be nothing to him. From Calais, she'd hired a coach, paid the driver twice his usual fee, and rode on to Paris.

If Nick proved to be alive, she would leave him where she found him and return home.

For a decade now, they'd been living the perfect facsimile of a Society marriage where they saw each other at arranged times of year—Christmas, Easter, birthdays—for the benefit of Geoffrey and Lavinia. Not ten words passed between them a year, and the children likely never noticed. It was the sort of marriage not uncommon to their social set, and it was not at all the sort of marriage she'd envisioned when she'd fallen head over heels in love with him.

She gave her head a tiny, clearing shake. That dream had been crushed years ago, a lifetime really. A better use of her time would be to focus on the present. If Nick proved to be dead, she would transport his body to London. At the very least, she owed the twins their father's decent burial at home.

Familiar panic rose, and the ground beneath her feet threatened to crater and give way. She wasn't certain what lay below, but she suspected it was a bottomless abyss from which she would never claw her way out. Even though she saw him no more than every few months, a world without Nick in it was too much for her brain to comprehend.

It simply couldn't be, and it simply was not. A force, intangible and mysterious, connected her to Nick. She would sense his absence if he'd left this world for the next. Except . . .

What if she couldn't? And he was dead? The doubt crept in and threatened to split wide into the unfathomable chasm of her nightmares, but she refused to consider that outcome.

Hands clenched into fists at her sides, a steadying wave of determination steeled her. It simply couldn't be. It simply wasn't. She would find him and prove it—for the children, and, yes, for herself. She could admit that much.

The playful rap of a silk fan across her knuckles snapped her back into the present. Helene leaned in. "I take it the tall drink of Viking water is no longer in Paris?"

Mariana quashed a sigh and replied, "He left soon after escorting me to Nick's hotel."

Helene shrugged a Gallic shoulder. "His loss," she said, returning her attention to her other neighbor.

Escorted all the way to Paris by the imposing Nylander—it was true the man resembled nothing other than a Viking in both bearing and temperament—Mariana's first order of business on her arrival yesterday had been to place herself on Helene's doorstep. Within the hour, Mariana and Nylander had followed Helene's directions to Nick's hotel in the Place Vendôme.

"I believe this is where we part ways," Mariana had said to Nylander, her tone purposeful and businesslike. "I'm not certain you needed to escort me *all* the way here."

She'd darted a covert glance at the captain. He was the sort of man who could give an unhappily, even happily, married woman ideas. Even though she was here for Nick, Mariana saw how easily she could pivot and pursue a different path. She could invite this gorgeous man into her suite of rooms. She didn't owe Nick fidelity, especially after what he'd done.

"Shall I escort you inside?" Nylander asked in a low rumble.

For a long moment, she met eyes the blue of a midsummer sky. "I think not."

"I shall be in Calais for a fortnight to have a few repairs done to the *Fortuyn*. Contact me at Le Blanc Navire if you need further assistance." Without another word, he pivoted and strode down the crowded sidewalk as casual passersby parted for him like the Red Sea.

Mariana found herself the lone occupant of Nick's set of rooms, which once picked apart inch by inch, yielded no clues as to his whereabouts or fate, an outcome at once wildly frustrating and oddly comforting. She didn't know he was alive, but she didn't know he was dead either. The man was nowhere.

Mariana worried the note between her fingers. Over the last few days, its texture had become as soft and supple as cloth. Yet, she kept it close for a reason: this note defied all logic. It was impossible to square with the dissolute life Nick led in Paris. Although the note was unsigned, it had originated from the Foreign Office.

How in the course of largely *ceremonial consular duties*—Nick's words—did one become missing and presumed dead in the eyes of Whitehall? She intended to ask Nick if she found him . . . No, *when* she found him.

"Mariana?" came Helene's voice.

As Mariana turned to reply, the fine hairs on her arms stood on end, and she hesitated. Her eyes darted left, toward the source of the feeling, but she found no one she recognized.

Heart pounding, she whispered, "Helene, may I use your opera glass?"

Helene raised a single eyebrow and handed the object over.

Mariana held the glass to her eyes and . . . saw nothing useful. Her overwrought mind was playing tricks on her. A phantom husband was the stuff of novels full of whimsy and scandal, not the stuff of real life.

The glow of the theater's lights dimmed, and the roar of the assembled dulled to a low rumble. The ballet was set to begin. All eyes shifted their focus away from the drama of each other and toward the impending drama to be enacted on the stage.

All, except Mariana. She couldn't succumb to the sugar-coated fantasy of the ballet. In an effort to relax, she exhaled every last bit of breath in her lungs and inhaled a slow, steady stream of air. But it was to no avail. Her heart a relentless tattoo in her chest, the walls of the theater threatened to close in on her.

She shot to her feet. "Helene, I need some fresh air."

Without a care for the other woman's response, Mariana darted out of the dark box and into a bright, empty corridor. Finally, blessedly alone, the walls expanded, and a self-conscious smile pulled at her lips. She was in danger of becoming the sort of excitable woman who tested her patience within thirty seconds of conversation. It was no state in which to conduct one's life. A restorative visit to a museum would do her a bit of good. Perhaps the Museum of Natural History . . .

An inconspicuous door flew open, and a hand shot out, closing around her upper arm with the strength of a steel vise. A scream caught in her throat as she was dragged into a pitch-black room, the door snapping shut behind her. Her heart hammered in her chest as if it was trying to break free of her body, and her mind raced in time with its frenetic rhythm.

Before another scream could gather in her chest, a leather-gloved hand clamped over her mouth, and an arm reached across her torso, trapping her arms to her sides and pulling her tight against a solid, muscular chest. She struggled, twisted, wiggled, and stomped—everything she could think of to free herself. But nothing succeeded, and her breath continued coming hard and fast through her nose.

It wasn't until her body stilled in frustrated exhaustion that she inhaled and *smelled*. Located in the scent surrounding her were notes she recognized—notes specific to one man. It was the scent of . . .

"Can I trust you not to scream?"

It was the voice of a dead man.

# Chapter 2

*Suds: In the suds; in trouble, in a disagreeable situation, or involved in some difficulty.*

*A Classical Dictionary of the Vulgar Tongue*
Francis Grose

Or, more accurately, it was the voice of a missing, and presumed dead, man.

Mariana gave a single, assenting nod.

One arm maintained its restrictive hold across her body, even as his other hand loosened its grip over her mouth. That hand hovered, just a whisper of a touch on her skin, so lightly she could speak if she wanted.

It occurred to her that she and her husband hadn't touched in ten years, just as another tension coiled in her body. But it was one not born of fear, it was more basic than fear. This was a primordial response, one specific to them. Did he feel it, too?

Once she'd been so sure he did. She'd been too sure. Of course, that was when she'd thought she was worth something to him.

A subtle arch of her back would reveal his desire, or lack thereof, even through several layers of silk skirts . . .

Every muscle in her body aligned in a rigid *no*. She wouldn't stoop to that level.

She cleared her throat, the sound a short, muffled scrape against the back of her throat. It achieved its intended effect when his hands fell away as if shocked into a similar realization. He stepped back, and her body swayed, suddenly too free. She heard the key turn in a lantern, and the dark transformed into dim, flickering light. She leaned forward to steady herself against a shelf of what appeared to be rags and various scrubbing implements.

Her blood rioted through her veins on a single emotion: relief. She could come apart with the ferocity of the feeling, but she wouldn't. At least, she wouldn't in front of him, not even in the near dark.

Nick was alive.

"I knew you would come looking for me."

Annoyed by his cheek, she whirled around and assessed the long, shadowy length of him dressed in unrelieved black. "Why are you dressed as a waiter?" she retorted. "And why do you have a beard?" She wouldn't mention that it was a sin against nature to obscure the strong line of his jaw and the subtle cleft of his chin.

His eyes, the gray of an overcast sea, met hers, and his head canted to the side, an arrogant angle to his right eyebrow. "It's better that you don't know."

Mariana resisted the temptation to reach out and slap that ridiculous beard off his face. Instead, she summoned the righteous indignation that had served her well over years of dealing with this man. "I received a message that you were missing and presumed dead, so I came to Paris to retrieve your dead body. To state the matter plainly, these past two days have been gruesome."

He leaned an indolent shoulder against the wall and crossed his arms, intending to put her on the defensive.

And, as she continued, it worked. "Have you ever experienced the pleasure of scouring the sick beds of La Salpêtriere for a missing, presumed dead, man?"

A slow, insufferable shake of his head was all the response he gave.

"Well, it's possible that I've conferred with every doctor and nurse in Paris, and every prostitute, too."

Amusement danced in Nick's eyes.

"And the stench." She couldn't control a shiver of disgust. "Well, we won't discuss the stench. Except to say, while we're on the subject of stench"—She couldn't seem to stem the flow of words, now that she'd gotten started— "have you enjoyed a trip to the morgue along the Quai du Marché-Neuf?"

"That particular pleasure, I *have* experienced."

"But not as a dead man, I assured myself earlier today. With bodies laid shoulder to shoulder like sardines in a tin, a more wretched place on earth I can't imagine."

"It was an *abattoir* before it was converted into a morgue," Nick stated, his tone that of a supercilious popinjay. She'd known this persona well over the last ten years. But it hadn't always been so . . .

She cleared her throat. "By my estimation, it never ceased being a butcher shop."

"Are you finished?"

Mariana's cheeks flamed, hot and mortified, and her mouth snapped shut. She'd been scolding him like a fishwife.

"Now," he continued, "I'm certain the letter you received was nothing more than a mere prank."

"*A mere prank?*" Mariana asked, unable to believe her ears. She swung around. She couldn't bear to look at him a moment longer. "*Foreign Office* was scribbled as the return address."

"Was it signed?"

"No."

A particular note sounded in his voice, a fine mixture of concern and curiosity she might have missed had she been facing him. Nick tended to overload her senses when she took him in all at once. His subtle, but commanding, physical presence . . . his overwhelming handsomeness . . . his direct gaze that held too many secrets, both his and hers . . . all sparked too much curiosity within her.

He was safer experienced one sense at a time, because only then could she see through the layers of deceit to ferret out the truth. And there was definitely a truth at the heart of his response.

"You must leave Paris," he stated, low and hard, his voice unaffected and real. Gone was the supercilious popinjay. This was Nick's true voice speaking.

"I must?" she bristled.

"You've accomplished what you set out to do."

"Which was?"

"To find me. It's time for you to go."

She swiveled around to face him. "I may make a holiday of Paris."

Now that Nick was safe and sound—well, *safe* might be a stretch—she could resume her long-established habit of opposing him when given half a chance. It was the only delight she'd derived from him in the last ten years, albeit a mean one.

"Everyone goes on at length about the shopping to be found in Paris these days."

"You find no pleasure in shopping, Mariana."

The assuredness of his words stopped her cold as a hot fury flared within her. "And what do you know about what does and doesn't give me pleasure? It has been over ten years since we . . ." She stopped herself mid-sentence. No good could come of speaking aloud what they hadn't done in ten years. "Parted ways."

Although separated by a distance of no more than five feet, a chasm the breadth and depth of the Atlantic Ocean expanded between them. It was a distance impossible to bridge, especially after his affair.

She cleared her throat—tight with emotion. "What have you been doing on the Continent all these years? Somehow I don't think it's *ceremonial consular duties*."

"Have you really not puzzled it out?" He raised his brows, speculation in his eyes. "I collect information for the Foreign Office."

"Collect information?" Mariana repeated. "That's almost as vague as ceremonial consular duties."

A charged silence stretched between them before Nick broke it. "If I tell you, will you promise to leave Paris immediately?"

"Why would I promise you anything?"

"Mariana."

"I promise to *consider* leaving."

A frustrated, sibilant breath sounded through his teeth. "Put bluntly, I'm a spy."

A short burst of baffled confusion transformed into rattled shock. "A spy?" she asked in a low hush. She'd been a willful fool all these years. She'd seen what she wanted to see in the man who had broken her heart: a frivolous dilettante.

But the Nick standing before her—whoever *he* was— was the real Nick. He was a collector of information for the Foreign Office. Nick was a *spy*. Obfuscatory beard and unfashionably shorn hair were all part of a role he played.

"Mariana, you've no idea what you're dabbling in."

"You still think of me as that eighteen-year-old girl, don't you?" she asked, bitterness twisting every word. She hated her inability to hide it from him. "The one so amenable to your wishes and requests?"

A wry smile curved his beautifully formed lips. These were the same firm, full lips that had ravished every inch of her during their short-lived union. He pushed off the wall and strode to the door. "I wouldn't dream of charactcrizing you as amenable."

She resisted the impulse toward distraction. Their past had no place in the present. "Why did I receive the note?" she pressed.

He paused and slid his gaze toward her. Her breath arrested in her lungs. He still possessed the power to stun and captivate her with a single glance.

"I shall fix this," he said as familiar, distancing reserve returned to his demeanor. "There is no reason to involve you."

With those parting words, he was out of the door. And out of her life for all she knew.

She slumped against a wall of shelving. She'd forgotten how devastating he could be, and how he could slice her open with a few words.

*There is no reason to involve you.*

No seven words better encapsulated the story of their marriage.

Rather than allow herself to become bogged down in emotion best left to the past, she stiffened her spine and focused on the present. She had experience in moving beyond a devastating moment: place one foot in front of the other and aim for a destination. In this case, Helene's box would do. Yet, as her feet carried her forward, a pair of refrains circled her brain like a whirlwind:

*Nick is alive. Nick is a spy.*

A statement of relief and truth: *Nick is alive.* A statement of bewilderment and intrigue: *Nick is a spy.* The clues had been before her the entire time she'd known him. Of course, Nick was a spy.

Within a matter of minutes—minutes which bore no resemblance to the steady tick-tock of time, given the torrent of conflicting thoughts and emotions that continued to swirl about her brain—she resumed her seat beside Helene.

"Did the air refresh you?" Helene whispered.

A quick, affirmative nod was Mariana's response. Her unseeing eyes were fixed on the drama playing out on the stage, even as she attempted to comprehend the drama just behind her.

Nick was alive, at least, as of five minutes ago, and she was free to pick up her life where she'd left it. London was little more than a boat ride away.

A subtle nudge of Helene's shoulder drew Mariana's attention. "*Ma chérie*," came Helene's delighted whisper, "you have an admirer."

As she brought Helene's proffered glass to her face and followed the direction of Helene's twinkling gaze, her heart banged out a hard thump in her chest. Was it possible that it could be . . .

Disappointment shot through her.

The wrong man returned her gaze. He inclined his head in a shallow nod, and his eyes shifted away.

"He may not be perfect," Helene murmured *sotto voce*, "but a flirtation with a most eligible younger man is refreshment for the soul, *non*?"

Mariana released a sigh and allowed the glass to fall to her lap.

"Why not?" Helene pressed, misinterpreting the cause of Mariana's pique. "The state of your marriage is no secret on either side of the Channel, *ma chérie*."

Vexed, Mariana averted her gaze toward the stage and focused on an unremarkable point in the middle distance. It was true: the state of her and Nick's marriage had become open for public speculation when his affair with an opera singer was splashed across every gossip rag in London ten years ago. With little recourse available to her—Parliament wasn't likely to allow her to divorce a husband who had only behaved like every other Society husband—she'd accepted that she would have the sort of marriage she'd vowed never to have: loveless and detached.

She'd anticipated a different sort of marriage with Nick, one rooted in love. But, in the end, that feeling had been hers alone.

A crowd of unfamiliar faces formed a continuous blur before and below her. By sheer accident, she caught the eyes of her young admirer. Something about him struck a flat note. His countenance held no hint of the playful or sensual. There was no promise of future delights should she choose him. A word came to her: *solemn*. Who ever heard of a *solemn* admirer?

Upon further reflection, solemn wasn't quite on the mark. His regard registered as deeper, more soulful, like a Parisian Lord Byron. In fact, this man's entire being spoke of the Romantic ideal: luminous brown eyes; dark curly locks; a general brooding air that belonged to a set of Mariana's peers for whom she never had an ounce of patience.

Still, he was handsome. And he was young.

Too handsome and too young.

What a night this was turning out to be.

She swung her attention back toward the stage and forced herself to concentrate for the rest of the performance. Part of the ballet's allure, aside from its breathless beauty, was its order and synchronicity. If everyone hit their marks, it flowed with a precision missing from life outside these walls. For the duration of the performance, she was allowed the fantasy that an ordered life was possible.

All too soon, the ballet ended, and reality—and disorder—was allowed to prevail once again.

*Nick is alive. Nick is a spy.*

Possessed of the proportions of a sturdy, little bullfinch, Helene took Mariana's hand and pulled her up. Times like these reminded Mariana how very much taller she was than other women. Not that she'd ever minded. She rather liked that she could see across a crowd on her flat feet.

Helene began guiding her through various groupings of Society acquaintances. Numb to it all, Mariana stepped through the motions of introductions and small chit-chat. She wouldn't remember a single person from this night.

Courtesies observed, Helene led Mariana down a dark and crowded corridor that spilled into a high-ceilinged room stripped of all decoration. It appeared to be a rehearsal studio with mirrors lining two adjacent walls and ballet barres bisecting all four walls.

"What is this place?" Mariana asked. She couldn't help feeling displaced, yet invigorated by an effervescence infusing the room's atmosphere.

"This is the Foyer de la Danse," Helene replied. "A select number of patrons have the opportunity to associate with the dancers after the performance."

Mariana observed the dynamics of the room. In England, dancers were regarded as little better than common prostitutes, and they were treated as such. Aristocratic Londoners kept every part of their lives distinct: their virtues located in Mayfair and Belgravia; their vices in Southwark and Whitechapel. The English didn't mix virtue and vice in the same neighborhood, much less in the same room.

Here, some patrons patiently watched the ballet dancers mingle with the crowd, while others seized the opportunity to engage the dancers and try their luck. In all, it was high and low, heavenly and sordid, an odd and conflicting atmosphere, and so very Parisian.

"I believe," Mariana observed, "you and I are the only two females not wearing tights and tulle."

A pleased giggle escaped Helene. "*Ma chérie*, I would never see my husband, the Marquis, if I didn't step inside this room from time to time."

Mariana couldn't summon a carefree rejoinder. She hadn't been so sanguine when it had come to her own husband's abandonment.

From the corner of her eye, she noticed a figure clad in evening black approaching. It was her admirer. Better to have this introduction over and done. Solemnly—again that word—the man bowed before her and Helene.

"Isn't this perfect," Helene stated rather than asked as she held out her hand to be kissed. "Lady Nicholas Asquith, may I introduce Lucien Capet, the Comte de Villefranche and heir to the Marquis de Touraine, to you?"

Mariana acquiesced to the request with a nod of her head and allowed the young Comte to take her hand. As his lips brushed the back of her gloved fingers, she braced herself for the suggestive eye contact that would inevitably follow when he straightened.

The inevitable didn't come to pass. In fact, his dark eyes barely glanced her way, hardly knowing where to rest as they darted from her to Helene, to coffered ceilings, back to her and Helene, and finally to his feet. Mariana was dizzy watching him.

This young man didn't seem to have the slightest understanding of the role he was attempting to play. This was no worldly French suitor with a trail of conquests in his wake. He was the very opposite.

"If you will allow me," he began, a callow crack in his voice, "I would be your escort for the evening. The Foyer can be a scandalous place for unescorted *mesdames*."

"Scandal?" Mariana asked, both bemused and irritated. "How very"—Oh, what was the perfect word?—"stimulating."

"Too much stimulation is not good for the delicate constitutions of . . ."

"*Mesdames*?" Mariana finished for him, warming to the subject. "My dear Comte, I understand that you are young and do not yet possess a working understanding of *mesdames*, but I can assure you that we—"

"We would be delighted to accept your company, Villefranche," Helene interrupted, smoothly shushing Mariana in the process.

Mariana bit back the rest of her sentence and acceded.

Three abreast, with Mariana in the middle, they began their turn about the room.

They had taken no more than two steps when a dancer approached and stopped before them, a playful light in her eyes. With careful precision, she positioned her arms and feet before performing a series of flawless pirouettes. She was the picture of grace and beauty. A delighted Helene clapped her hands.

After the dancer flounced away to perform for another group of patrons, Mariana turned toward the young Comte at her side. It would be rude to stay silent. "Do you frequent the Foyer?"

"*Non*," Villefranche replied, "it is not to my taste."

Her head canted to the side. "Yet you are here."

"There are times when a man must act outside his true inclinations," he replied, one word following the next in a passionate staccato.

Taken aback by his fervor, she asked, "And why would the son of a marquis ever have to act outside his true inclinations?"

Twin patches of scarlet brightened the young Comte's cheeks, and he glanced away. If she'd known him better, she might hazard a guess that he was flustered.

Unaware of the curious exchange, Helene continued greeting passersby as they progressed through the room.

Villefranche asked, "Have you yet shopped in the Palais-Royal?"

Mariana suppressed a surprised laugh at this conversational turn. This night grew stranger by the moment. "*Non*," she replied, disinterest rounding out the single syllable. Nick had been correct about one thing: she derived no pleasure from shopping.

"I shall escort you on the morrow if you like," Villefranche replied . . . solemnly.

Before Mariana could form a polite refusal, Helene nudged her. "Oh, *ma chérie*, you must experience the Palais-Royal before you leave Paris."

No other option available, Mariana replied, "I shall think on it."

She wouldn't, of course. She only entered shops out of necessity and with a clear objective. She couldn't think of a bigger waste of time than an aimless perusal of random wares for sale.

Villefranche leaned forward and caught Helene's eye. "You could join us for propriety's sake?"

Helene's eyebrows lifted. "I am fairly certain I have a previous engagement."

Mariana suppressed a smile. Helene would take great offense at the very suggestion that she was old enough to play chaperone to a woman of thirty years.

"In that case," Villefranche continued, "Lady Nicholas, I shall send a messenger for your definite reply on the morrow."

Without further preamble, the young Comte dipped in a shallow bow before pivoting on one foot and hastening through the arched doorway.

A short, astonished silence followed. "A shame his beauty is wasted on such a dull humor," Helene said on a wistful note. "I can't say I envy you your shopping excursion."

Mariana nodded in polite agreement and looked out across the room. Her eyes snagged upon a fleeting, and eerily familiar, figure. It wasn't Nick, but if she didn't know better, she would have thought she'd caught a glimpse of . . . Percy. He'd carried himself with a distinctive angularity.

She blinked, and the phantom was gone. Ridiculous. Percy had been dead these last eleven years. Two witnesses had testified to seeing him cut down at the Battle of Maya and buried in an unmarked grave. Just because Mariana's own husband had risen from the grave tonight didn't mean Olivia's had, too. Plenty of men were angular.

She must leave Paris. But not for Nick. She must leave Paris for herself. Any oblique dangers he might have referenced tonight were insignificant compared to the very real danger she presented herself.

Her marriage to Nick only operated smoothly if neither of them actively engaged with the other, maintaining parallel existences that intersected at appointed times. Yet her actions of the past few days had strayed off course and into Nick's territory.

While it had been necessary to find him and confirm he remained amongst the living, the matter was now resolved. Yet a pair of questions would quietly persist: When had he become a spy? And why was he missing and presumed dead to the Foreign Office?

She exhaled a forceful breath, attempting to release the questions from her mind. One thing was certain: this wasn't her mystery to solve, no matter how her curiosity would protest the opposite. She would leave Paris and her unanswered questions behind at dawn.

Nick's business was no business of hers. This was a refrain she would do well to repeat until she'd put a large body of water between herself and this new Nick who intrigued her all too much.

# Chapter 3

*Conundrums: Enigmatical conceits.*

*A Classical Dictionary of the Vulgar Tongue*
Francis Grose

"I can see myself to my suite from here." Mariana slipped a coin into the errand boy's hand. Eyes greedy and wide, he ducked a quick nod before skipping down the hotel stairs, coin clutched tight in his fist.

She considered the dim, narrow corridor before her and the set of rooms at its end, determined not to succumb to the weariness that had replaced the initial rush of relief at Nick's continued hold on his mortal coil. He was alive, and she and her newfound lady's maid, Hortense, had a night of packing ahead of them.

After all, she repeated to herself, she had a life to preserve in London: her children, her household, and The Progressive School for Young Ladies and the Education of Their Minds, the school she and Olivia founded a few years ago. Of course, Geoffrey and Lavinia were taken care of; her household lay in the capable hands of servants accustomed to the sporadic and prolonged absences of their employers; and the formidable Mrs. Bloomquist ran the school according to her own high and exacting standards. In all honesty, she would have to be absent from her life far longer than a few days before she would be missed. Sobering thought.

She slid her key into the door lock and twisted the handle. She was halfway across the threshold when she froze mid-step. Every lamp and candle in the sitting room was ablaze, illuminating Nick's rangy form sprawled across a peacock blue dupioni silk settee, an idle ankle balanced atop a muscular thigh. He lowered the book he was reading and silently regarded her as if she was the interloper. His ease with the situation set her teeth on edge.

"Your beard is gone." Her first observation was cool, steady, and at complete odds with the tumult she felt to her very core. "And your clothes . . . Now you look like a newly released prisoner."

"That was the idea."

She wouldn't mention how the short crop of his hair suited him as it framed the strong angles of his face and the thick, black lashes encircling his piercing gray eyes. As the flickering light cast his features in light and relief, it was a fact that he was unbelievably handsome. Not only handsome—it was too thin a word for him—but unbelievably appealing. Nick was the sort of man who drew women without an ounce of effort, no matter the length of his hair or the quality of his clothing.

She tore her eyes away, dropped her reticule onto the nearest table, and pushed the door shut with her shoulder. She pressed her back against it on the slender hope that her quivering legs would firm up soon. They weren't quite ready to move toward the sitting area . . . toward Nick.

He held up the book in his hands. "Interesting reading selection."

The book would be *that* book. A betraying blush flared to the surface, and, like a green schoolgirl, Mariana rushed to explain herself. "In my haste to depart London, I mistook it for another book and tossed it into my bag."

Nick's brows lifted in bemusement. "Is that so?" He opened the book. "I see from this dog ear that you've made it well into the C's." His voice softened as his gaze roved across the pages. "*Cotswold Lion. A sheep. Cotswold in Gloucestershire is famous for its breed of sheep.* Useful little tidbit. Your Uncle Bertie would certainly agree with that assessment of his beloved fold. Let's see . . ." He scanned further down the page. "Much of the page is given over to Covent Garden, famous, it seems, for its fruit, flowers, herbs, theaters, and brothels. One must be careful not to contract the *Covent Garden Ague* from a *Covent Garden Nun*. All seems to be in order there." A dry laugh scrubbed the back of his throat. "*Covey. A collection of whores. What a fine covey here is, if the Devil would but throw his net!*" Nick's amused gaze lifted and found her.

Impossibly, Mariana's blush grew hotter. "Mrs. Bloomquist confiscated the dictionary from one of the girls."

"That's quite an education the school is providing its students."

"And she entrusted it to me to dispose of properly." She wouldn't mention that the guilty party happened to be her precocious niece, Lucy.

"I'm not sure the word *properly* should ever be spoken in connection to *The Classical Dictionary of the Vulgar Tongue*."

"It's written in English, and there are no other books," Mariana snapped. "Besides, I've found it . . . enlightening." Oh, how she wished she could stop blushing and explaining herself.

"Right." Nick's fingers drummed a hollow tattoo across the leather book cover. "I see you decided to take my hotel suite."

"You weren't using it," she said. "Besides, you can have it back on the morrow. I depart for England at first light."

A puzzled smile reached his eyes. "Since when did you ever listen to me?"

Mariana bristled at his words, at the assumption that lay within them, but she refused to rise to it. "I listened to myself."

Again, his fingers tapped embossed leather, except now his lips had drawn into a firm line, humor evaporated.

She cleared her throat, hoping to clear the air of the sort of charged moment that tended to stretch between them, and summoned a healthy dose of self-righteousness. "You mustn't enter this suite at will. You relinquished your right to it when you went missing."

"A husband has rights," he said, his voice that of a perfect popinjay.

"You tossed those out with the rubbish some years ago," she stated with a bravado she didn't feel. Rather, an unsettled and exposed feeling charged her senses. How was it that he still continued to hold the power to reduce her to this state? A touchy girl composed of raw nerves wasn't the woman she'd spent the past decade cultivating. "What about my lady's maid? What did you do with her?"

"She has been dismissed for the night."

"Just like that?"

"A husband has—"

"Do *not* finish that sentence if you value your life." A related thought wedged its way in. "How did you convince her, dressed as you are? No servant would believe the likes of *you*"—She eyed him up and down—"to be the husband of me."

"Nothing is what it seems in this world."

"The last few days have been the strangest of my life," she said. "Can you just state plainly whatever the devil it is you're not saying?"

"I think you know what I'm not saying."

"Nick," she began on a whisper, her body inching forward, his words and the implication within them drawing her in, "are you telling me that Hortense is a *spy*?" She lowered to a perch on the edge of the settee opposite his. They were now separated by no more than the width of a small, inlaid walnut table.

Nick's right eyebrow shot up, but he remained otherwise silent. That eyebrow told Mariana all she needed to know. "And here I thought she was a godsend."

"If you prefer to think of her that way, I won't object," Nick cut in, a perverse smile playing about his lips.

"I was even considering taking her back to London with me," Mariana continued, choosing to ignore his quip. The man always did have a high opinion of himself. "Do you not understand how difficult it is to find a lady's maid who speaks English in Paris? She is as rare as a Woolly Mammoth in London."

"A Woolly Mammoth in London?" he asked with a confounded laugh.

"Given my involvement with The Progressive School for Young Ladies and the Education of Their Minds, I spend a good deal of time perusing London's museums."

Nick cocked his head. "I would have thought finding you in a stuffy museum would be as rare as finding a Woolly Mammoth in London."

"I enjoy it." Again, she sounded defensive. *Drat.* "And I happen to know that the Museum of Natural History in Paris has its very own Woolly Mammoth."

In fact, she was disappointed to have missed it on this trip. But Nick needn't know that. She'd revealed too much about her life already.

"That's," he began, a reflective note in his voice, "new."

"Actually, they acquired it more than one hundred years ago."

"I wasn't speaking of the mammoth."

Mariana's traitorous insides went light at his words and at the implication within them. The moment could grow soft, and a sense of ease could steal in, if she allowed it. It was an ease she'd felt the first time they'd locked eyes at a dinner party at Uncle Bertie's country estate—so very long ago.

She'd felt they were two halves of the same whole and had been waiting all their lives to be joined together.

She gave herself a mental shake. Such memories were a trap. Over the last decade, she'd done quite well forgetting what she liked about her husband. She wouldn't allow softness to shake her resolve. This was Nick. He was as soft as a razorblade. "You and I haven't bothered to have a conversation that doesn't involve our children in a decade. Now twice in a single night?"

The question hung in the air as he picked a piece of lint off tatty, old trousers. They would be here all night, if that was his purpose, as those pants appeared to be composed entirely of lint. Why was he dressed like a person who possessed neither lodging nor a place to bathe? Surely, *collecting information* had its limits.

"Isn't it a husband's prerogative to inquire into his wife's well-being?"

"Is that what we're doing? Inquiring into each other's well-being?" Mariana sank back into lush silk, even as stiff corsetry bit into her skin, and mirrored Nick's unconcerned pose. Two could play at this game. "Let us review," she began. "Since I arrived in Paris, I've been dividing my time between hospitals, morgues, and ballets. Would you like to hear about the twins?" she asked, forging on. "Lavinia is with Olivia and Lucy. The girl is as mad about horses as ever. Geoffrey is settled at Westminster. He's requested a kukri knife for his name day."

"He likely needs one at Westminster. That school has an unruly reputation. I would have seen him at Harrow."

"Westminster has been educating noble sons for centuries," Mariana defended. "As the parent who spends the most time in London, *I* would have him closer to home." She summoned a saint's own patience to get through this farce. "Your father and mother are well." With no small amount of satisfaction, she watched him shift in his seat. That movement spoke of discomfiture. "I spoke with them at a soirée just last month."

"In the same room?" he asked, caution in his words.

"Separately. Have I ever seen them in the same room together?"

"At our wedding." He paused to consider. "At Geoffrey and Lavinia's christening."

"They don't care much for each other, do they?" It was almost as if she and Nick were conducting a normal conversation. But the past had taught her where this conversation was heading: nowhere. Nick didn't speak about his family.

"That would be one way of stating the case," he replied, fiddling with a fingernail as if bored. "Another way of stating it would be to say that they would rather eat a dinner of glass shards than converse face to face." Hesitant, he asked, "And my brother?"

"I've seen Jamie at gatherings here and there," Mariana replied, her tone one of careful neutrality.

"In his cups?"

Now it was Mariana's turn to pause. She liked Nick's older brother Jamie, which was why she didn't wish to speak ill of him. Still, her answer would be the truth. "It did appear so."

"Have you heard any rumors of a courtship?"

She studied Nick closer. He looked strangely . . . vulnerable. "None."

"That sounds right."

"He won't ever marry, will he?" She'd long wondered about Jamie's seemingly solitary, even reclusive, life.

"Most doubtful, I would think."

"But he's the heir to the marquessate," she countered. "Your parents must . . ."

Nick's eyes flew up to meet hers, a fiery glow charging their depths. "Jamie owes our parents nothing," he stated, understated ferocity infusing each word. "You were brought up by the sort of family who laughs together over the breakfast table. Only our surname binds the Asquith family together."

"You love Jamie." She'd never seen him like this.

A subtle wince crossed Nick's otherwise impassive features.

Warnings about the Asquith family rose to the surface of memory. It was a good and noble family, a perfect match for her, but those parents loathed one another. On the night before her wedding, Olivia had even asked if she was certain she wanted to marry into *that family*. A blithe, "I'm marrying Nick, not his parents," passed Mariana's lips, the question buried beneath dreams of future marital bliss.

Tonight, she saw reality, a Nick visibly rattled by the conversational turn toward his family. Here lay the largest danger. This was where she would be drawn in by him, if she allowed it. And, oh, how easily she could allow it. A known entity existed between them, one she'd done well to suppress.

But in a room located in a foreign country where a sense of unreality could prevail? It was here that she could allow herself to be seduced into his web and be undone. She didn't want this.

She didn't want to burn with an intense desire to know about him. It had taken her too long to extinguish that particular flame, to convince herself that she didn't care, that she'd never really cared, that it was infatuation run its course. But, tonight, he'd revealed a concrete fact about himself: he was a *spy*. She yearned to know even more about this man.

She'd never felt more disappointed in herself. Hadn't the last ten years made her stronger than this?

She shot to her feet on a surge of resolution, intent on showing Nick the door. "You've gotten your wish. I leave tomorrow. We haven't anything more to say to one another until Geoffrey and Lavinia's eleventh name day next month."

He responded by settling deeper into his settee, and deep annoyance flared through her. His gaze raked up the length of her and held when it reached her eyes. She wouldn't squirm. She wouldn't remember the way that look used to snake through her until it reached the apex of her thighs. If she did, her legs might begin to quiver, much like they were now. That wouldn't do at all.

"A plot is brewing to assassinate the French king's heir, Charles, the Duc d'Artois."

Mariana retreated a step and fell back onto her settee in a puff of skirts. Within Nick's gaze, she detected a deadly serious light, and, just like that, she was caught like an impetuous grasshopper. "Why not assassinate the king?" she asked, at once ensnared by his web.

"The king is on his deathbed and has no heir except for his brother Charles, the Duc d'Artois, whose own heir was assassinated four years ago. With the death of Charles, the Bourbon line dies out, making—"

"Way for a new line," she finished for him, unable to help herself.

He nodded. "And new ideologies."

"The French rather have a history of that sort of thing." It was a glib and sorry attempt to diffuse the tension his intense gaze stirred inside her.

"These aren't revolutionaries, Mariana."

"Then who is plotting, if not revolutionaries?"

"A rebellious minority of nobles who do not share the Ultra-Royalist vision for France's future. These men fear Charles will turn back the clock as if the Revolution never happened."

"Can he?"

"Doubtful, but that isn't to say he won't try. These men are emboldened by last year's constitutional monarchist uprisings in Spain."

"Shouldn't we English support such a cause?" she asked. "After all, a monarchy limited by a constitution is our form of government."

"Over the past year, tens of thousands have died in Spain in civil war. Make no mistake, if the heir is assassinated, there will be war. It is in England and all of Europe's best interest that it be avoided at all costs."

"There must be a reason you're telling me this," Mariana cut in. She sensed a deeper truth rippling beneath Nick's words. "A spy doesn't reveal himself unless he receives something valuable in exchange. What is it that I have of value to you?"

He shifted in his chair and regarded her as if from a great distance. She could almost see the gears in his head racing to devise the best strategy for handling her. "You caught the attention of the Comte de Villefranche tonight."

"You were in the Foyer?" she asked.

"I have people."

"You have *people*?"

His eyes held hers. "Yes." He was absolutely daring her to look away first. "Villefranche is connected to the assassination plot."

"The Comte de Villefranche?" she returned, her voice dripping with disbelief. "You cannot possibly believe that . . . *boy* . . . is capable of assassination and revolution."

"I've seen *boys* do worse."

Her mouth snapped shut.

"The truth—"

"The truth?" she interrupted. "I wasn't aware you and the truth were acquainted."

"The truth is," he continued patiently—too patiently, "Villefranche fits the description of the sort of idealistic young man who powerful men manipulate into doing their dirty work. He wouldn't be the first."

Fraught silence stilled the air. "Before receiving the note that you were missing and presumed dead," she said, "your life appeared to be centered around the pursuit of the pleasures of our social set. I thought you played at politics and diplomacy here and there, but nothing serious. Nothing important."

Nick leaned forward and rested his forearms on his thighs, his entire demeanor taking on a distinct register of urgency as he breached the space between them. Anticipation sparked the air alive, and the room shrank away. It was just him and her.

The breath caught in her chest between an inhale and an exhale, holding the scent of him deep inside. She imagined sandalwood roots extending from her lungs into her veins to the very tips of her fingers and toes.

"Who do you think operates the government of England?" he asked, his voice hushed velvet. "Those with money, education, and land. The Lords, Mariana." The gray of his irises glowed with intensity. "Is it such a stretch that I could be one of them?"

Another unruly blush flared to the surface, its warm bloom heating her up by a few degrees. This one for her stupidity. Of course, Nick was the sort of man who kept governments operating. He possessed the intellect and the capability.

These were qualities she'd liked about him from the beginning. These were memories that had been banished to the past. Until tonight.

"Why are you *here*, Nick? In this hotel suite?" she whispered. He was close, so close. "Once Hortense returns, she will help me pack, and I shall be gone by daybreak. You will be free to resume the strange and mystifying life you lead here."

His gaze slid sideways, and he sat back in his seat. She almost ached for the loss of his nearness. Almost. She couldn't possibly be that foolish.

On a sigh, she tilted her head, first to one side to remove one diamond drop earring, then to the other side to remove the other. Next, she tugged open the clasp of her gold filigree bracelet. Her gaze lifted to find him following her every move.

Instantly, a specific sort of intimacy pervaded the air between them. It was the slow, familiar intimacy of a husband observing his wife make herself comfortable.

"What are you doing?"

If she didn't know better, she might think she'd unnerved him. "Readying myself for bed. It's what one does in the normal scheme of things. Or is *normal* completely lost to you?"

"Normal," he replied, "is a word deeply rooted in the relative. *Normal* is an entirely individual experience."

She resisted an incredulous shake of her head. "Philosophical musings aside, when did Hortense say she would return?" she asked, her tone all brisk business. She needed the distance such a tone provided.

"I asked her to take the night off."

Mariana opened her mouth and snapped it shut. Those words couldn't possibly mean what they sounded like, what her body, traitorous and hot, might hope they meant. "I have no lady's maid tonight?" she got out.

He nodded.

A riot of desire skittered through her. That nod had led them places in the past.

No. That wouldn't do.

She mustn't let her body rule her head.

She wrapped herself in righteous umbrage and shot to her feet in an exasperated shush of silk skirts, grabbing the candlestick to her right and purposefully striding to the French doors dividing the sitting room from the bedroom. She pulled them wide.

"Well, then, there is no help for it. You must play the part," she called over her shoulder. "Unbutton my dress."

# Chapter 4

*All-a-mort: Struck dumb, confounded.*

*A Classical Dictionary of the Vulgar Tongue*
Francis Grose

"*Unbutton your dress*?" Nick repeated. It wasn't possible he'd heard those words in that order.

"Yes," she called out, confirming his worst fear.

A nascent feeling of horror unfurled within him. Mariana had always been a provocative woman, which was precisely why he hadn't spent time alone with her in a decade. Her ability to upset his equilibrium remained absolute and effortless.

Still, he couldn't resist the pull toward her. He rose, and a few hesitant strides had him at the threshold of the bedroom, the vision of her propped against a bedpost before him. Mirroring her insouciant stance, he balanced a noncommittal shoulder against the doorjamb.

"This isn't a good idea," he protested . . . weakly. If pressed, his flimsy shred of resistance would give way to whatever wish she voiced.

"Have you spent a single minute of your life bound within layers of corset, shift, and tightly buttoned dress? Has this ever been required for one of your *spy* missions?"

He couldn't miss the scorn in her voice. "Never."

"Then you'll have to trust me when I suggest that it's a bloody fantastic idea for you to unbutton me. You've done it before, in case you've forgotten."

"I haven't," he said, his voice incapable of more than a low, gravelly rumble.

She blinked, and a moment passed. "You're the one who dismissed Hortense. Even if she is a spy, she's also my lady's maid."

As if to illustrate her seriousness, Mariana swiveled around and braced her hands on the bedpost, readying herself for him.

*Readying herself for him?*

Reason bade Nick exit the room, locate Hortense, and abandon the entire proposition. Under no circumstance should he close the distance between them and place his hands on Mariana's body. Paper thin layers of chartreuse silk and muslin between his fingers and her skin wouldn't be enough.

A few quick steps could carry him to her. A few quick steps could undo him.

His eyes swept down the length of gown draped elegantly across her body as if it had been sewn onto her. A brief count yielded fifteen glimmering, jet buttons racing down the ridge of her spine. *Fifteen.* With any other man and woman, this would be the scene of a seduction. A simple assenting nod of her head was all it would take for them to become those two other people with no past and no future—only tonight.

Except he and she weren't that man and woman. Not with their history.

He shook his head to clear it, lest he forget the mission that had brought him to this room tonight. Before him stood an opportunity, and in the world of espionage, one didn't spurn opportunity. One seized it. Second chances were rare and unreliable.

Somewhat fortified, he closed the requisite distance. The heat from her body mingled with his and enveloped them in a cocoon uniquely *them*. A bead of perspiration trickled down the hollow of his spine.

Oh, no, he hadn't forgotten what it was like to undress Mariana. A heartbeat later, he took the top button between thumb and forefinger. Smooth muscles contracted across her back, resulting in a slight arch just above her derriere. Impossible she didn't feel this implacable tension, too. The certainty didn't make his task any easier. Only a blindfold would.

The tiny button slipped its silken loop. Only fourteen more to go. He cleared his throat. "Mariana?" Her name came out on a rasp barely loud enough to stir the quiet stretch of air between his mouth and her neck. Beneath his fingertips, he felt her breath suspend in anticipation of his next words. He flicked the second and third buttons free in quick succession. "I have a proposition for you."

At last, he was speaking the words he should have spoken the moment she'd entered the sitting room. He was here in a professional capacity, not as a husband and certainly not as a lover.

"A proposition?"

He couldn't miss the lilt of interest inflecting her voice. The fourth and fifth buttons slipped free, and he tamped down a stab of disappointment when he saw that she wore a corset beneath her dress. He should have felt relief that another layer of fabric stood between his skin and hers, but he didn't.

Her corset was black. And lace. It was the corset of a trollop. Lust, pure and strong, shot straight to his cock.

He must ignore that he stood close enough that the fine strands of her upswept hair fluttered with each word he spoke. And that the heat from her body permeated him at an elemental level. And that she wore the corset of a trollop.

"It would be of considerable use," he began, hoping the formality of his words would neutralize the decidedly informal bent of his thoughts, "if you were to remain in

Paris and further your acquaintance with the Comte de Villefranche."

"Further my acquaintance?" she asked. "Why would I do that?"

"We have no agents so conveniently placed."

"Is that what I am? A convenience?"

"I wouldn't go quite so far as that."

Her response was a resounding silence. Nothing was ever easy with Mariana. She didn't wilt or defer to his authority. She stiffened her back and challenged his every word. Most men found this sort of woman exhausting. Not Nick. She tended to invigorate him.

The buttons were coming loose in a steady little rhythm now. *Six . . . Seven . . . Eight.*

"You would be in a position," he continued, "to collect information."

"Ah, a collector of information." A thread of mockery wove through her voice. "What sort of information?"

He began reciting possibilities as if ticking items off a list. "Names . . ."—*Nine*—"Dates . . ."—*Ten*—"Rendezvous points . . ."—*Eleven*—"Snippets of conversation you might overhear . . ."—*Twelve*—"Notes you might read by chance. Idealism often disguises the deeper motivations of the major players. You would place yourself in the position to get at the core of the intrigue."

"And how exactly will I accomplish this?"

"By earning Villefranche's trust."

*Thirteen.*

"And how do I go about that?"

*Fourteen.*

His fingers hesitated above the soft curve of her waist. Could he say to her the words he'd come here to say? After all, they were the same words he'd spoken to countless agents, both male and female, over the years. Never mind that the law stated she was his wife. That particular detail had been a minor technicality for years.

He let the words come. "By any means necessary."

The air went still in the way it did before a storm broke. Nick braced himself.

"By seducing him?" she asked in an incredulous half-whisper.

*Fifteen.*

"Any means," he repeated, his voice hollow to his own ears.

No buttons remained unbuttoned, yet his hands lingered at the small of her back.

"Now my corset," she said, her words a quiet command.

"Pardon?" Impossible that he'd heard her correctly. A litany of curses, he expected, but not this.

"Loosen my stays," she stated more firmly.

"Mariana . . ."

It was the plea of a desperate man, but he no longer cared how he sounded. Only a fool kept silent when he was drowning.

She presented him her stubborn profile. "I need a deep breath. Now."

Shaky fingers felt for the knot holding the stays together, and his mouth went dry. No longer could he ignore her effect on him. Blood ripe with anticipation raced through his veins, pervading his body with a specific craving that demanded to be assuaged in the specific ways only he and she had known.

Did he remember? How could he forget? His cock, hard and ready, certainly hadn't.

It would be nothing to reach down and gather up her dress, one silk fold at a time, exposing the long length of her legs inch by irresistible inch until—

No. He must resist. Who was he asking her to seduce anyway?

"About Villefranche," she began. Her voice held a matter-of-fact quality that served to stabilize the moment. "Have you considered that he will suspect I'm getting close to him at your behest? You and I *are* married after all."

"Society is well aware that we are estranged," Nick replied. His fingers began working at the knot again. He needed to finish this task. "Villefranche and his conspirators may think to play you against me, but it's an opportunity we mustn't pass up."

At long last, Nick's fingers tugged the knot free and loosened the stays. Task complete, nothing prevented him from stepping away from her and collecting himself before he ruined the entire mission. Except his eyes lingered on the transparent swath of muslin that did little to protect the supple, ridged line of her spine from his gaze.

Like nothing, the flimsy scrap of fabric would rend in two. His tongue would trace that exposed line all the way up to the sensitive, fine hairs of her neck . . . That was another sort of opportunity before him. But it was one he must pass up.

"You will answer me one question before you have my reply." She swiveled around to face him. Her dress draped forward ever so slightly, and he caught a glimpse of black lace peeking above chartreuse silk. She was a picture of womanly dishabille of the most delectable sort. "Why are you dressed in this manner?"

"I have gone underground."

"And this has to do with someone in the Foreign Office declaring you missing and presumed dead?"

"That makes two questions."

"Humor me, Nick. It seems that you could uncover the details of the assassination plot dressed as Lord Nicholas Asquith, alive and well. Yet you're not. What aren't you telling me?"

She leaned against the bedpost and crossed her arms in front of her breasts to prevent her dress from slipping to her waist. His eyes had no choice but to drop and follow the movement. In a slow blink, his gaze returned to meet hers and held steady. "Before your arrival in Paris, I was assaulted by two men in this suite. I managed to turn the dagger around on one of the assailants while the other fled the scene."

"You killed a man?" she asked, eyes wide, but lacking any trace of hysteria or fear.

"This can be a dirty business. Clearly, my investigation into the assassination plot has touched a nerve with the wrong people. I thought it best that I not be myself for a time." Frustrating Nick was that he'd told only the *right* people of this mission. This led to a single, unavoidable conclusion: his operation was compromised.

"How is Hortense connected to your mission?"

"After the attack," he began, "she was put in place as a maid to watch for suspicious activity around this suite in case anyone returned."

"You instructed her to spy on me?" Mariana asked. Her eyes held a mutinous light. Nick felt her slipping from him. He must tread with care.

"That was a stroke of luck." Truth would best serve the moment. "Once Hortense saw you check in to the hotel, she took it upon herself to become your lady's maid." He hesitated before making his next request. Mariana had never responded well to being told what to do. "I would ask that you keep her on. She would be useful in an unsavory situation."

Mariana's amber eyes searched his, and the distance between them became insignificant. The only world that mattered was the world he saw in there, threatening to reach beyond the carnal and into a realm he never did understand and never wanted to understand. In this intimate space lay the ingredient for his undoing, yet he couldn't resist its pull, even as he understood its potential for destruction. "If we are to work together, there is something you should know," he found himself saying. "Ten years ago—"

A forestalling hand flew up, and her eyes hardened into flat, brittle stone. Cold distance instantly dispelled any false sense of intimacy between them. "Don't," she commanded.

"Don't?"

"Apologize for your affair," she continued, her tone matching her eyes. "Or is it affairs? The gossip rags do so love to have a field day with your exploits. All done in the course of *information collecting*, I now see."

Even after all these years, her words hit him squarely in the solar plexus. Yet he would press on. "Mariana, the opera singer—"

"I shall do it," she cut in.

"Pardon?" She was turning him into a simpleton.

"I shall collect information for you." She spoke the words as if she was as surprised as he to hear them emerge from her mouth. "But not if you insist on dredging up the past. It's done. It has no place in Paris. Isn't that the way you've conducted your life this last decade?"

He cleared his throat, but found no available words. He nodded once, curtly.

"Besides," she began, the mean hint of a smile playing about her lips, "the Comte de Villefranche certainly is handsome."

The suggestion embedded within those words cut Nick to his core. But he deserved it, for it had been he who had set the idea of seduction into motion. She'd simply been the one to vocalize it. The matter was moot now.

Mariana was going to seduce another man. And he had no one to blame except himself. His blood boiled at the thought.

"I do have a request, though."

"Yes?" he asked, the monosyllable hesitant and wary. He wouldn't like whatever words next emerged from her mouth.

"You lose the voice."

He didn't need to ask. He knew the voice she spoke of. He'd long been aware of how his popinjay persona grated on her nerves. Now she was stripping his already meager arsenal of one of his most effective defenses against her. "As you like," he granted. Surely, he could devise other defenses.

Her smile brightened, dispelling the impenetrable fog of their ticklish past. "It will be a lark."

A prickle of foreboding raised the hairs on Nick's neck. "A *lark*?" The word rang false to his ears. He took a step back, hoping to gain a little perspective. "You're not the larking sort."

"No?" A daring glint lit her eyes. "For England. How is that?"

"I'm not certain," he said, the words emerging syllable by slow syllable in a weak effort to buy time.

What was happening? She'd turned the tables on him.

Of course, she had.

Arrayed before him in a state of partial undress, both impossibly sensual and impossible to ignore, stood the Mariana of his dreams and his nightmares: denuded of jewels; dress falling off her luscious form; gold locket temptingly nestled between her breasts; her face infused with a youthful eagerness he'd believed a memory. She looked so open . . . so Mariana . . .

A problem with his plan hit Nick with the force of a lightning strike: Mariana's open face. How could he have overlooked the trait that defined Mariana as . . . Mariana? Spies didn't possess open faces. At least, successful spies didn't. And definitely not the ones who lived.

A shot of regret tore through him. What had he begun?

"When do I begin?" she asked as if privy to his thoughts.

"Tomorrow you accept Villefranche's invitation to shop in the Palais-Royal." Was that panic in his voice?

"I suppose your *people* reported that conversation back to you?"

Nick nodded. "I shall be in touch." With that, he pivoted on a heel and fled the room.

Perhaps he fled her keen face.

Perhaps he fled his budding desire to tell her the truth about ten years ago. He definitely fled desire. Except, this desire had naught to do with the past. This desire lived squarely in the present, base and implacable.

And it wasn't the truth either of them needed.

~ ~ ~

Mariana lay atop the bed's soft damask coverlet, watching flickering shadows dance about her ceiling. As a child, she would imagine they were the shadows of fairies come to protect her as she slept. This twilight stage between waking and sleep had been her favorite part of bedtime. She hadn't been the dreamy sort of girl who frolicked about vast imagined landscapes. She'd been too grounded in the present. Except for this one bit of whimsy that came to her every night as she relaxed and sank into slumber.

She understood this would be her last stretch of stillness for some time. Once before, she'd experienced this singular feeling: the night before her wedding. She'd sensed then, as now, that she was about to step over an edge, and there would be no turning back. Gravity didn't work that way. It pulled one toward an inevitable conclusion, and she never was one to hesitate on the brink of a precipice. She simply went right over.

Tonight, she'd hesitated. She and Nick created a gravity of their own. And they'd reached their inevitable conclusion once before. *Ten years.* It was so very long ago, and, yet, it felt like yesterday.

When her eyes had held his and his fingers brushed the space between her shoulder blades as his breath caressed the nape of her neck, she'd longed, yearned, ached for the press of his body against hers. Not because she didn't remember, but because she *did*.

Her eyelids fluttered shut. As the fairies eased her into sleep, a hopeful note sounded. The grim past didn't have to push its way into the present. It was true that a gravitational thread linked them, one with no connection to their shared name or children. Nick had always been able to ignore it. Why not she, too?

The past was the wrong direction. The only direction now was forward.

# Chapter 5

*Caterwauling: Going out in the night in search of intrigues, like a cat in the gutters.*

*A Classical Dictionary of the Vulgar Tongue*
Francis Grose

Nick's feet hit the flat cobblestone sidewalk at a clip that could only be characterized as a near run. He flipped up his collar to guard against the dense layer of fog that now wrapped Paris in a shroud of mist.

How great was the temptation to find the nearest tavern and drink this night into oblivion in hopes of a clearer head tomorrow. But it wouldn't work. He needed to keep moving. A long and circuitous ramble through the city was the only way to rid himself of the panic rioting through him.

What had he been thinking? Mariana wasn't a spy. She might be the most obvious person he'd ever known. It was a quality that simultaneously charmed and struck a note of terror within him, but he couldn't deny that it was part of her appeal.

He exhaled a sharp gust of air through gritted teeth. It wouldn't do to think about Mariana's appeal right now. What he should do was return to the hotel, admit his mistake, and help her pack for London.

But he couldn't return to the hotel. He'd left her in a state of partial undress in her bedroom, and he didn't trust himself not to finish the job of removing her corset of a trollop, her gossamer muslin chemise, her stockings, her garters, her everything. Then what? His efforts of the last decade—to keep his distance, to keep her safe—would be entirely undone.

Not to mention he'd almost revealed the truth about the opera singer. *Blast*. What exactly did he hope to accomplish with that particular revelation?

Did he want to anger Mariana into leaving Paris? Or was it to win her back?

Ridiculous. The truth would likely upset her more than the original lie.

Ten years ago, it had been easy to tell himself that it was the necessary choice, the best choice to ensure her safety. He'd repeated words like *necessity* and *safety* to himself until he believed them—almost. A deeper truth lay below the façade. He'd taken the convenient way out of their marriage, and he knew why.

As his feet carried him forward across slick Parisian byways, his mind traveled back, beyond the night a lie ripped their marriage apart. It went toward the day he'd met Mariana, and she'd become an obsession from which he would never recover.

~ ~ ~

*The Cotswolds*
*5 March 1811*

Nick was late for the most important meeting of his nascent career. Over the course of the morning, what he'd thought would be a straightforward ride from London had devolved into a tangled knot of missed turns and wrong country roads. Every mile or so, he unleashed another round of invectives against his blasted bad luck.

Near the end of his tenure at Cambridge, a family friend, one Mr. Bertrand Montfort, had approached him at a social gathering with an interesting offer from the Foreign Office. He was riding out today to explore its possibilities.

A younger son, like himself, needed an occupation, and the church wasn't his calling. A position within Whitehall was worth investigating.

At long last, he found himself galloping across Montfort's Cotswolds estate, the sprawling house just ahead on the verdant horizon. Suddenly, his gaze snagged on a flurry of movement on the periphery of his vision. Some hundred yards to his right walked a young woman and a dog, skirting the edge of a copse of woods. He and his horse slowed to a complete stop while he watched this tall and willowy woman, long hair the hue of wild honey streaming down her back, locate an imperceptible trail and vanish inside the shadowy depths of the woods.

For a full minute, he watched the spot where she'd disappeared as if he could conjure her up at will. Something about her—her decisive stride, her air of determination, or the glimpse of the transcendent beauty of her profile— spurred his heart to race faster as she embedded herself into the forefront of his mind. Who was she? Had she been a figment of his imagination? He then heard the muffled baying of a hound, and the reality of her grabbed hold of him and refused to let go.

Even as he spent the remainder of the day closeted with the other three Foreign Office recruits in Montfort's study, receiving the details of their first mission on the Peninsula— Napoleon hadn't finished ravaging Spain and Portugal just yet—the knowledge that *she* occupied the same premises as he, completely overshadowed the proceedings. He was ravenous for any morsel of her.

Her name was Lady Mariana Montfort. She was his host's niece and would debut this Season. And, if he allowed it, she would be the ruin of him. No one had to tell Nick the last part.

If he believed in fancy and whimsy, he might have thought it love at first sight. Of course, he believed in neither fancy nor whimsy. And, love, well, he didn't believe in that either.

When she joined the small group at the supper table, he would have sworn the air in the room became lighter, almost effervescent. He avoided looking directly at her, even as he studied her from the corner of his eye. For most of the meal, she remained quiet at the table, her attention darting from conversation to conversation and her full lips occasionally tipping up into a quick smile at a witticism.

It was when she'd disagreed with an opinion that he'd first heard her speak. "What do you mean *those dirty immigrants*?"

"Oh, the Catholics from Ireland and those Latin countries. You know, Italy, Spain, and the like."

Nick watched her chin notch higher as she warmed to the debate. "Lord Farnsworth, where else would you have found the cheap labor to build your mansion in Grosvenor Square?"

"Precisely," Lord Farnsworth replied. "Montfort, your niece certainly has the right end of the stick. Well done, good sir."

A pink flush crept all the way up to the delicate tips of Lady Mariana's ears. "I'm afraid you misinterpret the meaning of my words. I was being ironic."

The men of the table chorused an indulgent chuckle, and Montfort patted his niece's hand, effectively silencing any additional ironies she might voice. Nick intuited she likely had a few.

Then her eyes slid sideways and found his. Her direct, amber gaze could have held him suspended until the end of time. In reality, the contact lasted no longer than a pair of heartbeats. But it was all he needed to know with certainty that she was as aware of him as he was of her. A lightning bolt of elation, unlike any he'd experienced in his two and twenty years, streaked through him.

Later, after the men had finished their cigars and were rejoining the ladies in the small salon, Nick watched her slip through a crack in the exterior French doors. In his defense, he had paused. A man like him had no business following virgins into the night for he had no intention of ever marrying. Marriage and children crippled a man involved in espionage.

Yet the hesitation had lasted only long enough for him to set down his brandy. In three short strides, he was through the doors and beneath an indigo sky dotted with a million stars, the sort of sky only possible outside the fog-bound city. He'd stood uncertainly on the stone portico feeling exposed and a thousand ways a fool.

Where had she gone?

Instinct guided him down the wide staircase and onto a crushed granite path lined with all manner of flowers. Montfort's was the quintessential English garden with its riots of overgrown blooms of every hue, tonight rendered monochromatic by the stark rays of the moon.

He'd begun to doubt his instinct when he rounded a bend in the path and spotted her some ten yards ahead, seeming to be in no particular hurry. Her ease was apparent in the relaxed set of her shoulders and the way her hand trailed idly above the flowers, allowing their velvety petals to brush the bare flesh of her palm. The way the light washed over and embraced her called to mind Selene, goddess of the moon. He should turn back before they ruined each other.

Just as he made to retrace his steps toward the house, she called out over her shoulder, "Are you going to skulk behind me all night?"

They were the first words she ever spoke to him. His heart kicked up a notch, and his tongue became a sodden blanket in his mouth as a series of facts occurred to him:

He'd followed her. He was alone with her. And he wanted nothing more than to touch her and know the scent of her. His stride increased in length to catch her.

"Do we need a formal introduction before you will speak to me?" she teased, presenting him her flawless profile. The moon above limned her features in a contradictory soft, yet crisp, glow. "Or are you simply shy?"

"You must know who I am," he called out to her back.

"He speaks." An enchanting giggle floated over her shoulder. "I know you are one of many young men who venture out to my uncle's estate to discuss England's politics. But who you are specifically, I can't say."

They reached the ha-ha, and he watched her clear its low wall with ease before turning toward the edge of the woods, him following at her heels like a lap dog hungry for the tiniest crumb of her attention.

He found himself close behind her, close enough to catch her scent of jasmine and neroli. It struck him that this wasn't the one-note scent of a debutante. On the surface, the floral jasmine indicated the shallow innocence of her peers, but the deep bitter-orange neroli complicated that assessment and made for a more interesting conclusion. She was different. "Why did you leave the house?"

His lips curved into a half-smile when she jumped at his words. Words so close she might have felt their dewy warmth on the nape of her neck.

"I was hot."

Three simpler words didn't exist in the English language. Yet that one simple word—*hot*—sent a spike of longing straight through him. "I suppose the air was a bit stale," he rasped.

They climbed a short rise that overlooked a small pond, wavy beams of moonlight rippling across its fluid surface. What was he doing in the woods with this moon goddess? It wasn't too late to turn back.

Then she spoke the next words, and he was lost.

"I wasn't hot from *stale* air." She faced him, her amber

eyes, clear and unflinching, gauging his reaction. "It was you. I was hot because of you."

No longer could he keep his emotions under a tight rein. She'd negated that control with a few careless words that struck his core with the precision of a well-aimed arrow.

"Did no one ever teach you not to say such things to strange men?"

"They tried," she said with the assuredness of a woman with far too much experience, or maybe it was far too little. "There is nothing strange about you."

"You should try those words on a different man," he said, straining for a tone of paternal guidance. If she believed it, he might, too. "One who would marry you."

"Oh, I care naught for that," she said on a laugh.

Instinctively, protectively, he reached out and pulled her close, her upturned lips a hairsbreadth away from his, her playful eyes inviting him to bridge the distance. "Society doesn't tolerate ladies who entertain loose morals."

With feelings of longing, desire, and bewilderment warring inside him, he lowered his head and touched his mouth to hers, unprepared for the responding punch of electricity. His hands slid to her waist, and her fingers found the back of his neck, her nails tickling across sensitive skin, her body swaying into his in surrender.

Kisses had the power to reveal truths about two people that extended far beyond trivialities like compatibility and incompatibility. This kiss revealed a single unshakeable truth: she was the only woman for him. It was a truth that shook him clear through to his bones. Nick had met his match. He would strive for the rest of his life to be worthy of her. And he knew he never would be.

His eyes flew open, and he broke the kiss, eliciting a tiny gasp of protest from her. He watched with a mixture of self-loathing and thwarted passion as she opened desire-glazed eyes and closed kiss-crushed lips.

"A girl like you is a girl one could marry," he murmured. They were heedless and dangerous words that fell from his lips, and he couldn't understand why he spoke them.

"A girl *like* me?"

"You."

"*One* could marry?"

"I."

"Careful," she whispered into the space between their lips. It was the only space that mattered in the universe. "I might hold you to such words."

"I might hope you do."

Again, words fell from his mouth of their own accord, and he'd proposed to her. There had been no biting it back. And he hadn't wanted to. At least, not for another five seconds. Then the enormity of the night crashed in on him.

They spoke not another word as they walked back to the house without touching. With barely a murmur of farewell, he left her at the French doors and strode toward the stables, single-minded purpose in every step. He'd proposed to Lady Mariana Montfort, a girl he didn't know.

That wasn't precisely true; in the ways that mattered, he *knew* her.

But it changed nothing: it was wrong. When the time came for marriage—*if* he chose to marry some years into the future—he needed a Society match. He needed the sort of marriage that relied on mutual goals of inheritance, procreation, and the continuation of civilized society. What he didn't need was a love match, or whatever it was that had sparked between him and Lady Mariana tonight.

A girl like her deserved to be with the sort of man who would know how to make a happy family with her. Nick barely knew how families functioned. In fact, he'd spent his entire childhood witnessing what happened when a love match made on short acquaintance turned to hate. He would yoke neither himself nor Lady Mariana to such a life. He must put distance between himself and the feelings she inspired within him. And the easiest way of accomplishing that feat was to put physical distance between them.

Quietly and efficiently, he saddled his bay stallion in the dark and rode for London like the hounds of hell pursued him. From there, he followed his orders and left for the Continent, where he remained for the next year, confident that Lady Mariana would be snatched off the marriage mart by the time he returned. It wasn't likely she'd taken his proposal, if it could be called such, seriously.

Of course, wishful thinking was all it had been. Fate had had other plans for him and Mariana. Yes, fate. No matter how much of a realist and pragmatist he was in his everyday life, an unfathomable universal power bound them together. As much as he'd tried, he couldn't reason it out of existence. The key had been to bury it deep beneath layers of resolve and willpower by focusing on reality. Mariana needed to be protected, and he'd taken the necessary measures.

They were measures which had been successful . . . until tonight.

Tonight, he'd involved her in the very world he'd vowed to protect her from. *By any means necessary*. A frustrated groan rumbled deep inside his chest, and he squinted against relentless mist that was thickening into a substantial rain. He pointed his feet in the direction of his modest set of rooms across the Seine on the Left Bank.

He did have one last defense in his arsenal against her. Unlike his twenty-two-year-old self from that long-ago night, he now understood her power over him. This understanding lent him his only advantage, and his only hope. For although it appeared he'd made a clean break of their marriage ten years ago, he alone understood the single, tenacious strand that had refused to be severed.

The desire to be worthy of her hadn't cooled a single degree. And she had no idea. She thought him cold and indifferent to her. If he planned to keep it that way, he needed to better prepare himself against her. But mostly, he needed to prepare himself against himself.

He could take a measure of comfort that in the coming days she would be spending her time with the Comte de Villefranche, not him. She would simply be another spy in his employ.

Before he next saw her, he needed to convince himself of the lie.

# Chapter 6

*Starched: Stiff, prim, formal, affected.*

*A Classical Dictionary of the Vulgar Tongue*
Francis Grose

*Next Day*

Twin slivers of anticipation and anxiety snaked through Mariana as she strolled the wide, crowded promenade of a Palais-Royal gallery. She unclenched the damp fists at her sides and attempted to soak in surroundings bright and pulsing with life, even as she watched for the Comte de Villefranche.

From the Rue de Richelieu, she'd passed through a screened entrance and into the rectangular interior arcade of bustling shops and cafés. While she could indulge in shopping and trade on the perimeter, she preferred the view provided by the interior grounds: perfectly aligned rows of apple trees and meticulously manicured gardens. In the center of the space stood a large circular fountain where Parisians of every class gathered to soak in a bit of afternoon sun to the mellifluous sound of bubbling water.

Here, the Revolutionary principles of *Liberté*! *Egalité*! *Fraternité*! shone like nowhere else. Helene's words were true: London had nothing on Paris.

The mix of high and low on display both refreshed and invigorated her. Coarse broadcloth mingled amongst superfine; dull woolens wove amongst vibrant silks. Tourists ogled fashionable Parisians; Parisians, in turn, pretended not to notice. The prostitutes, whom she chose not to directly acknowledge, cast jaded eyes over the entire tableau as they waited for second floor gaming dens to spit out the odd, flush gambler.

Mariana was just stepping aside to allow one such dissolute gentleman to pass when Villefranche appeared at the far end of the arcade. Her heart thumped a hard beat, and her stomach fluttered as competing emotions of fear, uncertainty, determination, and excitement washed over her. A tiny voice of calm attempted to tamp them down: she was here to shop and stroll with the man. Two activities she understood as they were two of the leading activities of her social set.

*Today is different*, the tiny voice reminded her. Today, she would be shopping, strolling, and *spying on* Villefranche. It was the last part that had her insides tangled up in knots.

She gave herself a mental shake. She was complicating the day, when in reality it was simple: she was here to play a role. The ability to become someone else seemed to be an essential element of navigating the world of espionage effectively.

Last night, Nick had come to her as a waiter and a fugitive in the space of a few hours. Although she would be none other than Lady Nicholas Asquith today, she would need to become a different version of herself if she was to finesse any closely held secrets out of Villefranche. She might have asked Nick for guidance on the matter.

Her head gave a tiny shake. It was impossible. She was an intelligent, capable woman. She could navigate this outing without running to her husband.

She'd told Nick she'd agreed to his plan for crown and country. But a deeper truth also lay at the heart of the matter: the prospect of entering his shadowy world of intrigue and besting him at it was a temptation too delectable to resist.

It was a world that frightened her a bit, a world that excited her no end. It was Nick's world. She would sooner streak down this promenade naked than implore him for help. But his words came to her: *by any means necessary*. Would *any means* really be necessary?

She pivoted to face the front window of a curiosity shop and feigned interest in its wares, even as she tracked Villefranche in her peripheral vision. Judging from his intensely gathered brow, she intuited he was too deep inside his own thoughts to have noticed her yet.

What sort of spy was the Comte de Villefranche anyway?

Just as he was about to stride past her, she silently counted *one . . . two . . . three* before swiveling around in a dramatic flurry of skirts, a bright smile pasted across her face. "Comte de Villefranche, it is you!"

As if startled out of a trance, he jerked to a stop, his eyes wide with surprise. "Lady Nicholas?"

"The one and only," she chirped like a brainless bird. Villefranche must be the same sort of spy as she: an inexperienced one.

"But," he began slowly, "you and I agreed to meet at Le Grand Véfour a quarter of an hour hence."

"Yet here we are . . . meeting." Mariana noted how rattled he was by this slight alteration to their plan, certainly an unpromising trait for anyone involved in espionage. "Shall we proceed with our shopping excursion from here?"

Villefranche's demeanor shifted in subtle acceptance, and he held out his arm for her. "Of course," he replied, his tone as wooden as his person. "Would you care to peruse this shop?" He glanced up at the sign. "Le Grenelle is renowned for its selection of eglomise boxes."

"How delightful," she exclaimed. In a fraction of a second, she assumed her role: Vacuous-Lady-Who-Lives-For-Shopping.

After just two footsteps inside the shop, however, Mariana regretted her blithe acquiescence. This particular shop was the breadth and depth of a horse stall—complete with its accompanying odor—and stuffed from ceiling to floor with all manner of bibelot, making it impossible for her and Villefranche to walk side by side.

Carefully navigating cramped aisles, she picked her way to the back, where the proprietor stood behind a counter. The two men exchanged a few words in rapid French, setting the proprietor into a flurry of motion with an obsequious smile pasted onto his mouse-like face. Soon, he'd assembled various sizes and styles of eglomise boxes for her inspection.

She singled out a box edged with lacy gilt and depressed its tiny lever, clicking open its ornate lid depicting the famed Medici Fountain of the Jardin du Luxembourg. Her gaze fixed on the box beneath her hand, she asked, "Are you an admirer of eglomise?"

Who knew espionage could be so deadly dull?

"I do not believe in accumulating material possessions for the sake of a collection. It is waste," Villefranche pontificated. "All objects must be of use; otherwise, what is the point of that object?"

Confounded by his absolute assuredness, Mariana felt her eyebrows lift. "How does art fit into your view of usefulness?"

A blush crept up his youthful cheeks. "You will have to forgive me, Lady Nicholas. Sometimes I forget that not everyone shares my beliefs." With an air of self-consciousness, he averted his gaze toward the velvety depths of the open box. "You look . . . comely . . . today," he added in a tone both conciliatory and strangely flat.

A bewildered smile found its way to Mariana's lips. Villefranche wasn't even looking at her. His skills as a suitor equaled his skills as a spy.

"Your eyes," he stuttered out, "they glow."

"Oh dear," she returned, "I hope I haven't caught a fever."

Eyes wide with alarm, he swung toward her. "You have mistaken the intent of my words."

"That is, indeed, a relief," she returned, the words dry as dust. She tapped the box and nodded at the proprietor. With a dramatic flourish, he swept up the box and began bundling it for transport. "So you aren't an admirer of eglomise?" She sensed a useful strand running through this particular conversational thread. "I would have thought you appreciative of a craft that requires such immense skill and expertise."

Villefranche averted his gaze. "Those who paint these tiny and intricate scenes for masses of rich tourists receive little pay, and their eyes fail at very young ages, leaving them with no livelihood and no eyesight. It is a tragedy," he proclaimed to the room empty of patrons save themselves.

In an attempt to prevent Villefranche from seeing the huge roll of her eyes, Mariana directed her attention toward the enormous sideboard to her left. She lay a hand on its marble surface and allowed its stone coolness to seep into her skin through the silk of her gloves. She glanced over her shoulder to find Villefranche righting an Oriental vase caught by his elbow.

"This is quite a massive structure," she began, hoping to lighten the conversation. "How did they manage to squeeze it inside this tiny shop? It must weigh a half a ton."

"Well actually, it's not so heavy, but heavy enough to gravely injure a man who has the misfortune to find himself on the wrong side of it. Every day, dock workers maim themselves while moving such structures."

Mariana heaved a frustrated sigh. Had the man never heard of hyperbole or idle chit-chat? Above every exchange with the Comte de Villefranche hung a rain cloud ready to burst. How was she supposed to finagle any useful information out of this man? Her only hope lay in the fact that he was clearly, blessedly, as unskilled in the art of espionage as she.

"Madame," the proprietor cut in with a discreet murmur, "your cigar box is ready."

Cigar box? What did she need with a cigar box? She reached inside her reticule for payment. Money and item efficiently exchanged between her and the satisfied proprietor, she faced the young Comte. "Shall we venture on?"

Villefranche nodded, and they began stutter-stepping through the cramped shop, each movement forward an intentional negotiation with the hodgepodge of furniture, stacked books, and various trifles and trinkets. Mariana glanced behind her and caught Villefranche restacking a column of books that he'd accidentally kicked over.

Nick was never so clumsy.

She shook her head. Where had that thought come from? The part of her brain that couldn't stop thinking about him after last night. That was where. Nick was alive, and he was a spy.

Nick was her . . . overseer? How best could she characterize this new twist in their relationship? Regardless of the title, she now spied for him, if one could call what she was doing *spying*.

She needed a new role. Vacuous-Lady-Who-Lives-For-Shopping wasn't working. Perhaps, flattery would. It usually did with young men. Lady-Who-Brazenly-Flatters-Younger-Men could be her new role. It was worth a try.

At last rid of the cramped and odiferous shop, Mariana rested her hand on Villefranche's extended arm and exclaimed, "Oh my, what hard muscles you have hidden beneath this superfine. Do you lift heavy objects?"

Polished and handsome, the Comte de Villefranche was the sort of man who set young girlish hearts alight, but who left hers cold. Yet, she was struck by an observation that should have been obvious from the start: in build and coloring, Villefranche was eerily similar to Nick.

Both men were tall, lean, and possessed a similar dark handsomeness that drew the eye. Still, a subtle, but distinct, difference in bearing differentiated them: Villefranche faced the world with a preposterously erect posture, while Nick held himself in a manner not precisely defensive, but in a way that kept himself to himself. It was one of the qualities that had drawn her toward Nick: the mystery of him.

"I labor at our family estate when I have the opportunity. A connection to the earth is vital."

His words brought Mariana back to the present. Memories of Nick's eternal mystery weren't helpful at all. "Those muscles combined with your commanding height make you one . . . healthy, young man."

*Healthy*? *Young man*? That was the most flattering response she could devise? Her improvisational skills sorely lacked panache.

"A healthy body is the foundation of a healthy mind," Villefranche returned, so certain of his own rightness.

"Of course," she replied. Did the man speak in nothing but aphorisms? She cleared her throat and pressed on, "You possess such wisdom for one so very young. Your years on this earth cannot possibly exceed twenty."

"I saw one and twenty years on my last name day."

"How the ladies of Paris must compete for you," she continued. "A striking aristocrat such as yourself must have his pick. And now, of course, aristocrats are back in favor in France."

Villefranche's step hitched, and a surge of hope shot through Mariana. Had she needled her way into a chink in his armor?

"*Oui*, my family is aristocratic," he began, "but we are French first. There are those who would have us revert to the *Ancien Régime*."

"Oh?" she asked, the question a blithe exhale.

"They refuse to admit the old way is unsustainable," he said, the volume of his speech rising with each word he spoke, echoing down the long, stone arcade before them. "Yet we have a king again."

"We have a king in England," she responded, maintaining an innocent tone.

"*Oui*, but you also have a Parliament for balance. We French have trouble with balance." An ironic laugh escaped him, taking Mariana by surprise. She wouldn't have thought him capable of irony. "We like extremes."

"But isn't that human nature?" she asked.

"A government, Lady Nicholas, must be above extremes," Villefranche expounded, instructing her as if she were a child. "It must be above human nature, pettiness, and whim. When one man rules without checks and balances, as the Americans would say, he becomes corrupted and a tyrant. Even our great Napoleon succumbed to it."

Mariana watched the Comte de Villefranche transform before her eyes. No longer was he an awkward pretend suitor. He was a confident man passionate about his beliefs.

"If we are to have an aristocracy," he continued, "then we must have a constitutional monarchy, like your England. Otherwise, good riddance to the aristocrats."

"Yours is a powerful branch of the Orléans family," she countered. At last, she was getting somewhere. "It seems your family would lose a great deal."

"My family is French first," he repeated on a rising note. As if shocked by his own fervor, he came to an abrupt stop. "You must pardon me," he said, his voice hollowed of the passion that had infused it seconds ago. The moment was lost. *Drat.* "At times, I become too . . ." he trailed off as if unable to find the correct word.

Mariana took pity on him and exclaimed, "Oh, this is the shop I've been searching for. My son, Geoffrey, simply adores"—She glanced up at the sign, and her stomach dropped to her feet—"tobacco."

Villefranche's brows knit together. "You cannot possibly have a son old enough—"

"Who do you think the cigar box is for?" Mariana asked, her eyes locked onto his, all but daring him to contradict her. It wouldn't do to mention that Geoffrey would reach his eleventh-year next month.

Or that, in the letter she'd retrieved from Helene today, he'd made a shopping request that she bring home a box of French bon-bons. He was trying to convince a sweet-toothed cook at Westminster to give him larger dinner portions. The boy certainly possessed a fundamental understanding of what made the world go round. In fact, he was much like his father.

No, none of that would do presently.

In for a penny, in for a pound, she went on, "Geoffrey is a connoisseur of the fogus."

Villefranche cocked his head. "*Fogus*? I'm not acquainted with that word."

"Tobacco is characterized as such in certain areas of London." She would keep to herself which areas of London and that she'd never once ventured into any of them.

Oh, how Francis Grose's little dictionary was infecting her mind. The thought provoked a tiny smile that wouldn't be bitten back.

Villefranche's mouth drew into a silent, grim line, and he pushed the door open. As Mariana stepped inside the shop to the delicate tinkling of bells, she regretted her bravado. Feigning interest in the various forms of tobacco on display, her mind raced to find a usable angle for how to proceed. Flirtation hadn't succeeded. She floundered about for yet another role.

"Lady Nicholas," Villefranche began, "would you like me to sample a particular . . . *fogus* for your son? It is my understanding that ladies have difficulty appreciating cigars."

How Mariana longed to reach inside one of the many open boxes on display, pull a cigar from its depths, and puff it alight before his scandalized eyes. Perhaps it was the paradox of Paris calling out to her, but last night's foray into the Foyer de la Danse slipped into her mind. *Heavenly and sordid.*

A frisson of excitement trilled up her spine, and her next role came to her. *Seductress.* Hadn't it been Nick's idea to use *any means necessary* to finesse information out of Villefranche? She could transform into a hedonistic, amoral Parisienne. Morals, it must be admitted, could be so tiresome . . .

Quickly on its scandalous heels followed another thought: Nick had been spying on her last night, Nick could be spying on her *right now.*

Impelled by a bold and unfamiliar brazenness, she propped her elbows on the display case behind her and allowed a flirtatious smile to play about her lips, thoroughly channeling the role of hedonistic, amoral Parisienne. If such a position forced her breasts to thrust forward and draw Villefranche's eye—or any other eye that might happen to be watching—then so be it.

*Any means.*

"Have you never pulled out your cigar and invited a woman to appreciate it?" she asked.

Shock mingled its way into Villefranche's bland features. "Never."

"Have you never longed to watch a woman—"

His eyebrows arched toward to the ceiling.

"Puff your cigar alight?"

His throat moved up and down in a gulping motion. She almost wished she could give him a glass of water and a pat on the back—almost. When he finally regained his capacity for speech, he sputtered, "I have not experienced the pleasure—"

"*Non?*" she interrupted. "I thought every sort of pleasure was to be experienced in Paris."

As Villefranche averted his gaze, she considered Nick's eyes possibly lingering on parts of her body long left untouched. A mixture of unanticipated excitement and desire flowed through her, casting a warm glow down the winding length of nerve endings aching to be used again, furthering her sense of unreality.

Memories of a past best forgotten threatened to descend upon her. Memories London would suppress; memories Paris would ignite. Even after all this time, they could consume her in a fire that had never been convincingly extinguished.

In an effort to pull herself together and allow reality a foothold in the present, she dragged a breath deep inside her lungs and released it on a slow exhale.

Villefranche's gaze stole toward her décolletage for a fraction of a second before darting away. "It seems I was mistaken." He shifted his weight to the left, then right, then left again. "Since there is nothing you don't seem to know about cigars—"

Mariana blushed at the unintended barb.

"—I shall bid you *adieu*." He inclined his head in a shallow bow.

Alarmed, Mariana discarded her role of seductress, pushed off the counter, and reached out to grab Villefranche's upper arm. She couldn't allow him to leave. Impossible that this day would end in failure. "Perhaps we could meet again on the morrow and further our"—She wracked her brain for a word, any word—"delightful"—That wasn't quite the right word—"friendship." Neither was that one.

Villefranche hesitated, his gaze unable to meet hers. "I have a previous engagement."

Mariana felt a thin sheen of perspiration coat her body. *No, no, no.* "What a shame. Then the next day it shall be," she pressed. She was making an utter fool of herself, but she cared not. Nick could be watching.

"I'm afraid—" he began.

"Then the next day." Her fingers tightened around his arm. "You must show me the sights of Paris." Rigid metal bit into the tender flesh of her other hand—the cigar box. "Perhaps the famed Jardin du Luxembourg?"

As if Villefranche sensed the only way to extricate himself from their increasingly awkward interaction was to relent, he said, each word clearly a negotiation with his rational mind, "It will be my pleasure. I shall send a note—"

"I shall meet you at the Medici Fountain at half past three on the dot," she interrupted. She wouldn't allow him to wiggle out of it later. Her fingers released their grip around his arm, and she rushed out of the shop, her mind racing faster than her feet.

Shame assaulted her from every angle. She'd made a tactical error with Villefranche. He had no desire to be flirted with, flattered, or seduced. And her behavior in the tobacconist shop . . . Her shame flared hotter.

Her enthusiasm to best Nick had blinded her to the fact that she knew nothing about his world and the methods she would need to navigate it with success. Her willfulness and overconfidence had ruined this day. How could she face Nick again and retain a measure of her pride? For surely, he knew. He had *people.*

As her heels clicked across the cobblestone arcade, she nearly groaned aloud as another thought occurred to her. When she'd engaged with the phantom Nick of her imagining, it had . . . *excited* . . . her. Had she forgotten what she'd felt when he'd melted away from her life a decade ago?

A black void. And voids longed to be filled.

The thought sobered her. She couldn't give him that power over her again.

As a girl, she'd prided herself on learning her lessons the first time around. And she'd learned her lesson regarding Nick ages ago. Once was enough, yet she needed further guidance if she was going to continue with this adventure.

She squared her shoulders and faced the gallery before her. Over the last few years of patronizing The Progressive School for Young Ladies and the Education of Their Minds, she'd come to understand something fundamental about knowledge: it was easy to attain if one was willing to set aside one's pride and admit ignorance. This was what she must do.

Tonight, she would put her pride behind her and streak naked in front of Nick, in the metaphorical sense, of course.

And after she picked up a box of bon-bons.

# Chapter 7

*Born Under a Threepenny Halfpenny Planet, Never To Be Worth a Groat: Said of any person remarkably unsuccessful in their attempts or profession.*

*A Classical Dictionary of the Vulgar Tongue*
Francis Grose

Mariana alighted from the cramped and noisome hackney, tilted her face up to the open night sky, and basked in the muted brilliance of the moon's rays. Refreshed, she glanced about the street, her eye drawn to the red lanterns hanging singly above the row of doorstops.

This was a side of the city, an area known as the Left Bank, she hadn't yet experienced. Every surface from cobblestone street to slate rooftop glistened with midnight light that danced to the competing rhythms of music from opposing open windows, creating a cacophonous symphony of sound not unpleasant to her ears.

And on the street below those windows, where she stood, a pace and demeanor that belonged to the night replaced the hustle and bustle of daytime activity. It was a pace no less hurried, but one that spoke of hidden intentions and secret destinations.

How stark was the contrast between this place and the bright and vivacious environs of the Palais-Royal. Every city had two versions of itself: one version openly displayed with a pride of ownership, and a second version that filled in the shadows, even within a bold and candid city like

Paris. All one had to do was take a carriage ride out of one's comfortable life to see the shadows hiding in plain sight.

This was a Paris that both unnerved and delighted her.

As a girl, she hadn't been allowed to leave the family's property unescorted. Any number of cutthroats and thieves surely lay in wait for a little girl like her to happen along. As an adult woman, it embarrassed her to admit that she still adhered to the instructions of her youth when she ventured forth in London.

What had she been missing all these years? This raucous Parisian night didn't feel unsafe; it felt alive. Paris was adventure.

Her amoral, hedonistic Parisienne returned to her, accompanied by the familiar wash of shame that had plagued her all afternoon and into the night, which wouldn't do. She must put aside her earlier failure and submit to learning her lessons like a good student, even if they had to come from Nick. Impetuosity and pride had led to her humiliation this afternoon. She wouldn't let it happen again.

A few doorstops away, she spotted a lantern different from the others. This one shone purple and dim, its light extending no farther than its own doorway. Intuition carried her to its solid, oak door. She gave it a few discreet taps and recalled Nick's terse response to her request—sent via an unquestioning Hortense—that they meet:

*Rue de la Huchette. La Coquine Violet. Midnight sharp. Memorize and burn.*

*La Coquine Violet.* Mariana understood the word violet easily enough, which explained the purple lantern hanging low above her head. But *la coquine*? Years of French lessons had never taught her that word. Of course, she never had any patience for French, thus her retention of its vocabulary and grammar had been negligible.

Again, she rapped on the door, harder this time. Hand suspended mid-knock, the door swung open, startling her.

Before her stood an enormous wall of man of African descent. Silently, his eyes swept up and down her person before he stepped aside and waved her into a dark foyer that offered no view into the room beyond. Only the muffled vibrations of boisterous music and men's voices, followed by women's laughter, reached her from the interior. The door clicked shut behind her.

"Your overcoat?" the doorman intoned in an accent that spoke of a complex past.

She nodded and allowed him to remove her coat.

Every fiber in her being tingled in anticipation of what lay beyond the door before her. "This is *La Coquine Violet*?" she asked, an irritating note of uncertainty lacing her tone.

The doorman brushed aside her nerves simply by smiling and pushing the door open in response. She was across its threshold before anticipation could evolve into panic. Once inside, however, there was no room for ninny-ish considerations like fright or ambivalence.

The blue-tinged room presented every sort of tableau requisite for a gentleman's entertainment: gaming tables dominating all four corners; whiskey carts scattered throughout; reclining sofas tucked into discreet shadows.

One might think this place a gentlemen's club, except for two distinguishing features: the jangling piano which produced a convivial style of music conducive to frolic and fun, and the women. They were everywhere the men were. Ever listening. Ever agreeing. Ever nodding. Ever smiling. Ever at the ready, and ever on display.

And, oh, how they displayed themselves. The dark-eyed beauties draped in bold colors, the pale-eyed blondes in pastels, all swathed in diaphanous fabrics that left little to the imagination.

Mariana felt distinctly drab, clad in the serviceable boots and gray dress Hortense had insisted she borrow for the occasion. A servant balancing a tray of champagne and wearing nothing more than a chemise and pantalettes glided swiftly past. Mariana lifted a glass and took a cooling sip.

Her body flush with excitement, she stood enveloped by a Paris unlike any she'd experienced in her usual genteel circles. Not even in London had she ever stepped foot in a room like this. Maybe, especially not in London.

*La coquine*. There was a reason she'd never been taught this word in classroom French. This place was surely a—

From across the room, a pair of dark, sharp eyes drew her attention. She couldn't look away from the sturdy woman clad in unrelieved black if she wanted to. Besides Mariana, she was the only woman in the room not smiling up at a man. She must be *la Madame*.

In the next instant, the Madame sprang into motion, agile and quick in her navigation of the room. The woman was coming for her. Mariana gulped down the remainder of her champagne in an attempt to gird herself. She knew a formidable woman when she saw one.

The Madame stopped in front of her and bluntly eyed her up and down before showering her with a tirade of rapid-fire French that Mariana didn't bother attempting to translate. The Madame snatched the empty champagne glass out of her hand and pointed toward a nondescript door on the other side of the room. Through a haze of shock, Mariana gathered that the woman was absolutely livid. At her.

When the Madame finally ran out of words, Mariana asked, hushed and polite, "Could you speak more slowly? I am certain we can resolve this matter amicably."

The Madame's mouth snapped shut, and her eyes narrowed. "*Anglaise*?"

It was more statement than question. Mariana answered a simple, "*Oui*."

The fire left the woman's eyes. "Zeese way," the Madame called over her shoulder, on the move again.

Mariana had no choice but to follow the woman through the room. Every couple she passed exuded their own unique and erotic scent—jasmine coupled with cloves, lavender with sandalwood, rose with almond—underlain by continuous notes of cigar smoke and whiskey, reminding her that despite the flowery wallpapers, quivering cleavages, and ornate furnishings, this was wholly a man's world.

Behind the Madame, Mariana ascended a dark stairwell, the sounds of revelry growing more distant with each step upward. At the end of a corridor of tightly shut doors, the Madame knocked once and pressed an ear against oak, presumably listening for permission to enter.

"*Oui*," the Madame called through the door, reaching for the jangly ring of keys at her waist. She slipped the correct key into the lock and pushed open the door. Mariana stepped through the threshold and stifled a gasp at the sight of an at-ease Nick lounging behind what appeared to be a gaming table.

"You are dressed as yourself tonight," she said, unable to state anything other than the obvious.

With the fluid grace of a cat, he stood, his fingertips brushing across the felt tabletop. "In this establishment, it is necessary."

The cold distance infusing his words brought her down to earth. Yes, he was himself tonight. Dressed in crisp whites and blacks, he was a vision of aristocratic English male. Ice wouldn't melt in his mouth. Before her stood the man she'd assumed him to be until last night. Except he wasn't that man, and possibly, he never had been.

She watched him approach the Madame and begin conversing with the woman in her native French. She couldn't help admiring his cool, collected confidence. Nick had ever been so. He knew how to handle a moment capably without trying to prove himself to anyone.

Yet another attractive quality about her husband she'd willed herself to forget. Yet another attractive quality about her husband she again remembered.

Aware that she was staring, Mariana redirected her gaze and took in the room around her. To her right stood the gaming table. Seated in one of its five chairs was a gray-bearded croupier, who sat with his face bent to the task of fuzzing the cards. All beards now suspect, she narrowed her gaze on the man before determining this one was genuine as the man's hair was the same gray.

Her gaze swung left toward the room's other dominant feature: the most massive and ornately carved bed she'd ever seen. With its scarlet and velvet coverings, it looked like a caricature of a bed one would find in a bordello.

A hot flush crept up the cleft of her décolletage, and her eyes squeezed shut. A specific memory from last night came to her: her hands braced against the bedpost, Nick's body positioned behind her, short bursts of his breath on her neck, capable fingers unraveling the flimsy scraps of cloth separating her naked skin from his . . .

The door clicked shut, blessedly drawing her attention away from the bed and a memory that served no good purpose. The Madame was gone.

"Madame Larousse has a place for you," Nick said, "if your arrangement with me ever sours."

"She thinks me a strumpet?" Mariana felt not an ounce of surprise or outrage at the Madame's assumption. In fact, it might even delight her.

"What other kind of woman would you be?" he asked, eyes wide and guileless.

A short laugh escaped her. "Life as your spy is infinitely more interesting than life as your wife." She wasn't certain when they'd last engaged in light banter, but it felt new. If she wasn't careful, it could feel like a beginning. She would be more careful.

"The meaning of *la coquine*?" she asked in an attempt to right the conversation before it went completely sideways.

"Minx." He paused before continuing, "Or hussy, depending on your point of view."

"So this place is what I think it is?"

"Yes." Nick stepped to a side bar and poured two tumblers of whiskey neat.

"I don't drink whiskey," she said, assuming one glass was meant for her.

"Tonight, you might reconsider."

He offered her a half-full glass, and she took it. "Is there a reason I might need the fortifying effects of whiskey?"

An enigmatic smile curved his lips. "After receiving your request that we meet tonight, I decided this was the perfect place to begin your . . . *lessons* . . . regarding the fundamentals of espionage."

"You're giving me spy lessons"—He winced at her phrasing—"in a *brothel*?" She thought he would teach her a few tricks of the trade tonight and send her on her way.

"We have three nights until your next *tête-à-tête* with Villefranche." He set his whiskey on the nearest table and slipped his right hand into the interior pocket of his evening jacket, pulling from its depths a long and slender object.

It was a cigar.

The sudden blaze of mortification fired through Mariana as Nick snipped off the end before striking a match and puffing the cigar alight. A thin and winding column of smoke wafted toward her, its acrid scent of earth and decay filling the room. Cigar secured between thumb and forefinger, he asked, "Would you care for a puff? It is my understanding that life thus far has denied you the pleasure of *appreciating* a man's cigar. Although, if memory serves—"

"You were there today." Her heart threatened to thunder out of her chest.

The cherry end of his cigar began to gray with ash. "I have—"

"*People*," she finished for him.

He tapped the ash into a crystal dish. "You will never be alone or unsafe, Mariana. Never."

His words elicited a powerful charge of emotion within her, and she glanced away, lest he see it within her eyes. The moment elongated as neither of them spoke. Nick did enjoy prolonging a moment. In fact, she remembered just the sort of moment he most enjoyed prolonging . . .

*Years.* It had been years since she'd indulged such thoughts about him. She wasn't one for dwelling on past failures, but with one touch of his body last night, those years threatened to fade into irrelevance.

Nick cleared his throat, breaking through her unhelpful reverie, before stubbing out his cigar in the dish. His point made, he held up the glass in a toasting gesture and tossed back the entire contents of his glass. She took a compliant sip and couldn't help a grimace.

"It's bourbon whiskey from the Americas," he explained as he began walking toward her. She instinctively braced herself. "Tonight, we will play poker."

"Poker? It sounds menacing."

"It's a card game played on Mississippi riverboats," he explained in the patient tone one would use with a toddler. "One must employ duplicity and guile to win at it. You mustn't give yourself away."

"That's tonight's lesson? Duplicity and guile? And where did you pick up bourbon"—She held up her glass—"and Mississippi riverboat games?"

"On a Mississippi riverboat."

"Nick"—And she'd thought he could never shock her again—"when were you on the Mississippi River?"

It occurred to her that she must forget everything she thought she knew about this man and start from scratch.

Before her stood a spy who made secret ocean voyages, drank exotic whiskeys, and played cards on Mississippi riverboats.

Oh, and he happened to be her husband.

Three taps sounded on the door.

"I shall save that story for another time," he called over his shoulder.

A shrill, excited squeal from downstairs burst into the room alongside two saucy young strumpets who sauntered in with arms linked, each gripping an open bottle of champagne. Their dark flashing eyes flitted between Mariana and Nick before one whispered into the other's ear, and they giggled in unison. Mariana's hand felt for the chair beside her, and she searched Nick's face for a clue about tonight's proceedings. But he betrayed not a single thought.

The subject of the strumpets' matching smirks and giggles became immediately apparent to Mariana. They were speculating about her and Nick, and what such a couple would require of them. In their place, she would wonder the same. Actually, now that she thought about it, she *did* wonder the same. What would be required of these two strumpets tonight?

One fact was obvious: they weren't innocent virgins, and this situation was neither new nor shocking to them. In fact, she was likely the only person in this room to whom this particular circumstance would be . . . *fresh*. Every muscle in her body tensed at the perverse notion. She readied herself for the night with half the contents of her glass.

"Yvette and Lisette will be playing with us," came Nick's low voice, closer to her ear than she expected.

*Playing with us?* Mariana turned to find him at her elbow. "Are you on a first name basis with every strumpet in Paris?"

A quicksilver grin crossed his lips as he pulled out the chair beside her. "Shall we?"

She bit back a responding smile. She liked the way that particular smile transformed his serious and intense visage into that of a carefree boy. She'd made herself forget all about that smile, and now she remembered it. She was remembering too much.

If she knew what was good for her, she would hasten to Calais and board the next ship bound for England. But she didn't know what was good for her, because she lowered herself onto the proffered seat and arranged her skirts as if settling in for a long evening. Nick sat to her left, Yvette and Lisette to her right, and the croupier across.

One could almost forget the croupier, so quiet and understated he was, eyes cast down, face obscured by the beard so characteristic of a certain class of Parisian. Yet a familiarity hung about the man that she couldn't lay a finger on.

The thought was replaced by matters more urgent when Nick nodded, and the croupier began dealing several sets of five cards arranged in various combinations.

Nick made no move to pick up the cards. "Poker is a vying game, similar to Brag."

"Brag uses three cards," Mariana pointed out.

"Similar. Not the same."

Again, that patient note sounded in his voice. It found its way beneath her skin and nestled there.

As Nick proceeded to explain the rules of the game and its winning combinations, Mariana only caught every other word. Yvette and Lisette, with their ceaseless whispering and giggling, provided constant distraction. They, too, had found their way beneath her skin.

Uninterested in the words coming out of Nick's mouth, they displayed a most definite interest in him as a man. One strumpet leaned forward in feigned curiosity, when really she was offering him a view of her décolletage, while the other strumpet skated her tongue across her bottom lip in a brazen attempt to draw his eye to the nature of its potential charms. Mariana had seen it dozens of times. Women simply couldn't help themselves around Nick.

"Shall we?" he asked once he concluded his tutorial. He distributed three bags of small coins around the table before the croupier performed a quick shuffle and dealt. The game was on.

Mariana picked up her cards and hid an unruly smile. A straight flush. Even though the cards were low, it was one of the best combinations in the game.

She added a few coins to the pot and glanced around, trying—and likely failing—to mask her elation. Nick's face, on the other hand, gave nothing away as he changed two cards. Meanwhile, Yvette and Lisette drank champagne straight from the bottle and giggled, not bothering to hide their cards from each other.

When the time came to reveal her cards, Mariana's heart raced at the prospect of a win. Yvette and Lisette showed one pair each before Nick laid out a full house. Relief stole through Mariana. If anyone could have bested her straight flush, it would have been Nick.

"Well done."

"Beginner's luck, to be sure," she allowed as she reached for her winnings. All she wanted to do was crow in triumph.

It felt good to best Nick. Always. Obviously, there was nothing to this game.

The croupier dealt the next hand. This time she was but one card away from a straight. How lucky.

She slid her nine of hearts facedown toward the croupier, who changed it for a different card. All she needed was a Jack of any suit to complete her straight. With bated breath, she lifted the new card. Nine of diamonds. The Curse of Scotland—Grose's appellation for this particular card— wasn't at all what she needed. Now what?

Unwilling to admit uncertainty, therefore weakness, she pushed more money into the pot.

"You're raising?" Nick asked as he tossed enough coins into the pot to check her bet.

"Of course," she replied, hoping her voice didn't ring as hollow as it felt.

In the end, it was Yvette—or was it Lisette? Oh, who cared—who won the round. Of course, their response was to giggle and whisper and giggle some more. What a pair of bubble-brains. Mariana wouldn't have minded taking the pair of strumpets by the shoulders and shaking some sense into them.

Instead, she turned in her chair and trained her gaze on Nick. "This ridiculous game is supposed to provide an instructive"—Her voice lowered to a murmur—"lesson?"

Eyes fastened onto his cards, Nick's reply was a curt nod.

On the next hand, she went for the straight. Again. And she lost. Again.

Nick won. Yvette won. Lisette won. Mariana lost. She lost every hand, except for that first one, which was beginning to feel like a lifetime ago.

She glanced down at the freshly dealt cards now resting in her hands, and her heart accelerated. She held a flush, yet . . . she was so close to a royal flush. How every instinct called out to her to throw caution to the wind and trade the nine of spades for a chance at the ten. She resisted the call and stayed, all but assured of a victory if she sat tight. Her fingers constricted around her tumbler of whiskey. With each sip, it went down ever more smoothly.

Nick raised the stakes by tossing in a handful of coins, and the strumpets matched him. That pile of coins was exactly what Mariana needed to reestablish herself in the game, and this was just the hand that would take her there.

She reached down to check their bets and found nothing but green felt, sleek and empty. She was penniless.

The room went airless, and her cheeks warmed. This was it. She was so close, and yet she was done. Her eyes refused to meet Nick's. Would she fail at everything today?

To her right, Yvette and Lisette whispered into each other's ears. The exchange was noteworthy because this time they didn't giggle. Instead, matching impish grins lit up their faces as they spoke a few words to Nick in rapid French. His lips an unyielding line, he shook his head. Yvette and Lisette giggled and again pressed their point. Again, Nick shook his head, this time punctuating the gesture with a firm, "*Non.*"

"Nick?" Mariana asked, unable to keep her curiosity at bay a moment longer. "What are they saying?"

He swiveled in his chair and leveled his serious gaze upon her. "If you wish to stay in the game, Yvette and Lisette have a proposal."

"Yes?" Mariana prompted. What could a pair of silly strumpets with air for brains have to propose to her?

"Since you have run out of funds, they suggest we wager articles of our clothing."

"Our clothing?" Mariana asked in a stunned whisper. Her gaze shifted right and found the strumpets warily observing her, awaiting her reaction. They wondered if she had the nerve.

Well, they didn't know her at all.

# Chapter 8

*Devil's books: Cards.*

*A Classical Dictionary of the Vulgar Tongue*
Francis Grose

Fascinated, Nick watched a parade of emotion march across his wife's face. Shock . . . Perplexity . . . Disbelief . . . Those were the expected ones. When the disbelief evolved into thoughtfulness, however, he experienced a jolt of surprise. She was considering the proposition. Of course.

If Mariana had an Achilles' heel, it was her inability to resist the call to adventure. It was this quality that had brought her to Paris. It was this quality that had brought her into this room. And it was this quality he'd sought to exploit by involving her in the assassination intrigue.

His plan for tonight had been to allow her to deplete her funds and then to supply her with more coinage before beginning their *spy lesson* in earnest. It hadn't been necessary to repeat Yvette and Lisette's proposal.

Why had he deviated from the plan? He knew why. Because he couldn't help himself. Because he'd partially undressed her last night, and the basest part of him would see the job done tonight, however cheaply. And because, given the opportunity, he would undermine himself time and time again when it came to her.

*That* was why he'd arranged this lesson here of all places. And *that* was why he'd repeated Yvette and Lisette's proposition.

Her eyes fixed on the kitty in the middle of the table, Mariana nodded once in assent. Yvette and Lisette squealed in delight. "What's the old saying? When in a whorehouse, do as the whores do?" Her legs swung right, toward Nick. "A little space, if you don't mind?"

His mouth went dry when she bent forward and untied the laces of her boot. She kicked the boot off her foot and paused, possibly having second thoughts. "You don't have to do this."

Her gaze shot up to meet his. "But Yvette and Lisette are so impressed."

"A dubious honor, at best."

Her eyes lit up with humor before they darted away, and gratification surged within him. How he delighted in amusing her. He was in trouble.

From the edge of his peripheral vision, he watched Mariana take her dress in hand and lift it fold over fold until the hem rested on her thigh. In a thrice, she freed the stocking from its garter and slipped it down the smooth length of her leg. Secured between forefinger and thumb, she tossed the delicate stocking, allowing it to flutter to the table. Yvette and Lisette clapped with glee.

Nick needed a large dose of spirits for his suddenly parched mouth. He reached for the whiskey and refilled his tumbler before setting the decanter on the felt. He suspected he would need several more top ups before this night was finished.

Play resumed, and Mariana lay a flush face up, a shy, sly smile curling about her rosy lips. Delectable was that smile. He wanted a nip of it. Of course, she wouldn't give him one, not once he showed his cards.

Yvette and Lisette laid down two pairs each, and Nick hesitated. Mariana had agreed to potentially strip naked based on the strength of her hand, and his full house was one of the few combinations that beat a flush.

Like ripping a bandage off a fresh wound, he slapped his cards face up onto the felt tabletop. He half expected Mariana to throw her cards at his face or, perhaps, never speak to him again.

She did neither. Her lips firmed into a straight frown—he experienced a pang of loss for her cute, curly smile—and she fixed him with an intense glare. "How do you know of this place?"

Impressed by her restraint, he cleared his throat. "In my *métier*, one learns of such venues." He tugged his cravat loose and tossed it into the pot as his wager.

"Paris," she began in a conversational tone that he didn't trust, "must be ripe with *such venues*."

He nodded a terse response, hoping to suppress this particular conversational thread, and pretended to focus on the game. Yvette and Lisette tossed one garter each into the kitty. Mariana reached down and again gathered up her dress fold by fold before unhooking the garters on her other leg, her movements quick and efficient as if this situation was mundane, banal even.

Like a green boy on the verge of his first view of female flesh, Nick's heart doubled its rate. He should avert his gaze. It was the gentlemanly course of action, but all hope of the high ground was lost when his gaze snagged on the instep of her narrow foot. The bones of her feet matched the rest of her: long and lithe. Elegant. The woman had elegant feet.

He must gain control over himself. This was an example of how a moment could spin out of control around Mariana. How easily he could ask if her feet ached, if they required a massage. It was this sort of moment he'd been avoiding for most of their marriage. No matter how he feigned indifference, he wasn't. The word *cheap* came to him again.

Finally, she straightened and tossed both stocking and bright pink garter into the kitty. It was an unusual pink of the sort one would expect to find in the tropics where everything and everyone ran just a bit hotter . . .

In a desperate bid to regain control of this night, Nick picked up the discarded remnant of their conversation and began stating facts in the hope they would rescue him from the erotic fiction his mind was creating. "In the thirteenth century," he began, his tone brisk and matter-of-fact, "Louis the Ninth decreed prostitution legal on nine streets in Paris in an effort to control its spread throughout the city. Rue de la Huchette was one of those streets. Today, more than one hundred and eighty brothels populate Paris."

"Such a precise number," she said. "One might think you a *connoisseur*."

Her voice had grown cold and distant. Just where he needed it to be. Hot and close was too distracting. "*Connoisseur* isn't the correct word for my interest. And you know it."

"Do I?" she countered. "Do I know a single true thing about you?"

"Yes," he stated, daring her to look at him.

Her gaze, however, remained steady on her cards. She was processing his response and, more specifically, that word. *Yes*. Wouldn't it have simplified matters to have said *no*? Implicit in that word would have been that she'd never known him.

But he'd replied the opposite. It was as if he had a basic need to preserve the thread of their old connection, a thread he'd severed. Or so he'd convinced himself. One day in her presence outed the lie.

Her brows lifted to her hairline, and she gasped, bringing her fingertips to her mouth. Nick followed the direction of her gaze, and a far more cynical response escaped him in the form of a short, single-note chortle.

Yvette and Lisette had stood and were now slinking around each other, slowly unbuttoning one another's dresses.

In unison, they shimmied their shoulders and allowed their dresses to fall to the floor. Neither wore a chemise, only short pantalettes and small corsets that served to lift exposed breasts, nipples immodestly puckered.

Waves of tension radiated off Mariana as the trollops tossed their dresses into the pot and giggled. Nick knew better than to react.

All eyes swung toward Mariana, even the croupier's. Hers was the next move. A flush of deep rose crept along the delicate ridge of her collarbone as she did the unexpected: her fingers reached across her body and found the three buttons located on the side of her dress before flicking them out of their loops.

The night might have gotten away from him.

"Mariana"—He spoke up, because he must—"you don't have to do this."

"Don't I? I must abide by the rules of the game if I'm to stay in the game, correct?"

Nick's hand shot out and trapped Mariana's fingers on the table. Her eyes widened and flew up to meet his as a spark of electrical current raced up his arm. She must have felt it, too. "This is your game, Mariana. You make the rules."

"How will I learn to play the game if I'm a delicate flower for whom allowances must be made? I thought you live in a harsher world than that."

"I do."

Sudden awareness caught Nick by surprise, the bare flesh of their hands pressed skin to skin. He pulled his hand back as if scalded. She rose to her feet and wiggled out of her dress, allowing it to fall to the floor in a heap of coarse wool. Yvette and Lisette first gasped, then collectively cooed at the sight of her.

The dress was dull as used bathwater, but *dull* wasn't the correct word for the garments that lay beneath. He wasn't certain the fuchsia of the corset and garters existed in nature, but the color came alive against Mariana's honey-toned skin, even as the corset embraced her lush body, pushing ripe breasts up and forward, curving in at her waist and subtly flaring out at her hips. She was a hothouse flower in bloom. She was incomparable.

His mouth again went dry. He must busy himself if he was to keep his head, the one atop his shoulders, in the game. Slowly, as not to startle this exquisite confection before him, he shrugged off his jacket and added it to the pot. His contribution felt meager compared to Mariana's.

She settled into her chair with an insouciance as if nothing of consequence had occurred. Very French was that insouciance. Very unlike the Mariana he knew. The croupier dealt the next hand.

As they changed cards, it was undeniable that the tone of the room had altered. How could it not? Mariana had thrown down the gauntlet.

No longer did Yvette and Lisette whisper and giggle. Instead, they became more . . . *tactile* . . . with one another. Yvette feathered light fingertips across Lisette's collarbone before reaching up to remove an earring. She repeated the motion on the other side and tossed the pair into the pot. Lisette responded in kind.

And Mariana? Captivation writ plainly across her face, she watched Yvette and Lisette play out an erotic scene for which patrons paid outlandish sums of money to witness and even join. For the uninitiated, it could be overwhelming. Yet Mariana's cool response was to reach up, remove the silver brooch holding her simple chignon in place, and drop it into the pot.

The action itself was simple; the effect was anything but. Her hair tumbled about her shoulders, stray tendrils finding their way to the cleft between her breasts, transforming her into the most alluring woman in Paris. Nick added his waistcoat and averted his gaze. Play was ready to resume.

The round that had begun so dramatically concluded with a whimper when he showed his hand. Mariana sighed and folded. As he gathered his winnings, he watched her attention again stray toward Yvette and Lisette, who were now caressing one another's faces. Then, one whispered into the other's ear, and they both angled their bodies toward Mariana. Likely she'd never seen such a display between two women. Or even considered its possibility.

Lisette reached out a hand and tenderly cupped one side of Mariana's face, while Yvette cupped the other. Mariana sat stone still as if bewitched by a spell. Experienced fingertips began tracing a path down her cheeks and neck, inch by inch, trailing lower before hesitating at the space just above her breasts. Suddenly, the equilibrium of the room felt balanced on the tip of a needle with no margin for a wrong movement. One either toppled over, or one was pricked.

It occurred to Nick that blood might be drawn tonight.

Emboldened by Mariana's lack of response, Yvette and Lisette sidled closer. The three women looked like they were forming a sacred pact, its secrets known only to them. And all Nick could do was watch, helpless on his side of the table. He glanced at the croupier whose attention remained fixed on the whispery fuzz of his cards.

Fingertips resumed their progress ever lower toward the curve of Mariana's scantily clad breasts. He could see the outline of her nipples puckered beneath her white chemise.

Before Nick had a chance to consider what this night might reveal, Mariana's hands reached up and grabbed each trollop by a wrist, eliciting annoyed whines from each. The pact was broken.

A relieved Nick shot to his feet. At last, he could be of some use. "That will be all," he told the visibly bewildered Yvette and Lisette in their native language. Petulantly, they grabbed their discarded apparel and stomped out of the room, slamming the door behind them.

He made eye contact with the croupier. "You must go, too. And leave the cards." The man nodded and was through the door in a thrice of heartbeats.

Nick turned the lock behind him and faced a Mariana altered from the one who had entered this room an hour ago. This woman could be the most sought after and expensive courtesan in Paris.

"There is nothing those women won't do, is there?" came her first words in what felt like hours, but must have been no more than five minutes. Anything could happen in five minutes.

"No."

"Must that be me as I *work* for you?"

Her voice emerged quiet and soft, and he detected an uncharacteristic strand of uncertainty running through it. "You will never be forced to do anything you don't want to do," he responded with a fervid earnestness he hadn't expressed in years, if ever. He sat in the croupier's vacated chair across from her and pushed a stack of coins across the table. "Ready?"

She pushed the coins back toward him. "Let's keep the stakes high, shall we?"

# Chapter 9

*Sharp: Subtle, acute, quick-witted; also a sharper or cheat, in opposition to a flat, dupe, or gull. Sharp's the word and quick's the motion with him; said of anyone very attentive to his own interest, and apt to take all advantages.*

*A Classical Dictionary of the Vulgar Tongue*
Francis Grose

Even with all the twists and turns the night had delivered, Mariana gleaned from Nick's startled expression that he wasn't prepared for this one. He'd expected her, like any sheltered lady of her class, to accuse him of subjecting her to a night filled with vice and perversity. Instead, she'd chosen to keep playing, to further the game, to push it to its edge. She would learn tonight's lesson before their game was done.

Her hand reached beneath the table and emerged dangling her other garter. He unclipped sapphire and gold cuff studs and tossed them onto the felt. Play was ready to resume.

Silently, he shuffled the cards. Silently, he dealt them. Silently, he won when she folded. Silently, he slid the winnings into his growing pile.

Silently, Mariana stewed.

Gathering her composure, she finally spoke. "Tell me what I'm doing wrong."

"Show me your cards."

She lay them face up on the felt.

"You were going for a straight."

"Yes?"

"I know your hand by the way you bet. If you have a pair, you raise with two coins. If you have a better hand, you raise with five coins. You're too predictable. You cannot be predictable in espionage."

She wanted to bristle at the word *predictable*, but she didn't rise to it. "Then how did Villefranche become embroiled in this intrigue? He's one of the most predictable people I've ever encountered."

"Perhaps that was why he was chosen."

"Chosen?"

"He reports to someone with more power and connections. On the other hand, he could simply be a bloodthirsty anarchist."

"That's one theory. Try another."

"He's a scion of the Orléans family. They're a powerful family, but not *in* power. He may wish to correct that imbalance."

Mariana shook her head. "That doesn't ring true either. He doesn't strike me as hungry for power. Tell me," she continued, "have you visited the museums in Paris?"

Nick's eyebrows crinkled together in confusion at the sudden conversational switch. Then his eyes narrowed. "Is this about the Woolly Mammoth?"

"They're woolly and have large tusks. How was that question for the unpredictable?"

Nick dropped his cards face up on the felt. She showed a pair of sevens and felt a sly smile tilt the corners of her mouth. He'd folded with a pair of Jacks. She'd won the hand and caught her first windfall of the night.

Duplicity, guile . . . She was beginning to understand how to win at this game.

Nick glared down at his mistake and conceded with a grudging, "Well done." He took in hand a newly shuffled deck of cards, ready to deal.

Riding a gratifying wave of triumph, Mariana was just about to slide his cuff studs into the kitty when she hesitated. A nervy feeling began to get the better of her, a feeling that made the room feel bright and shiny and teeming with possibility.

She would stake her locket. She didn't need to. And she most definitely didn't want Nick to have it or see what lay inside, but she couldn't resist wagering her most precious asset. She *wanted* to play for high stakes. She hadn't felt this alive . . . ever. Perhaps the bourbon had been going down *too* smoothly.

"In the last few years, I've discovered something about myself." Blood zinging through her veins, she unclasped her locket and dropped it into the kitty. "I am quite taken with the history of our earth. It seems that The Progressive School for Young Ladies and the Education of Their Minds has worked its magic on my mind, too. Can you imagine?"

"I can imagine," he replied, meeting her wager with the sapphire and gold buttons that matched his lost cuff studs.

"There's a word for what I am. *Autodidact*. It's my dirty little secret." She could ignore the fact that his shirt fell the scantest inch open, revealing the fine trail of hair running down the hollow of his ridged stomach to the top of his trousers. "Check."

Charged up with a feeling of invincibility, she lay her cards face up on the felt—a full house.

"Well done—again," he bit out.

With a simple nod of acknowledgement, she accepted his paltry congratulation and slid her winnings toward her growing pile of loot. "That isn't to say I'm suddenly a bluestocking." She picked up the thread of their conversation as if the hand she'd just won was a triviality, as if she wasn't exhilarated by it. It was a heady feeling, beating a man like Nick.

She reached for the decanter of bourbon at her elbow—
when had that appeared on the table?—and topped her glass
before shooting it back like a seasoned riverboat gambler.
She might be developing a taste for hedonism.

"If I may be blunt?"

She liked the way his voice sounded just now. All
affectation was gone, and there was no hint of patronization
either. The tone conceded they were two well-matched
adults. "Are you ever not blunt with me?"

"You're dressed like the most expensive courtesan in
Paris." His intense, gray gaze held hers. "It's a fair bet that
no one would mistake you for a bluestocking."

Her lips stretched into a too-wide smile. She should be
offended by his words, but they delighted her. He'd only
confirmed what she'd known for some minutes now. He was
distracted by her state of dishabille.

Her fingers absently toyed with the top of her chemise,
brushing against the exposed skin above her corseted breasts.
Nick averted his gaze and shifted in his chair.

She leaned forward. "I really want to see that Woolly
Mammoth." The words might sound playful in the moment,
but she couldn't be more earnest.

"Be careful where you voice your wishes," he began
in a voice low and intense and utterly serious as his gaze
again captured hers. "There are men who would stop at
nothing to give you what you want. Men break laws, walk
across flames, and even start wars to give a woman like you
*everything* she wants."

"A woman like me?" she whispered from inside the
spell he'd woven around her with his words. "A man like
whom, Nick?"

The air went completely still. The world could have
stopped spinning on its axis, and she wouldn't have noticed.

"I think you've mastered duplicity and guile," he spoke

into the quiet before shooting to his feet and breaking the spell.

Mariana assessed the man towering over the table. He was agitated, which perversely calmed her. "You think me so without guile?"

She rose, one slow inch at a time, until they stood facing each other like combatants. His eyes remained steady, too steady, on hers. He was trying not to glance down at her scantily clad body. She liked to think she'd chosen tonight's undergarments without him in mind, but she knew the truth.

She leaned across the table to retrieve her clothing. If he received an eyeful of the effect of gravity on corseted cleavage, then so be it. She reclined in her chair and lifted a foot, slipping her toes inside a stocking and unrolling the length of silk up her leg. His eyes lingered hot upon the bare skin of her thigh just above where the stocking ended.

She reached for the other stocking. "It feels as though we haven't discussed anything substantive."

"There are many ways to have a conversation," he said, his voice rough and intimate. "Sometimes we communicate more about ourselves by what we don't say." A moment passed. "And in the language of our bodies."

A lightning bolt of desire shot through Mariana. And she'd thought she was in control. Rather, intoxication, bright and pervasive, flowed through her, as if she'd downed the entire decanter of bourbon in a single swallow. Its hot glow had found its way into her bloodstream, transforming her body into a vessel incandescent with brilliant light. She lifted her other leg and touched toes to silk.

Her eyes lifted and met raw craving within his. The space between their bodies no longer mattered. "And what is my body communicating right now?"

"Mariana . . ."

The rest of his words slipped away. His eyes did his

talking when they lowered to her pointed toes and raked up her ankles before lingering on her exposed thighs for a moment too long. Her core throbbed and ached. Unhurried, his gaze continued over her hips, her breasts, her collarbone, and her parted lips before reaching her eyes. Piercing gray burned into her, leaving no doubt about the message she'd communicated, and the one he'd received. Her breath came shallow and quick as exhilaration surged through her. Contrary to what she'd assumed for the past decade, Nick wasn't immune to her.

In three decisive strides, he moved to her side of the table, erasing all distance between them. She remained in her chair, her head tilted back to take in the length of this gorgeous man—all long lines and strong angles. He reached over and lifted her necklace off the table. Its locket swung like a pendulum between them.

Her hand flew to her chest for confirmation that the locket wasn't there. How had she forgotten it? The man before her was how.

"Do you mind?" she asked, rising to her stocking feet. *Oh.* Scant inches separated their bodies. The outside world felt as distant as if they'd created a world of two, its sole occupants her and him. She couldn't look away.

~ ~ ~

Nick could have handed over the necklace. He *should* have handed over the necklace. Instead, he reached for the curve of Mariana's hip and guided her around until her back faced him. He stood poised to drape the necklace around her elegant neck and allow its locket to resume its rightful place between the ripe curve of her breasts.

It was another instance of what he should have done. But a feeling too basic to deny overrode his intellect: he wanted her—badly.

Without thought for their past or their future, he lowered

his head and touched his lips to her bare skin. Her back arched, and her shoulder blades slid together. His hand reached around her waist to the flat of her belly, steadying them both as his tongue flicked across her salty flesh.

"Nick . . ." His name emerged from her lips, not on a scold, but on a sigh. She was waiting, anticipating. She felt the same intense desire.

He sensed it in the stillness of her body and heard it in the hitch of her breath. His tongue traced the ridge of her spine and up her graceful neck until it reached her earlobe, drawing the tender flesh between his lips and teeth for a testing nip. Her head tilted to the side, granting him access to more of her. He released a soft groan into her ear, and goose bumps rose beneath his touch. The rigid length of his cock thrummed in anticipation of what came next.

That ridiculous bed behind them dominated this room for a reason. It wasn't a bed constructed for a good sleep. It was a bed constructed for a good tup.

She was a single ragged breath away from giving in to this need . . . But that breath never came. Her hand covered his. At first a feather light touch, it became viselike as her fingers clamped around his hand and lifted it off her body.

Reactively, he took one, two steps backward. She turned to face him, a rosy blush tinting her skin, her breath coming fast and hard.

Oh, yes, she wanted it, too. But it was she who had put a stop to the madness. Her lips were a firm, determined line as she reached for her dress and slipped the drab garment over her head. Her movements, quick and efficient, contrasted sharply with the soft and languorous moment just left behind.

Thoroughly unbalanced, Nick felt like a rank amateur. And he was supposed to be the teacher. He'd lost focus, pure and simple. It was the sort of gaffe that could cost him his life in more tenuous circumstances. His body aching and bitter with unrequited desire, he snatched up his evening jacket.

*Blast*. Tonight had served but one useful purpose: a reminder of the man he became around her—the man who could never have enough of her.

A rapid succession of knocks sounded on the door, turning into a haranguing of the door. Necklace still in hand, he pocketed it as he strode to answer before the door came off its hinges.

After a short exchange with a drunk who had the wrong room, Nick turned to find a dressed and expectant Mariana standing with reticule primly held before her. The previous interlude had been wiped from existence. Wasn't that the fiction best for them both?

"My apologies for the necessity of such dicey accommodation," he pronounced superciliously, breaking last night's promise. He needed to batten down his defenses against her. "This place must be quite a come down from your usual *milieu* for entertainments."

He caught a glimpse of bewilderment on her face, but before he could examine it, it turned into something else— something harder and less vulnerable. "I am certain you know nothing of my *milieus*, Nick."

With those words, their past was again their present, implacable and insurmountable. He could forget that for a wild moment a different outcome had felt possible, even inevitable.

"I believe we've covered duplicity and guile sufficiently," he found himself saying.

"Until our next lesson?" she asked. "Soon, the seduction begins." She swept past him and out the door.

He rushed to the doorway and peered down the corridor's narrow distance long after she'd disappeared down the stairs, leaving behind only a faint wisp of her scent and a familiar desire that neither time nor distance had erased.

*Soon, the seduction begins*. Or had it already? He'd

never met a more seductive woman in his life.

Never met? Of course, they'd *met*. It was such a small word for everything they'd done. They were married, after all. Except the Mariana he'd left ten years ago hadn't yet developed into *this* woman. She'd always been irresistible to him, but not a seductress.

*Seductress*. The word landed with a crash. She wasn't here to seduce him; she was here to seduce another man. The smack of reality struck him hard.

He would do well to remember its impact.

# Chapter 10

*Island: He drank out of the bottle till he saw the island: the island is the rising bottom of a wine bottle, which appears like an island in the center, before the bottle is quite empty.*

*A Classical Dictionary of the Vulgar Tongue*
Francis Grose

*Next Day*

One word for the state of Mariana's being this morning came to mind: crapulent. Hedonism had its drawbacks.

A woman was entitled to slumber the day away when she'd spent the previous night drinking and gambling in a bordello with a pair of strumpets and her estranged husband. She'd earned the right to sleep, and Hortense should have let her. But Hortense happened to be the sort of lady's maid—and spy . . . they still hadn't discussed that development properly—who believed in an invigorating and early start to the day.

The girl had taken one glance at her this morning and released a little cry of distress. "*Mon dieu*! Zee puffs beneath your eyes . . . I shall fetch you a mirror."

Eyes closed to relentless morning light, Mariana had held up a hand. "*Non*, Hortense, no mirror. If my head looks anything on the outside like it feels on the inside . . . just *non*." She needed more time to wallow in her crapulence. Last night's flirtation with whiskey might have gotten the better of her. Yesterday hadn't been the most auspicious start to her life as a spy.

She heaved a deep sigh of relief when Hortense's footsteps receded from the bedroom. How on earth could she possibly call on Helene to collect the twins' letters today? She would have to send the hotel's errand boy. She couldn't face Helene in this condition.

Efficient footsteps sounded outside the bedroom, and Mariana stifled a groan of annoyance. Hortense was returning. Through a forest of fuzzy eyelashes, she watched the girl pour a pitcher of cold water into a washbasin before taking a knife to a cucumber and slicing off two thin slivers.

At Hortense's insistence, she left the comfort of her warm bed and washed her face in the cooling water before taking a seat on a firm chair, allowing Hortense to tilt her head back and place the slices over her eyes. The girl maintained that she not lie back down.

"*Non, non*, your head must be elevated. Zee bad puff must flow down, down, down."

It was here Mariana remained for the next thirty or so minutes. She had to admit to feeling somewhat less crapulent sitting here with her head resting back on a firm, cushioned surface with vegetables covering her eyes. They felt nice.

*Soon, the seduction begins.* Through the fog of day-after crapulence, the words came to her, echoing through her head like a gong. Why had she spoken them? To *him*.

She knew why. She'd hoped those words would imbed themselves under his skin like little, sticky burrs.

Hortense began fluttering around the bed, straightening blankets and pillows. "Zee green fairy, *non*?"

Mariana peeked out from beneath a cucumber. "Pardon?"

"Zee absinthe, *non*?"

"*Non.*"

"You don't know of zee absinthe?"

Mariana shook her head and immediately regretted it. "It was zee whiskey." She sensed now might be her opportunity to discuss Hortense's *other* duties. "Have you been in your other line of *service* very long?"

Hortense's gaze met hers, and Mariana saw that the girl understood this turn in the conversation. "Since I was fourteen years of age."

"How many years have you now?"

"Twenty."

Shock traced through Mariana. At twenty, she'd been a married woman with a pair of twins to care for, a household to run, and a philandering husband to ignore. "Is Hortense your real name?"

"Zee answer to that question is . . . complex."

"How did you become—?" Mariana hesitated.

"Your husband saved me from a bad family situation."

"Nick casts a wide net, doesn't he?" Mariana said, unable to hide her sarcasm.

"Your husband is a great man," Hortense said, her dark eyes flashing. "You are lucky to call such a man yours."

With a start of surprise, Mariana understood this girl knew nothing of her relationship with Nick. He'd certainly succeeded in keeping his two lives distinct.

As if realizing she'd overstepped the mark, Hortense blushed bright scarlet and busied herself fluffing pillows that had been fluffed minutes ago. She must say something to put the girl at ease. "Your loyalty to Nick does you credit." Strangely, she meant it.

Hortense nodded once in acknowledgement, and the mood in the room lifted. Mariana snuggled deeper into her robe and again covered her eyes with the cucumbers.

What had gotten into her last night? What had gotten into Nick?

Whiskey.

But that wasn't all there was to it. To blame the spirits was too easy of an absolution. The whiskey had simply made it easier to remember what she liked about her husband. Too easy. In the future, she would stay away from whiskey around Nick.

A soft, but insistent, tap-tap-tapping sounded on the exterior door to her rooms. Mariana's ears strained toward the sound of Hortense turning the key in the deadbolt and opening the door on smooth hinges. Hortense had no time to ask for a calling card before a cacophony of voices filled the rooms. Mariana knew those tones, rhythms, and cadences nearly as well as any on earth. Family had arrived.

More irritated than alarmed, she flicked the cucumbers into a rubbish bin, cinched the belt at her waist, and strode through the doorway to her sitting room. She could ignore the mild, persistent throbbing at the base of her skull. "Uncle Bertie? Aunt Dot?" Their names emerged in the halting staccato of bemused disbelief. "How extraordinary to see you." It was the politest way she could think to ask what they were doing here.

With her characteristic cloud of unruly white frizz puffed about her head, Aunt Dot rushed across the room and took both of Mariana's hands in her own slightly damp ones. Aunt Dot ever had moist palms. "Oh, my dear. Oh, my dearest." She rotated back and forth between Uncle Bertie and Mariana a few times. Mariana likened Aunt Dot to a spinning top once she got worked up. Today, she was in top form. "Oh, my dearest dear."

"Has something happened?" Mariana asked, genuine alarm beginning to creep in.

"Has something happened? Has something happened? Oh, my dear."

Mariana glanced up at Uncle Bertie, a ponderous man whose great jowls sagged lower than ever, and lifted her brows in query. "Uncle?" she asked in a weak voice, bracing herself for the worst.

"Oh, my dearest, your face—"

"My face?" To be sure, she wasn't looking her best this morning, but she was quite certain that she hadn't sprouted a wart on the tip of her nose overnight.

"Your face says it all. Oh, my dearest dear."

Mariana reclaimed her hands from Aunt Dot and began to worry that she'd walked into a scene straight out of bedlam. She only questioned whether it was she or they who belonged in the padded room.

"Why don't we all take a seat and perhaps ring for tea?" Uncle Bertie suggested in his usual proper and diplomatic manner as he settled his cumbersome body onto the sofa.

"Of course, Uncle," Mariana replied, following his lead and perching on the edge of the opposite settee.

"And have you a dollop of French cream to accompany tea?" Aunt Dot asked, eyes wide and innocent.

Mariana nodded once toward Hortense and returned her attention to Uncle and Aunt, who watched her with twin expectant looks on their faces. It occurred to her that they may all need more than a dollop of brandy before this visit was through. "Have you recently arrived in Paris?" It seemed like a fitting question. Their disheveled appearance suggested they'd arrived this very moment.

"Have we recently arrived? *Have* we recently arrived? Oh, my dearest dear. On a wave from Noah's flood, I daresay."

"Is it raining?"

"Is it raining? *Is* it raining? Oh, dearest, is it raining. We have nothing like this in England. I can assure you of that, indeed. Oh, the French—" Hortense entered the room bearing tea service, and Aunt Dot lowered her voice. "How do they live the way they insist on living?"

"Aunt," Mariana began, resisting a sigh, "the French can hardly control their weather." Out of the corner of her eye,

Mariana noticed Hortense stiffen as she commenced her task of arranging the tea tray for service.

In a loud whisper, Aunt Dot asked, "Does the chit know how to make tea?"

"Yes, Aunt," Mariana replied, her patience beginning to run thin.

"*Proper* English tea?"

Impatient to redirect the conversation, Mariana turned toward Uncle Bertie. "Are you in Paris for long?"

"We do not yet know the duration of our stay." His gaze locked onto hers and held. "And you, my dear, have you found what you must so desperately seek?"

Alarm bells sounded inside Mariana's head. "I suppose—"

Her reply was cut short when Aunt Dot, who wouldn't cease monitoring Hortense's every movement, called out, "Girl—how do you say *girl* in French?"

"*Une fille?*" Mariana supplied the word and instantly regretted it. She was only feeding the beast. "Aunt, Hortense speaks perfectly serviceable English."

Aunt Dot, however, had had enough. She rose in a huff and rushed around the sofa, her hand extended. "I'll take that," she commanded, referring to the tea strainer held by a stunned Hortense. She released the instrument and took a step backward, allowing Aunt Dot ample room.

"Now, *fille*," Aunt Dot said as she began advising Hortense on the intricacies of making a *proper* English tea, enunciating every word loudly and clearly as if Hortense was both deaf and mentally slow, instead of simply French. These were one and the same for Aunt Dot.

Every so often, Aunt inserted an incorrect French word, and Hortense corrected her, saying, "Madame, I speak English fluently." But Hortense's protests were all for naught; staunch English ladies were neither swayed nor changed.

Meanwhile, Uncle Bertie leaned forward in a confidential manner. "I came as soon as I heard," he intoned on a low note that wouldn't carry beyond the few feet separating them.

A prickle of foreboding tingled down Mariana's spine. "Heard what?"

"About Nick, dearest."

Mariana glanced around, caught Hortense's steady eye for a fraction of a second, and leaned in closer to Uncle. "I've seen Nick."

"Alive?"

Mariana recoiled from Uncle's narrow gaze. A sense that she'd said the wrong thing snaked through her. The glint in Uncle Bertie's eye was keen, too keen.

He reached out and covered her hand with his. It took every ounce of her resolve to leave her hand where it lay, even as her instinct would have her snatch it away. By sheer force of will, she returned Uncle's gaze and felt a moment of connection. A knowledge lay within his eyes . . . It was a knowledge that shouldn't be there, unless—unless, he'd received a note, too.

Aunt Dot interrupted this disconcerting line of thought when she swept around the sofa in a peevish flurry of muslin skirts. "Oh, my dear, you simply must keep a sharp eye on that girl," Aunt Dot proclaimed in a less than discreet voice.

"Aunt, she speaks English," Mariana repeated, "and she can hear you perfectly well. I would ask that you lower your voice or, better yet, keep such thoughts to yourself," she finished on a firm note. Years spent alongside the stern headmistress, Mrs. Bloomquist, hadn't been lost on her.

Hortense brought the tray around and began pouring. A much-chastened Aunt Dot watched in silence, even as her unsparing gaze caught every nuance and stored away every perceived mistake for future conversation. A small prick of guilt jabbed Mariana's conscience. "Was your journey in good order and comfortable?"

"Oh, my dearest dear, the roads."

Mariana awaited further clarification, but that was all her aunt would say on the matter. *The roads* spoke volumes.

Not a sip of tea later, Uncle Bertie pushed off the settee to a stand. "Well, we must be off."

Aunt Dot reached out and squeezed Mariana's hand. "My dear, will you be well in our absence?"

"I shall manage," Mariana replied as Aunt released her hand. She ushered the pair to the door. "Thank you for your visit and for your . . . concern."

The instant the door clicked shut, Mariana called out, "Hortense, will you pour me a bath?" Partially obscured by a silk chinoiserie screen, stood a claw-foot tub, soft and inviting with mid-morning light.

Once again, she settled into the familiar chair and rested her head against its firm cushion, eyes closed, while the bath was readied.

Uncle Bertie knew something about the life Nick led on this side of the Channel, of that she was certain. Ever since she could remember, he'd been involved in vague governmental activities, like so many second sons of their class. In fact, it was Uncle Bertie who had paved the way for Nick, another second son, with the consulate.

She felt in her gut that her earlier suspicion was correct: Uncle Bertie had received a note, too. Why hadn't he said so? She couldn't slough off the feeling she'd mishandled the situation by telling him that Nick was alive. She kept getting it wrong at every turn when it came to this spy business.

She released a groan of frustration. Nothing was what it seemed. First Nick, then Hortense, now Uncle Bertie . . . Who *wasn't* involved in this intrigue?

Of course, she shouldn't feel all that surprised. Nick had always withheld the core of himself from her. In the early days, she'd felt it with a deep certainty in the way only a girl wholeheartedly in love for the first time could intuit every straight and curve of her lover's heart. And, in the way of a young girl, she'd accepted it. He was five years older; of course, he would have a past. Wasn't his mystery part of his allure?

Now that past was out of the shadows and in the light, but still between them. It was a whole new, strange world that unfurled before her. An image of Yvette and Lisette kissing sprang to mind. What sort of life did Nick lead?

Her finger ran along the space between her breasts where her gold locket should lie. A stab of regret for its loss pierced her. What had possessed her to gamble her locket away?

Not whiskey. Rather, it was a dangerous high-spiritedness that at times overtook her good sense and led her down paths wild and unknown, sometimes destructive. In all likelihood, and at this very moment, her locket was gracing the décolletage of a French strumpet named either Yvette or Lisette. She squeezed her eyes tight at the thought of what activity said French strumpet could be engaged in—

"Madame, your bath is ready," came Hortense's soft, husky voice.

Mariana stood and shrugged off her bathrobe as she closed the few steps between her and the blessed pleasure of a piping hot bath. No click of a ring sounded as her fingers closed around the tub's edge, and she lowered herself into its steaming depths. She'd stopped wearing her wedding band years ago, the moment she'd learned about Nick's affair, not from the gossip rags—they traded in lies, after all—but from his own lips.

But she'd never stopped wearing the locket with the cameo inside. Not for a single occasion. The cameo represented an ideal, one they'd achieved together for a single perfect moment in time. She sank further into the water's sultry embrace, banishing the thought and the regret.

Eyes closed, her mind traveled to a different time and place, far away and long ago toward a memory long-suppressed. It was out of self-preservation, to be sure. But here, in the foreign environs of Paris, she could indulge in the luxury of such a memory—not just any memory, her favorite memory. The day she'd known Nick was hers forever.

# Chapter 11

*Arsy varsey: To fall arsy varsey, i.e. head over heels.*

*A Classical Dictionary of the Vulgar Tongue*
Francis Grose

*The Cotswolds*
*24 March 1812*

Unlike her twin sister Olivia, Mariana didn't fall in love with her husband at a ball or anywhere near the glittering flow of the *ton*. If she were to characterize Society as a set of colors, its palette would glow bright gold and hard platinum.

In direct contrast stood the place where she fell for Nick: a color palette of soft ambers and gentle greens, the palette of the countryside.

As the younger brother of Mariana's father, the Earl of Surrey, Uncle Bertie had been entitled to the Cotswolds estate that had been part of their mother's dowry. From the earliest age, Mariana loved traveling to Little Spruisty Folly.

To get to the heart of the estate, one turned off the main road and rode for more than half a mile down a wide lane flanked on either side by stately horse-chestnut trees before one caught sight of the main house. Although neither house nor grounds were "little," and neither a single folly nor a solitary spruce pine were to be found anywhere on the entire estate, the name somehow fit the sprawling house constructed with various architectural styles, ranging from the original Tudor to the latest Georgian. It was a patchwork quilt of a house, and one not soon forgotten. One could easily become lost inside its jumble of rooms for hours, days, and even weeks.

Mariana loved the Folly in a personal way none of her other family did, not even Olivia. As a result, she'd spent many a fortnight in her youth as Uncle Bertie and Aunt Dot's lone girl visitor. No one—not even Uncle and Aunt, she suspected—could comprehend Mariana's abiding love for the place since its bucolic solitude seemed so at odds with the bold, social girl London knew. For Mariana, the Folly was a place where she never felt the need to prove herself. She could just *be*. The Folly was her oasis.

One morning, no different from any other, Uncle Bertie began going on at length about a promising chap making some excellent connections on the Continent. "The boy has the right ideas," Uncle continued. "Just the sort England needs with Napoleon getting ready to march again."

The conversation occurred on the periphery of Mariana's consciousness for she'd been entirely focused on the estate's retired hunting beagle, Horace, who slyly snapped up every bit of ham she slipped beneath the table to his ever-patient chops. Uncle was ever rhapsodizing about one promising chap or another, which was why his remark about "the chap's" return to England went right over her head. If she'd been more attentive, she might have been prepared for the sight greeting her eyes thirty or so minutes later. Likely not.

Aunt Dot had other plans for the breakfast conversation. "Dearest Mariana," she cut in, silencing Uncle Bertie, who directed his attention to his *Morning Chronicle*, "have you devised a strategy for the upcoming Season? You must make your second go around count. Did no young lord catch your eye?"

Mariana inwardly cringed and exhaled a noncommittal, "Hmm."

"Well, Olivia made the most of *her* first Season," Aunt continued, oblivious to Mariana's increasing discomfort. "A love match with the son of a duke. Even if he is a younger son, Percy Bretagne was something of a catch. And married before the end of the Season . . . I daresay, I never knew the chit had it in her," Aunt Dot finished on a note of grudging admiration.

Unable to take any more chatter about strategies and "catching" husbands, Mariana stood and excused herself from the table. With a low, short whistle she summoned Horace to accompany her on their morning walk. Sometimes he trotted alongside her; other times his sensitive nose picked up an interesting scent that claimed the entirety of his attention and off he trotted in a direction all his own. Scents were neither good nor bad to Horace. They were either interesting or not.

On this particular morning, he stuck close as they lit across the stone portico and onto the closely-cropped grass that provided a carpet for the formal garden. Once past the ha-ha, Mariana cut right and found the narrow trail that led into the copse of woods forming the northeast boundary of Uncle's land.

Soon, they reached the bubbling creek, which ran through the estate. They continued parallel alongside until it flowed into the small and secluded Duck Pond, a name first optimistically, then ironically, bestowed upon the mass of water no duck had ever deigned to set feather upon. It was here that Horace usually strayed, but not on this day.

This day, he stuck with Mariana as if he knew what they would encounter on the other side of the small rise that formed the southwest bank of the pond. She thought nothing of Horace's unusual steadfastness. Instead, her mind wandered elsewhere.

It was true that she was on the verge of her second Season. It was also true that she would have to face it without Olivia this go around. Horrifying thought.

The thing was this: she couldn't imagine the selection of potential husbands would be any better this Season. After all, they would be the same young men from last Season. It wasn't that they were horrible young men with no prospects, they just hadn't been . . . *Him.*

He'd ruined her. Or, more accurately, she'd ruined herself on him. In the span of a single moonlit night, he'd become more than the standard by which she judged other men; he'd become the only man.

She gave herself a mental shake. A year had passed, and she may never see him again. She must purge him from her mind. After all, aside from his accidental proposal that hadn't truly meant anything, he'd given her no reason to believe that he would be part of her future. She must give up the idea of him, for that was all he was. An idea—a ghost, really.

Horace saved her from further exploring that bleak thought, when, just before they reached Duck Pond, he stopped, lifted a front paw, and tilted his head. "What is it, boy?" she asked, unconcerned, her feet striding forward. This was typical Horace behavior, a hound to his stout, little core. It was likely a rabbit. Then she saw it: a shock of bright white glinting in the morning sun on the bank of the pond. It was the white linen of a shirt.

She stopped in her tracks and noticed a few more anomalies: starlings weren't trilling through oak and elm, and crickets weren't chirruping in the grass. Utterly still, she listened for any sound which might proceed from the direction of that white shirt.

Her feet inched up the rise at a snail's crawl, carrying her toward it bit by bit, nature's mulch of dead leaves and rotten twigs crunching dully beneath her feet. She was like a needle drawn to a lodestone, so acute was her curiosity.

At last, she heard what her ears had been both expecting and dreading: a splash. Could it be an estate worker? It was a possibility. But her ambling morning strolls were well-known at the Folly, and no worker would take that risk. She braced herself for the likelihood that someone unknown to her was splashing about the pond. Her feet stumbled across a decent-sized branch, and she picked it up, fingers clamped around one end. Horace raced to the top of the rise and again lifted one paw off the ground, intent on whatever or whoever he saw.

Just shy of the top, she stopped to inspect the layers of clothes at her feet: navy silk cravat, white lawn shirt, buff trousers, riding boots, and navy overcoat, all folded in a single compact pile. These weren't the clothes of an estate worker. These clothes belonged to a man of her class.

It was then her ears picked up a rhythm in the splashing. The man was . . . swimming?

Her grip tightened around the stick, and she took the few remaining steps to the top of the bank. Her stomach dropped to her feet. Her suspicions had been correct. It was a man, and he was swimming.

Except . . . the man was *him*. And *he* was . . . naked.

A quick patter of heartbeats, and it set in that *Lord Nicholas Asquith* was swimming *naked* in Duck Pond. Her eyes darted away before a stronger, more elemental, instinct pulled them back in.

With every stroke, his long, muscled arms cut through the water like blades, carrying him fluidly across the water as if he'd been born to it. Rills of water streamed across his tanned skin like transparent silk, down the length of ridged muscles before dipping at the small of his back and whooshing over his taut, muscled buttocks to flow over long legs kicking in effortless rhythm with his arms.

She'd never imagined a man's body could be a thing of beauty. Looking at this . . . *Adonis* . . . she understood she'd never possessed the capacity to imagine this sort of man's body before now.

The feeling radiating out from the juncture of her legs told her something else about a man's body: it was a thing of desire. *This* was the feeling that inspired scandal. *This* was the feeling that upset the balance of the world. *This* was the feeling that *ran* the world. For the first time in her inexperienced life, she understood desire as more substantial than flimsy impulse or weakness.

Her fingers loosened their grip on the stick, and it fell to the ground before rolling into the water with a tiny splash. Horace raced to retrieve it, but rather than bring it back, he found a soft patch of mulch and began lazily gnawing on it, Lord Nicholas Asquith forgotten.

When Mariana's gaze swung back toward the pond, everything was changed. No longer was he swimming. Instead, he was treading water, his eyes trained on her. Dark, wet hair slicked back and drops of water running down angled cheekbones and chiseled jaw, he was gorgeous. Eyes the hue and intensity of an afternoon storm cloud stared back at her, running up and down her length in silent query and evaluation. A frisson of excitement purled down her spine.

She liked the idea that a man like Lord Nicholas Asquith was curious about *her*, an eighteen-year-old nobody on the verge of her second Season. A girl would never tire of being the object of attention of a man like him. Her pelisse became hot and constrictive, and she suddenly wanted—nay, *needed*—it off her body.

As she began backing away from the pond, her feet stumbled over an object. It was his stack of clothes.

Still, he watched her, silent and self-possessed.

Annoyance stabbed through her. It was difficult for her to control the impulse to break through someone's self-possession. As a child, she would pinch the ever-poised Olivia just to ruffle her feathers a bit. That same urge poked at her now.

Fueled by whim, she seized the pile of clothes and hugged them close to her chest. A scent of deep, rich spice and utter male reached her nose, and she inhaled, eyes closed as her lungs filled to capacity with him.

On the exhale, her eyes flew open. The right corner of his mouth tilted up into an almost-smile. His arms began moving in a languorous breaststroke motion, pulling him toward the shore . . . toward *her* . . . in slow, deliberate increments.

Mariana's heart became a hammer in her chest, imploring her to run away. Whatever was she thinking? She was out of her depth.

Her capacity to reason through the situation evaporated when his feet found purchase on the pond's floor, and he began emerging from the pond. Water streamed down rivulets formed by the sinewy muscles of his arms and chest, descending ever lower to his corded belly, following the fine trail of hair that coursed even lower.

Heart racing, she lifted her eyes to meet his already upon her, daring her to again feast her eyes upon him. He may have been as naked as a Greek god, but she felt like the exposed one.

She wanted to look away. No, that wasn't true. She didn't want to look away. She *should* look away. Propriety and modesty demanded it. But she was neither proper nor modest, ever drawn toward the wild and unknown. Even so, she was shocked by his unhurried stride toward her . . . naked.

His gaze held hers within its enigmatic grasp, and her knees went to putty. He and she might be the only man and woman on Earth. She'd never been especially attentive to her catechism, but the tale of Adam and Eve came to mind. Except standing before her wasn't Adam, but a man both serpent and fruit, both tempter and temptation. All she had to do was reach out and . . .

The spell broke when he stopped within a foot of her and removed his clothes from her compliant hands. His fingers brushed hers, sending a tingling sensation through her body. An emotion unfamiliar to her crossed his features, but it was gone before she could consider it.

Later, she would know it as his responding desire. On this day, however, her thoughts moved on when he turned and strode to a sun-soaked patch of grass, softly intoning Horace's name, and reaching down to ruffle the loose skin beneath the traitorous beagle's chin.

Trance-like, she watched in fascination and horror as he lay his greatcoat flat on the ground and then himself atop it—on his back, eyes closed as his body, every single inch of its long length, soaked in the dewy sunlight. Not once had he displayed a care for her presence or concern that she might feast her eyes upon him. And what a feast on display. All of him was long and lean except for, well, his male member was certainly long, but lean it wasn't. In fact, it seemed to be growing . . . *thicker* . . . by the moment.

A wave of hot, wet embarrassment swept over her, and she swiveled around, her back decisively to him, her cheeks burning. "Lord Nicholas, I must ask that you clothe yourself."

Her ears picked up the rustle of movement behind her, and she felt both relieved and strangely let down.

"It's safe to turn around now," she heard after a minute or so.

She risked a glance over her shoulder before turning fully to face him. He'd donned his trousers and shirt, but the shirt was open to his waist, revealing the fine trail of hair that led directly to his—

"You are," she began, her voice cooperating only with great difficulty, "returned."

"Just yesterday." He stretched his legs out in front of him. "Would you care to join me down here?"

For all his casual and confident display, she detected a note of apprehension in his tone. It was appealing, that apprehension. It made him more human, less god-like, accessible. It drew her in, and before she knew it, she was sitting beside him, her shoulder just brushing his. Her entire universe collapsed to that single point of contact.

"I have something for you that I happened upon during my travels," he said as his hand reached inside the pocket of his greatcoat and emerged holding a shiny object in his open palm.

She leaned in closer. It was a necklace, given the length of gold chain coiled within his palm. But that wasn't what drew her interest. Within the nest of gold lay an oval-shaped pendant that appeared to be a cameo of . . . her.

On a gasp, she straightened and met his gaze. "You didn't just *happen* upon this during your travels."

Opaque, stormy gray held her in its thrall. "I commissioned Pistrucci to engrave it when I was in Rome."

"Rome," she whispered, her breath caught in her throat. "But how did he render my likeness so accurately?"

"I provided him a sketch."

"Done by?"

"Me."

"From the memory of one night?"

He nodded once.

He was so different from every suitor she'd had to endure over the last year. Lord Nicholas Asquith wasn't consumed with promoting himself. He was thoughtful, considerate, and beyond handsome. That was the moment she knew: they were destined for each other.

"Yes," she stated simply, boldly.

"Yes?" An amused light entered his eyes. "But I haven't asked you a question."

"You asked a year ago." She wouldn't let him go. Not ever. "And now you have my answer."

With that, she snatched the cameo out of his open palm and sprang to her feet. She trotted down the embankment, her pace increasing with each step. When she reached the edge of the clearing, she couldn't resist one last look back to confirm he was real.

There sat her future husband, the very model for Adonis. *Powerful. Confident. Thoughtful. Considerate.* Those were words for him. *Beautiful* was another. *Older* was yet another. But not too much older. He was experienced older, not aged older. *Just perfect older.*

In that instant, her fall was complete: she was headlong in love.

"And Nick"—She decided that very moment he would be Nick to her—"you must make haste to London and ask my father for my hand. I won't endure another Season on the marriage mart."

Then she'd whistled for Horace and hastened down the trail before Lord Nicholas, *Nick,* could contradict her and say his proposal a year ago had meant nothing. With every step she took, she felt not the earth beneath her feet, but clouds. Her feet might never touch terra firma again.

Even now in Paris, with so many years between that day and this one, what she'd felt then—the desire in her belly, the confirmation in her heart—echoed within her when its memory beckoned. She could hate herself for it.

Nick broke her heart once; she wouldn't allow it to happen again.

His first love was espionage. She didn't figure into the equation, never had really, and she'd never known why. Now that she did, she wasn't certain knowing was any better. Along with knowing came understanding. And she didn't want to understand Nick because close on the heels of understanding could follow sympathy.

She must protect herself from that insidious feeling, a feeling that could lead her nowhere good or safe. It might lead her to believe in the possibility of perfect moments again. And possibility was a delusive feeling to pair with Nick.

Tonight's second spy lesson needed to remain a business partnership. She was his spy. Any other partnership was unthinkable.

Last night, she'd mastered duplicity and guile. In the coming days and lessons, she would use them to her advantage, not only for the mission, but for her heart.

Her fingers slid along her clavicle and traced a path down to the place where the locket usually lay. She no longer believed in the hollow lure of possibility, but a small part of her, a part secured inside a lost locket, was grateful for proof that it once existed.

# Chapter 12

*Tackle: A mistress; also good clothes. The cull has tipt his tackle rum rigging; the fellow has given his mistress good clothes. A man's tackle; the genitals.*

*A Classical Dictionary of the Vulgar Tongue*
Francis Grose

"His inner circle is certain King Louis will not rise again from his bed," the agent spoke from the shadow of a shuttered patisserie. "We must discuss the plan."

"Later," Nick murmured. Through late-evening mist he watched a figure step down from a hackney two blocks in the distance. He stole a glance at his pocket watch, the only remnant of his recently abandoned genteel life that he kept on his person. A few minutes past the hour. A dash late. She was, as ever, a dash late.

"Are you certain about involving her?" The agent jutted his chin in her direction.

"She stays for now." Nick valued the agent's judgment, but he had the final say in this matter.

The agent nodded, conceding the issue. "I'm meeting with Villefranche two hours hence. You and I can discuss the outcome later in my rooms."

The agent melted away into the sodden night while Nick's gaze remained trained on Mariana's brisk figure.

Even wearing the dress of a low-born, Parisian trollop, Mariana, with her efficient, determined stride, retained an ability to be purely Mariana. It never failed to inspire a measure of envy within him. To be purely oneself was pure luxury—a luxury he couldn't afford. He wasn't certain he even knew how anymore. Except . . .

He could still taste the salt of her skin on his tongue. He hadn't entirely lost the ability to be himself.

Last night, he'd lost control and forgotten the first rule of this game: he must view her with professional dispassion, like any of his other agents. Which meant he mustn't lick her spine all the way up her elegant neck. Never before had he come close to licking one of his agents. Of course, none of his other agents were Mariana.

It was a truth he continued to repress, because he needed her. Whoever had sent her the note from a Whitehall address was the key to the assassination plot. She was his opportunity to draw this person out, and he wouldn't give it up lightly. He mustn't forget that his primary role was agent of King and Country. *Not* as lover to his wife.

Now a city block's distance away, her gaze locked onto him. A niggle of uncertainty persisted. Mariana . . . a *spy*? What was he thinking?

He pushed off the wall and set his feet into swift motion, closing the distance between them in five strides. He slid his arm into the crook of hers before curving a left and redirecting them toward tonight's venue. From the outside, they must look like the devoted couple they weren't.

"I see you've returned to the newly released prisoner look tonight," she observed once their feet settled into a steady rhythm.

Nick brushed self-conscious knuckles across day-old stubble. "I was aiming for bohemian revolutionary."

"A different costume every night?" He detected a caustic note in the question. "What are we to do tonight? And why am I attired like a Bartholomew baby?"

Nick couldn't resist the tug of a smile. "I take it I have Francis Grose to thank for that bit of color?"

Mariana cleared her throat. He suspected he might have seen a blush pinking her cheeks in the light of day. "It's another way of saying I look tawdry. I mean this dress, Nick."

He didn't need to look to know what she meant by *this dress*. "It's necessary that you dress in this manner for your *spy lesson*." He felt silly speaking those words aloud. "Unlike London, much of the intellectual life in Paris takes place in cafés. Tonight, you are my *lorette*."

"*Lorette*?" she asked, her gaze hot on the side of his face. "Do I want to know?"

"Neither wife nor whore." He hesitated. "Mistress."

"So this is what we've come to? I am now your mistress? I've often wondered what skills mistresses possess that wives don't." A short laugh escaped her. "No one would mistake us for conventional. And, pray tell, what new skill am I to learn tonight? If last night's lesson was duplicity and guile, tonight's is"—She indicated the twin rounded mounds of her breasts with her free hand—"what?"

"Invisibility."

Another laugh sounded, but this one possessed a fine, sharp edge. "In this dress? With my waist cinched tight and my breasts up to my ears?"

His gaze raked over her. "The latest Parisian style suits you."

Blessedly ignoring that last bit, Mariana continued her complaint, "Pray tell, how am I supposed to be invisible when so much of me is visible? Besides, I thought the purpose of my spying activities was to make myself *noticed* by Villefranche."

"Mariana, you've done admirably well in making yourself *obvious* to the man." Her body stiffened at his side. "Sometimes you need to be inconspicuous in this game we're playing. It's important that you're able to transition between being seen and *un*seen at will." He paused. "You've never been a wallflower."

"Let me make certain I have the facts straight. You think I will be *un*seen with my bosom exposed in this lewd manner?"

"What else will any male within a mile be able to see?" He came to a stop on the empty sidewalk and faced her. "But they won't see *you*."

Her eyes narrowed before she exhaled a soft, "Ah," and kept the rest of her thoughts to herself.

Nick cleared his throat and held out his arm, indicating his readiness to resume their progress. "The intent of these *spy lessons* is to introduce some artifice into your dealings with the world." He paused. "Your gaze is too curious, too assured, too aristocratic, and too direct."

"You make it sound as if I'm entirely too much."

It was true: she was entirely too much. But he wouldn't confirm it for her. "An agent must make herself invisible at will. It could mean the difference between life and death in this game. You must commit to it."

"So," she began, "that was what you were doing when I spotted you just now? Making yourself invisible to the world?"

"Pardon?"

"And the man with you? Was he being invisible, too?"

Nick remained silent. Better to let her make her point.

"His bearded profile bore a striking resemblance to that of the croupier from last night." Amber eyes, wide and unflinching, watched him for a reaction, and a smug, little smile tipped up the corners of her mouth.

She had him.

Nick weighed his next words and decided to speak the truth. "I trust him."

"I thought no one could be trusted."

"I trust him with my life." He hesitated before adding, "And with yours."

The words came out with a finality that brooked no argument. But Mariana wasn't finished. "Uncle Bertie and Aunt Dot paid me a visit this morning."

"Oh?" Nick replied, caution in the monosyllable.

"What does Uncle Bertie know about your activities on the Continent?"

A gusty laugh erupted from Nick. It was intended to make light of her question. Instead, it landed with a flat thud between them.

"Nick?"

"Why would your beloved Uncle Bertie *know* anything about your estranged husband?"

"There is something I need to tell you." Mariana planted her feet and stopped them both in their tracks. "Uncle Bertie knows you're alive."

"Why would he have thought otherwise?"

"That was my first thought, too. But, Nick, he *knew*."

"What did he know?"

"That you're missing."

"Anything else?"

"And now that you're alive."

"We're talking in circles."

"I seem to have confirmed to him that you're alive." Uncertainty and guilt hung about her. "I think I handled it wrongly."

Her naked vulnerability reached out and grabbed Nick in the chest. "Mariana," he said, low and insistent, "you did nothing wrong."

"Then why does it feel so?"

"Too much information will endanger you. You're going to have to trust me."

She flinched. "That's asking too much."

"There is trust, and there is *trust*." His eyes searched hers. "You know you can *trust* me."

"Do I?"

"Yes."

She focused on the wall beside them where miniscule beads of mist collected and fattened into round drops. Too heavy for the pull of gravity, at last, they fell in random vertical streaks to the ground. "You sound so genuine that I could believe you. I could even believe that you believe your words." Her eyes, cloudy with emotion, met his. "It's better if we don't speak of trust."

Her words, soft and clear, struck him square in the solar plexus. She'd spoken the truth; he didn't deserve her trust. That was the trade-off he'd made a decade ago. By avoiding meaningful interaction with her all these years, he'd been able to avoid his culpability. Until now. He deserved her words. And more.

Yet, she remained silent and began moving, the click of their heels the only sound between them, as block by block the sidewalk became ever more crowded with an increasingly spirited Parisian nightlife.

Just shy of the entrance of a lively café, its patrons spilling out onto the street in small groupings, Nick pulled Mariana into a quiet alcove. The space was snug enough that he felt the heat radiating off her body. "There is something you need to know about this place," he said, willing her to follow his lead and put their past aside for now. "It doesn't serve traditional drinks."

"That's a relief after last night's whiskey binge," she said on a light note.

Even if it did ring a bit hollow, she was playing along. Good.

"This place serves absinthe. Have you heard of it?"

"The Green Fairy? Of course," she said, blithe and dismissive.

"The *Green Fairy* comes in small doses," he explained as if she'd never heard of absinthe, which, of course, she hadn't. He did admire her bravado, though. "Under no circumstances drink it down in one go. It must be sipped very slowly. In fact, it would be best if you only pretend to drink."

"I left my leading strings behind in London," she snapped.

"Then you must know"—He paused, considering the best way to phrase his next words—"it produces a state of euphoria."

"A state of euphoria?" Her head tilted to the side. She was intrigued. *Blast.* "Have you tried it?"

He nodded once, his eyes darting away from her too intrigued gaze. "And the feeling it produces the next day—"

"One of crapulence?" she interrupted. "After last night, I know something about that feeling."

"It's the very opposite of euphoric. Best to stay away. Agreed?"

~ ~ ~

Oh, how he willed her to agree.

"Perhaps," she replied. That was all the satisfaction she would give him. She inhaled a steadying breath and backed out of the alcove, unable to tamp down an unruly smile.

The front door swung wide, and long, protective fingers curled around her hand. Giddy pinpricks of excitement wended their way across her skin from that small point of contact as he swept her inside the café and guided them past a cluster of haphazardly strewn tables. They ventured to the back of the café side by side, a genuine couple to the crowd around them.

"This café," he said in a muted voice meant for her ears only, "is populated by indulged and moneyed sons looking to show off their educations and their *lorettes*."

Without another word, they found two open seats at a long table that ran the length of the back wall. Mariana took the corner seat Nick offered and attempted to follow any one of several heated conversations swirling through air dense with cigar smoke and a certain humidity specific to enclosed spaces brimming with animated people.

"This is quite a public place," she observed.

"Cafés are where individuals of like-minded, usually extreme, political persuasions congregate."

Mariana's voice emerged in a secretive hush, "These people are revolutionaries?"

"At one extreme."

"Villefranche said the French like to live at extremes."

"He's not entirely wrong."

Of a sudden, everyone in the café became suspect. "Won't the wrong people know you're alive?"

"They don't really think I'm dead. The note you received in London was a ruse, I'm convinced." Although, he hadn't worked out why. "I'm simply unreachable for the time being."

Mariana nodded and allowed her gaze to roam the room. She gave up on understanding what was being shouted around her. The French spoken was too informal and too fast. She leaned in close to Nick. "Translate his conversation for me." She jutted her chin toward a young man with the wildest, reddest head of hair she'd ever seen, surpassed only by his complementing wild, red moustache.

"He is speculating whether the king's new throne is solid gold or gold plated."

"Does it matter?"

"To the French? Absolutely."

Next, she indicated a fervent young man to Nick's right.

"He is declaiming the merits of oil paints over watercolors. Watercolors speak of an artist's lack of fortitude, substance, and gravity. They are an insubstantial and moral void."

A half-smile lurked about Nick's lips and responsively, nay, *instinctively*, she matched it. "Good to know," she responded, but his attention had strayed away from her.

She tamped down a flicker of pique. Her rational mind understood that it was part of their act tonight. Still, it irritated her that Nick played his role so convincingly well.

Left alone to her thoughts, she settled back and soaked in the atmosphere. She couldn't help feeling a little let down. She'd thought pressing matters of importance were discussed in the cafés of Paris. And, perhaps, they were. But not with her, a mere woman. Judging by the arrangement of the table, it was glaringly obvious that a woman was to be seen and not heard. The men sat flush up to the table—the better to hear one another and insert an opinion when necessary—while the women sat positioned slightly behind their men.

She formed a sympathetic bond with the other women, the *lorettes*, that transcended their cultural and lingual barriers. In London, women of her station would find a quiet nook and conduct their own conversations. These Parisiennes, however, remained glued to the sides of their men. Content to be displayed in an ornamental capacity, they maintained a specific disinterested mien that only French women could properly deploy. In fact, it was this French insouciance that managed to salvage their dignity.

The women's attire snagged her attention. Indeed, Nick had been correct to send this crimson monstrosity with tonight's instructions. It integrated her seamlessly into her surroundings with its cinched waist, revealing neckline, and garish color. She scanned the row of women clad like jewels in hues of sapphire, ruby, emerald, and amethyst, arrayed like a rainbow of sin.

Oh, how very moralistic, Mariana chided herself. Perhaps she should step down from her high horse. After all, she didn't fully understand these women's lives or livelihoods. It was a tough world for women with no means. She would do well to remember that.

Nick had been correct . . . again.

Even with their revealing clothing, or because of it, these women were invisible in every meaningful way. She shifted her body toward Nick, attempting to emulate their specific pose of sophisticated insouciance. But she had difficulty deciding where to place her hands. Her neck felt oddly angled, and she desperately longed to cross her legs. What looked entirely natural on the *lorettes,* felt entirely *un*natural on her. It struck her that their entire demeanor and comportment was a subtle art form. It would take more than a single evening for her to become one of them.

A sudden touch pulled her attention toward her ungloved hand. The tip of Nick's finger had begun tracing soft figure eights on the tender skin of her palm, tickling nerve endings that in turn sent signals across her body. The competing cacophonies of jangly music, shouted conversation, and riotous giggles were reduced to muted background noise when his finger began a feathery ascent up her arm to her shoulder before languorously descending to the tip of her middle finger. Her body longed to sway toward him like a cat, encouraging, even begging him to do it again.

Her eyes popped open. When had they drifted shut?

She glanced at Nick to find him still engaged in conversation with the other men. He hadn't even broken conversation to stroke her. This was the sort of treatment these men doled out to their *lorettes.* It was like a statement of ownership toward a beloved object . . . or a favorite pet. By claiming her in this way, he was rendering her ever more invisible. Even if it was a role for one night, she couldn't help bristling at the treatment. She most definitely wasn't anyone's pussy cat.

Nick repeated the motion, and her nipples tightened into hard buds. Her body didn't seem to understand what her mind did. Of course, it was possible that her body simply didn't care. The memory of another sensation came to her. One of his velvety tongue gliding across her skin. Oh, last night . . .

Mariana sat up straight and clasped her hands together. There would be no more of that.

A carafe of green liquid and a small accompanying glass appeared before her. The glass was topped by a sugar cube nestled within what appeared to be a tiny sieve.

Nick leaned back and cocked his head, so his lips almost brushed her ear. "Meet the Green Fairy."

"Absinthe?" She abandoned her earlier pretense that she was well-acquainted with the substance. "How does it achieve that particular green glow?"

He inclined his head a fraction, and his serious gaze found hers. "Follow my lead."

As she watched, he took the carafe in hand and poured the unearthly—there was no other word for it—substance over the sugar cube. As the liquid filtered through the sugar, the two substances melded together in the glass.

"We're to drink that?"

She thought she saw a quicksilver smile flash across his well-defined lips, but she could have imagined it so seriously whispered were his next words. "Remember what I said. You must *pretend* to drink it."

It wasn't only the content of his words that riled her, but the way he spoke them as if he was telling her gently, but firmly, *no*.

Well, that wouldn't do. It was time for her to remind him who she was.

Without a second thought, she reached for the glass. Nick's hand shot out and closed around hers. She brushed him off and lifted the glass to her lips. Strong notes of anise met her nose. It wasn't her favorite scent, but there was no turning back from here.

Her gaze met his above the rim of the glass—she had his full attention now—and her lips curved into a smile. "*Vive la France*!" she sang out and tipped her head back, downing the absinthe in one swift gulp before slamming the glass onto the table.

# Chapter 13

*Fox's paw: The vulgar pronunciation of the French words* faux pâs. *He made a confounded fox's paw.*

*A Classical Dictionary of the Vulgar Tongue*
Francis Grose

Within the space between one heartbeat and the next, Mariana's world transformed into a wonderland composed entirely of helium and ether. She wasn't certain it was exclusively the effect of the absinthe, either, instead suspecting it might be her act of disobedience fueling the feeling.

No, that wasn't the best characterization of the feeling or herself. Disobedience was the act of a child attempting to assert power and control.

She was no child; she was an adult woman. Perhaps downing a glassful of an unfamiliar liquid emitting an unearthly green glow wasn't the most adult way to assert her independence, but Nick's steady, gray gaze told her she'd gotten her point across loud and clear. Except, how utterly unsurprised he looked.

She took a self-conscious glance around the table. A dozen pairs of eyes regarded her with equal parts bemusement and astonishment, awaiting her next move. Then the moment evaporated as they seemed to realize in unison that she had no more moves.

The men continued their conversations while the mistresses' eyes lingered half a beat longer, assessing, indulgent, but not warm. The peculiar Englishwoman was dismissed, her novelty gone as quickly as it had come. Raucous music and the general cacophony of café esprit roared back to life, and the outside world tumbled in.

It mattered not. Particularly not when the air around her became as light and weightless as if gravity no longer had a claim on her. Her fingers wrapped around the seat of her chair as a cascade of floaty warmth washed over her. She had imbibed a bit too much wine—or whiskey, as the occasion allowed—more times than a lady would dare admit, but this feeling was that and more.

"Where does it come from?" she heard her voice asking.

"Grande wormwood," Nick tossed over his shoulder.

"No. Not where, but *where*? What world? Surely not ours. I feel as if . . . as if I've lassoed a shooting star."

She might have detected a roll of Nick's eyes before he turned away, but it mattered not. She had no use for the here and now, but for epiphany, bright and true: only Nick had done the touching. These last three nights, he'd touched some part of her body, but she hadn't touched his. It had been years since she last felt him.

Her eyes traveled the broad width of his back. Was he different now? He'd been lean and angular, but the angles these days cut a little sharper. This was a harder man from a decade ago. How had it escaped her notice all those Christmases, Easters, and birthdays? She wanted to feel him. Not through layers of jacket, vest, and shirt, but skin to skin.

Her gaze wandered over the other women, the other *lorettes*, her odd sense of kinship with them increasing. Then, she noticed it: they weren't simply on the receiving end of being stroked. These women gave back in subtle ways: fingertips feathering against a thin sliver of bare skin at the back of a neck; rouged lips pressed against an ear, whispering a promise for later that only the two of them would ever know; hands finding their ways inside jacket pockets, inside trouser pockets . . .

A tingling sensation fluttered out from her belly. She didn't have to sit here like a demure little nothing all night. Before her was an opportunity to take what she wanted. And right now what she wanted was a touch of Nick.

She moved her chair closer to his and half draped herself against him. The muscles in his back went rigid. Good. Still, this level of touch wasn't enough to satisfy.

With that thought in mind, her hand found its way to his thigh, and, like the muscles in his back, those, too, contracted beneath her touch. She resisted the urge to test their rigidity with a squeeze. Instead, her hand began snaking its way up the solid length of muscle, her fingers soon locating his trouser pocket. It slipped inside.

Shocked by her own boldness, she hesitated, her breath hitching in her chest. She watched his profile for a reaction, any tic or tell that revealed an effect on him, *her* effect on him. Nothing. His face remained frustratingly impassive. But his heart—which she felt, pressed as she was against his back—revealed the opposite of impassivity. His heart beat hard and fast, mirroring the thunder of her own. Oh, he felt it, too.

Her fingers resumed their progress, feeling their way deeper inside his pocket. Did he feel a light increasing in luminescence inside of him until he was glowing with a warm river of sensation, wet and wondrous?

Hmm, that last bit might have been the absinthe.

Oh, delicious anticipation. An image of his manhood flashed across her mind. She remembered it as hard and true and ever at the ready. Was that still the case?

"Am I invisible enough now?" she whispered into his ear.

A vise grip, sudden and steely, clamped around her wrist and removed her hand from his pocket, firmly returning it to her lap.

He half-turned in his chair and faced her. His eyes gave nothing away, and it occurred to her that they should. They should show anger, dismay, desire, disgust . . . *something*. Yet they revealed nothing, which could be a tell in itself. He wasn't allowing himself to reveal himself. How was it that she'd never perceived this particular skill in her husband? She'd thought he felt nothing, but she was beginning to suspect it was rather the opposite.

"I don't feel an ounce of shame for what I just attempted," she whispered. She'd never been the sort of girl who minded very much getting into trouble. "Wasn't I behaving like another one of the mistresses? Like another one of *your* mistresses?" He remained stoic and silent. "Indignation and shame are such *muddy* emotions. In fact, I feel the opposite of muddy. *In fact*, I've never felt so pure in my life."

"That is the absinthe speaking."

"Is it? And is your absinthe speaking to me right now?"

"Mariana—"

"Oh, stuff the scold. I wasn't being serious. Well, not entirely."

No longer did she feel like remaining hostage to Nick's too-steady gaze. She wanted to enjoy the night. Never in her life had she felt so at one with the people around her. It was as if they stood together on a plane of existence known only to them. It felt miraculous.

Her musing was cut short when her gaze fell upon a familiar figure. At first, she didn't believe her eyes. She was viewing the world through the lens of the Green Fairy, after all. "Nick," she whispered, enough urgency in her voice to regain his attention.

"Yes, Mariana," he returned. She didn't care for his long-suffering tone.

"Aren't you concerned this is the sort of place someone you know would frequent? Perhaps someone like the Comte de Villefranche?"

"Villefranche wouldn't be caught dead in a place like this," Nick returned. "His elevated ideals don't venture far from on high and down into the realm of reality."

Mariana felt an unruly smile bloom across her face. She knew something Nick didn't. "Then how is it that I just watched him walk through the front entrance?"

Nick froze. "Is he alone?"

"Yes."

"Has he spotted you?"

"Not yet." Her eyes locked onto Villefranche's tall, wooden form as he navigated the room between various groupings of people with whom he was clearly acquainted. "I do believe you've underestimated your opponent."

"Is he behind me?"

"Directly."

"Look at me," Nick commanded.

Mariana tore her gaze away from the Comte de Villefranche and found Nick's steely gray eyes. He reached out and cupped the back of her head, his long fingers threading through her loose hair, fingers warm and capable and distractingly male.

"Follow my lead," he said for the second time tonight.

Without another word, he pulled her into him, and his mouth was upon hers in what only outwardly could be characterized as a kiss, so cold and unyielding were his lips.

It lasted no more than a thrice of seconds before she broke away, panting. "I thought we were better at kissing than that," burst from her.

"Has he passed?" Nick asked, refusing to be distracted by their utterly, utterly terrible kiss.

Mariana had never felt so disappointed in her life.

But she remembered her role and located Villefranche's receding back. "He's just stepping outside through the front entrance"—Bemusement crinkled her eyebrows together—

"with a woman. I guess his high ideals take a roll down in the hay every once in a while."

Nick pushed away from the table and stood, dragging her up with him. Without a single *adieu*, they were off, navigating the haphazard café at a pace surely never seen in its loose environ. Her flimsy scrap of a shawl slipped off her shoulders, forgotten forever to the night as there was no stopping Nick's forward momentum. And all of this done without a single disturbance to the firm set of his features.

In a thrice, they were speeding down a short, back corridor. Nick's hand still clamped around hers, he used the other to push open the door at the corridor's end.

Two strides later, Mariana found herself in a narrow, dark alley devoid of light and dense with soft, feathery mist. Even as the uneven rhythms of her breath raced in her ears, the world slowed, and stillness enveloped them. The raucous café faded into a past that was becoming increasingly distant, even as the absinthe pulsed lightning flashes through her veins. Only the present where his hand held hers mattered.

"Are we following Villefranche?"

Nick shook his head, a wild light flickering in the gray depths of his eyes. Through the fog of their shared past came the memory that his wildness had always driven her equally wild for him.

"You thought we were better than that?" he asked on a step forward. Inches separated them. His hand held onto hers as the other reached up and stroked the side of her face. His fingers felt wonderfully cool against her cheeks, hot with inebriation and . . . desire.

She opened her mouth to speak, but words refused to form. There was nothing left to say. Only something left to do. Her hand reached up, found the back of his neck, and pulled his mouth toward hers.

A soft growl sounded as his lips claimed hers with a pent-up ferocity that had been vibrating between them for three straight nights. A kiss never felt so good, so ravishing, so hedonistic, so *right*. No, it wasn't right. Yet somehow its very *wrongness* made it all the better.

The full, unforgiving length of his body pressed forward and pinned her against the damp, stone wall. Her eyes fluttered shut, and all she could do was *feel* the contrasting sensations of pleasure and pain swirling together. Her entire being transformed into a bundle of exposed nerve endings whose only function was to give and receive pleasure. What else was there?

His fingertips trailed down her neck, across her clavicle, and hesitated at the swell of her breasts. A plaintive cry erupted in her throat, and her back arched, pressing her further into his body. She wanted more than a kiss.

One hand cupped her bottom, pulling her into full, erotic contact with his erect shaft, the other slipped inside her bodice and lifted a breast out of the confining fabric before squeezing her taut peak between thumb and forefinger. Instinctively, her leg wrapped around his waist as his manhood ground into her. Her body alternately screamed and ached for more . . . for everything.

Drat these layers of clothes between them.

He broke the kiss and took her breast into his mouth. Her head arced back, and a long moan escaped her.

"We *are* better than that," he murmured, his hand snaking up her bare thigh. "Do you require additional proof?"

"Yes," she exhaled, a plea to the heavens above.

The heavens ignored her entreaty, for the next moment, Nick went stock still and pressed a staying finger against her lips before she could cry out in protest. She followed his gaze and found what had caught his attention. A gendarme stood, not five feet away, patiently awaiting their attention.

Mariana knew she should feel absolutely mortified, face flaming with embarrassment and shame. But she felt not a bit of it. She'd only just coaxed Nick into lowering his defenses and revealing something true about himself—that he desired her . . . madly, wildly—and this officer of the silly law had come along and denied her. She didn't feel ashamed; she felt thwarted.

The gendarme motioned for Nick to step aside with him. "*Monsieur, s'il vous plaît?*"

Nick straightened and locked eyes with Mariana for the briefest moment, the message in them clear: she was to stay put and keep quiet. She was to prove she'd learned her lesson and make herself invisible.

Ha. That ship had sailed.

She watched his wildness recede and the civilized take over as his fingers ran through his shorn hair and smoothed it down. She suppressed the desire to reach out and stay his hand. Desire and possibility faded fast, replaced by a devastating sense of impossibility. Desire wasn't enough to fix what ailed her and Nick. It never had been.

She instantly sobered. "Neither wife nor whore," fell from her lips.

~ ~ ~

Nick felt the words with the force of a slap, but he had no time for them now. The gendarme was waiting. Appeasement must be his first concern. Mariana would come later.

He closed his eyes and inhaled. No, Mariana wouldn't come later. Not like that, anyway. There would be no appeasement tonight, or ever, for them.

He moved away from her. "You may want to"—He darted a glance toward her bare breasts—"adjust yourself." The gendarme was getting an eyeful.

Nick stepped toward the officer of the law, a practiced, sheepish smile on his lips. *Oui*, he knew this wasn't the place, but sometimes a man had . . . *needs*. It was the gendarme's turn to smile sheepishly, tapping an empty hand against his thigh. *Oui, oui,* but next time. *Oui, oui,* next time. The gendarme's hand returned to his pocket richer than it had been a few minutes earlier.

The gendarme strolled away, a satisfied whistle on his lips, and Nick again faced Mariana. There couldn't be a next time. As he watched her arrange her hair, slender arms raised and breasts all but exposed to the night sky, and anyone else who happened along, the resolution rang hollow.

"This scheme isn't going to plan." He adjusted his cravat. "You're not exactly spy material."

"Ah, I see."

Startled, he glanced up, expecting to find her vibrating with betrayal and disappointment—it seemed his destiny ever to disappoint her—except he read neither emotion there. He read challenge in her eyes.

"I find Paris suits me," she continued.

"This is bigger than us," he pressed, except even he could hear that his words lacked conviction. He wasn't certain anything was bigger than he and Mariana. Not even the fates of France and England were more important—not in this moment.

"There is no *us*, Nick. There never was."

He flinched. Even he knew that wasn't true. Once upon a time, there had been a *them*, and it had been a glorious frolic in delusion—until reality had come knocking.

Again, he called upon the requisite words. "The stability of Europe is at stake here."

A brittle laugh escaped her. "And, of course, you're the only man who can insure Continental stability. You always did overestimate your control over a situation."

A sudden, hot urge to tweak her overcame him. "Not always." The words came out a hard growl. "There are certain situations I control very well."

~ ~ ~

A blush warmed Mariana's cheeks, and she glanced away, hoping to hide her body's reaction to his words, to the promise in his eyes when he spoke them. It was a desire that must be quelled. They had gone too far tonight.

*Not far enough*, her body protested.

Nick stepped out into the street and hailed an approaching hackney. A staying hand held out to the driver, he turned and waved her toward the conveyance. Her feet felt mired in sludge as she crossed the few feet between where she'd stood and the open door. The absinthe had sailed away into the ether without her, leaving her earthbound and deflated.

Yes, absinthe. She wouldn't consider what else could bring on this feeling of gloom. What was the word from earlier? *Crapulent*. It was the perfect word. Absolute crapulence.

His arm, angled at the elbow, extended and awaited her hand, so he could assist her into the carriage.

Memory, unbidden and unwelcome, pushed at the corners of her mind. Once, she'd stood like this, her hand poised above his forearm; she'd been dressed in virginal ivory and he in tailored blacks and whites. Their "I do's" just spoken, they'd faced the aisle before them, friends and family to each side. Her shaky, silk-gloved hand had lowered to a light rest on woolen superfine, and the gratification of having well and truly caught him swelled up. This gorgeous, cunning, untamed man was hers, forever.

Bitterness mingled with memory. A flash was all it had been; there had been no substance, no lasting truth in it. She ignored his waiting forearm and grabbed hold of the carriage's open window frame, mounting the first step unassisted.

"It was a foolish idea, Mariana, to think that you—"

"Could be useful?" she finished for him.

"You are useful, just not to—"

"You?" She stood perpendicular to him, her gaze fast on

the interior of the carriage. "Well, isn't it your job to make me so?"

"Mariana—"

"One more lesson, Nick," she said, hating her inability to keep an imploring note out of her voice.

After a moment's hesitation, he said, "One more lesson."

She finished her ascent into the carriage, and Nick shut the door behind her. He gave the boot two quick taps, and it lurched into motion.

Mariana resisted the urge to peer out the window and watch Nick recede into the distance until he blended with the shadows. Instead, she pressed her back flat against unforgiving leather and turned her thoughts to her nerve endings.

Not ten minutes ago, she'd been focused on their pleasure. Yet it was the other side of a raw nerve ending that claimed her attention now that the pleasure had receded: *pain*. As a midnight Paris streamed past her window, she sensed a nascent, yet familiar, pain held at bay, a pain she would rather avoid.

If this was truly the case, then why had she all but begged for another lesson? She knew why. It was for the same nervy, hedonistic reason she'd staked her locket last night.

While there was a fifty percent chance she would find pain once she reached the end of this particular nerve, there was another fifty percent chance she would find pleasure there. After all, she'd vowed to follow Nick's example and ignore their past. Such a gloomy past was better left in gloomy London. This Paris idyll was a time and place for unreality to rule the day.

And if a few nerve endings were pleasured along the way, well, wasn't that what Paris was for? People risked more for less.

She shifted uncomfortably on her seat.

*A risk greater than a heart*? a tiny thought nagged.

# Chapter 14

*Comfortable importance: A wife.*

*A Classical Dictionary of the Vulgar Tongue*
Francis Grose

Feet cutting a brisk clip across the mist-slick cobblestone byways of an early morning Paris, Nick dared not let up the pace. He'd kissed her.

No, kiss was too simple a word for what he'd done. He'd ravished her mouth with his and would've done more if the gendarme hadn't appeared.

But the gendarme and even the kiss itself weren't what troubled him most. He'd lost control . . . again. From the moment she'd whispered the taunt, *"Am I invisible enough now?"*, he'd had to have her. There had been no question of it in his mind. He'd wanted her to understand precisely how invisible she *wasn't.*

His first instinct upon seeing her inside La Grande Salle had been correct. Trouble had arrived. And here his prediction was playing out as he'd envisioned. Only the passing gendarme had saved him from himself tonight. Who would save him from himself next time?

He looked up and slowed his pace. His feet had carried him to the banks of the Seine, where he inhaled air ripe with sewage and river stench. How smooth its murky black surface appeared in these last hours before dawn, as if its façade of tranquility continued deep below the surface, but nothing could be further from the truth. Just beneath that calm surface roiled a river teeming with vibrant life, straining to arrive at its final destination, the Channel.

How like a person a river was. How like Mariana.

Her surface was a sleek and sophisticated exterior similar to so many ladies of her class. A cursory glance might tempt one to assume her depths uncomplicated by the world outside her rarified orbit. After all, in that way she slotted in seamlessly with her peers. One, however, would be mistaken.

Strong currents lay below Mariana's surface. Many had dipped in a toe, only to find themselves swept along by the force of her tide. Like the Seine, Mariana, too, had inevitable destinations. Only she willed where they led.

And one of her inevitable destinations was him. Indeed, they were fated in certain ways.

He turned away from the river and set out across the bridge. *One more lesson.*

*Blast.* Why hadn't he followed Villefranche into the night? If he'd come into the café, wasn't it possible he'd have other unexpected stops on his way to meet his agent?

But these weren't the questions that bothered him most. A different question plagued him: why had he agreed to *one more lesson*?

He knew the answer, too. He was losing focus, unable to resist the pull of her current. He'd never been able to, not really.

Eleven years ago—eleven years next month, in fact— that reality had come home to roost, belying the half-truths he'd been telling himself about his feelings for his wife.

~ ~ ~

*London*
*10 October 1813*

Inside Whitehall, Nick had sat, pen to paper, writing a brief, the banal reverse of espionage that little boys playing at cloaks and daggers never dreamed of.

He'd just gotten into the meat of the report when the low-level agent he'd assigned to keep an eye on the house burst into the office. "Sir, they're coming," the man exclaimed.

A low buzz expanded inside Nick's head, providing a buffer between him and the outside world. No one needed to explain who *they* were, or why it mattered that they were coming.

*They're coming.*

On the move, he snatched his overcoat off its knob, his feet gobbling up great swathes of yardage with each stride. Several city blocks and two parks stood between him and Mariana. He would reach Half Moon Street in twelve minutes at a steady sprint, having prepared for this day with a run-through last week. Twice.

"Sir!" he heard behind him, his heels already a swift click-clack across a blessedly dry sidewalk. "Your carriage!"

The plea fell ignored on his back. The carriage wouldn't cut the time—it would likely take longer—and he couldn't sit passive inside while the minutes ticked by.

He hooked a quick right at the Horse Guards, his figure a phantom along the meagerly populated paths of St. James's and Green Parks. By the time he reached the reservoir in Green Park, he was a winded, sweaty mess, but a focused one, too. He was only a few blocks from home now.

*They're coming.*

Mariana wasn't overly concerned about giving birth to twins. "After all," she'd repeated more than once, "my mother came through just fine, and, like her, I'm not a small woman."

The logic had done little to allay his fears. This was *Mariana* who was about to give birth to twins. What had he been thinking by getting her with child? With *children*? A twin herself, he'd known the danger.

He flew through the front door of their townhouse, taking the stairs three at a time, a bevy of servants at his back, all calling out, "Sir, Sir." It wasn't until he reached Mariana's closed bedroom door, the bedroom kept up for appearances as she spent every night in his bed, that he stopped, gathered breath in his lungs, and attempted to collect himself.

*They're coming.*

"Nick," sounded Olivia's low, calming voice at his side, "she's doing great."

"I'll be present for the birth," he said, pugnacious, ready to fight his way inside if need be.

"It's most irregular," she said, a half-smile in the words.

A long, keening wail sounded through hollow birch, and instinct took over. Nick pushed open the door, past the retinue of doctors and nurses he'd hired for this day, and past the frowning midwife who first scolded, then mumbled over and again, that his presence was *quite unnecessary*.

White knuckles gripping the blankets at her sides, sweat streaking in thin rivulets down her face, Mariana's eyes met his across the room. "You're not supposed to be here."

His feet froze in place. He hadn't considered the possibility that she might not want him present. "I could leave."

"Don't you dare," she said, equal parts levity and steel.

His feet closed the distance in two strides, and he took her hand. "Squeeze as hard as you can. Transfer your pain into me. I can take it," he said, wondering at the words emerging from his mouth. They were words born of fear, of powerlessness.

"Nick," she said, "everything will come out all right."

"Now," the midwife called out from her place at the foot of the bed, "when I say push, you push until you feel like the top of your head is about to pop off. Understood?"

Mariana nodded, and Nick sensed her go deep inside herself, leaving him behind at her side, helpless, unable to protect her from here on out. This was between Mariana, her maker, and the midwife.

Mariana's grasp on his hand tightened, and the midwife said, "All right, milady, the contraction is coming"—Another persistent wail emerged from Mariana, gaining volume on a rise—"Get ready . . . to . . . *push*," the midwife commanded.

Mariana's torso crunched forward, her heels dug into the bed, and she crushed Nick's hand. How he wanted her to squeeze harder, even take his hand off, if it would ease her suffering a jot.

Her body released, and she collapsed back into feathery pillows, her breath a shallow, rhythmic pant. The doctor stepped forward, and the midwife waved him away.

"Two more like that, milady, and we'll have a babe screaming down the house."

Another groan gathered in Mariana's chest, demanding release, and Nick remained helpless at her side, unable to reach her inside the deep, womanly place she'd gone.

"Another contraction already? All right, milady, start panting."

The still room filled with the sharp, staccato shush of breath whooshing in, out, in, and out of the rounded "O" of Mariana's pursed lips.

"Now, again, *push*," the midwife commanded.

A moan, the deepest, loudest yet, rose from the depths of Mariana's guts and threatened to rattle the windows loose. A fresh layer of sweat beaded her forehead. Nick's heart pounded in his chest at the pace of a thousand thoroughbred horses. Fear, stark and bright, threatened to drive him out of his skin.

"The head is crowning," the midwife shouted out. "Now, rest a moment."

The sound of panting filled the air, and Nick felt a cool, damp cloth being pressed into his hand.

"For her forehead," Olivia said at his back.

He swiped cotton across Mariana's forehead, down cheeks flush and hot.

"It's time this baby was born. The one behind him won't appreciate him dillydallying," the midwife said. It was clear she relished her occupation. "Now, bear down and *push!*"

Again, Mariana crunched forward, and Nick's world went white. Fear and helplessness pressed in at every angle as he returned Mariana's crushing grip with his own. He'd never felt so linked to another person, so dependent on another, for his happiness, for his entire being. There was no point to being without *her*, this brave, formidable woman who strode through life without fear.

But that was all right. He felt enough fear for them both. He felt it, so she'd never have to. He vowed to move heaven and earth to keep her safe, always, and without fear. So long as they got through this day.

A haze, black at the edges, coated the periphery of his consciousness. First came Geoffrey, then Lavinia, one right after the other. "The Lord's work is done," the midwife intoned, standing and plunging her hands into the washbasin.

Mariana took the twins, one in each arm, and pressed her lips to their wrinkled, red foreheads, back and forth between the two. Awed amber eyes met his, inviting him to share in the wonder.

It was only then that Nick realized he stood apart. Carefully, he lowered his body onto the bed and snugged in close, but still not touching. He didn't have the right to ruin the perfection of this scene with his hulking, unworthy presence.

Mariana reached out, took his hand in hers, and pulled. Instinct guided him as he wrapped one arm, then the other, around this trio of perfection, his entire world encompassed within his arms. His fall complete, he was lost.

Actually, that wasn't true. His fall wasn't complete. He kept falling, helpless, powerless to stop the feeling.

Even so, his rational mind kept asserting itself. He may not be able to control his interior world, but the only world that now mattered was the world within his arms. He would stop at nothing to protect them, to keep them safe.

And he'd managed it with success. Until two nights ago when he'd invited Mariana into his world.

Nick looked up at a nondescript building whose dilapidated state even the darkest night couldn't conceal and found that he'd arrived at his destination. He stepped inside and began the five-story ascent to the attic rooms.

A casual glance down revealed a small family of three—a mother, or possibly an older sister, and two small children—nestled into the hollow crook of the staircase. He bent over the rail and dropped a gold sovereign into the eldest's tattered overcoat pocket. He could acclimate to many of Paris's dismal conditions, but never to the deprived lives of so many of its young.

He took the stairs two at a time and soon found himself standing before a nondescript door at the top of a cramped landing. His knuckles struck a single knock, followed by a five second pause, then three muted taps in quick succession.

A key turned in the lock, and he slipped inside a room lit by a solitary candle, the space dim and spare. The descriptors of his native world, words like *gilded* and *lush*, didn't apply here. The beeswax candle sitting atop a small, rectangular table was, in fact, the only element in the room that suggested all wasn't what it seemed. This single, white candle was luxury, the sort of luxury, for instance, unavailable to the building's other inhabitants, who likely burned cheap tallow.

This was the room of a British agent who passed not as French, but as a Spaniard with his dark, flashing eyes and lean, rangy form that appeared not to have encountered a decent meal in a number of years. The operative embodied the role of a revolutionary escaping persecution in his home country. It wouldn't be a stretch to believe this man was looking to start a revolution in the name of democratic ideals. The Comte de Villefranche had certainly been drawn in by him over the course of a week's worth of "chance" meetings inside cafés and coffee houses.

If he hadn't known this man continuously for well over a decade, Nick never would have connected him with the man he'd met in a crowded ballroom all those years ago. War changed men, and it had certainly done its work on this man. The thin, silvery scar running along his left cheekbone would be the most obvious ravage of war. One would assume such a distinguishing feature a deficit in the world of espionage. Not so. There were missions in which the scar conferred a measure of authenticity.

The agent poured them each a glass of whiskey before settling into a rickety chair on the far side of the table. Nick chose to remain standing. "Bertrand Montfort arrived in Paris today," he stated without preamble.

The agent swallowed a finger of the amber liquid before replying. "Villefranche introduced me to his *recruiter* tonight." The agent paused for an uncomfortable second before pushing the other whiskey across the table. "You might want to have a drink before I continue."

At the look in the other man's eye, Nick downed the fiery liquid in one gulp and waited.

"It was Bertrand Montfort," said the agent, eyes carefully trained on Nick. "He's running a rogue operation."

"It's not going through the Foreign Office?"

The agent shook his head.

Certain elements began to make sense. "Villefranche is the perfect scapegoat. Get a member of the Orléans family to do the dirty work and take the fall, if necessary."

"No one would ever link Villefranche to Montfort. But to what end? The assassination will only incite revolution."

"Perhaps that is the intention."

"And how does another French revolution benefit Montfort?"

The question hung in the air, unanswered, even as the revelation winded Nick like a blow to the gut. Bertrand Montfort . . . Uncle Bertie. A deep sense of confirmation settled inside him.

It fit. Pieces that his biases had been too blind to see fell into place. Certain intricacies of the operation only he and Montfort knew now became clear. Nick's brain rifled through the past fortnight piece by piece: the attack in his rooms; the note to Mariana; the visit to Mariana.

*Mariana.*

Hot blood turned to ice in his veins. Montfort had used her to draw him out. Even after all this time and distance apart from her, Montfort knew she was his Achilles' heel, a fact that had likely been evident to all but him over the years.

And he thought he'd created an insurmountable distance between himself and her. It was laughable how completely the last few days had proven the opposite true.

The agent poured another two fingers of whiskey. Of course, Nick wasn't the only man in this room with a connection to Bertrand Montfort. "Tell me he didn't recognize you."

The agent allowed a long, assessing moment to pass. Nick alone hadn't sacrificed in the name of England. Before him sat a man who had sacrificed *everything*.

"It was dark. I was cagey. He didn't recognize me," the agent said, laying on a thick Spanish accent. "I'm not easily recognized these days." A bitter edge laced his words.

Nick had no interest in pursuing this line of conversation. He had a more urgent concern. "Was anything said about Mariana?"

"Only that Villefranche would continue engaging her until King Louis expires."

Nick should allow the conversation to pivot toward their mission—the agent had given him the opportunity by mentioning the dying king—but he was fixated. "Montfort is playing Mariana against me. He thinks wherever she is, I won't be too far away."

The agent lifted his eyebrows. "He'd be a fool not to."

"Blast."

Nick slammed back another round of whiskey beneath the agent's passive gaze. If there was an agent better than him, it was the man sitting before him. Even with the scar, which could be minimized or maximized to effect, the man was a chameleon, lost inside every role, equal to every circumstance. All those years ago in England, Nick couldn't have predicted such a frivolous youth would transform into the hardened man before him now—a man who had fought beside him in battle. This was the only man in the world he trusted with his life.

A thought occurred to him. "How would you feel about a new assignment?"

"You want me to follow her?" the other man intuited.

Nick nodded.

"I could do that." The agent leaned forward and rested his elbows on the table, head cocked at a speculative angle. "Or—"

"Or what?"

"You could take her home." The agent leaned back in his chair, surely testing every limit of its flimsy construction. "*You* go home."

Nick's stomach tightened. "The assassination plot—"

"Will resolve itself," the man finished for him. "As these situations do."

"I hadn't realized you'd become so cavalier about our work."

"I won't allow you to redirect the conversation." The agent paused, choosing his next words. "Has it ever occurred to you that your marriage wasn't doomed from the beginning?"

A familiar sliver of dread snaked through Nick. "I don't catch your meaning." Although he did.

And in the next moment, the agent confirmed it. "Just because your parents' union combusted into a ball of flame—"

Nick took an aggressive step forward, stopping the agent mid-sentence. Only their shared history prevented him from doing bodily harm to this man. Instead, he stated in a controlled voice, "This topic isn't open to speculation or discussion. My family have naught to do with—"

The agent held out his hands in a conciliatory manner. "You know better than I, to be sure." Nick chose to ignore the hollow ring of disbelief in the words. The agent continued, "This is about you and Mariana. Go home. You've done enough for England. It's time to reclaim your life."

"Ridiculous. She doesn't want me in her life."

"Tonight, and last night, I saw the way you watched her. Shall I describe it for you?"

"I think not."

"Anyone with eyes can see that you're not as immune to her as you would like to believe," the agent pressed.

That showed how much this man understood. Nick understood on a fundamental level that he had absolutely no immunity from Mariana.

Instead of correcting the agent, he tried a different tack. "Why don't *you* go home and reclaim *your* life?"

"I have no home and no life to reclaim. I gave up both when I followed this path. Don't make the same mistake. There is a chance for you, Nick. *That* is what I saw in your eyes tonight."

"You don't know Mariana—"

"I know a bit about Lady Nicholas Asquith. I knew her when she was Lady Mariana Montfort, if you'll recall."

Nick held his tongue. Of course, this man knew a bit about Mariana. He gave a single brisk nod. "If that is all for tonight."

The agent poured another whiskey and silently toasted Nick before tipping the bottom up to the ceiling.

Nick vacated the room without a word of farewell and quickly found himself outside, bracing against a sudden north wind. Daggers of sharp, clean air were what his disordered mind needed at the moment. He must lay out his thoughts singly before they made a stew of his brain.

Bertrand Montfort presented the most danger, well beyond the Comte de Villefranche. Blast the man. What was he playing at? It was Montfort who had recruited him to the Foreign Office in the first place. Now, Montfort was hiring thugs to attack him in his hotel? The two didn't jibe together.

And then there was Mariana, Montfort's niece and Nick's wife. Of course, it was through Montfort that Nick had met her. Oh, Mariana . . .

All rivers led back to her. She was his inevitable destination, no matter how he tried to influence fate otherwise. He'd been running from it these last ten years.

The agent's words echoed in his mind. *It's time to reclaim your life*. His insides had done a flip at those words. It was a reaction worthy of a green boy. It was a reaction born of hope. Hope? To what end?

The answer lay hidden in the potential of the force connecting him and Mariana. It was a force he'd never squarely faced, because he'd insured that he never had to. How convenient it had been to convince himself that the Foreign Office suffered no competitors. That by abandoning his wife, he'd ensured her safety. He'd convinced himself that all these years were worthy of his sacrifice.

Deep below that surface lay another reason for denying the connection between him and Mariana, one he'd carefully kept hidden . Until tonight when the agent had hinted at its root. *Just because your parents' union combusted into a ball of flame—*

Nick hadn't allowed the agent to finish that sentence. It was clear the man had never watched a marriage combust from the inside.

Nick had.

He'd just reached his fifth year when his older brother, Jamie, had gladly abandoned the ancestral pile in Suffolk and claimed his rightful place at Harrow, the boarding school that had been educating Asquith sons since the reign of King James I.

Left to his own devices, Nick spent the next five years mostly in the company of house servants and an ever-changing series of governesses. One after the other, the governesses replaced each other three or four times a year. The next was always the same as the last: young, pretty, and timid. Nick had blamed himself for their desertions and tried to be better, but better had never been good enough to make any of them stay. Only later did Nick understand about his father's predilection for young, pretty, *vulnerable* girls.

Worse than the parade of governesses had been holidays when his mother deigned to leave her beloved London and visit Suffolk. Unable to control their mutual animosity, his parents spent the entire time sniping at each other and attempting to rip each other to shreds over one or the other's latest infidelity.

And this was in the privacy of their home. Their public bouts were the stuff of legend.

As soon as Nick came of age and was finally, blessedly, old enough to have himself shipped off to Harrow, he'd joined Jamie amongst the ranks of the student population, and he never looked back.

Nick understood at an elemental level what came of love matches when the love went sour and curdled into a noxious, stinking heap of acrimony. And as much as he tried to convince himself and others that his and Mariana's was a Society match, he knew exactly what sort of match they'd made.

Shoulders hunched and braced against another gust of northern air, he dug his hands deep inside his overcoat pockets. The fingers of his left hand hooked a long chain and yanked from its depths a locket—Mariana's locket. He clicked it open, expecting to find miniature portraits of the twins inside, when a different image met his eyes. It was the cameo.

His pulse jumped in his veins, and his pace slowed. Yet another memory came at him—there seemed to be an endless supply of them tonight—and his thoughts flashed backward to that long-ago day when he'd claimed the cameo from Pistrucci. He'd held the carved sardonyx in his hands, awestruck by its beauty. Mariana's alabaster profile underlain by a rich, dark red and encircled by a band of rose gold. The world-renowned cameo maker had surpassed his reputation in the execution of it.

The man had asked Nick what words he would like inscribed on the back, and he'd gone mute. What sort of words?

For the entire previous year, he'd struggled to find the words that captured his feelings for Lady Mariana Montfort. There were too many emotions to count and most of them conflicting. But that wasn't to say he'd left the space blank.

He clamped the locket shut and turned it over in his hand. The backing was nothing more than a smooth gold surface. She'd had the cameo set inside the locket for none to see. Only she and he knew the words he'd had inscribed. And she kept them close to her heart . . .

Right.

If he truly knew what was good for him, he would break his promise to Mariana and refuse her another *spy lesson*. But he wouldn't break his promise to her. Too many promises had already been broken.

Tonight, he would teach her one of the most fundamental elements of espionage, and in doing so give her the one thing she wanted in Paris. Never mind that he would be giving himself the gift of watching her face light up with joy when she beheld it.

From a lone corner of his mind, he saw that his spiral out of control had already begun. His words from last night came to him: *Men break laws, walk across flames, and start wars to give a woman like you* everything *she wants.*

Nothing he'd done tonight had come remotely close to any of those acts, but that didn't mean he wasn't capable of each and every one. For her.

This was what he'd fled all those years ago: the knowledge that there was nothing he wouldn't do for this woman, to be worthy of her. It was absolute weakness, worse than opium, and, despite ten years spent trying to outpace and elude it, it had caught him.

# Chapter 15

*Nack: To have a nack; to be ready at anything, to have a turn for it.*

*A Classical Dictionary of the Vulgar Tongue*
Francis Grose

*Next Day*

Mariana crouched down into a dark, filthy corner and attempted to make her body as inconspicuous as possible. Nick's instructions tonight had been as succinct and paltry as those from the previous two nights:

*Rue de Buffon. Small black door behind the iron railing.*

After skulking up and down the avenue a few times, she'd finally located the small black door behind the iron railing, but she hadn't known how to proceed from there. So, she'd ducked into an unobtrusive alcove on the opposite side of the street where she could wait and watch. Now twenty minutes later, she was still waiting and watching. Tonight might be a complete failure—another one.

On the bright side, at least, Nick had been wrong on one account: the absinthe hadn't affected her head this morning, and she'd been able to call on Helene to collect the twins' letters. All seemed right in their respective worlds with Geoffrey reminding her about the bon-bons and Lavinia buying new ribbons for her ancient mare's mane. What a sweet, patient old thing Bessie was, and what a horse-mad, dreamy girl Lavinia was. To be sure, it was the perfect match of horse and girl.

Mariana poked her head out and scanned the street up and down. Thankfully, she remained its sole occupant, save a few rats she'd spied scurrying along walls. She shifted her cramped bum from left to right and clutched her knapsack tight to her chest.

Tonight's note had been accompanied by a long, slender piece of metal resembling a hat pin and the set of clothes she now wore. Nick seemed to have developed a penchant for dressing her, but this time he'd gone beyond the pale. Of course, it didn't escape her notice that these clothes were the reason she was able to blend with the shadows, dressed as she was in unrelieved black: black knit cap, black woolen sweater, black leather gloves, and snug, black . . . trousers.

What could tonight's lesson possibly be? Duplicity . . . guile . . . invisibility . . . now *trousers*. To what end?

As far as she was concerned, trousers were a functional and boring article of men's clothing. Some men wore them better than others, but she'd never given them a moment's thought. They didn't feel terrible, but not quite right either. The fact was she couldn't help feeling exposed. Trousers were so *fitting*. They left a woman no secrets.

There was something else, too. After she'd slid them up her legs and began tentatively circling her bedroom in an attempt to adjust to their fit, an odd feeling had stolen over her. She'd felt light . . . free. If she wasn't careful, she could easily adapt to this particular feeling.

Stranger still, once she'd donned the full costume and tucked her hair into the knit cap, her reflection in the full-length mirror had revealed a man. Well, not a man precisely, rather an ambiguous person who could be anyone. The idea was . . . liberating. It was another feeling to which she could grow accustomed. She was coming to understand what attracted Nick to espionage.

She opened the knapsack, dug out the long pin, and glowered across the deserted street at the innocent door.

She had a feeling about this long pin, that door, and the task before her. Namely, Nick was setting her a task doomed to failure. She felt it in her bones. He hadn't wanted to agree to *one more lesson*. Most likely he figured that if she failed, she would tuck her tail between her legs and flee Paris.

Captain Nylander, the path not pursued, and his boat came to mind. He could sail her to Margate and on to London, where she would forget the last few, strange days and resume her life as normal.

Except it wouldn't do.

She'd asked for one more lesson and gotten it. She wouldn't fail tonight.

On a fortifying wave of pique, she pushed off the wall and out of the shadows, her feet beating a quick tattoo across cobblestones. Within seconds, she stood before the unobtrusive door, long pin in hand and no idea how to use it. The word *dolt* sprang to mind.

A bead of sweat trickled down her forehead to the tip of her nose. She swiped it away with the back of her hand and squatted to better inspect the challenge before her. She inserted the pin into the keyhole and jiggled it to no great effect. On a huff of frustration, she removed the pin and thought for a moment. She needed to slow down.

Bit by hesitant bit, she reinserted the pin and listened . . . and felt. Again, it struck unrelenting iron. This time, however, her steady hand guided the pin across the unforgiving surface until the tip found a tiny hole and slipped inside. Gently, she pressed forward as she turned the door handle. Like a miracle, the lock gave way and the door creaked open.

From her stooped position, she hobbled inside and pressed back against the door until it closed behind her on a soft click. Her eyes squeezed shut, and she sucked in a relieved breath. The sudden dissonance of hands clapping broke through her relief. Her eyes startled open, and she shot to a stand. Directly across the room stood Nick.

"Why you're a right rum kate, if ever I saw one," he said, a smirk curving his lips.

Annoyance at this man struck Mariana at every angle, from his smug expression to his patronizing words. Yet . . . She also couldn't help feeling gratified. In the cant language, he'd just called her a clever picklock. Four days ago, she wouldn't have known what those words meant, much less have felt flattered by them.

Discomfited by the thought, she cleared her throat and shifted on her feet. "Tonight's lesson?"

"Breaking and entering. You, darling, are a natural."

Even as she chafed against his condescending *darling*, she experienced a surge of pleasure at the compliment. She was forever at odds with herself when it came to Nick.

She glanced around at the hundreds of tiny drawers lining the walls from floor to ceiling.

"What is this place? An apothecary?"

"You don't know?"

She shook her head. The familiar quicksilver smile flashed across his face, and a corresponding jolt of excitement streaked through her. She couldn't help it. That smile did things to her insides.

"Follow me," he instructed, on the move.

In a snap, he stepped through an adjacent door and out of sight. Mariana dashed into motion to catch him. His brisk clip never once relented as they navigated a maze-like series of narrow corridors.

Finally, they reached a set of double doors locked with an iron padlock larger than her two hands put together. This was a far more formidable lock than the exterior one. She would wager it weighed half a stone.

"What is this place?" she asked again, her curiosity nearly tripping over itself to find out.

He leaned a shoulder against the doorframe. "Time to work your magic again."

She tore her eyes away from the dratted man and considered the challenge before her. Luck had been on her side with the first lock. With this lock? Her luck had just run out. She risked a glance at Nick. An intent gleam flickered in his eyes. It was as if he was impatient to have her succeed. How unexpected.

She reached for the lock and allowed its heft to sink into her hand. She released the hunk of metal and felt inside her knapsack for the pin. Its long, elegant length didn't appear equal to the challenge. She suspected Nick caught her hesitation, which strengthened her resolve to succeed. She wouldn't fail in front of him. Not again, anyway.

With renewed focus, she crouched low on her haunches to better examine the lock. Indeed, it was large, heavy, iron, and formidable. She slid the pin inside, increment by careful increment, and pressed her ear to its cold, hard surface. Just as with the exterior lock, the tip of the pin found a tiny hole and slipped inside. This time, it refused to release.

Frustrated, she raised her head and immediately realized her mistake. Positioned before her face was the closure of Nick's trousers. All that stood between her and his manhood was a foot-long patch of air and a flimsy length of wool.

"Mariana?"

At the sound of his voice, she startled and tipped backward onto her bottom. Would the humiliation of this night never end? The somewhat mollifying thought occurred to her that, at least, she was wearing trousers. A flash of her bits would have been entirely too much.

Her eyes flew up to meet his, expecting to find amusement there. She didn't. He remained intent on her in a way that called to mind the Nick she once knew. As he lowered to a crouch beside her, she pushed herself up and mirrored his position. Their eyes locked and held on an equal plane.

Into the short distance between their lips, he said, "You're almost there."

"Oh?" It was a moment she could sink into and allow to happen, but the reality was he referenced the lock and not . . . other possibilities.

"A quick, hard twist left should do it."

Although her brain received his instruction, she could hardly process it. His closeness, his warmth, and the way they combined to conjure last night distracted her so completely. Given *that* kiss, a kiss now didn't seem outside the realm of possibility. It occurred to her that it might even be an inevitability . . . An inevitability?

She tore her gaze from him and focused on the lock. A quick, hard twist left and—*voilà!*—the lock released, clunking open. Triumph raced through her, and an irrepressible yip of joy escaped her throat.

Beside her, Nick remained serious and clam. Her smile faltered, and suddenly those *other possibilities* felt inevitable.

"Now what?" she whispered.

~ ~ ~

*Now what*? Her lips were the obvious place to start—too obvious.

He would move toward her, and her eyes would close in anticipation of his lips upon hers. At the last moment, he would switch course and press his mouth to the vulnerable space between her jaw and neck, where he would feel the race of her pulse beneath his skin. A surprised gasp would sound, followed by the release of a soft, slow sigh . . . That was one possible outcome.

Her question was the shock of reason he needed. It was imperative he rein in his thoughts about possible outcomes. "Open the door and find out," he managed.

Her fingertips pushed off the ground and long legs uncurled, her body rising to a graceful stand. She nudged the door open as her feet carried her measure by measure into the room, his gaze trained on her profile, unblinking. This was the moment he'd been anticipating since last night.

In stops and starts of alternating disbelief and awe, her expression bloomed with rapt pleasure. He'd never forgotten how he enjoyed pleasing her.

Beneath a roof composed of opaque glass, black with night, stood an open central floor surrounded on all sides by four stories of wrought-iron balustraded galleries showcasing animals and environments from all seven continents. The meticulously rendered exhibits ranged from the butterflies of Amazonia to the predators of the African savannah.

"Is this—" She cleared her throat. "Is this the Museum of Natural History?" She advanced down the center aisle slowly, reverently, her fingertips smoothing along the fur of a stuffed, South American jaguar. "How did you manage this?"

Nick stood and followed her into the room. "You broke in, remember?"

Her head whipped around. "I'm not so certain of that. I believe your *people* may have had something to do with this."

He shifted on his feet beneath the acuity of her gaze. "Do you like it?"

Her face tilted upward to a ceiling populated by skeletons of dinosaurs and stuffed birds of prey. "*Like* is such a tepid word for what one should feel inside this room. If one merely *likes* it, then he or she doesn't deserve to be here." Her gaze swooped down to meet his. "What do you feel about this place?"

Her question was a test with one correct answer. "What I see before me is nothing short of glorious."

The import of his words turned the air intimate and hot. A heartbeat, then another, thumped inside his chest. She swiveled around, and her feet began moving.

The minutes ticked by as he kept a discreet distance while Mariana explored one aisle after another: this aisle displaying Arctic life; the next, apes inhabiting their trees; while yet another aisle exhibited reptilian bones from too many millennia ago to count. Her clear joy infected him with a responding elation both automatic and unavoidable.

Although he didn't fully understand how the woman he'd known a decade ago had transformed into one captivated by old bones, it mattered not. Those ancient skeletons gave her pleasure. *That* was all that mattered.

As he followed, an inevitability occurred: his baser nature prevailed, and his gaze sank below the supple curve of her waist to a curve more generous. He'd never encountered a woman wearing trousers, therefore hadn't anticipated their enlivening effect on his person.

He'd thought, perhaps hoped, they would render her masculine, but the opposite was true: coarse wool lovingly encased the curve of her derriere before outlining the length of her legs. She'd never looked more feminine.

A delighted "Oh!" called Nick's attention away from the increasingly prurient direction of his thoughts.

Of course, she'd found the Woolly Mammoth.

"It's magnificent," she whispered. She slowly approached the skeleton, as if she was afraid to startle it. "This is quite a large male. Thirteen feet long, at least. Did you know"—Nick watched a pronounced confidence replace her awe—"a specimen like this would have weighed seven hundred stone?"

She moved around the massive and long-deceased pachyderm to better explore him from every angle: her hands reaching down to span the creature's sturdy feet; her head ducking beneath for a different view of the animal's massive ribcage; her fingertips brushing along the length of extravagantly curved tusks.

"Just look at these tusks," she instructed. It was apparent by her assured tone that she had, indeed, been spending considerable quantities of time in the company of schoolmarms and museum guides. "Their curve disguises how long they truly are. Fourteen feet, at least. Some scientists would suggest that a Woolly Mammoth with a pair of impressive tusks like these would have his pick of the ladies." She jerked as if coming out of a trance. "Females," she corrected.

Nick chose to show mercy and let the moment pass. He had other concerns on his mind. For example, he couldn't take his eyes off the contours of her derriere through the fabric of those trousers. He sidled closer to her on the pretext of inspecting a tusk. In reality, he was ridding himself of the distracting view.

Closer wasn't better, for now her intoxicating scent of jasmine and neroli drifted over and enveloped him in a cloud of Mariana. If he didn't know better, he would deduce from his reactions to her tonight—and the last few days, if he was being dead honest—he was enamored of his wife. Again.

No, it couldn't be. He'd vowed never to let that happen.

*Amor* hadn't motivated his plan tonight. Mariana had voiced an interest in this museum, and it just so happened that it was the perfect setting for her third spy lesson. There didn't have to be anything more meaningful to it.

He thought somewhat sheepishly of the next phase of this night and the garden just beyond these walls. It wouldn't do much to disprove the previous thought. "Would you care for a light repast?"

She shot him a quizzical glance. "Here?"

"Follow me." He brushed past her, his pace a decisive clip as they wound through two small, adjacent rooms before reaching a wide door. He pushed it open and stood aside, allowing Mariana to step past him onto an exterior landing.

His inhalation as she passed him was pure instinct. He was unable not to help himself to a breath of her.

Once through the door, she came to a sudden stop and gasped even louder than she had at the sight of the Woolly Mammoth. "Nick," she began, her voice a halting whisper, "what is *this* place?"

"The Jardin des Plantes."

Below them twinkled hundreds—two hundred, he recalled approving—of globe candles lining a crushed granite path and hanging from trees and shrubs at varying heights.

"This is more than a light repast." Golden amber fell on him. "This is magic."

Nick suppressed a surge of pleasure at her words. The caterer may have gone a bit overboard. All he'd requested were a few courses for a light supper, an open-air tent, a few reclining sofas, and a few candles. Two hundred, to be exact.

It was entirely possible that the caterer had followed his instructions to the letter.

Nick followed Mariana as she descended the short flight of stairs before stepping onto a path that curved through the garden created for both pleasure and research purposes.

Once they reached a table set beneath the dimly lit tent, she asked, "I wasn't really breaking and entering tonight, was I?"

"No." He pulled out a chair for her. "The museum and its grounds are ours for the night."

"This is perhaps the loveliest *light repast* I've ever encountered."

The moment Nick took his seat opposite hers, a parade of attendants appeared with a first course of oysters presented with small plates of varied and colorful tidbits of cuisine.

"Are we meant to eat these enchanting creations?" Delight sparked an amber glow in her eyes. "What are they?"

"*Amuse-bouche.*"

"*Amuse-bouche*?"

"Mouth amuser."

"Oh, the French." A charmed smile quirked her lips. "They simply can't help themselves, can they?"

"A single *amuse-bouche* is typically served at the start of the meal or between courses, but I wasn't certain of . . ." he trailed off. He didn't like the pull of this conversation toward the past.

"My tastes? So you had several brought out," she finished for him. She was one to meet a difficulty head-on. "This garden is too bewitching for the past."

She brought an oyster to her mouth and tipped it back, allowing it to slip inside her mouth and slide down her throat.

Nick sat, transfixed.

She patted her lips with a napkin and asked, "Did I pass this spy lesson?"

He cleared his throat. "With flying colors."

She tucked a stray tendril of hair behind her ear. "I must confess," she began. He caught an unexpected glimpse of nerves. "The Woolly Mammoth took my breath away."

"Was it more massive than you imagined?" The question was out of his mouth before he considered it. One could locate a double entendre within if one looked closely enough. Her case of nerves infected him as he anticipated her response.

"Not the *size* of him"—She hesitated a heartbeat—"The gift of him."

Nick shifted in his seat. "Well, you mentioned him, and I thought to—"

"Surprise me?"

"Actually," he began, "I have a connection within the museum—"

"Of course, you do."

"—And since this place is known for its thousands of locks, I merely thought it a suitable venue for your lesson."

The parade of servers returned with a course of roasted meats and vegetables.

Mariana's eyebrows drew together, and Nick grew alarmed that he'd made a mistake, but they released and a rare, wondrous smile lit across her face.

"Is this," she began, her fork poking at her meat, "is this *rabbit?*"

Memory, sharp and sweet, raced between them. The Isle of Skye. Their honeymoon.

"What a lark we thought it would be," she said on a wry laugh, "to arrive at the lodge three days before the servants and have the entire place to ourselves."

"But we forgot one essential detail," he said, drawn into the memory with her.

"Food," she supplied. "In my defense, I thought I'd spent enough hours in my family's kitchens as a child that I'd picked up the bare essentials of cooking." She speared a new potato. "The first day wasn't so bad."

"That was because the innkeeper in Kyleakin saw fit to send us on our way with a loaf of bread and a Scotch pie."

She swallowed her bite and laughed. "We took care of that in short order."

"The next day was cured meats and the remainder of the stale bread loaf."

"But the third day," she began, slicing off a bite of rabbit and bringing it to her mouth.

"Starving."

"Ravenous," she added around the bite. "How did we come by the groundskeeper's cottage?"

"We thought to alleviate our hunger by taking a walk." He left unsaid what else they'd done to keep the hunger at bay.

"That's right. We happened upon his house. Mr. Budge, a grumpy, old Scot, if there ever was one."

"He was just pointing us back in the direction of the lodge—"

"When, like a miracle," Mariana cut in, "the front door opened and emitted both the man's wife and the most heavenly aroma of roast—"

"Rabbit."

Their gazes met and held on a smile.

"How did we finagle our way into their dining room?" she asked.

"Our wolfish leers must've done the trick."

"I'm fairly certain Mrs. Budge fed us her entire pantry."

"Without a doubt."

Mariana's smile went dreamy and thoughtful in a way he hadn't seen in years. It reminded him of the best moments of their marriage when she would open herself to him and reveal the softness at her core. Only he knew this part of her, and it warmed him. Her smile was a gift.

"I send Mrs. Budge a Christmas goose and a box of oranges every year," she said.

"You do?" he asked, the rasp in his throat hopefully obscuring the emotion behind it.

"Of course. She was part of one of the happiest memories from our—" Mariana bit off the rest of the sentence, and the present brushed away the past.

"Marriage," Nick finished for her, vowing at once not to finish anymore of her sentences.

Her smile skittered away, and she nodded.

Once again, the parade of servers returned to clear their plates and set the course of *fromage*. Nick dismissed the attendants for the night.

Mariana ran her fingers up the stem of her glass, and Nick had to look away. While he related to the impulse for more champagne, there was a different appetite that had been awakened and required but one meal to reach satiety.

One meal? No. Once with his wife had never been enough. Their Scottish honeymoon attested to that fact.

"About the Comte de Villefranche?" she began, pulling him away from thoughts that could reach no satisfying end.

"Yes?" he asked, clipped, curt. He shouldn't feel annoyed that she'd brought up the mission. After all, she was his agent.

"I've given my encounters with him a bit of thought. He may be young and idealistic, and perhaps a bit brash, but he doesn't strike me as a revolutionary bent on anarchy."

"What sort of revolutionary is he?"

"The well-meaning sort, I think."

"The *well-meaning* sort?" Nick asked, unable to hide his skepticism.

"Perhaps the misguided sort."

"Are you willing to wager the lives of England's sons on conjecture?"

Mariana held her tongue and averted her gaze.

"Don't allow a handsome, young idealist to turn your head."

"Handsome? *Young*?"

Nick detected the insinuation in her tone. "Impetuous," he continued, hoping that settled it.

"Ah," she drew out. The subtle lift of her eyebrows spoke of disbelief.

The Mariana who said, "*Ah*," and kept the remainder of her thoughts to herself was new, the opposite of the gallivanting girl who stomped across the Skye countryside proclaiming her impending starvation to the world. He wasn't sure which version he preferred.

She pushed away from the table and stood. Champagne glass in hand, she stepped toward a patch of peppermint dahlias in bloom. "While on his famed expedition to Mexico," she began, changing the subject, "Alexander von Humboldt sent dahlia seeds to Paris, London, and Berlin."

She glanced over her shoulder, a glimmer of mischief in her eye. "Perhaps you encountered Humboldt on one of your Mississippi riverboats?"

"Humboldt and I don't travel in the same circles."

She returned her attention to the effulgent blossoms. "Kew Gardens has maintained a lively dahlia patch from Humboldt's seeds."

As Mariana continued with a botany lesson about the edible tubers—apparently ancient South American civilizations used them for food—it struck Nick that her education, and her need to educate, was a device intended to place distance between them.

"The effect of the candlelight on the flower petals is lovely," she continued. "The way they absorb the light, yet reflect it with a soft, deep glow. Like little scraps of velvet beneath a night sky."

"Have you become a poet, Mariana?" Given her response to turn away from him, would he have detected a blush in the light of day?

"If I didn't know better," she began, a hitch in her voice that only he knew, "I would think this the scene of a seduction."

Unable to remain seated quietly when such words issued from her lips, he rose. "If you didn't know better?"

She caught his eye over her shoulder. "Yes."

"Are you so certain it isn't?" He wasn't so certain himself.

"Yes."

It was the jagged fray in her voice when she spoke that simple, "*Yes,*" that sent him over the edge and set him on a course both foolish and inevitable, possible outcomes suddenly fated.

# Chapter 16

*Titter-tatter: One reeling, and ready to fall at the least touch . . .*

*A Classical Dictionary of the Vulgar Tongue*
Francis Grose

Would Nick let the provocation pass?

She could see by the determined set of his mouth and the narrow slit of his eyes that he was analyzing her words, deciding whether or not to respond. She may have even detected a slight flaring of his nostrils.

A tiny frisson of panic raced through her, alongside no small amount of excitement.

Gently, perhaps too gently, he placed his champagne flute on the table and stalked toward her in slow, but inevitable, increments. The South American jaguar she'd stroked earlier flashed across her mind. The jaguar was a solitary and opportunistic apex predator, the sort who was the king of his jungle. Inside the eyes of the man before her, she saw the kinship between man and jungle cat.

"You know the scene of a seduction so well?" he asked, his voice as smooth as a purr.

"Of course."

His mouth crept wider, as if he sensed her false bravado. "*A seduction*," he repeated, continuing his advance on her.

She stood her ground, unwilling to retreat backward beneath the intensity of his gaze and the steadiness of his step.

"The phrasing suggests a lack of agency on your part. I never found you wanting in that department." A forefinger tapped his lips once, twice. "Let us analyze the elements of a seduction, shall we? We are engaged in a *spy lesson*, after all."

Her mouth went dry, but she couldn't look away. Apex predators understood averted eyes as submission. She would not submit.

"Champagne? Check."

Even as a healthy dose of wariness braced her against his steady advance, she didn't feel as cautious as she should. After all, this was Paris, where a sense of unreality underlay and influenced every moment. In London, this night . . . this scenario wasn't possible.

But in Paris? Here, possibility abounded.

And in this garden? *Everything* was possible.

"Oysters? Check. I wonder"—A wicked gleam entered his eye—"has your autodidacticism extended into the realm of the sensual? Mayhap an empirical inquiry into the efficacy of aphrodisiacs?"

A curt shake of her head was all the answer she trusted herself to give as her senses awakened to anticipation. No aphrodisiac on earth was more powerful than Nick, his words . . . his voice . . . his dominant presence casting a spell of sensuality around them. It could be true that *everything* was possible in this garden.

Perhaps she could be granted a special dispensation: one night free of her shipwreck of a marriage where she could pursue a seduction with her husband. Oh, the irony . . .

"What do you think?" he murmured.

A meager stretch of grass now separated her from him. "What do I think?" she asked, managing a raspy whisper. "This is madness."

His gaze all but dared her to look away. "And which words shall I use for this seduction?"

"For *this* seduction?" she whispered.

He nodded once in confirmation. It was no longer a seduction in theory. It mattered not if she'd goaded him into it or if it had been his intention all long. *This* seduction was happening at this very moment. He stood not a foot away from her, the air between them thick with the undeniable reality of it. She tilted her head to hold his gaze.

"Words of love?" he asked. "Words of lust?"

Her legs threatened to give way. His hand reached out and, before she understood his intent, he flicked the cap off her head. Loose tendrils of hair tumbled about her shoulders, his eyes went as dark as the indigo sky above, and she knew: the wanting between them was mutual. He wasn't toying with her in the way a jaguar toyed with his prey only to release it once he grew bored. Instead, his eyes suggested a different narrative: he wouldn't release her.

To have Nick in her thrall was a feeling she was incapable of resisting. A cresting surge of audacity emboldened her to reach across the insignificant stretch of space separating their bodies. She considered caressing the back of his neck before pulling his mouth to hers. But such an action was expected . . . ordinary.

Rather, her hand reached forward and stroked the fabric of his trousers. His jaw clenched, and a sharp inhalation of air sounded through his teeth. The tip of her finger began tracing the outline of his manhood through coarse wool, her fingernail grazing its rough surface. She stepped forward, their bodies a hairsbreadth away from touching, and rose to her tiptoes. Her lips found his ear. "Oh, I think actions, rather than words, will do."

His body tensed, and she sensed the last remnant of his rational mind asserting itself. He was attempting to regain control. That wouldn't do.

She'd made this man lose control before. Those three

starved, glorious days in Skye, for example. It was nothing new. Yet . . . it felt new.

Her stomach fluttery and light, the world became clear, crisp, fresh. She hadn't yet experienced Nick as the person she was today. And she wasn't leaving this garden tonight until she had experienced every last inch of him.

Her fingers found the waistband of his trousers and hesitated at the closure. "Don't you want this?"

"It's not that simple."

"It is that simple." She unlooped the buttons, one . . . two . . . three, freeing his swollen manhood, her point punctuated.

Unable to resist, her fingers wrapped around the naked length of him, her thighs instinctively squeezing together in response. It had been so long, too long, since *this* had been inside her. She could push him down onto one of the reclining sofas and have him straddled between her legs, poised to take him inside her within a matter of seconds. But that wasn't the way she wanted him.

She unwrapped her fingers from his shaft and registered a note of protest in his eyes. Good. It was a start. "I have a confession."

"You're a long way from a chapel," he all but growled.

"I secretly admire scandalous women."

"Some might call you a scandalous woman."

"Those people have no imaginations." She paused a heartbeat, just long enough to stoke his curiosity about what she might say next. "I've been quite genteel and abstemious all these years. Tonight, I long to be a hedonistic Parisienne." She reached for the bottom of her sweater and pulled it over her head. His eyes lowered to feast on her naked torso. The raw lust charging his gaze increased her desire tenfold. "I've always wondered"—She kicked the slippers off her feet—"what would it be like"—She unlaced the closure of her trousers—"to shed all inhibitions and be completely, utterly free?" She wiggled her hips and shimmied free of the trousers—her last stitch of clothing.

"Mariana," his voice rasped, "what do you want from me?"

"Isn't it obvious?" She was absolutely intoxicated. And it wasn't from champagne. "I want you to lose control."

A canny light sparked within his eyes. "That isn't what you want."

His words sounded an alarm bell in her head, but she had no care for it. "It isn't?"

"It isn't." He pulled her into him and dared her to look away. His manhood pressed against her naked pelvis, dissolving her body into a pool of molten lava. "You want me to fuck you."

A tremor of shock rocked her. *Fuck*. A vulgar word, but a word ripe with carnality, too. Alongside the shock coursed a thrill of pure lust.

"Isn't that the same thing?" she asked breathlessly.

"No. Say it."

"Say what?" she whispered. The power of the moment seemed to be sliding away from her, and she cared not.

"Say, *I want you to fuck me*."

Without consideration for possible consequences, or perhaps because of them, she whispered fiercely, "I want you to fuck me," before immodestly and wickedly adding, "*right now*."

One hand curled around her upper arm, the other released and stole down the tight space between their bodies until it reached the intimate slit of her sex, his eyes refusing to release hers, their breath mingling in the small space between their lips.

His hand hesitated, and she thought she would burst into flame if his fingers didn't reach their inevitable destination. His irises flared as his fingertips feathered across the sensitive nub of her clitoris, a word she'd learned not too long ago from an anatomy book deemed too indecent for females of all ages.

Her eyes closed on an involuntary gasp. All she was capable of doing in this moment was *feel*. A soft mewl of longing escaped her as his fingertips stroked back and forth, eliciting one crest of pleasure followed by another, the next higher than the last. While one long finger continued stroking her, another slipped inside her, inch by exquisite inch.

His lips moving against her ear, he whispered, "You're so wet for me."

Pleasure at his words and the feel of him rippled through her body, yet it wasn't enough. She wanted . . . needed . . . *more*. She reached around and cupped his tight buttocks with both hands as she pulled him toward her, his ready manhood grinding into her pelvis. Her hips gave an impatient thrust.

It wasn't enough. It wouldn't be enough until—

He stepped forward, forcing her to step backward. They repeated the cooperative little dance until her legs bumped against the edge of a sofa. A tiny cry of protest escaped her when their bodies separated, and he lowered her onto lush, down cushions.

From her prone position, she watched the clothes fly off him in a quick succession of efficient movements, his delicious body a feast for her eyes. The hardened muscles flexing across every lean inch of him were nothing short of splendid. Wild with pleasure, desire, and greed, she opened her legs and bared herself to him, a feeling of delicious sinfulness overtaking her. Never in her life had she felt so much assurance within her femininity as when he froze at the sight of her.

"Mariana . . ." he trailed off, apparently unable to complete a sentence. Craving, dark and sinuous, stole through her, causing her sex to quiver in anticipation of *him*. The corners of his lips tipped up ever so slightly.

Again, he was a jungle cat, and she wanted nothing more than to be his capture.

When he dropped to his knees between her legs, she rose onto her elbows. She would watch as he entered her.

He wrapped long fingers around his shaft and pressed his hips forward, slowly, deliberately, until his manhood pushed against her sex. Her body tensed with anticipation, and the breath suspended in her lungs. She sensed a hesitation within him. He wanted her. That she knew. But he didn't want to want her. That she also knew.

"Aren't you going to *fuck* me?" she whispered, the question a demand and a plea.

His manhood poised at her opening, he pressed forward, inch by excruciating inch, his eyes drifting shut. He looked utterly lost in the moment. At the sight and feel of him, she teetered on the edge of orgasm, another recently acquired word.

Deeper and deeper he sank into her, rills of sensation streaming through nerves focused on a single purpose: pleasure. Encased to the hilt, his eyes opened, and she, too, was lost. Unable to restrain herself, she wrapped her arms around his neck as her legs encircled his waist. She would feel all of him.

A muffled groan escaped her when he drew away; a sharp gasp filled her when he pushed forward. With each deliberate thrust of his hips, his fingers biting into her skin, steadying her, spurring her on, she no longer knew or cared where he ended and she began.

Yet something wasn't right. They hadn't kissed. With a craving, sudden and desperate, she needed the touch of his lips on hers, the whisper of his ragged breath across her skin, mingling with hers.

She reached up, pulled his head down, and claimed his mouth. Her tongue found his and toyed with it as her hips responded to his increasingly frenzied rhythm. The moment transformed from one of mindless indulgence to one complicated by an unexpected rush of intimacy, a closeness familiar and new.

His hips thrust harder, faster, deeper, ravishing her, destroying her, breaking her into a million pieces of light and air and exquisite nothingness.

Incapable of holding the kiss, her head arched back as his shaft drove relentlessly into her, and an elusive feeling of wildness began to overtake her, driven by a fever nearing its breaking point.

She needed more, *more*, her sex winding tighter, her fingernails digging into his back as the tension refused to release. "Oh, Nick," she gasped.

An image of an iron lock, stubbornly clamped shut, came to her. It had been so long . . . Perhaps too long . . . A groan of frustration escaped her.

"Come"—He pulled out of her—"for"—He drove into her—"me."

On a cry, her body slipped free of its locks and release overcame her on wave after pulsing wave. Her essence separated from her body and soared above, high on the wing of wantonness, as he pressed toward his own climax, meeting her there in the realm of abandon and oblivion.

Shaky arms unable to support her, she collapsed back into lush cushions, where she lay, eyes closed, thoroughly, deliciously fucked. Nick's enervated body followed hers down, and they lay skin to skin, heartbeat to heartbeat, breath to breath, in unison, the known world fallen away.

It could have been the errant flicker of a candle or a night bird's song in the trees, but the world began to reassert itself, to remind her of its existence. Her eyes flew open, and panic, blind and self-preserving, rose.

She pushed his hard, muscular chest. "What have we done?"

# Chapter 17

*Sixes and sevens: Left at sixes and sevens; i.e. in confusion: commonly said of a room where the furniture, &c. is scattered about; or of a business left unsettled.*

*A Classical Dictionary of the Vulgar Tongue*
Francis Grose

*Nothing we shouldn't have kept doing all these years* was Nick's first thought. But it wouldn't do to speak that thought aloud. Or think it again, for that matter.

On a groan both sated and irritated, he slid off Mariana, ignoring the scream of protest inside him. His body had no desire to separate from hers, but he couldn't think in a straight line otherwise. Her gaze held his in a moment both tense and tender, and he felt an insuperable chasm open up and yawn between them, the sense of intimacy growing more elusory with each second that ticked by.

He sat back on his heels, suddenly as naked as Adam after he ate the forbidden fruit.

Mariana rolled onto her side and curled into herself, denying him the unobstructed view of her body he craved. "Have you seen Yvette and Lisette since . . ." she trailed, ". . . since that night?"

At once and unaccountably hurt, he responded with a defensive, "Of course not."

In a gesture of reassurance, she reached out and touched staying fingers to his arm. "I'm missing my locket and hoped it was in your possession."

He shot to his feet and began dressing beneath her unflinching gaze. "I don't recall a locket." He'd intended to return the locket to her tonight. Instead, he'd lied, and he knew why. He didn't want to let any part of her go.

Without another word, she slipped off the sofa and strode past him. He allowed her to pass, affording her a measure of privacy as she retrieved her discarded clothing.

He knew what he must say next. "You are ready to engage your *handsome* and *well-meaning* and *misguided* revolutionary tomorrow."

A blank pause stretched between them before a brittle laugh burst from her. "Don't forget *young*."

The interlude that had just occurred was gone forever. He would pretend that a pang for its loss hadn't just stolen through him.

"I passed the seduction lesson as well as breaking and entering?" Mockery sounded in her voice. "Two birds with one stone, to be sure."

He matched her tone with a sardonic one of his own. "You always were efficient."

Steeling himself, he faced a fully dressed Mariana, her eyes glittering hard as diamonds. "If you don't have any further instructions, I shall show myself out."

"Around that corner"—He inclined his head—"is an unlocked gate."

Their gazes held for a moment longer than he would have expected. She was angry at having been dismissed so casually. He wouldn't blame her for slapping his face, given all that had been said and done tonight. He might even want her to slap his face, just for the contact of her skin against his.

She gave a curt nod and disappeared down the path.

Once she was out of sight, he grabbed his overcoat and traced her footsteps down an aisle of shrubbery, around a sharp limestone corner, and through the open gate. At a distance of about twenty feet, she strode ahead of him and cut across the street.

"Do not follow me," she called over her shoulder.

He elected not to respond verbally, letting his feet do his talking. He would see her safely back to her hotel since his agent had been given instructions only to follow her to the museum tonight.

Had he anticipated the outcome of the night?

He was being disingenuous with himself. Of course, he had. His skin still pulsed with the electricity of her skin against his.

How many years had it been since he'd last felt her? How many years had he spent trying to forget the feel of her?

His eyes trained on her fleeting form, his mind traveled back to the night he'd put a stop to the electricity between them.

Or had tried.

~ ~ ~

*London*
*Midnight, 6 May 1814*

Nick stepped across the threshold of his foyer and gave free rein to the impatience and anxiety that had been plaguing him during tonight's tedious evening of pretend.

For nigh onto a fortnight now, he'd been attempting to draw out an enemy agent who possessed a legendary jealous streak by publicly engaging the man's lover, an opera singer whose loyalty, and affection, could be sold to the highest bidder.

Tonight, the ruse had finally begun to yield a result in the form of a hotly worded note from the agent. The man had stated in no uncertain terms that Nick was to drop the dalliance. This was expected and played into Nick's hands.

Yet one thinly veiled sentence negated any triumph he might have felt at the breakthrough.

*Remember: unlike lovers, beloved wives aren't disposable.*

A single fact was clear: Mariana was in mortal danger. His mission faded into the background, and nothing else mattered. All that mattered was that Mariana was safe, and that he keep her so.

*Beloved.* The enemy agent's use of the word nagged at him. For here was what he'd known since the twins' birth: it wasn't outside the realm of possibility. All he wanted to do—all he ever really wanted to do—was steal into his wife's warm bed, snug his body against hers, and never let her go.

In his and Mariana's case, familiarity wasn't breeding contempt. He didn't understand how it was possible, but their marriage seemed to be a happy one. It was easy to see how an outside observer might think so, too. Another surge of anxiety pulsed through him.

A stray ray of moonlight streaming through a high window, he stopped and listened, ears attuned to any untoward sound. He followed the soft orange glow emanating from the family drawing room just off the central corridor. Mayhap a servant had forgotten to extinguish the lantern, mayhap not. He reached beneath his overcoat, and his fingers wrapped around the hilt of the dagger hidden at his waist.

Just outside the room, his hackles rose. Someone lay in wait for him on the other side of the wall. He counted backward from five and swung around the corner, hoping the element of surprise was in his favor. A single, sweeping glance revealed that he shared the room with one other person: Mariana.

He exhaled a gust of relief. No more than five feet away, she sat with her robe closed tight at her neck and her hands folded in her lap, observing him, eyes wide and strangely unfathomable. She looked not herself. But he hadn't fully processed that observation just yet.

"Mariana, what are you doing up at this hour? Is everyone well?"

"A late night at the opera?"

"Oh, you know how these things go," he answered in his usual evasive way.

Mariana never pried all that deeply into his business. He didn't like the feeling of guilt that had begun to worm its way into these evasions. They'd begun to feel more like lies, and, more and more, he didn't want to keep his other life from her. It was a problem, admittedly, for a spy whose wife was seen as *beloved* by him.

Her head cocked to the side. "I'm not sure I do."

He kept his tone light and easy, but something wasn't right. "Diplomacy consists of little more than showing visiting dignitaries the sights and bonding over hard whiskey and fine—"

"Women?"

"—Cigars," he finished.

How pale and drawn she looked. It could be the lateness of the hour or the twins having a rough night.

"Olivia paid me a visit this morning," she said, matching his light and easy tone note for note.

"Is that so unusual?" Mariana and Olivia were close, especially after Olivia's foolhardy husband, Percy, had joined the army and left for the Continent on a doomed wave of idealistic fervor.

"She was at my bedside with the latest edition of *The London Diary* before I'd even drawn a sip of my morning brew. Have you read it?"

"You know I don't read that rubbish." He noted a studied casualness radiating off her, and his eyes narrowed.

"You might reconsider. After all, you feature prominently in their most recent edition."

That was when he heard it: the tremor of barely restrained emotion in her voice. Something was wrong—direly wrong.

"Would you care to read it? I have a copy right here." Her lips set in a tight line, she lifted the paper off her lap and extended it toward him.

Nick stepped forward and took the offensive object from her hand. He had no way of knowing that when his fingertips brushed hers, it would be the last time he touched her for ten years.

He quickly scanned the offensive rag until he found what he was looking for, dead center of page two in the "About Town" section:

*A chip off the old block?*
*Lord N——s A——h spotted intimately acquainting himself with the Italian tongue thanks to noted soprano A——a N——i.*
*This particular lord's penchant for the opera clearly runs in the family. Just ask his father, the M——s of C——e.*

Even though they were a lie—admittedly, one he'd gone to great lengths to encourage in certain circles—those four sentences struck him to his core. His entire existence centered around being as *un*like the Marquess of Clare as possible with one glaring exception . . . And he was staring straight at her.

Like his father before him, he'd made a love match. Mariana was beloved by him—thoroughly and desperately.

During their mad dash of an engagement and year of marriage, he'd evaded his feelings for her. She was young, beautiful, provocative, and an appropriate match in the eyes of family and Society. Like so many men of his social set, he'd never spoken of love. It was entirely superfluous to the institution of marriage.

Even when the feeling filled him full to bursting at times, he'd never given himself over to it. The weight of his parents' union hung over his head like an ax suspended just above his neck, poised to drop.

Now, the feeling of dread that had hung about the edges of his marriage from the very beginning, and particularly since the birth of the twins, started to coalesce into something concrete. He'd known this life had never really been his. His happy marriage was nothing more than a mirage.

"I explained to Olivia," Mariana said, "it is a vicious bit of unsubstantiated gossip from London's lowest rag."

Nick met her eyes wide with equal parts hope and fear and saw that she was giving him the benefit of doubt. She was giving him a chance to tell her the truth.

But it was a different truth that gnawed at him. Before him stood the opportunity to right the wrong he'd done Mariana by marrying her. He'd known from the start that he was endangering her heart, but the enemy agent's note made it clear that this marriage was endangering her physical person, too. That couldn't be stood.

In a single stroke, he could protect Mariana from the increasingly dangerous underworld he navigated on a daily basis, and he could save her from the inevitable collapse of their marriage along with the bitterness and hatred that would follow. He wouldn't repeat the mistakes of his father.

"The column is true," he stated. "Every word of it."

His heart pounded so hard in his chest that he thought it might rend in two. But she couldn't see that. She only saw the supercilious smile pasted onto his face.

"How can that be? I thought we were—"

"Happy?" he finished for her, his tone ripe with distancing notes of condescension and disdain.

Although it killed him, this was the right measure. One he should have taken from the start. He would do anything to protect Mariana and keep her safe—even if it meant breaking her heart.

Acid rose in his throat for what he must say next, and for the way he must say it. "We've been happy, darling. But I fail to see how my having a sweet bit on the side has anything to do with you."

She flinched as if he'd physically struck her, and another part of him died. "I wasn't aware that we had a—"

"Society marriage?" He forced out a laugh, mean and abrasive, ripe with ridicule. "Pray tell, what other sort of marriage would we have? Don't be daft, darling."

She blinked once, twice. Betrayal, hot and wounded, shone in her eyes. He'd succeeded. He'd made her hate him and ensured her safety.

"Get out," she commanded low and hard. Her brows crinkled together in disbelief as if she'd stunned herself with her own words.

"My darling Mariana," he began in that supercilious tone that irked her to this very day, "I thought you were aware of the sort of marriage we have."

Eyes glaring at him through twin pools of unshed tears, she pulled her robe tight like a protective shield. "Get out," she repeated louder and stronger, her resolve clearly gathering steam, "and don't come back until I say you can." She'd hesitated before adding, "Unless it's to see Geoffrey and Lavinia. In which case, you will alert me ahead of time when you will arrive, so I can be out."

Like that, the mirage of his happy marriage evaporated, and the future pattern of their marriage was established.

He'd immediately taken himself off to the Continent before he could change his mind and beg her to take him back. A single ten-minute conversation had set in motion the trajectory of his life for the last decade.

In the name of England, he gave up Mariana. In the name of truth . . . Well, that was a different matter. No longer did it feel like he was waiting for the axe to drop. It had dropped, and he'd survived.

Little did he know that survive was all he would do for the next decade, that surviving wasn't the same as living. A part of him, the only part that mattered, had died that night.

Ahead, Mariana's pace slowed as she approached the well-lit hotel, and without a backward glance his way, she allowed herself to be ushered inside by obsequious attendants. How would she explain her trousers? In a luxurious hotel, discretion was everything. Likely, she wouldn't have to.

Nick's pace doubled its rate as he strode past the entrance. Unable to resist, he risked a quick look left toward the lobby and saw her needs being met by no fewer than three attendants. Once past, he further increased his pace until he nearly jogged, as if he could outpace both the present and the past.

But the past wasn't through with him yet. The momentum of that long-ago night had propelled him ever forward and away from her. At least, it had until three nights ago when he'd spotted his wife at the ballet.

Except the woman he'd just made love to wasn't his wife, not exactly. The Mariana he was coming to know in Paris was a woman apart from the girl she'd once been. She was a woman who had picked up the pieces of her life, after having been abandoned by her husband, and carved out her own paths and experiences. With her sister, the woman had even created a vocation for herself by founding a progressive school for girls.

Her irresistibility, when he'd first beheld her energetic, lissome form entering a copse of woods with a stout hound at her side, was nothing to her irresistibility tonight. This Mariana—a woman composed of flesh and bone and fantasy—wasn't a woman who a man released from his grasp once he held her within it.

Yet it wasn't that simple. Between them stood an insurmountable mountain range the height and breadth of the Himalayas: their history—a history riddled with half-truths, outright lies, and impossibility.

He rounded a corner and a blast of north wind met him full in the face. It was the slap he needed as he traveled a Paris murky with a billion dots of newly-arrived fog. Just as the fog began to dissipate beneath the glare of the sun's first rays, so, too, did the night's uncertainty.

An essential truth remained unchanged: he couldn't have Mariana. It was too dangerous. But he was having trouble remembering for whom it was most dangerous. Was it for Mariana? Or was it for him?

# Chapter 18

*P's: To mind one's P's and Q's; to be attentive to the main chance.*

*A Classical Dictionary of the Vulgar Tongue*
Francis Grose

*Next Day*

Mariana picked her lone way across a crushed granite path flanked on each side by towering rows of horse-chestnut trees. The wind breezing through the high canopy, sending fall leaves spiraling in graceful pirouettes to the ground, called to mind a carefree midday stroll down Little Spruisty Folly's long, undulant drive.

Reality was anything other than carefree. She suppressed the groan that longed to be set free on the breeze. Last night—what had she done?

She took a deep, steadying breath. Focus was required for the matter at hand: her *tête-à-tête* with the Comte de Villefranche.

But focus was impossible. She'd even arrived at the sprawling Jardin du Luxembourg half an hour early, hoping to clear her mind of the one thought that kept spiraling round and round. What had she done . . . *with Nick*?

Conflicting feelings of elation, desire, and panic charged through her in a competitive rush, each making a compelling case for primacy.

How the same he was from ten years ago. How *different*.

His intensity. His engagement. His . . . hardness. A hot flush crept up to the tips of her ears. He'd always been a hard man. But, now, he was . . . *harder*.

She must be pink all over by now.

She'd opened Pandora's box. Now all of life's pleasures were available to her. So, too, were its pains. What had she done? What did she still want to do?

*Shameless*. *Hedonistic*. No other words better described it.

Her eyes drifted shut, and a sensory memory pushed forward. His capable fingers clutching her hips . . . the press of his unrelenting body against her forgiving flesh . . . sharp stabs of his breath on her nape . . . Her foot caught an exposed root, and she stumbled, her eyes flying open.

It might be better if she didn't close her eyes for the time being, possibly ever. If she kept moving, she might be able to outrun her shameless, hedonistic self.

As troubling as her utter capitulation to her desire was, something else disturbed her more. It was the utter confusion of him. One moment they were making love like their lives depended on it, the next, he was telling her that she was ready to seduce Villefranche.

Nick was forever drawing her in and forever pushing her away. She'd convinced herself that all the emotional flotsam from their shipwreck of a marriage had risen to the surface years ago, but apparently not. All it took was five days in Paris to jar more wreckage loose. There seemed to be an endless supply of it.

She gave herself a mental shake. She was decidedly unfocused for a woman presently engaged in a spy mission. *Spy mission*—whatever *that* was. Espionage was a terribly ambiguous business.

Just as she emerged from the tree-lined path, a pair of gentlemen caught the edge of her vision. She side-stepped off the path and slipped behind a thick horse-chestnut, her heart beating an unrelenting tattoo. She poked her head around the trunk, committing what felt like her first true act as a spy.

Silhouetted against the backlight of a stone archway stood Villefranche, engaged in conversation with another man. She could act the innocent and "happen upon" the pair, but the close positioning of their bodies implied a discussion private, even covert.

Furthermore, another problem occurred to her: she recognized the other man. Even though his distant profile revealed a clean-shaven jaw, she knew him for the bearded croupier from the poker game. This was the same man whom Nick trusted with his life.

Villefranche glanced from side to side, but not far enough to spot her, and held out a thin, flat packet. The croupier efficiently pocketed it and strode away in the opposite direction, shoulders hunched, head down.

Villefranche pivoted in her direction. Mariana ducked back and tried to think. The crunch of his booted heels grew louder as he fast approached. She had approximately three seconds. *Think.* She willed herself to do just that, and an idea came to her. It had worked once, why not again?

Braced against the rough tree trunk, she counted one . . . two . . . three . . . before rushing forward and literally happening upon him. As their bodies collided, her reticule skittered across the path. Like the gallant he was, Villefranche sprang into action and retrieved her bag.

"Madame, I believe"—His eyes widened with shock— "Lady Nicholas? Are you injured?"

"Oh, *non*, Comte," Mariana replied as she retrieved her bag from his slack hands. "I am quite sound."

"It was my understanding that we would meet at the Medici Fountain half an hour hence."

"Sometimes I enjoy a contemplative stroll in a garden." It was Nick who had told her that for a lie to be believable, it must be threaded with truth.

"You are unaccompanied by your lady's maid?" Villefranche asked, prim shock made evident by his raised eyebrows.

"She succumbed to a sudden fever this morning and was unable to escort me," she replied. Hortense was, in fact, in perfect health and had protested most vociferously against Mariana venturing to the garden without her. "I am so looking forward to my first view of the Medici Fountain. I've heard it's glorious. Do you know the way?"

"Of course, it will be my pleasure to show you."

She rested her hand on his forearm, and it struck her that she was touching the wrong man. What a silly and unwelcome thought.

She should distract herself by flirting with Villefranche, but she couldn't muster the will. And since he lacked the capacity for light conversation, they perambulated through the famed Jardin du Luxembourg as if they were on a grim death march instead of a pleasure stroll. It then occurred to her exactly what she needed to say.

"Lucien . . . may I call you Lucien?" At his hesitant nod, she continued, "I must apologize for my *curiosity* regarding cigars."

His only response was the betraying splotch of red that crept up his neck.

"After you bid me that hasty *adieu*, I realized how the topic may have been misconstrued to mean, well, I'm not certain how to finish that sentence."

They were the words of a flustered ingénue. She risked a shy glance up at him, and her eyelashes might have fluttered. This was the moment that would make or break her mission.

"Think nothing of it, Lady Nicholas. Misunderstandings can occur."

The words were stiff. His tone was stiff. But the Comte de Villefranche was nothing if not stiff. In other words, she might have mollified him, but it was too early to tell.

"You are the very soul of graciousness," she said obsequiously. She squeezed his forearm for good measure. "Do you often venture to the garden for rendezvous?"

"Rendezvous?" he all but exclaimed. He must be wondering if she'd seen him with the other man.

She pasted a bright, flirtatious smile onto her lips and returned, "Well, what would you call what we're doing?" The rigid muscles beneath her hand released the slightest increment. She tried again. "Do you know the history of this garden?"

A history lesson would have to do. Clearly, neither of them was in the mood for a flirt.

"Marie de' Medici," he began, "created the garden two hundred years ago in the Italian style to remind her of her childhood home, the Palazzo Pitti in Florence. Two thousand elm trees were planted at her behest."

As his lecture—Villefranche didn't know how to speak in any other fashion—began to take shape, Mariana's mercurial focus blurred around the edges, softening its borders, allowing other thoughts entry. On a usual day, she would soak in every word, delighting in newfound knowledge that might never be useful, but wasn't useless either. This informal acquisition of knowledge was how she'd educated herself over the past decade.

But this was no usual day. This was the day after she'd *fucked*—oh, that wicked word—Nick.

But it had been more than simple physical pleasure. She'd experienced an emotional pleasure last night, too, that could be summed up in two words: Woolly Mammoth. It was an example of the tender, thoughtful man she'd married, a side he'd only ever revealed to her; she was sure of it. It was a gift in itself.

This last decade, she'd never allowed herself to remember that side of Nick. She would have missed him too much. And now she remembered.

Villefranche waved an instructive finger in front of her face, effectively cutting into her reverie. "Marie de' Medici referred to the palace"—His finger remained pointing toward the building to their left— "as *Palais Médicis.*"

"Her own Italian paradise," Mariana replied, the statement bland and indifferent.

"Perhaps," Villefranche allowed. Mariana sensed a storm cloud about to break over her head. "But this is Paris, and she was the Queen of France. She built her *Italian paradise*, as you call it, with French money and on the backs of French laborers without a care for any but her own desires. Do you know she was the grandmother of King Louis the Fourteenth?"

"I've never given it a thought."

"*Le Roi Soleil.* That was the name he gave himself. The Sun King."

"I might have read something—"

"And the palace at Versailles? An utter waste of the French collective wealth," he spat.

Mariana's gaze locked onto him. "You certainly have strong opinions about . . . everything."

Sheepish misgiving stole across his features. "My apologies, Lady Nicholas. I tend to let my principles carry me away."

Mariana held her tongue. In the implacable determination in his eyes, in the tone of his voice, in the set of his jaw, she recognized herself in Villefranche. She'd allowed her principles to carry her away more than a few times. Her work at The Progressive School for Young Ladies and the Education of Their Minds was the fruit of one such principle. It was a quality she respected in others. She respected this man for it.

He was the sort of man who formed the backbone for revolutions. He had the intellect. He had the connections. He had the resources. And, most important of all, he had the will.

His words, and his fervor in their delivery, confirmed another impression of him, too. This was a man ensnared in a role for which he was supremely unsuited. He wasn't a revolutionary; he was a pawn to be used and discarded at the whim of more powerful players.

There was no doubt in Mariana's mind that Villefranche was careening straight toward Nick, who understood the game and its larger implications better. Nothing in Nick's covert world was black or white, right or wrong.

This was going to be a problem for the idealistic young man at her side. Villefranche *only* saw the world in black and white. While she sympathized with that view, her adult life had taught her that world existed only in fairy tales and dreams.

Neither man was wrong. Yet neither seemed to have the right of it. The time was long past for them to come to terms. She didn't know what the conversation between Villefranche and the croupier entailed, but there wasn't a doubt in her mind that the stakes were raised when those two men exchanged that package.

Nick needed to know. But, then, he had *people*. Likely, he already knew.

She put the thought behind her and walked on in silence with Villefranche until the sky opened above them and the trees fell behind. As if provided an instructive metaphor, her mind, too, opened, and a possible solution to the problem of Villefranche and Nick began to coalesce.

She shook her head. The idea was too bold. And there was the strong possibility that it just might be a terrible idea, maybe even disastrous, like so many of her ideas since she'd arrived in Paris. She should do the job given her and leave the bold ideas to the seasoned professionals.

The vista before her widened, and she allowed herself to be distracted by the view. Before her stood a massive grotto both high and wide, composed of a brown stone that gave the impression that it had sprung directly from nature. This must be the Medici Fountain.

Her eye followed the line of the four impressive columns all the way up, up, up to find the requisite—this was an Italianate fountain, after all—classical imagery of lounging gods overseeing all from on high. And even though the fountain itself was an unimpressive stream of water that flowed into a small pool at the grotto's base, when taken as a whole, the Medici Fountain possessed a majesty that spoke volumes about the colossal power of the woman who had commissioned its construction.

Mariana's gaze wandered back to earth, and her eye happened upon a shadowy form some thirty yards in the distance. Her breathing went from relaxed to shallow in the space of a second, her heart an unrelenting hammer in her chest, frozen blood sloshing through her veins.

Instinctively, her gaze darted away and settled on an arrogant Greek god. When she detected no movement at the periphery of her vision, she stole a glance, and the figure was gone. Her stomach lurched in relief, and her eyes fixed on the pool at her feet, so as not to reveal the receding burst of anxiety and paranoia.

Villefranche's voice came into tune once again. "It was Napoleon who rehabilitated the Medici Fountain after it had fallen out of fashion and into disrepair. No one had a use for a picturesque, Italian fountain in the last century."

"I suppose it wasn't gilded enough," she replied, a caustic, distancing edge relieving a measure of her interior tumult.

"*Exactement*," Villefranche exclaimed. "Tastes, as we know, are fickle. We are currently enjoying a recent return to the sublime."

"Lord Byron couldn't have said it better."

"Ah, but it was Byron who said it first."

Mariana regretted conjuring the late poet, already a hero to idealistic young men everywhere. That word, *idealistic* again stole into her thoughts, conjuring ideas of black and white, right and wrong.

The solution to the problem of the Comte de Villefranche returned to her, and she couldn't remember why it would be best if she left it to the professionals to solve. Wasn't *she* a professional . . . of sorts?

Before she could again reverse on herself, she opened her mouth and said, "There is something you must know." She waited for Villefranche's full attention. "You are terrible at this. We are both terrible at this."

His brows knitted together in confusion before releasing. "We are? Lady Nicholas, to understand the mind of a poet is perhaps too rigorous an undertaking for the delicate constitution of a mere—"

She held up a silencing hand. "At spying. You. Me. *We* are terrible spies."

His poetic eyes grew bright and serious.

"We are being used in a game neither of us fully understands."

"You have me confused with another." He disengaged his arm from hers and inclined his head. "I bid you good day."

He began to turn away. She had to think fast, or she would lose him. She glanced about to insure no attentive ears were near before calling out, "The king is dying, *non*?"

Villefranche swiveled around, bewilderment clouding his handsome face. Buoyed by his dismay, she continued,

"It is no secret that the Bourbons and your Orléans relations have little use for one another. Perhaps you hope for a fresh start."

"Nothing will be gained from Louis's death," Villefranche stated flatly.

"That isn't completely true. You will gain a new king in the Duc d'Artois," she said, her words a testing inch forward.

"As I said, nothing will be gained," he repeated with the emotional complexity of a block of wood. His eyes narrowed. "You show a keen interest in France's politics."

It was time for her to be bolder yet. She felt like a conductor, influencing the rises and falls of a symphony. "There will be war if the Duc d'Artois is assassinated, making it most difficult for your family to claim the throne."

"Is it your implication that my family would stoop to assassinating a future king for personal gain?"

"Some might believe it," she said. "But not I. I believe the Duc's assassination would be for nationalist purposes, not materialist."

Villefranche blanched as the implication of her words sank in.

"But at what cost?" she pressed.

"Is there a cost too high for *liberté*?"

"Hasn't enough young blood been shed on France's fields?"

"There will be no war," he stated with finality.

Mariana couldn't contain a cynical laugh at his certainty and his naiveté. "With power, money, and control hanging in the balance? There will be war." She cut the distance between them in half. From afar one might think them engaged in a lovers' quarrel instead of a struggle for life and death. "Like me, you're a pawn in their game."

"And who are *they*?" He scoffed dismissively. "You are deranged."

"They will use you," she said, her words an insistent whisper, "and they will discard you. It is what they do. Do you want England involved in your country's politics? Once you let Whitehall in, good luck getting them out. Would your countrymen welcome such a radical step?"

"Lady Nicholas, you know nothing—"

"What was in the packet you handed that man?"

A sheen of perspiration glistened against his pale skin. "You saw?"

"I told you that neither of us is any good at this."

Again, the analogy of the conductor came to her. There was a time for bombast and drama, but also a time for subtlety and sensitivity.

Her voice emerged on a low and steady note, the sort sounded through a woodwind instrument. "Is it too late?"

His eyes went wide, calling to mind a spooked horse. She knew enough about spooked horses to tread with light feet.

"You will lose everything," she continued. "Your family will lose everything. France will lose everything. And for what reason? For the actions of a naïve and spoiled boy?"

She took a step back to allow him a measure of space for reflection. A heady feeling grew and expanded within her. She saw how one could become addicted to it, this influencing the fate of nations.

Her gaze returned to Villefranche, expecting to find him reflective and possibly penitent. Instead, she found a man intently and singularly focused on a point above her shoulder.

A sensation stole over her as if the very air she breathed had changed its molecular composition. This must be how wild animals felt the moment they realized they were being stalked. She glanced over her shoulder and followed Villefranche's gaze across the pool and down the opposite path.

She blinked. Then she blinked once again for confirmation that her mind wasn't conjuring visions. If Villefranche was seeing him, too, it must not be fiction.

It must be true that approaching them was none other than Nick, returning their twin dumbfounded stares with a polished aplomb uniquely his own.

# Chapter 19

*Dimber: Pretty. A dimber cove; a pretty fellow. Dimber mort; a pretty wench.*

*A Classical Dictionary of the Vulgar Tongue*
Francis Grose

Yes, Mariana decided, *polished* was the correct word for Nick, impeccably dressed in a sage green cutaway jacket, buff buckskins, and a freshly laundered, starched linen shirt complete with an intricately knotted silk cravat. He was a vision of the fashionable English gentleman, except for his unfashionably cropped hair, which only heightened the angular beauty of his face. The whiff of French prison that had hung about him a few days ago was gone.

It struck Mariana that this was the first time she'd seen him in the daylight since her arrival in Paris.

He stole her breath away.

She'd made love with this man last night.

Just before Nick stepped within polite speaking distance, she snuck a glance at Villefranche. He'd arranged his features into a mask of utter disregard. She almost felt badly for him. Villefranche didn't know it yet, but he didn't stand a chance against Nick.

Of course, she wasn't certain she did either, not when the entirety of his attention was focused on her as if the outside world had ceased to exist. She might have experienced a wobble in her knee.

It was only when he came within three feet of her and showed no sign of stopping that she realized his intent. In the next moment, she was enveloped in his strong embrace. Her upturned chin nestled into the crook of his neck, she had no choice but to breathe him in. He smelled delicious.

"Play along," came a duo of words, low and hot, whispered into the cup of her ear. The touch of his velvety lips sent goose bumps skittering across her skin.

Once at a lecture, she'd learned the scientific word for goose bumps: piloerection. The audience had collectively gasped, ladies' fans fluttering in outrage. She'd been delighted at the time. At the moment, however, she wasn't.

*Piloerection.* A blush flared at the suggestive nature of it.

Nick's arms released her as suddenly as they had embraced her, but he kept her close by, pulling her hand through the crook of his arm. She'd been thoroughly claimed. An unruly part of her thrilled to the treatment, while another part of her, the one accustomed to opposing him, bristled.

"My love," he began, supercilious popinjay on full display. "I received your thoughtful note that I would find you here, and—*voilà!*—here you are."

"Here I am," she replied, at once bemused and intrigued. "And here *you* are."

What was he playing at? Wasn't he supposed to be missing, presumed dead to the operators in his world of shadows and intrigue?

"I see you've had no problem finding a young gallant to escort you through the wilds of Paris," he said with a winking, vacuous irony the English fop played so well.

A watchful Villefranche remained silent.

Fussy French custom dictated that an introduction could be made only if both parties agreed to it. Clearly, these two men working so assiduously against one another had never been formally introduced.

Mariana swept an arm toward Villefranche. "Lucien Capet, Comte de Villefranche"—She decided to leave out the ritual naming of forebears—"may I introduce my husband"—The word nearly stuck in her throat—"Lord Nicholas Asquith, to you?"

The two men bowed and wordlessly assessed one another. Nick was the first to speak. "In my absence, I must thank you for being of such attentive *service*"—Twin scarlet blushes pinked Villefranche's cheeks at the clear innuendo— "to my wife."

"It was assumed," Villefranche returned in a tone that could only be described as belligerent, "you fled Paris when word reached you that your wife had arrived."

A shocked laugh escaped Mariana at Villefranche's bluntness. She wouldn't have suspected him capable of it.

"On the contrary," Nick returned smoothly, bringing Mariana's gloved hand to his mouth for a quick brush of his lips. She didn't feel like laughing anymore. "I returned as fast as my horses would ride when I received news of her arrival. We are ever at cross purposes, it seems."

He gazed upon her lovingly, as if his entire world depended on her . . .

She caught herself. A less experienced woman might mistake that look for the genuine article, but not her. This was a farce. She mustn't forget.

"In uncertain times such as these in Paris," Nick continued, "one cannot be too careful, to be sure."

"*In uncertain times such as these*?" Villefranche repeated. "France has enjoyed peace these last nine years. I can assure you that your wife is perfectly safe in our city."

"Of course, my good sir," Nick returned. He angled his body toward Mariana. "To be young and idealistic again."

"Ah, yes," she purred, "he is *young*, isn't he?" There would be no mistaking the womanly appreciation in her voice. Nick's eyes narrowed and held hers for a long second. She'd hit her mark.

He shifted his attention back to Villefranche. "My dear

sir, we seem to have gotten off on the wrong foot. I simply refer to the uncertainty regarding the king's health."

"There is nothing uncertain about his health," Villefranche snapped. "The man is dying."

"That should bode well for your family, *non*?"

"Have you met the heir Charles, the Duc d'Artois?" Villefranche asked, fire in his voice.

"I have. The man is a—" Nick paused as if searching for the correct word.

"Popinjay, as you English say," Villefranche supplied.

Nick's eyes narrowed, and the blithe smile fell from his lips. The air turned deadly serious. "This rogue operation to assassinate Charles will never succeed. Have you any idea who you're dealing with?"

Shock marched across Villefranche's face. The man lacked all ability to hide his feelings from the world. He could use a night of poker with Nick and a pair of strumpets.

"How . . . you," the man sputtered, "you know nothing of—"

"Oh, I know a few things," Nick cut in. "Let's say your plan works, and Charles is assassinated. Who do you think the blame will fall upon?"

"There are any number of people who wish for the death of the Bourbon line."

"But who would benefit most? Your Orléans family. That's who."

Villefranche's lips drew into a straight, stubborn line.

"Come down from your high ideals and think, man. Make no mistake, if you decide to see this calamity through, I shall stop you, one way or another."

Mariana's mouth went dry. She believed him, and if Villefranche had a jot of good sense in his idealistic head, he would, too.

He drew himself up to his fullest height and cleared his throat. "Lord Nicholas, you and your wife make an

unexpectedly"—He visibly searched for the correct word—
"*unified* pair. Perhaps the rumors surrounding your marriage
lack substance?"

Mariana inhaled sharply, and Nick's expression went
carefully blank.

"My family," Villefranche continued, "is hosting a
soirée tonight. I shall have your names added to the guest
list. A few of tonight's invitees might be of interest to you."

With that, he pivoted on his heel and strode down the
wide gravel avenue, leaving Mariana and Nick alone. She
couldn't help noticing that with Villefranche gone they stood
facing each other like combatants.

It was he who broke the charged silence. "His invitation
could be a trap to draw me out into the open."

"It isn't," she replied with a quiet assurance that she
almost felt.

"We make an *unexpectedly unified pair*?" he asked
without missing a beat.

"I had a word with him."

"A word?"

"Sometimes plain language is what is needed, not
subterfuge. Seduction isn't the only weapon in a woman's
arsenal."

"That's a large bet you placed."

"A bet that you matched."

Another one of his quicksilver smiles flashed across
Nick's lips, and Mariana's belly fluttered. Her composure
threatened to slip. "There is more," she said, her voice a
raw scrape against her throat. "I saw Villefranche with the
croupier. He handed the man a packet."

"You're certain?"

She nodded. "You still trust the man?"

The question hung between them on an open note. When
Nick answered, his voice carried only far enough to reach
her. "As I said before, nothing in this game is what it seems."

He stepped forward, and her body's awareness of his rose to the surface. He made no move to touch her and, instead, held out his arm. She intuited that they were to stroll. There was no help for it. She must touch him.

She directed her gaze at some indistinct point in the distance before reaching out and resting a light palm on his solid forearm. If a pulse of electricity jumped between them, she could ascribe it to the dryness of the air.

Their feet fell into unified step as they navigated the peaceful grounds in silence, taking in the exterior of the palace and its formal gardens so unlike the wild informality surrounding the Medici Fountain. Here, every shrub and flower was placed with meticulous care to maintain rows perfectly straight and predictable. If only life could be arranged with such precision, but life was nothing, if not imprecise.

"Have you collected the twins' daily notes from Helene today?" Nick asked in a familiar retreat to the last ten years when they'd only discussed their children.

"Just this morning. In fact," she said, too happy to play along with this return to order, "Geoffrey has requested the kukri knife that we procure for him for his name day be of the Eastern, rather than Western, variety. He would like, and I quote, *a more easily transportable blade*."

Nick snorted. "What sort of school have you sent the boy to that he needs transportable weaponry?" he asked, the question not a scold, but a tease.

"As I'm sure you know, Geoffrey could fend for himself with his bare hands. The boy is most resourceful."

"A trait he shares with his mother, to be sure."

Gratification, warm and liquid, spread through Mariana, and her mouth clamped shut. She no longer thought herself capable of easy banter.

In a move born of sudden necessity, her hand slid off his arm, and her feet stepped off the path before wandering into the heart of Marie de' Medici's famed elm thicket, the only sounds the crunch of mulch beneath their feet and the wind rustling the leaves in the trees.

Although she experienced a pang for the loss of him, it couldn't be helped. Complete and rational thoughts refused to form when any part of her body touched him. And she most definitely needed to be rational when it was only he and she and the trees.

"You don't prefer we walk together?" he called out to her back.

His words stopped her in her tracks. Within them she detected a note at once open and vulnerable. It was a note that made her insides go light.

When she turned around, she saw that she'd raced some twenty yards ahead of him. They stared across the verdant expanse at one another until she broke the silence. "No one can see us." She paused a beat and gathered the courage to speak a truth that they both needed to hear. "Villefranche is gone. There is no need to pretend here."

His eyes held hers another moment. The intensity within them caught her unawares. At last, he asked, "Pretend what?"

"That we're truly man and wife."

~ ~ ~

Across the open expanse of leaf-strewn forest floor, Mariana was the picture of a startled deer poised to flee at his slightest movement. She could very well slip through his fingers, and he could lose her, forever. He couldn't let that happen. He must do or say something, anything to hold her in place.

From beneath the weight of his desperation slithered a possibility: the truth. He could correct a lie, the very lie that had torn them apart in the first place. No longer would it stand between them.

"Ten years ago," he began. Her head canted to the side in curiosity. She was listening. He must make his next words count. "The opera singer was a ruse."

Her eyes went flat. She didn't feign ignorance and ask which opera singer. Instead, she closed herself off to him. He saw it in her face and felt it in the air. They'd never once discussed the opera singer beyond that fateful night.

At last, she broke the silence, her voice hollow and unsteady. "A ruse?" He wasn't certain she was aware that she'd taken a step forward. He responded in kind—any excuse to close the distance between them. "And for whom was this *ruse*?" she continued. Bitter sarcasm laced her words and marred her lovely face. He'd done this to her.

"We needed to draw out a vicious enemy agent, and the opera singer was his lover. Among his many faults, the man also happened to be extremely jealous."

"Ah, I see." Her features went hard.

"I'm almost certain you don't." He might have just made matters worse.

"It's an easy puzzle to sort out," she continued as if he hadn't spoken. "It began as a ruse, but soon cold calculation turned into a red-hot passion that wouldn't be denied. Am I close?"

"Not remotely."

"It seems," she barreled on, "last night wasn't such an anomaly for you. Your *métier* has certain perquisites."

A mean left hook from Gentleman Jackson himself couldn't have floored Nick more effectively. "I never made love to her."

Mariana's mouth snapped shut, her eyebrows knit together, and a heartbeat passed. "It occurs to me that you had the opportunity to explain this pertinent fact ten years ago. Or during any of the time since."

He could walk away. There was yet time for that.

Or he could speak the truth. He wasn't ready to walk away from her.

"I needed you to toss me out, and I needed it to be real." As if to foreground his revelation, the wind stopped breezing through the trees, offering him a still and quiet confessional. "Your life was in danger, and I made the choice to keep you safe."

Her eyes widened in incredulity. "Do you expect me to thank you? You made the decision alone to end our marriage—"

"Family men are vulnerable," he cut in. "It makes their families vulnerable. I should have never brought you into that world."

"Didn't I deserve a choice in the matter?" she asked, betrayal and hurt quaking her voice. "I thought I meant more than that to you."

"You did."

He paused. Should he uphold the status quo and leave her?

He couldn't. Even if she didn't know it yet, he understood that these last few days, and last night in particular, had shifted the parameters of their relationship.

"You meant everything to me."

"And what of the rumors concerning your exploits and conquests?" she pressed on as if she hadn't heard him.

"Simply rumors. Some were ruses and bait, others were fabrications by bored Society wives. But none were true. I was never unfaithful to you." He took another step forward. An elemental part of him needed to be closer to her. "Not once," he said, finally speaking the truth they both needed to hear. "Never." A terrible weight lifted off his shoulders.

"Never is a very long time," escaped her lips.

"Ten years."

"You robbed us of a life together." Her fragile whisper carried far enough to reach him before her spine visibly stiffened, and she drew herself up to her fullest height. Her next words emerged on a stronger note. "It seems my work in Paris is done."

"What do you mean?" He felt as if he'd been dropped from a great height, and the only way to break his fall, the only way to hold her in place, was to keep her talking.

"I mean"—Her words and the latent anger within them gathered steam—"I am leaving Paris."

She pivoted away from him, her skirts swishing about her ankles with the force of her intention.

"Stay," he called out, the note a raw scrub of his throat.

What was that in his voice? Desperation? Was he *desperate* for her?

The word, or the desperation contained within it, did its job when she stilled. Her eyes caught his over her shoulder.

"Mariana"—He closed the distance between them, even going so far as to place a staying hand on her arm, so she would have to face him—"we *are* man and wife."

"Not in a meaningful way."

"Then what was last night?"

They were the wrong words. Last night wasn't about their status as husband and wife. Last night was about pent-up, irrepressible desire.

She gave a short, bitter laugh. "Certainly not meaningful." She shook off his hand and retreated a few steps to steady herself against the nearest elm. "You lobbed a grenade into our marriage and blew it to smithereens. Now you're claiming marriage after one night of passion? Do you think me such a weak-minded woman that one night could turn my head and undo the past?"

He caught an emotion in her eyes that he didn't expect to find there. Fear. What was she afraid of?

The answer followed before he'd fully formed the question. She was afraid of herself.

Another question occurred to him, one he was almost too afraid to ask. "Do you think yourself that woman?" He took a step forward, drawn toward this fragile possibility.

"Can't you leave me be?"

"I don't think I can."

"What is happening between us is insanity." Her eyes searched his. "Haven't you proven enough?"

"I don't think I have," he replied. He'd never known how addictive truth-telling could be. "I think I have a great deal more to prove."

Last night had done nothing to slake their desire for one another; it had only whetted it. Certain desires weren't mitigated by the passage of time.

She flashed him a look, a question in her eyes he couldn't interpret. There was a time when he'd known her thoughts before she did. No longer was that the case. The *spy lessons* had worked too well.

The thing was this: he wanted to be able to read her. The debutante he'd met at the Folly had been in the first draft phase of womanhood. Now she was a completed manuscript, one new to him. At least, she was mostly new. Certain pages he'd read quite thoroughly.

"We both know this—whatever *this* is—can lead nowhere," she said.

Did she believe her words? Last night told a different story of precisely where *this* could lead.

"Why are you asking me to stay?" she asked, the question racing along the serrated edge of a rising panic that he heard in her voice.

"Isn't it obvious?"

Her teeth bit down on her plump bottom lip for the space of one . . . two . . . three heartbeats. At last, she released it and relented. "Perhaps."

# Chapter 20

*To Milk the Pidgeon: To endeavor at impossibilities.*

*A Classical Dictionary of the Vulgar Tongue*
Francis Grose

*Perhaps.* Located on the periphery of that word was an open door Nick could slip inside.

"This is happening too fast," Mariana said, her words a protest at odds with the new light that had entered her eyes—a light that hinted at not only possibility, but also hunger.

"Is it?" He pushed the door of opportunity wider. "Or perhaps it was ten years in the making."

A dozen rapid heartbeats sped by, and she remained silent. She cleared her throat in a decisive manner, and the air froze in Nick's chest.

"Last year, I attended a lecture," she began, and his hope sank, possibility dimmed. The woman did manage to attend a good number of lectures. "The topic was religions of Asia. Do you know the subject?"

He shook his head, feeling at once foolish and not a little despondent.

"Take Buddhism, for example," she said. "At the core of this belief is the idea that one shouldn't dwell on the past or dream of the future. Instead, one lives solely in the present moment. No other moments matter."

"And?"

A canny light sparked in her amber eyes. "And in certain circumstances such a philosophy can be useful."

Understanding dawned on Nick. "No past. No future."

She nodded once, a slow up and down motion. The subtext of her words rising to the surface, nearly a tangible thing.

She wanted him. Now. The past and the future had no bearing on this present want.

And if his mind suggested that he could wrest a better deal from her, one that would last beyond the present into the future, his body decided to focus on having her now. The future could wait.

He pressed forward on this unexpected wave of possibility. "Perhaps I could demonstrate for you how such a philosophy might be of use to you," he said, his voice a deep rumble in his chest.

He braced himself on one forearm against the sturdy elm, just to the side of her head, and leaned in without touching her. She had to tilt her head back to hold his gaze. Her scent reached out and encircled him in its warm jasmine and neroli cocoon. He touched his lips to her ear. "But let's not be hasty and let go of the past entirely."

"Oh?" she asked, the monosyllable a breathless exhalation, the distancing sarcasm of minutes ago forgotten. Short, warm bursts of her breath on his neck sent shivers tingling down his spine.

He took her delicate earlobe between his teeth and nipped, eliciting another breathless, "Oh," but this time it didn't question. It conveyed release and permission.

He held his body at a determined remove from hers. If he pressed into her, his intent would be lost to his own desires. The very thought made his cock jump against the constraining fabric of his trousers. And that wasn't what *this* was about. This was about Mariana and her pleasure.

He allowed his fingers to touch her body, beginning at the soft indent of her waist, tracing upward until they reached the ripe flare of her breasts. His palms forming a cup beneath, his thumbs moved over taut nipples, teasing them through gossamer layers of silk and muslin. Unable to help himself, he tugged at her short bodice until her breasts fell free. With their plump fullness and matching dusky peaks, they were the embodiment of temptation.

"Even better than I remembered," he murmured before inclining his head, and taking one tight bud into his mouth and the other between thumb and forefinger, squeezing.

A soft moan escaped her, and her head arched back. Her breath now came in shallow pants, and it was all he could do to restrain himself from ravishing her.

He could do better. He would give her what she'd all but explicitly requested: pleasure uncomplicated by the past or the future—pleasure that mattered only in the present. If last night was about loss of control, this moment was its exquisite opposite.

He kneeled before her and grabbed her lush derriere with both hands. On a low growl, he pulled her into him, his face nestled into the soft juncture of her legs. He inhaled her warm, erotic scent, and exhaled slowly through thin layers of muslin, his hot rush of breath finding her quim. From his supplicating position, he watched her lips part and her eyes close to all sensation but the promise of his mouth. Still, he could do better.

"I remember something you like very much. The past has its uses."

He sat back on his heels, ignoring her sob of protest at the separation, and grabbed the hem of her skirts before lifting them fold by fold, revealing ankles . . . calves . . . thighs . . . clad in alabaster silk stockings held up by simple blue garters. Ever higher inched her hem, exposing the naked flesh of her upper thighs and her mons pubis covered by nothing, except a wild patch of curls the color of honey. Again, he blew a stream of humid breath onto her sex.

His intention clear, he lifted her foot and guided it onto his shoulder, her quim opening for him like a hothouse flower in bloom. Her body quivered in anticipation of what came next. One steadying hand clamped around her thigh before he leaned in and flicked the tight pink bud of her sex with the tip of his tongue . . . once . . . twice . . . Her fingers threaded through his hair on a long moan.

"Again," she demanded, her voice a sensuous combination of ecstasy and ache.

His body her servant, his tongue found a rhythm that rendered her incapable of speech, only pants and groans and whimpers as her quim grew luscious beneath his tongue, her hips tilting forward even as she counterbalanced the motion by pressing harder into the elm at her back. She was nothing more than a creature composed of carnality and lust.

His hand found its way up her thigh, and his forefinger entered her slick and hot cunny. He wanted to feel her pulse around him when she exploded in release. His tongue began alternating between hard and soft flicks, encouraging her desire ever higher, as his finger dove deeper until finally, inevitably, her body tensed for one . . . two . . . three fraught seconds before she broke and cried out her climax to the leaf-dappled blue sky above. His hands steadied her as she collapsed back against the tree, replete with satiety.

He sat back on his heels and took in the delectable and irresistible mess that was Lady Nicholas Asquith. His wife. A fierce need to possess her nearly overtook him. But this wasn't about his need, it was about hers.

Her lust-glazed eyes slid open and locked onto his. From above, she regarded him with a wonder that he hadn't been worthy of in years, if ever. He still wasn't worthy of it.

Reluctantly, he placed his hand on her ankle to remove her foot from his shoulder. He would set it on the ground, and her dress would fall into place as if nothing of note had happened between them. It was one of the hallmarks of their class that they could. Already he regretted the loss of the present to the past.

"What are you doing?" she asked, her enervated body drawing up into a firmer line against the tree.

He halted. He wasn't certain if he was viewing her through the lens of his raging lust, but he read in her eyes a desire for a different scenario.

"We aren't finished," she said, a subtle command in her voice.

Her forefinger reached down and hitched beneath his chin. He followed it up until he stood before her, her dress caught between them, preventing it from chastely falling to the ground. There was nothing *chaste* about this situation.

It was all he could do not to moan in frustration at the idea of nothing but the lacings of his trousers standing between his cock and her naked, desire-soaked quim.

"This was for you." He ground out the words through sheer force of will.

She reached between them and pressed her hand against his cockstand. "*This* is for me."

Her fingers made short work of the lacings of his trousers and reached inside to wrap around him. He closed his eyes and exhaled a deep groan.

A long leg wrapped around his waist, brazenly opening her to him. The length of his throbbing cock slid indulgently along her wet slit. "And I want you to fuck me mindless with it."

His hips responded with an instinctive slow thrust, and he slipped inside her, his eyes locked onto hers, daring her to look away. She didn't. He slid his length out and thrust inside her again, this time slower, her silky tightness both a tease and a promise. Still, he held her eyes, but he detected a mixture of pleasure and frustration in their depths.

"Tell me what you want," Nick demanded.

"I want—" she began on a pant.

He silenced her when he pulled out.

"I want . . ."—Her heel dug into the small of his back—"
. . . it . . ."—Her hips ground against his—". . . harder."

His leg bent so he could angle in further. "Like this?"

She moaned an, "Oh, yes," and he repeated the motion. She reached around and grabbed his arse with both hands, her nails digging in, spurring him on. "Yes," she whispered, her hips matching his rhythm.

With a will of its own, a sort of animal instinct took over, his hips thrusting harder and faster, his lips and tongue claiming hers with an untamed ferocity that matched the rhythm of their bodies. He couldn't get enough of her.

He sensed a specific sort of intensity begin to wind within her. His strokes became short and shallow.

"Oh, yes," she uttered with mindless abandon.

She was close. Again, he deepened his strokes, driving into her with a matching abandon.

"Come with me over the edge," he groaned into her mouth. He was close, so close to the precipice.

"Nick," she cried, her quim convulsing in release, pulsing her climax around his cock. One . . . two more thrusts, and he followed her into the wild freedom of release. It was a moment he never wanted to end. Yet his hips gradually and inevitably stilled, and beat after beat, his heart slowed its urgent tattoo.

"Nick?" came her voice.

*Not yet*, he silently implored. It wasn't his name on her lips that he minded; it was the question in her voice. He sensed distance in that question. He lifted his head from the curve of her damp neck and accepted that the future was upon them.

He pressed a palm against rough bark and pushed away, catching a quick flash of her quim before her dress fell down and into place. His fingers reached down to cinch the closure of his trousers. The moment slipped into the past.

His eyes found hers, and in their depths flashed uncertainty. A future might be located in that misgiving, if he managed it right. The possibility rekindled a light he'd thought extinguished. Perhaps the space between them wasn't insuperable. "Mariana"—A silly and uncontrollable note of optimism sounded in his voice—"do you feel—"

"I'm not certain what I feel."

"But you feel it, too."

"And *it* is?" she evaded.

"More certain than you would admit," he replied, but he wouldn't press the issue. He hadn't yet earned the right.

Her gaze broke from his. In an efficient flurry of movement, she began dusting off and smoothing down her skirts.

He tilted his gaze up and followed a large bird of prey as it cut across the sky above them. How much time had passed? It hardly mattered. For a single, glorious moment in time they'd soared above the realm of reality.

"Are we husband and wife now?" she asked, refreshed and ready to meet the world's scrutiny. If he detected the slightest hint of a wobble in her voice, the rest of the world wouldn't. They didn't know her like he did.

The temptation to misinterpret her words nearly superseded all good sense. This coupling could be a consummation of sorts, a renewal, a beginning. But that interpretation would be disingenuous. She was, of course, speaking of their game of pretend. "Yes," he replied. Simple was best at present. "Will you attend the Capet family's soirée tonight?"

With a quick nod of her head, she gave her assent. Relief flooded through him, even if he'd sensed her reluctance. "Tonight, we will be loving husband and wife," he said recklessly. Why was he pushing his luck?

"Loving?" she scoffed. "There aren't many people who would believe that."

"It only takes two."

The words were bold, too bold, but were they true?

Her fingers fidgeted with her reticule, again calling to mind a skittish deer.

"My carriage awaits me at the end of the avenue," she stated and pivoted on her heel, the very heel that had dug into the small of his back not five minutes ago. "Until we meet tonight, *husband*."

Like last night, he followed her at a respectful distance while she picked her way through the small, but dense, copse of trees and onto the dusty granite avenue that led to her waiting carriage. On a tidy, little hop, she slipped inside and rolled away. At the periphery of his vision, another conveyance jerked into motion. His agent would take it from here.

Where had the present gone?

To join all the other moments in their past that he'd allowed to slip away.

The familiar encroaching darkness of his parents' doomed union crept toward the edges of his consciousness. For years, he'd allowed that past free rein over his future, but not today. Today, he pushed it away and turned toward the truth, unavoidable and clear: he was in love with his wife.

It was that simple. It was that complex.

What he felt in his body extended beyond physical sensation. There was a fullness . . . a lightness . . . a wholeness . . . a rightness.

As selfish as it might be, he wasn't about to let her go. Not a second time. He would have more than simple physical satiety from Mariana. He would have a future with her.

The past be damned.

# Chapter 21

*Knave in Grain: A knave of the first rate: a phrase borrowed from the dyehouse, where certain colours are said to be in grain, to denote their superiority, as being dyed with cochineal, called grain.*

*A Classical Dictionary of the Vulgar Tongue*
Francis Grose

As the carriage transported her across a grid of indifferent Parisian streets, Mariana sank into brittle leather upholstery and allowed her head to thump back against the unforgiving cushion.

What had she done? Again.

Yet, even as mortification blazed through her—had she really just done *that . . . again . . .* with Nick in the *Jardin du Luxembourg*?—regret refused to take hold. She'd wanted Nick. Despite their past. Despite everything.

And she'd had him.

In all honesty, she wanted him again. She *craved* him the way an opium eater craved the poppy. The more she had, the more she wanted. Her transformation into an amoral, hedonistic Parisienne seemed complete.

Her gaze found the river Seine to her left as the carriage rolled alongside. Tonight, she was to play wife to Nick at the Capet family's soirée. Hysterical, even unhinged, laughter bubbled up her throat. If the libidinous feeling flowing through her veins was any indicator, it seemed she and Nick excelled at playing husband and wife.

She shouldn't go. Her dealings with the Comte de Villefranche were done, for better or for worse. And her dealings with Nick?

A flood of nervous energy filled her. She would burst if she remained trapped inside this confining carriage a moment longer. She tapped the roof twice and was through the door before the wheels came to a complete stop.

"*Monsieur*," she called up, "I shall meet you on the Rue de Rivoli outside the Louvre Palace one hour hence."

"Madame," the outraged driver called down in his thick French accent, "it is not so safe—"

"My safety is my concern," she snapped. Without another word of protest, the driver set the carriage into motion.

The breeze from the river swirled off the water and gusted over her. As she took in the magnificent view of the Notre Dame, she willed the riot of emotion to release and flutter away. What remained were two prevailing, and conflicting, emotions. One, expected and correct; the other, unexpected and utterly wrong.

Correctly, she was angry at Nick. His mistresses hadn't been opera singers and dancers all these years. Rather he'd had one formidable mistress: the Foreign Office. The man had blown their marriage to smithereens to play at cloaks and daggers. But . . . He hadn't betrayed the intimacy between them.

*What if it's a lie?* her rational mind nagged. The man told lies for a living.

But it wasn't. Her irrational heart knew his confession for the truth, a thought not easily dismissed or erased by anger. In fact, this knowledge led her directly into the other unexpected and utterly wrong emotion: hope.

Hope was an emotion she hadn't allowed herself to feel for a decade. It would have crushed her. But now that Nick had revealed the truth to her, hope expanded within her heart to bursting. It seemed a few days in Paris with Nick were all it took to spark the inconvenient emotion alive.

*It only takes two.*

Unable to process the enormity of those four simple words and her reaction to them, she'd run. Still, she ran, but she couldn't outpace them no matter how hard she tried. Within those words lay the dashed dreams of her twenty-year-old heart.

And her thirty-year-old heart? How did she feel about them?

Mariana had had to get away from him as fast as her legs could carry her . . . before he saw the truth in her eyes. It seemed her heart hadn't aged past twenty. Hope competed with the anger, and the hope might be winning.

An involuntary groan escaped her, and she spun away from the river, as if her mind could match the motion and change her thought pattern as readily as she changed her view. The trick didn't work. Nothing worked. Truth, and hope, refused to be avoided.

Why had her heart chosen this man all those years ago? And why was she even thinking about hearts after having it ripped from her chest all those years ago?

Weary of standing still and thinking too much, she set her feet into motion and soon found herself rambling through a jumble of narrow lanes. As her heels clicked across medieval cobblestones, her confusion of energy found an outlet in the brisk walk. She'd never walked so much in her entire life as she had in Paris. This trip had revealed to her an unexpected pleasure in the activity. It cleansed. It revivified.

In fact, not only had she never walked so much in her life, she'd never *thought* so much in her life. She wasn't a thinker; she was a doer. Yet in Paris she found herself inside her own mind more often than she would like, sorting through thoughts that refused to be sorted.

*Twice in less than twenty-four hours.*

She groaned aloud. It seemed everything she did lately elicited a groan. Oh, that didn't sound right.

*Twice in less than twenty-four hours.*

Soon she found herself in the heart of a vaguely familiar neighborhood, and her pace slowed. Perhaps the absinthe café was around here. Or was it the brothel?

The atmosphere had transformed with the daylight: bustling, vibrant—a man's shoulder clipped her—rude. The distraction of people rushing around her, getting on with their individual days, was a welcome one. These people were doers, not thinkers. When one stripped away the trappings of class and wealth, she saw they were her people.

In the next block, she happened upon a fruit stand offering assorted varieties of juicy fall apples and pears. Of a sudden, she was ravenous.

"*Bonjour, Madame*"—She wracked her brain for the correct French phrasing—"*combien coûte?*" She was certain she'd left out a connective word or two, but it would have to do.

The fruit seller—who hadn't yet acknowledged Mariana as she polished her wares one by one—tilted her head, finally gifting Mariana with her attention. She shifted on her feet beneath the intensity of the woman's brown-eyed scrutiny.

"*Anglaise?*" the woman all but spat.

"*Oui,*" she replied, reconsidering the offerings of this particular fruit seller. This woman might not be her people.

She eyed Mariana up and down for a solid minute before saying, "*Un* sovereign."

It was the woman's use of English that first struck her, but it was the woman's price that took her completely aback. A *sovereign* for a piece of fruit worth less than a penny?

She noticed a few sets of curious eyes observing the transaction. Of course. She looked every bit the lady.

Instead of voicing her opposition to this highway robbery, she reached inside her reticule and pulled out a single, gold sovereign. A canny smile stretched the woman's thin, cracked lips as she reached for the coin. Mariana held onto the sovereign for a beat longer than necessary and watched the woman's smile slip as they engaged in a subtle tug of war.

"*Duex*," Mariana said, holding up two fingers with her free hand.

The fruit seller shrugged an indifferent shoulder, and Mariana released the coin, somewhat mollified. At least, she would have an apple *and* a pear out of the deal.

As she took her time selecting the biggest, juiciest fruit, and the fruit seller resumed ignoring her, Mariana noticed a motionless male figure on the periphery of her vision. It might have been her imagination, but it seemed the man was intent on . . . her. Her eyes darted right, and he was gone.

The tension bunching her shoulders together released and slid down her back. These spy games were creating menace where there was none. No choice but to act like a reasonable adult woman, she crunched down on the apple and set her feet into motion.

As she wound through the Left Bank, her thoughts settled, and a *giddy* pleasure fizzed through her. Ladies didn't eat apples whilst perambulating foreign cities alone. Two, possibly three, rules broken, she was certain. Her etiquette teachers had never explicitly enumerated these rules, but she was certain they didn't think they needed to.

She took another bite of apple. *Scrumptious*. This forbidden apple might be the best she'd ever tasted.

When she paused to better peruse the wares of a book shop, her peripheral vision again caught a glimpse of the male figure. The tiny hairs on the back of her neck stood on end. It was most definitely the same man.

She tossed the half-eaten apple into an alley and searched the lane for a hackney. When none was to be found, she thought to pick up her pace. That would be the height of stupidity. The man would know that she knew she was being followed.

She cut an instinctive left into a dark sliver of an alley and immediately regretted her decision. She would be alone with her stalker. She had only a few seconds before he caught up to her.

She scanned the ground for a weapon before chancing upon a thick plank of wood. Her fingers closed around one end, and a rotten chunk crumbled in her hand. Likely, it wouldn't inflict enough damage for her to escape. But it was too late to explore other options. It would have to do.

Her back against the damp, stone wall, she went stock still and waited, the flimsy plank raised above her head and at the ready. Just as her arms began to tire, the man slinked around the corner. Without a second thought, she swiped the plank of wood across his head, knocking him off balance. Before her would-be assailant could recover his equilibrium, a surge of adrenaline propelled her down the alleyway, her heart racing faster than her feet.

She'd already fled a good ten yards when she heard, "Christ almighty!"

She stopped dead in her tracks. That voice was most definitely not that of a Parisian cutpurse. In fact, it was unmistakably English.

Slowly, she turned to face the man, who was now hunched against the patch of wall she'd just vacated and rubbing the back of his head. She recognized him as the croupier, or whoever he was today. But that wasn't what arrested her attention: she knew that voice. His was a voice from her past. But where from her past?

Against her better judgment, she began moving toward him, picking her way across murky puddles of filth she hadn't noticed a few seconds ago. The alley had gone eerily silent.

Her hand tightened its grip on her wood plank, which she hadn't realized she still held until now. He began to come into focus.

He was a tall man. Rangy . . . Wolfish. His head was topped by a flat cap with dark curls peeking out from beneath. The gray light of the alley and the brim of his cap conspired to obscure the details of his face.

"Are you injured?" she called out from a cautious distance.

A dry laugh escaped the man as he cut her a sidelong glance and removed a blood-smudged hand from the back of his head. Still, he didn't utter a word. And she needed him to speak. She needed confirmation of what her ears had told her.

Her feet inched closer, as if she approached a wild and unpredictable animal, and she began to discern a familiarity in his profile, not only in his voice. Even though this was the same man she'd seen with both Nick and Villefranche, this feeling of familiarity ran deeper: she knew this man. But from where? Context continued to elude her.

"I should have known better," the man's deep voice sliced through the silence, "than to underestimate Lady Mariana Montfort Asquith."

He turned his head and faced her square.

The rotten plank fell from her suddenly slack hand as context hit her with the intensity of a gale force wind coming off the North Sea. Her brain refused to accept what her eyes and ears were telling her. It couldn't be. That voice and that face, although both much altered, were long dead.

"Percy?" She had difficulty comprehending the name even as it passed her lips.

Percy was her sister's long-deceased husband. Percy was an impetuous young man who had sped off to war and his death at the first opportunity. Percy was buried in a field in Spain. Percy was dead.

"Percy?" She repeated herself like a simpleton when the proof stood clear before her eyes: Percy was alive.

He straightened and pushed off the wall, and she stepped backward. "Captain Lord Percival Bretagne"—He performed a bow worthy of a ballroom—"at your service."

Was that irony she detected in his tone and in his manner? When had Percy developed irony? "*You* are not Percy," she whispered.

He was Percy . . . But he wasn't.

His eyes went hard and unreadable. It struck her that she didn't know a thing about this man standing before her in a dark alleyway. She longed for her rotten plank of wood. She might need it.

"Follow me," he said and added over his shoulder, "or don't." In a few long strides, he ducked around the corner and out of sight.

*Drat.* Before she could consider the foolishness of her actions, she scrambled to follow him. It was an opportunity she couldn't afford to squander. Her gaze swept the crowded street and finally located his swift-moving back half a block ahead. He was zigzagging through the streets at such a fast clip that she had to trot to keep pace.

After several blocks and street crossings, he hooked a sharp right into a dingy and disreputable building. By the time Mariana reached the entrance, she was out of breath, and Percy was already at the top of a decrepit staircase that didn't look fit to hold the weight of a child, much less that of a full-grown man. She glanced about the wretched pile and placed a tentative foot on the bottom step. When she looked up for confirmation from Percy, he was already gone.

It was her choice.

Well, she hadn't much of a choice. She must follow. Her skirts hitched up to her calves, she allowed her breath to catch up with her and began her ascent, fleet feet springing up the steps in his wake. He wouldn't get away so easily.

At last, she arrived at the very top landing and stood before a cracked door. Once she entered this room, nothing would be the same. Uncertain footsteps stuttered forward as she reached out and pushed wide the door. Three steps later, she found herself at the center of a dim, attic room the size of a garden shed.

The door clicked shut behind her, and she swiveled around to find Percy watching her, his stony expression inscrutable. She resisted the urge to reach out and touch him, to confirm the reality of his corporeal form. Instead, she clenched her hands into fists and kept them at her side.

Her eyes locked fast onto his, she spoke first. "Aren't you supposed to be dead?"

An unreadable emotion flickered across his face, but he remained silent. It was too big a question. This conversation couldn't be swallowed whole. It must be taken in small bites.

"What happened to your hair?" she asked, beginning anew. "It was gray when I saw you in the brothel. I truly didn't recognize you." It seemed a simple enough opening.

"I'm not recognizable when it suits me." He crossed the room and poured them each a measure of amber liquid.

This man didn't move like Percy. The Percy she remembered moved with an upright bearing, like the horses he'd so loved displaying on Rotten Row. This Percy slipped and slid like a shadow, never taking the straightforward path.

He set one glass on the tiny table below the room's lone window and silently toasted her with the other. She reached for her glass and followed his lead, downing the whiskey in one fiery gulp. A gusty, "Oof," escaped her.

He indicated with a flick of his wrist that she sit. She moved to the proffered chair, but stood behind it. She wasn't ready to make herself comfortable for a civilized discussion of, *And how have you been faring? It's been a dreadfully long time since we last spoke. My, oh my, how time does fly!*

That wouldn't do.

"What happened to you?"

"Is that a general or specific inquiry?" he asked before settling back into a creaky chair.

"Either." She glanced at the thin, silvery scar running the length of his right cheekbone. "Both."

"The Battle of Maya."

A seed of frustration cracked open within her. "The Battle of Maya ended eleven years ago."

"For some." He lazily traced a finger around the rim of his empty glass.

This was blatant evasion. Her frustration sprouted roots. "You owe me more than that. It isn't only the scar, Percy. You are altered."

An unhurried hand reached for the whiskey, and he poured them each another few drams. She watched him take a sip and left her own untouched.

How was this Lord Percival Bretagne? Sitting opposite her was a rangy wolf of a man. The sort of man one instinctively crossed the street to avoid. *This* was Percy?

The Percy she remembered was a high-spirited youth who was the life of every party. She would have even gone so far as to describe him as frivolous. Honestly, she'd never understood what, beyond his dashing good looks, Olivia saw in him. Mariana had always thought him shallow as a puddle of water. And when he'd run off and gotten himself blown to bits on the Continent, she hadn't been at all surprised.

The man before her was no brash, shallow youth. His face had shed any trace of boyishness. It was still a handsome face, but one long accustomed to deprivation. The word *wolfish* returned to her. One's eyes wouldn't linger long enough on this man's face to take note of its rugged handsomeness. This man possessed depths that ran as deep and dark as those of a Scottish loch.

"Shall we start at the beginning?" she asked, grasping for some sort of opening.

"And where is the beginning?" he asked, the question a laconic drawl.

"Why did you lead me here only to be deliberately obtuse?" She couldn't keep a frustrated rush from jumbling her words. "How is it you're alive? That would be a beginning."

He picked up his glass of whiskey and downed its contents in a swift swallow. Here was something else she was learning about this Percy: he was difficult. The Percy she remembered had been eager to please. Not this one.

"My death, it turned out, wasn't long-lived. Eventually, I was found somewhat alive, if a bit worse for wear." A dark laugh escaped him, and a chill raced up her spine. "Turns out I'm far more useful dead than I ever was alive."

"Why would you say such a thing?"

"So many indelicate questions for a lady. But, then, you never were one for mincing words." He absently tapped the side of his empty glass. "If you must know, a government has many uses for a dead man."

A sick feeling of dread crept into her stomach. His eyes slid away from hers, and she knew. His government . . . Whitehall . . . the Foreign Office . . . *Nick*.

Nick knew. Of course, he did.

She'd seen them together twice. She'd even spent an evening in the same room with this man. A dark thought came to her. She wasn't certain if it was born of fear or . . . hope. "I've seen you with Nick *and* the Comte de Villefranche. Perhaps you are playing both sides. Perhaps you sent those men to attack Nick."

He mulled her words before answering, "And if I did?"

It was tempting to give in to the possibility of his confession. After all, if Percy was a double agent, the situation would be black and white, and easily concluded. As quickly as the thought came, it was replaced by another consideration, one grounded in reality. Nick trusted this man, *Percy,* with his life. Nick trusted no one.

Percy wasn't behind the attack. Furthermore, it was clear that he was providing cover for Nick. The black and white swirled into gray again.

"Your loyalty to Nick runs so deep that you would allow me to think the worst of you so I don't think it of *him*?"

Percy's gaze glimmered with an intense light. "Nick is finished."

A surge of protectiveness swelled within Mariana. "Nick knows his business very well. When he sets his mind to something, he is the—"

"Best?" Percy finished for her. "He *was* the best before"—She braced herself. She knew how this sentence would end—"you arrived. Now, he is finished. He simply hasn't realized it yet." He shifted forward. "Do you know why he is finished? Can you admit *why* even to yourself? Allow him to come home, Mariana."

"You have the temerity to speak those words to me?" She threw back at him. "What of *your* home, Percy? What of Olivia? What of your daughter whom you've never met? Or do you even know of Lucy?"

He flinched. She'd hit her mark. "I know of her."

"Have you considered how Olivia suffered?"

"Not as much as she would had I returned."

"Help me understand. Why do you and Nick choose *this*?" She spread her arms wide to indicate the ramshackle room surrounding them. "You're the son of a duke."

"I am a son of England. My surroundings"—He mirrored her gesture, arms splayed wide—"are of no consequence. But the work I *do* is." He cocked his head, and a shrewd light sparked within his eyes. "It's the same work you're doing. This work seduces you in. It invigorates and makes you feel alive. You feel it, *non*?"

Her mouth snapped shut as she remembered the heady sense of power she'd experienced *conducting* Villefranche.

"Not everyone in this world can make the easy choice or take the straightforward path. Your tidy Mayfair world depends on it. Society's ease comes with a price for those who will pay it. And make no mistake, Mariana, someone must pay the price. Have you ever taken a good look around you in London? Have you ever noticed the hordes of maimed men littering the sidewalks? Those men paid the price and are still paying it."

"But, Percy"—This conversation had taken a sharp turn, and she was determined to right it—"you owe . . ." His eyes snapped fire, and the remainder of her words died in her mouth.

"You know nothing of my debts," he said. "I owe you nothing."

"But Olivia—"

"My wife, yes."

"Your wife?" The question startled out of her. "Percy, you were declared dead. Olivia is a widow. You don't get to call her your wife."

A stab of concern for her sister cut through her. After years of widowhood, Olivia had settled into a measured life of peace and routine. It wasn't the sort of life Mariana could tolerate for more than five minutes, but Olivia had chosen it. That was enough for Mariana. And, now, here was Percy, alive to muck up the past. And the present.

His chair a sharp, strident scrape across the floor, he stood. "Allow me to escort you to the door."

"You never answered my question," she protested. "Why did you choose this life over your family?"

His head canted to the side, his eyes an onyx glint in half-shadowed light. "You think this life a choice? You're not asking the right question."

"Tell me what question to ask." A strange idea occurred to her. "Are you here against your will?"

Although he hadn't been moving, somehow his body went yet more still. It was as if she was a gorgon who had turned him to stone with her question. "Someday you and I might debate Aristotle's meditations on free will and fate, but not today. It's time for you to leave."

He placed a guiding hand on the small of her back and all but pushed her along. Nearly through the door, she planted her feet into rotting floorboards. She must say something more to this man, and he would hear it. She swiveled around to face him. "Whatever comes of this, leave Olivia be."

A strange mixture of curiosity and vulnerability shone in his eyes, but he kept silent.

"Stay dead, Percy."

He flinched. Good. She pivoted on her heel and strode down the corridor, her footsteps a decisive echo behind her. The old Percy was in there, but buried deep—too deep for her to fathom.

By the time she reached the outside of the building, her feet beat a harder, more decisive tattoo, her thoughts racing toward the source of her burgeoning wrath: Nick. She'd been a fool for the man . . . again.

A storm of anger swept through her, body and mind, before settling into a cold fury. Her furies usually ran fierce and hot, obscuring the world around her for the length of time it took to drink a pot of tea, but this one was unlike any she'd ever experienced. Through this cold fury the events of the past week showed crisp and clear.

She could have forgiven Nick the opera singer ruse. In fact, she saw now that it had been an inevitability. Perhaps she'd been on her way to reconciling with him. Perhaps that had been an inevitability, too.

Now she knew the truth about Percy, a truth Nick had

kept secret, not only from her, but from Olivia. Forgiveness and reconciliation with Nick were impossible.

Bitterness frayed the edges of her crisp and clear fury. She should have known better than to be seduced by that most insidious of emotions: hope.

Hope had no place in the lexicon of her relationship with Nick.

No longer was this a game they were playing. Real life had been happening all this time, directly beneath her nose. She'd been playing fast and loose with a ruthless man, one who would watch others grieve when he knew a truth that would save so many from heartache. The good of the many outweighed the good of the few. That was Nick's belief. What were a few lives worth when so many more were at stake?

But what about those few? What about those individuals who sacrificed so much without any knowledge of their act? What about Olivia?

To harm Olivia was to harm Mariana. It had ever been so. And ever would be. The man who had inflicted that harm had once held her heart, a heart he may once again hold . . .

She swept aside the remainder of that unruly thought and returned to her cold fury, a fury that included herself. She'd gone into her dealings with Nick with the full knowledge that she played with fire. Yet she'd played on, foolishly thinking she could separate the emotional from the physical. She'd thought she wouldn't get burned. That she'd learned her lesson the first time around. Well, she was scorched.

And she had no one to blame except herself, not even Nick. Past behavior was the best predictor of future behavior, after all. Absurdly, she'd fallen into the trap of believing it could be otherwise and that a new pattern could develop.

Ha.

Nick would always be Nick. And she would always be Mariana, the girl who fell hopelessly in love with him any time he glanced her way. How easily she'd allowed herself to forget.

But now she remembered. And now, once again, she must find a way to forget and carry on with the rest of her life. Dark possibility snaked in alongside the thought, and a way of forgetting came to her. Even as her stomach dropped to her toes, cold intellect pressed forward. It might be the only way.

To forget one man, one could seduce another. Nick himself had given her a few lessons toward that end.

Like a domino tipping over, the perfect candidate for her seduction fell into place: Captain Nylander.

What was Helene's description of him? A tall drink of Viking water.

Her own? The path not pursued.

Well, it was her prerogative to pursue that path now.

Captain Nylander was gorgeous and discreet, and he'd given her his address in Calais. She could be there within the day.

But she knew the answer must be *no*. The man clearly had a code of honor regarding women, and she wouldn't take advantage of it.

She needed someone else, someone who couldn't threaten her emotionally and vice versa. She needed . . . the Comte de Villefranche.

She couldn't stand the man, which made him perfect. And she'd already put in the effort with him. Furthermore, he wasn't exactly repulsive.

With Villefranche, the sexual act would be a cold and sterile affair. She would walk away from him completely unscathed. That was the most important consideration.

Villefranche would do.

Tonight's soirée would provide the opportunity she needed. Never mind that Nick would certainly find out. *That* wasn't her motivation. Of course, it wasn't. Through the haze of her cold fury, she saw that she would be doing this for herself. She needed this to forget Nick, to break her bond with him.

She should have taken a lover years ago. Never mind that Nick had never taken one. He should have. They each should have. It was the only way to protect their hearts from each other.

The past was done. A new future opened itself to her. It was a future she would embark upon tonight. She should feel optimistic.

And if she didn't? If the future stretching before her felt as bleak as the tundra of her cold fury?

Well, there would be more lovers.

# Chapter 22

*Kiss mine A-se: An offer, as Fielding observes, very frequently made, but never, as he could learn, literally accepted.*

*A Classical Dictionary of the Vulgar Tongue*
Francis Grose

"I do not deal in politics. I am a mere woman," Mariana said.

A passing tray of champagne floated within reach, and she snatched a glass. She took a rather deep sip, one that could be characterized as a gulp, and attempted to ignore the persistent little Frenchman hovering at her side.

He'd been there since she'd stepped foot inside the Capet family's soirée, set inside their private Palais-Royal garden. Within this exclusive preserve, the principles of *Liberté! Egalité! Fraternité!* didn't exist. This opulent garden, replete with flowing champagne, sparkling gems of every hue, and coldly sophisticated smiles, was reserved solely for the pleasure of the reestablished aristocracy.

"But, Madame, you deal in politics for that very reason," the man insisted with an exhausting earnestness. "Everything about a woman is political. And this school you speak of, The Progress School—"

"The Progressive School for Young Ladies and the Education of Their Minds," she supplied for him, unable to keep a weary note out of her voice.

"*Exactement*," he exclaimed, his arm gesticulating

theatrically up into the air. "Theese ees politics. Education ees politics."

The man's protuberant eyes snagged on the line of her décolletage, and he went mute. Mariana cleared her throat, startling his eyes upward. Politics certainly didn't render a man sexless.

"To base a school on the precepts of *Émile* by our own Rousseau is political," he resumed, inching closer and creating an intimate space ripe with breath that must have partaken of raw onion and garlic. "Such boldness only proves that you are, indeed, a rare Englishwoman."

Mariana took an instinctive step backward in subtle rebuff. She had two men on her mind, and this little toad wasn't one of them. Her gaze swept the garden for the hundredth time tonight. Nothing.

"Your eyes," began the little toad, "they shine with the clear light of a flawless diamond."

Some nights this sort of man, servile and obsequious, amused her. Not tonight. A frigid smile curved her lips. "Doesn't that particular metaphor better describe blue eyes? My eyes are, in fact, plain brown."

"Brown? Your eyes are no common *brown*"—The little toad all but spat the word—"Just look how the pink of your dress—"

"I do not own a single pink dress," she cut in. "This dress is coral."

"Ah, *oui*, my paltry English cannot capture the nuance of color. But the way the *coral* brings out the amber of your eyes reminds me of a ray of morning sun piercing a honeycomb with its warm glow."

"*Warm glow?*" she repeated on a joyless laugh that sounded brittle even to her own ears. "I think you were closer to the mark with the diamond metaphor."

She wasn't certain about the flawless or brilliant parts, but the comparison cut strikingly close to her transformation over the last few hours. She may have been soft coal this morning, but, tonight, she was a hardened diamond. Tonight, she was adamantine.

Once again, her gaze scanned the garden lit by particolored star lanterns composed of translucent *papier-mâché*. Small flames flickered and danced on the whimsical breeze, creating illusory images reminiscent of the fairies who once danced across her childhood ceiling. On a different night, this garden would enchant her.

Tonight, it did nothing of the sort. The cold fury from earlier had given way to an odd sense of distance from herself.

As her gaze darted from vibrant string quartet to perfectly manicured rows of fall flowers and on to the fleet of lanterns floating on the black void of the garden's central fountain, she still detected no sign of either man. It would be easiest, of course, if Villefranche appeared before Nick arrived. Then she could get the seduction out of the way without any potential interference from Nick.

Of course, it didn't escape her notice that her plan might have one flaw. Namely, how was she supposed to seduce a man who wouldn't come within seducing distance?

She nabbed another flute off a passing tray, efficiently trading her empty for a full. The French made it entirely too easy to overindulge.

Sensing an opportunity while she gulped down half of the flute's contents, the little toad tried another angle. "Your eyes shine with the fiery light of an avenging goddess."

"Careful now," Mariana began, "or you'll deplete your entire repertoire of clichés before the night has a chance to truly begin."

She was being insufferably rude, but she cared not one jot. In fact, the little toad's eyes only shone brighter.

She glanced away from him in disgust, even as the word *fiery* called to her. This afternoon, she could have streaked across this garden like a ferocious, avenging goddess. Tonight, however, the emotion necessary to fuel such a dramatic flight lay just out of reach. In short, she felt numb and heavy, divorced from her emotions and bound by the lead weight she'd tied around her own neck: this seduction. She wanted to get it over with as quickly as possible.

If a little voice protested that seductions weren't meant to be chores, that seductions were to be savored and enjoyed, she suppressed it with yet another gulp of champagne.

The little toad opened his odiferous mouth to undoubtedly spew yet another round of noxious, hackneyed flattery, when Helene fluttered to her right side. At the exact same moment, Aunt Dot came at her from the left. The little toad was entirely squeezed out. An awkward and uncertain silence stretched with the three women uniformly staring the man down. At last, he heaved a resigned sigh and shuffled off to try his luck elsewhere.

Mariana's relief at his departure was short-lived when she noticed a palpable tension radiating off the two women flanking her sides. "Aunt Dot, you are acquainted with my honorary aunt, Helene de Vivonne, the Marquise de Chevreuse?"

"Oh, my dear," Aunt Dot began, her eyes straight ahead. "I am, of course, your aunt by blood"—There was no mistaking the umbrage in her voice—"and we all know blood is thicker than water."

"How true, Madame Montfort," Helene intoned smoothly, her gaze, too, fixed in the distance. "I am merely Mariana's aunt by choice." Helene squeezed Mariana's arm. "What is the saying? You cannot choose your family, but you can choose your friends?"

Aunt Dot's mouth snapped shut, and Mariana began to long for the little toad. Abhorrent breath and leering gaze might be preferable to spending an evening wedged between two women who loathed one another for no better reason than one was French and the other English.

"Shall we take a turn about the garden?" Mariana asked, unable to summon the emotion to care one way or the other. They just seemed like the polite words to say.

"*Ma chérie*," Helene exclaimed as their feet found a sedate, collective pace, "do you see our dear Charlet? One cannot miss him. So talented is he with his lithographs."

Mariana followed the direction of Helene's gaze and found the painter. He was indeed unmistakable with his towering height and ever-present smile. A small crowd gathered around him, basking in the warmth of a boyish good humor evident even from this distance.

"You are aware, of course, that Charlet was a dear friend to Géricault," Helene said in a reverent tone. "Such a tragedy was the death of Géricault. The boy was only a few steps into manhood."

"A tragedy?" harrumphed Aunt Dot. "When is a painter's death from dissipation and licentiousness so uncommon as to be tragedy?"

"No, Aunt," Mariana spoke before Helene could respond. "Olivia mentioned Géricault's failing health when he showed *The Raft of Medusa* in London a few years ago. He suffered from a persistent lung ailment, if I remember correctly."

"Oh, *The Raft of Medusa*—" Helene began.

"Obscene," inserted Aunt Dot.

"—*Tragique*," Helene continued as if Aunt Dot hadn't spoken. "Those poor souls . . . to be abandoned after a shipwreck by their own captain."

"Speaks of a certain national character, one would think," Aunt Dot cut in.

"And Géricault's depiction of those poor, lost souls on the raft was so—"

"Animalistic," Aunt Dot again interrupted, a dramatic shudder quaking her generous bosom. "All those writhing limbs and bodies clad in only the loosest scraps of cloth, I daresay."

"—*Sympathique* to their plight and their suffering," Helene pressed on. Mariana had never seen Helene so determined. "Géricault understood the human condition well beyond his years. His loss . . . oh, what tragedy for Charlet. Friends are the family we choose." She paused, allowing her latest jab to sink in before asking, "Mariana, do you know that our great Delacroix—I wonder if he is here tonight?—posed for Géricault as one of the poor unfortunates?"

"Oh, dearest dear, Delacroix," Aunt Dot exclaimed. "That young reprobate? No thank you. Give me a painter like Mister Turner. Mariana, have you viewed *The Battle of Trafalgar*? Now, *that* is a national treasure of which to be proud."

"It is my understanding," Helene began, "a controversy surrounds this painting. Perhaps Monsieur Turner's depiction isn't so accurate? Is it possible that a looseness with the truth speaks—how did you say it, Madame Montfort?—*of a certain national character*?"

So stiff did Aunt Dot's body go, it was a wonder the woman was able to continue placing one foot in front of the other. If emotion had been available to her, Mariana might have felt badly for her aunt. Perhaps. Likely not.

"Duchesse," Helene exclaimed of a sudden before lowering herself into a deep curtsy. Mariana's gaze lit upon a tiny, yet somehow statuesque, woman approaching them without a single stir to her features or person. Not even her skirts moved as she progressed forward. Mariana and Aunt Dot followed Helene's lead and dipped into their own curtsies.

"What a *magnifique* soirée," Helene sang out as she rose. "The stars. The fashion. The soirée of the year."

The Duchesse inclined her head and granted the three women a smile that could only be characterized as condescending. She was a *duchesse*, after all. The daughter of an earl, Mariana wasn't especially impressed. Still, this woman was Villefranche's mother, and this was their Paris residence.

Like that, a solution to her problem struck her, and it became clear exactly how she could seduce a man who wouldn't come within seducing distance.

After Helene went through the requisite introduction ritual, Mariana exclaimed with all the grace of a country ingénue, "Duchesse, the beauty of your garden overwhelms me with its splendor." She may have been laying it on a bit thick. After all, she'd been presented at court, and none other than the current King George himself had named her and Olivia *Milk and Honey*, due to their respective complexions. A moniker that had followed them everywhere their debut Season. "If I may be so bold"—She leaned in ever so slightly—"our English styles pale in comparison."

Helene gave her a smug pat on her right hand while Aunt Dot bristled to her left. If Mariana ever wanted to see the Folly again, she would find a way to make it up to Aunt. But that was a task for future Mariana. Tonight, she had a larger game at play.

"I wonder if . . . oh, this may be asking too much," Mariana faltered, willing a blush to rise to her cheeks. The Duchesse eyed her with all the verve of a dead-eyed fish. "But I wonder if a tour of your residence would be a possibility? Of a sudden, I'm feeling inspired to renovate my London townhouse in exactly this style."

The Duchesse's eyebrows lifted in surprise. "Indeed?" With an elegant flick of her wrist, she summoned an attentive servant.

While a muted conversation ensued, Mariana glanced to her left to find a beet red Aunt Dot staring straight ahead.

She turned right to find a quiet Helene studying her closely. "What is this all about, *ma chérie*?"

The Duchesse rescued Mariana from having to devise a lie. "Lady Nicholas, when you are ready, summon Gaston"— Her delicate fingers fluttered in the direction of the servant to her left—"and he will show you all you wish to see."

Mariana stepped forward to implement her plan and leave the three women to negotiate the rest of the evening without her. She had some exploring to do. Gaston was going to show her every inch of this residence, including the room where Villefranche slept. Before this night was finished, it was entirely possible that she would employ every single one of her newfound spy skills—duplicity, guile, invisibility, lock picking, and seduction . . .

Unexpectedly, her eye caught on the figure she'd sought all evening, standing in a secluded alcove at the far end of the grounds: Villefranche.

Two facts became immediately apparent. He wasn't alone. And, if the impassioned nature of his hand gestures was an indicator, he was angry.

Intrigued, Mariana took in the figure opposite Villefranche. Towering form . . . massive belly . . . sagging jowls . . . She knew that man.

It was Uncle Bertie, engaging in a heated argument with Villefranche. Theirs wasn't a polite acquaintanceship made at a Society function. What on earth did Uncle Bertie and the Comte de Villefranche have to discuss *heatedly*?

Another question followed quick on its heels: did Nick know of Uncle Bertie's connection to Villefranche? Where was the dratted man anyway?

As if her unspoken question had the power to conjure him out of thin air, another familiar figure caught the edge of her vision. A collective gasp met her ears, and her body froze. A frisson of anticipation skittered through her veins.

One steadying inhalation of air later, she pivoted to face fully what her body already knew. Across the garden stood Nick attired in crisp whites and blacks, surveying the garden like he owned it.

Society's eyes flitted between him and her as they awaited what would come next. Would he acknowledge her? Cut her? Embrace her? What a delicious *amuse-bouche* of gossip she and he were serving Society.

Meanwhile, he remained seemingly oblivious to the hushed silence. How had she been fooled for so long by his façade of supercilious popinjay?

She knew how. She'd chosen to see it. In that way, it had been easier to dismiss him and fashion a new life for herself. And now she knew the fop was a disguise for the real Nick, a deceitful bastard.

As his gaze continued its thorough sweep of the garden, her heart hammered in her chest, her traitorous body winding up in expectation of the moment his eyes would land upon her. For the first time tonight, she felt alive. She could hate herself for it, even more than she hated him.

At last, his gaze found her. A quick smile quirked up his lips and lit his eyes, and her breath caught. How easily she could become enthralled by his smile. It was the sort of smile that had the potential to erase an entire past. This smile was so utterly unlike Nick—open, loving, genuine—as if his entire world centered around her.

Too open. Too loving. Too genuine.

And she wasn't his entire world. She never was and never would be. His smile played for the hundred pairs of eyes surrounding them on all sides, not for her.

The thought was the splash of cold water she needed. Tonight, she had a role: loving wife to Nick's loving husband. A smile matching his in brilliance curved her lips, even as she felt it didn't quite reach her eyes.

In the next heartbeat, the quiet broke, replaced by the buzz of bees swarming. It was the sound of gossip, excitable and relentless.

The curious numbness of the evening gone, her sleeping fury reawakened and began to rise. As she took her first step forward into this uncertain night, duplicitous smile pasted onto her face, she allowed her fury to enshroud her like a protective cloak. She wouldn't be distracted from her intention to take a lover.

Never mind that she'd never shared a bed with a man other than Nick. Tonight, she would remedy that. She was a diamond, unyielding and multi-faceted.

And if within those illusory facets hid a weak spot that had never sufficiently hardened, only she needed to know of it. She would see the seduction through. Tonight was the beginning of the rest of her life without Nick.

Only he didn't know it yet.

# Chapter 23

*Carry witchet: A sort of conundrum, puzzlewit, or riddle.*

*A Classical Dictionary of the Vulgar Tongue*
Francis Grose

Nick spotted Mariana across the starlit garden, and confirmation, deep and true, settled in his gut. She was his.

A smile that refused to be suppressed opened wide across his face, stretching muscles that hadn't been used since childhood, and possibly not even then. If he appeared foolish, then that was the price he must pay. He wanted everyone to see his feelings for her, but, even more, he wanted her to see them.

With every step he took toward her, his world shifted into balance by increments. His feet ticked along at a pace, swift and sure, as he navigated through the party, maneuvering around effusive waiters, knowing Society smiles, and obstructive topiary animals.

With only a dozen feet to go, the path to Mariana cleared, and it was only him and her beneath a low-slung crescent moon that shone solely for them. Even if the moon had shone full and bright tonight, it couldn't match the tide of her smile inexorably pulling him toward her.

He hesitated just shy of her and silently held her gaze. Words weren't necessary. Not after this afternoon.

"Nick," she began, "there is something you must know."

Unable to resist the feel of her, he stepped forward and slipped his arms around the supple curve of her waist. He tipped his head and met the pulsing bend of her neck with his lips. A soft sigh released from her. Emboldened, his mouth trailed up to her ear, and beneath his lips a light dusting of goose bumps rose. "Play along as nicely as you did earlier," his voice rumbled, "and I'll reward you . . . again."

A duo of heartbeats later, her body stiffened into a rigid line, and she slipped entirely out of the circle of his arms. Perhaps she thought they were scandalizing Society?

Strangely exposed and uncertain, he opened his mouth to question her when yet another hush descended over the crowd, drawing all eyes. He quashed his unease and followed the collective gaze, where he found the king's heir Charles, the Duc d'Artois. Nick couldn't help a grudging respect for the pretentious coxcomb. It was a savvy and bold move, walking into the lion's den, even as his brother, the Bourbon king, lay on his death bed.

Nick glanced down to find Mariana quietly taking in the scene. They would have to set aside their future until the matter of the Duc's assassination was put to bed. He angled his mouth toward her ear. "Louis is expected to die tonight."

"And the Duc d'Artois is attending an Orléans soirée to shore up the support he needs for his claim to the throne," she finished for him.

"If the death is announced"—He needed to ask one more favor of his wife—"rush over to the Duc and create a little scene."

"Why?"

"We need a distraction at that precise moment."

"And who are *we*?"

His eyes narrowed on her. She held herself with a mien of disinterest, but a closer inspection revealed the opposite. Her eye held a sharp light. There was a correct answer to her question, but he wasn't certain what it was. "I have another agent placed in the garden," he said carefully.

"Ah," she said, a brittle smile curving her lips. "Should I seduce the Duc right then and there?"

"Over my dead body," he stated, sudden ferocity rearing up within him.

The smile froze on her face. "I thought I was to use *any means*," she threw back at him. Before he could reply, she continued, "Since we're on the subject of cloaks and daggers, I feel somewhat obliged to tell you that I saw Villefranche engaged in a rather heated discussion with my Uncle—"

"Bertie," Nick finished for her.

"Of course, this isn't news to you. Who in my family isn't involved in your spy intrigues?"

It dawned on him that something was wrong. How was it possible?

They'd been about to confess their love for one another this afternoon. Now she acted as if she couldn't stand the sight of him. His sense of balance shifted away. "What happened between this afternoon and now? This afternoon we—"

"*We?*" she cut in, her voice a shard of mockery. "There is no *we*. There never was."

Nick felt winded as if he'd been gut punched. He moved closer to her. He wouldn't leave her side until they sorted this out.

A sudden and cacophonous tapping of metal against glass rang out and demanded everyone's attention. An expectant silence descended as the collective gaze swung toward the raised dais where the Duc d'Artois sat, coolly staring out across the garden. A frustrated Nick had no choice but to wait.

A courtier stepped forward, a grave expression on his face, and proclaimed, "*Le roi est mort, vive le roi!*"

In unison, the gathered sank into low curtsies before their new monarch, the man who would be crowned Charles X.

Mariana finished off the last of her champagne in a single swallow. "Actors take your places."

"Hang the assassination plot," Nick found himself not only saying, but also meaning with every ounce of his being. "You and I are—"

"Far less important than the fate of two nations, correct?"

"Not even close." His fingers wrapped around her arm when she made to step away. Her eyes flashed fire over her shoulder, and his stomach sank.

"You must do as you will. Just as I must." She shook off his hand and fled toward the dais to set the plan into motion.

He'd been delivered a message in no uncertain terms. His suspicions coalesced into a fully formed conclusion, unavoidable: something was again broken between them.

This line of thought was interrupted when Percy, in the guise of a ubiquitous, faceless server, caught his eye. Nick's feet sprang into motion. He located Mariana in time to see her barrel into the new king of France. The startled smile lighting up her face combined a flawless mixture of vacuity, sheepishness, and awe. He couldn't resist a swell of pride, even as the prickle of anxiety remained constant. He must focus on the task at hand and see this night through. Mariana must come later.

His feet accelerated into a light sprint as he and Percy converged on the fringe of the crowd just rising from their deep curtsies and bows. Their footsteps fell into a unified rhythm as they rushed toward the same destination: the Comte de Villefranche.

"Get Villefranche out of here," Nick spoke under his breath.

"For how long?" Percy asked.

"Tonight, at the very least. A few days would be ideal."

"Consider it done."

"Your cover will be blown," Nick continued. "It is only a matter of time before Montfort knows that you are alive. Perhaps it is time for you to go home, too."

"Perhaps," Percy allowed, his tone indicating the opposite. Percy would follow his own path. "But Nick," he continued, "we must discuss your wife."

"Now isn't the time." Eyes trained on Villefranche some twenty yards away, Nick didn't want to halt their forward momentum.

"There is something you must know," Percy pressed.

"Not now, Bretagne," Nick snapped. They were so close. Villefranche was in his sights, and nothing short of a force of nature would stop him from completing this mission.

As he and Percy closed in, Villefranche's body shifted and visibly tensed. The inevitable was striding toward him, and there was no avoiding it.

Villefranche's gaze met Nick's for a fleeting second before the man excused himself from his guests and beat a hasty retreat to a nearby dark passageway. Percy, then Nick, followed. Nick took one last backward glance, his senses on the alert for a trap. Perceiving nothing untoward, he slipped into the shadows.

The three men standing in a close, uneasy triangle, Nick spoke first. "The assassination won't be happening tonight. Your new king only awaits his crown."

Villefranche hesitated, his wide gaze shifting back and forth between Nick and Percy. His chin jutted toward Percy. "He was your agent all this time?"

"*Oui*," Nick replied. A watchful Percy remained silent.

A humorless chortle escaped Villefranche. "Your wife was correct about my espionage skills."

"Leave Mariana out of this," Nick said, his body suddenly tensed for battle. Percy's fingers discreetly closed around his upper arm.

"Is there more we need to know?" Percy asked.

"I told Bertrand Montfort to leave France with no delay, or he would be charged as an enemy of the state for plotting the death of the king." Villefranche drummed impatient fingers on his thigh. "My part in the plot is done, but it is the Englishman who will decide if it is truly finished."

Nick switched his attention to Percy. "You know where you're taking him?"

Percy nodded, and Villefranche began to protest, "I refuse to be told what—"

Percy's gaze shot toward Villefranche. "You will follow me. And you will not leave my side until I allow it. Understood?"

Villefranche remained stubbornly silent.

"Or will force be necessary?" Percy asked in a voice at once eerily calm and utterly capable, leaving no doubt that the man behind the words could carry out the implicit threat.

A wary Villefranche shifted on his feet before assenting with a single nod. Percy threw a farewell glance Nick's way before striding down the stone passageway, Villefranche close at his heels. Nick pointed himself in the opposite direction and stepped out of the shadows as he scanned the interior grounds for Bertrand Montfort.

His gaze landed on the massive and imposing man . . . already watching him. Montfort was the perfect spider, and spiders didn't appreciate having their webs destroyed. He would be out for revenge over tonight's destruction of his carefully laid plans.

Bertrand Montfort was now his enemy, a fact Nick understood with crystal clarity. He also understood what was needed in this situation: proof linking Montfort to the plot to assassinate the new king of France. It was his best, and only, insurance policy.

But where did such proof exist?

As his gaze held Montfort's patient one, it came to Nick. Villefranche's rooms. He must find the proof before one of Montfort's agents did. Montfort never left a job unfinished. But, then, neither did Nick.

He tipped an ironic nod toward the man before setting his feet into motion. First, he must lose the agent surely tailing him on Montfort's orders. Then he could finally finish this mission.

*And Mariana?*

As if pulled by a magnet, his gaze once again locked onto her. Even from this distance he could see her skillfully handling a visibly charmed King Charles. Again, pride surged. The woman standing there with a king wrapped around her pinky was his wife. He would make her so again.

The time had long passed for him to allow the specter of his parents' doomed union to fade away. He should have spoken the words this afternoon, but he'd wanted to give her time to reflect on the whirlwind of the last few days.

The hard glint in her eyes returned to him, and he experienced a note of portent. He shook it off. All would come out all right. It had to. The universe had given him another chance with her. Just a few minutes more and they would start planning the rest of their lives together.

But there was no future until this last piece of business was settled.

Then he would finally be free to speak the words to her he'd never had the courage to speak.

# Chapter 24

*Knot: A crew, gang, or fraternity. He has tied a knot with his tongue, that he cannot untie with his teeth; i.e. he is married.*

*A Classical Dictionary of the Vulgar Tongue*
Francis Grose

Nick slid open yet another desk drawer and blindly groped inside.

Empty. Not even the smallest scrap of paper that would give him leverage against Montfort could be found. *Blast.*

A frustrated breath escaped him. Then he heard it: the quick pick of a lock followed by the low moan of hinges turning. An agent working for Montfort must have tracked him. He ducked down and waited, expecting lanterns to be lit and exposure to follow.

The room remained pitch black. Whoever shared this room with him didn't know he was here.

A few tense seconds passed before the other intruder began moving noisily. The sound was familiar. It was the swish of silk skirts. He peered around a solid walnut leg just in time to see a long swath of coral silk rush across the sliver of moonlight cutting through a cracked window.

*Mariana.*

It must have occurred to her to search Villefranche's rooms, too. Except, she barely paused in this room, clearly Villefranche's office. Instead, she strode straight through to the bedroom. Clever woman. She was beginning to think like a spy.

Of course, Villefranche would keep his closest secrets near him in his bedroom. Nick experienced another surge of pride for this quick, intelligent woman who was his wife.

Gingerly, he rose to his feet, stretching his long, cramped body, his ears trained on the sounds emanating from the other room—skirts shushing, bedcovers rustling—as she searched nooks and crannies for evidence. But why was she here in the first place? The question only just occurred to him. Didn't she understand the danger was passed now that the plot to assassinate King Charles had been foiled?

Curiosity whetted, Nick padded softly toward the room. Her skirts went silent. She'd detected his tread, but didn't yet know the other occupant was her husband. Unless . . . unless she'd followed him and saw him slip inside the room. That was the most likely scenario, but . . . Why hadn't she acknowledged him if that was the case?

An unhelpful thought occurred to him: Mariana was in a bedroom. *Blast.*

*Focus.* He wasn't here to make love to her in a bed. He was here to find evidence and wrap up this mission. There would be time for beds later.

Just beyond the doorway, he slowed to a stop when she came into focus. His brain needed a moment to process the vision greeting his eyes.

Stretched atop the Comte de Villefranche's massive four-poster bed reclined a Mariana clad simply in a transparent white shift and stockings held up by silver garters. The shift reached just far enough to cover her . . . quim.

His breath caught in his chest. She resembled nothing so much as the world's most delectable courtesan.

Her eyes trained on the doorway, she called out in a hushed whisper, "Lucien?"

One salient detail became instantly clear: she hadn't followed him into Villefranche's rooms. In fact, judging by the tentative expression on her face, she had no idea that her husband stood just outside the frame of light.

A riot of emotion assailed Nick as he stepped forward into a moonbeam. Her cautious smile froze, then fell, revealing more than she might want to tell. He could no longer deny the conclusion that had been staring at him from the instant she'd swished into these rooms. Mariana was here for Villefranche.

Through the noise of anger and betrayal, one last shred of hope sounded: perhaps she thought she still needed to seduce the man to obtain information. She could be confused.

Which made no sense. Mariana didn't get confused.

But a drowning man would grasp at anything to prevent himself from going under. He forced himself to loosen his stance, lean a relaxed shoulder against the doorjamb, and paste an easy smile onto his lips. Nothing had ever been more difficult in his life. "I feel like an addendum to our last *spy lesson* is in order."

Her arms crossed defensively. Good.

"When seducing a mark in his own bed, make absolutely certain he still is on premises."

"He was here when last I saw him."

"So you no longer need to exercise," he continued as if he hadn't heard her, his hand sweeping toward the bed, "*any means*."

Her head tilted inquisitively to the side. "Who says I no longer *need* to seduce Villefranche?" she asked, her eyes burning with the combustible light he'd detected earlier. "What about what I *want*?"

Nick's insides went heavy with dread, her question confirming his deepest fear: she was indeed arrayed atop the Comte de Villefranche's bed to seduce . . . the Comte de Villefranche.

Hurt and betrayal swept through him with the force of a

tidal wave. "Did last night and this afternoon mean nothing to you?" he asked unable to curb the impulse.

"Last night and this afternoon meant pleasure to me. Pure and simple."

"No, Mariana, it meant more to you than lust. I was there, remember?"

A laugh sounded from her. It resonated across his eardrums the way a bitter quince would across his tongue. "That was then," she began, "and this is now. I seek a new experience."

He stepped closer. "I may not know every detail of your mind, but I do know exactly who you want to *experience*." He'd thrown down the gauntlet.

"I am here to *experience* a different man," she replied, picking it up.

Cold determination tore through the hurt and betrayal. "You won't be seducing Villefranche tonight."

"Won't I?" she asked, defiance writ clear across her face and in her words.

"No."

Villefranche wouldn't have her. No other man would. She was his.

He unknotted his cravat.

"What are you doing?" she asked, startling forward, her eyes wide. "I'm not here for you. Didn't you hear me?"

"Oh, I heard you." He shrugged off his evening jacket and allowed it to drop to the floor. His fingers began on the buttons of his shirt.

In the near dark, he could see her eyes brighten, even as she dragged her feet closer to her body, effectively cutting off his view of all but her feet, shins, and luminous eyes. "It occurs to me that we haven't yet made love in a proper bed. Not in years, anyway."

"This isn't about you, Nick."

"Isn't it?"

"It's about what I need. And I need to break free of you."

He took a step closer, slowly, deliberately. "You are free to leave."

Her response was to take her bottom lip between her teeth and bite down.

"I won't stop you." He halted at the side of the bed, the long length of her body within reach. "You don't want the uncertainty of a green fopling. You want a man who knows exactly what to give you and how."

"Tastes change," she said, a breathless hitch in her voice.

"Not those kinds."

"What if I want to change my tastes?"

"You want what I have to offer. You always will. Mariana"—Each syllable of her name sounded an urgent and desperate plea—"let me touch you."

"It won't solve anything," she whispered, her eyes at once imploring and wavering.

"Maybe not," he said as he reached out to touch his fingers to her toes.

He bent forward and replaced his fingers with his lips. A measure of resistance drained from her body as her knees parted slightly and her eyes met his. He saw reflected there a burn of emotion mirroring his own: betrayal and anger, yes, but above all, desire, raw and unfiltered, so strong it rendered all other emotion insignificant until it was slaked.

He should stop now, he knew. He should investigate why she was so angry with him, and what had changed between this afternoon and this evening. He knew that, too. But he couldn't.

His eyes lowered to upthrust peaks discernible beneath transparent silk before sinking ever lower to the view inches from his face: her naked quim tantalizingly visible beneath the hem of her shift. It was possibly the most erotic view of his life.

"Tell me what you want," his voice rasped, his gaze lifting toward hers. He met a wildness there, one he'd never been able to resist. He wasn't about to start tonight.

Her eyes shifted away, as if weighing her words, before returning to him, resolve in their depths. "Lick me," she exhaled, "all the way up until I say stop."

Without hesitation, he touched his tongue to the delicate arch of her foot and trailed it over ankle, up long leg, over bent knee to dewy, inner thigh. Her intoxicating, female scent had just reached him when he heard the word, "Stop."

He obeyed, even as his swollen cock throbbed in protest. His eyes locked onto hers, but his focus remained on her bare quim, inches from his mouth. Wet and ready for him. She must feel every exhale of his breath across her sensitive flesh.

Audacity brightening her eyes, she brought her forefinger to her parted lips and licked it. Through the valley between her breasts, down her soft, flat belly, ever lower it trailed. "Now I want you to"—Her resolute finger slid to the glistening nub of her sex—"watch."

As if he had a choice.

Slowly, her finger began to move, sliding down, then up, over the sensitive flesh, pink and swollen with desire. A moan sounded from deep within her throat. How easily his tongue could join her finger and double her pleasure. He shifted to the side and reached down to unbutton his trousers, intent on easing his aching cock.

"What are you doing?" she asked, her finger ceasing its erotic motion.

His gaze flew up to meet hers. "I think you know."

"I haven't given you permission to touch me . . . or yourself."

"Is it your intention to torture me?"

"Perhaps."

As if to illustrate her point, with her other hand she took a cherry-hard nipple between forefinger and thumb as she resumed rubbing the nub of her sex. Another moan escaped her, and her neck arched back.

It was all too much.

In a raspy, desperate voice he didn't recognize as his own, he murmured, "I can help you with that."

Her brows lifted, and she pinned him with a lust-glazed stare. "Oh?" was all she spoke, but he heard, *Impress me.*

He stretched forward, languid and sure, her flesh separated from him by a thin stretch of air. "I would do this."

He touched his lips to her quim, almost primly, before his tongue flattened and moved against her in a long, slow stroke, eliciting a long, slow groan from her.

"Then I would do this."

His hand slipped beneath her to slide one . . . two fingers inside her.

"Followed by this."

His tongue stiffened to a velvet point and began tapping, finding a quick rhythm as his finger moved in and out of her.

She melted beneath his tongue even as muscles began tightening, a palpable tension clearly overtaking her as her head arced back and her hips thrust forward. A few more taps of his tongue, and her release would engulf her . . .

And then what? She would be done with him. He wasn't ready for that.

His tongue abruptly stopped its motion, and his fingers slid out of her.

A groan of frustration, rather than one of release, poured out of her.

Her eyes flew open and fixed him with a fiery glare. "I didn't give you permission to stop."

"I know."

# Chapter 25

*Tat: Tit for tat; an equivalent.*

*A Classical Dictionary of the Vulgar Tongue*
Francis Grose

Mariana froze.

*I know.*

With those two simple words, Nick shifted the power balance. And he knew it, she suspected. But she was too far gone to care. He knew that, too. Drat the man.

"I want you to need me," he said.

Something about the way the word *need* scraped against his throat nearly undid her.

He slipped off the bed and stepped out of his unlaced trousers. Her unblinking gaze dropped to his hard shaft, and she felt the slide of her tongue against her lower lip.

"All of me," he finished.

She observed him from across the length of the bed, and a dark hunger took shape within her. Too much distance separated them. She tipped forward and came to her hands and knees. With a sense of unhurried purpose, she began crawling across the silk expanse, her gaze holding fast onto his. Just at the edge, just shy of him, she stopped, her mouth a fingerbreadth from his ready member, her head and back deeply arched so she could hold his gaze.

"Is *that*"—They both knew what *that* was—"all you are?"

"At the moment."

Anticipation skittered through her veins.

"And the moment is all we have."

Her gaze still locked onto his, her tongue reached out to lick the tip of his manhood before circling it once . . . twice . . . thoroughly wetting the crown. Her eyes drifted shut as her body pressed forward, and he slid inside her open mouth one exquisite inch at a time.

Never in her life had she been so brazen, so wanton, so uninhibited. A deep moan of pleasure vibrated through her even as she squeezed her thighs together to relieve the ache between them.

He went utterly still. "Do that again."

Again, she moaned, longer and louder this time, the vibrations of the moan pulsing through his hard, velvety column. His fingers threaded through her hair, and his hips rocked forward and back. She fell into a rhythm with him as his manhood slipped in and out of her mouth. Again, she moaned.

His fingers clutched tighter, his hips rocking, now thrusting, into her mouth. She sat slightly back as her fingers gripped the base of him, her mouth sucking his crown. She glanced up. He was completely gone, his body tensing, reaching . . . Her hands grabbed his hips and held, effectively bringing the momentum to a screeching halt, his breath coming fast and hard. His fingers released their grip on her hair and began caressing her scalp in tiny circular motions.

She almost felt undone by the unconscious measure of comfort. She'd denied him release, yet it was she who was being soothed.

But she wouldn't be undone. She rocked her hips backward, allowing the length of his surely painfully erect phallus to slide from her mouth. She sat back on her heels and faced him.

They could stop here. They both knew it.

But she wanted more. She wanted everything.

She reached out and pressed her palm against the muscular flat of his chest as her legs swung around to the edge of the bed. Positioned in the corner behind him, she noticed a small chair. She hadn't formulated a plan for what would come next, but one suddenly formed as she came to a stand.

Her arm stiffened, one foot moved forward, and she prodded him backward. She repeated the motion until the backs of his legs met the chair. With one final nudge, she pushed him down.

"Even when there's a bed in the room," he said, "we can't manage to use it."

Another time his words would have elicited a flirtatious response, but not now. Not when the moonlit length of his body offered such exquisite distraction. Defined muscles, at once sinewy and substantial, stretched down him, leading her eye across a man's body hardened by time and energy. Speaking of hard . . .

Her gaze locked onto his thick manhood. "Hard and true and ever at the ready," emerged from her mouth. Her eyes startled up to meet his. She hadn't meant to speak the words aloud.

A knowing smile tipped up the right side of his mouth and sent a shot of lust straight through her. He'd been right: he knew exactly what she wanted and how. There was no use denying herself any longer.

In a pair of efficient motions, she straddled him and the chair. Poised inches above the glistening head of his manhood, her sex throbbed in anticipation of the press of him against her flesh. She leaned forward and braced one hand on the chair back, her loose hair falling around their faces and forming a silky curtain. Her other hand wrapped around the base of him. His pupils dilated, nearly extending to the outer edge of his irises.

Her hips lowered until the crown of his manhood touched the entrance of her sex. A heartbeat later, she began taking him inside her, his length a delicious, hard slide, until, at last, he filled her to completeness.

A breathy, "Oh," fell from her lips.

Impossibly, he felt better now than he had last night or even this afternoon. He kept getting better and better. She needed him more and more. He was the opiate, and she the addict. She would never get enough.

Her fingertips brushed across the patch of hair at the base of his cock. Lightly, almost reverently, they trailed up the ridged muscles of his stomach and across the wide expanse of his chest. Finally reaching his broad shoulders, she dug in her nails, tilted her hips forward, and ground further down onto him.

Fluttery waves of pleasure and pain shot through her. Nothing beyond the points where their bodies met mattered. This must be how an addict felt the moment the drug filled the lungs.

She wanted to take him in slowly and deliberately, but each thrust of her hips stripped her resolve away until all that was left was an overwhelming urge to feed this desire that refused to be slaked. Still, she would try, her thighs tensing and releasing, sliding her up and down him. Her forehead met his, her hair encircling them, her sweat mingling with his as it dripped between their bodies.

"Fuck me, Mariana," he whispered into her ear, impossibly notching up her lust for him.

His long, capable fingers reached out and gripped her hips, steadying her before he increased the rhythm of his thrusts. Mariana's sense of control spiraled away as his body demanded more of her. She was reduced to a raw nerve capable of nothing other than giving and receiving pleasure.

And she cared not.

Not when the pleasure spiked ever higher and higher, winding her sex ever tighter and tighter until she reached the sweetest spot of anxiety.

"Nick," she cried out, "please."

His fingers found her face and pushed her hair back. "Look at me," he demanded. Her eyes found his. "And do not look away."

His gaze holding her in thrall to him, he returned his hands to her hips and began measuredly moving her atop him as if rationing out his strokes one . . . at . . . a . . . time.

Sudden and unexpected intimacy flared between them as their gazes held fast onto each other. Her sex began to curl inward and tighten. Storm cloud gray held and steadied her as a glorious and unstoppable momentum accumulated in her core and began to overtake her. She reached, she strived up toward a freedom that only he could provide. A few more strokes and her sex shattered in climax, tiny earthquakes of pleasure rippling through her as she shook off the bound world and tumbled into ecstasy.

"Mariana," fell from his mouth as his hips continued their relentless thrust into her once . . . twice before he shouted out his own release.

All that remained of him and her was a confusion of breath. Lungs expanding, lungs contracting in arrhythmic pants. Her chin fit perfectly into the hollow of his collarbone. She'd known that once. Now she knew it again.

"Mariana," she heard as if from a great distance. Her eyes squeezed shut in protest. *Too soon.*

His hands reached up to gently cup her face. She resisted the urge to nuzzle into their warmth and, instead, followed their direction. She shifted her weight back and faced him square.

He pressed forward and touched his lips to hers.

It was an almost chaste kiss—the sort of kiss that shouldn't follow such an animalistic coupling.

It was a perfect kiss.

It was just the sort of kiss that could weaken a woman's resolve.

Without deepening the kiss, he broke away, a shy smile on his lips. "It occurred to me that we hadn't yet done that."

Mariana felt exposed. How did a simple kiss have the power to shatter her after what they had just done?

Yet it wasn't simply the kiss. It was the coo of his voice, too. Soft and sweet, she didn't recognize that voice . . . because she'd never heard it. Nick had never spoken to her thus. Or looked at her thus.

Actually, that wasn't true. He had the same look earlier tonight. It was a look that could give a woman hope . . . If she didn't know better.

Her spine stiffened, and her feet hit the floor. When she pushed off him to a stand, her traitorous body experienced a momentary pang for the loss of him. At least, she hoped it was momentary.

*Hope.* How recently she'd experienced that emotion. How soon it had crushed her.

She moved to the foot of the bed and perched against its edge. Eyebrows drawn together, a bewildered Nick stared out at her.

"What changed between this afternoon and tonight?" he asked.

She should've been glad he'd spoken the words first. But she wasn't. A naïve part of her thought she could seduce Villefranche and leave Paris without an accounting with Nick.

"We must talk about why you are here in Villefranche's rooms."

She forced out a dry laugh. "I prefer to be dressed for that particular conversation."

Drained of the fiery energy that had propelled her

through this day and night, she stood heavily and trod to the dressing table where her clothes lay.

He reached for his discarded trousers and proceeded to jerk them up his legs. "Mariana"—

Notes of frustration infused his voice. Good. That was a start.

—"we must discuss your intentions tonight if we are to salvage—"

"Salvage?" she shot out as she swung around to face him, reinvigorated by the coming confrontation. "There is nothing between us to *salvage*." A confounded silence stretched between them. "How long have you known Percy is alive?"

The question seized control of the room, sinking in and settling between them where it would remain forever. The flummoxed expression clouding his features told her that he didn't understand that yet.

"Ten years," he stated flatly. He sounded . . . unapologetic.

Like that, Mariana's anger returned like an Arctic fury. It was an anger that would sustain her through this conversation, through this night, and on through to London. "How could you keep it a secret?"

Nick grabbed his shirt and shrugged it onto his shoulders. A pang of loss for the sight of his gorgeous body shot through her. It sank in that this was really happening. Impossibly, a part of her had been hanging on to the hope that there were correct words to fix this situation—that he and she could be salvaged.

"It wasn't my secret to tell," he said, pitching his body into a deceptively lazy sprawl in the chair opposite hers.

"Olivia is my sister," she began righteously, "and I am your—"

"Wife? Make up your mind." His gaze held hers. "Percy was in too deep, and I couldn't risk exposing him. Then time kept passing, and he kept staying buried. It was never my place to tell."

"How could you be so ruthless?" she fired back. "Are you so without feeling? Are you so without humanity?"

He pushed to a stand, impatience evident.

"Do not come near me," she stated, slowly enunciating each word.

He stopped cold. "Percy has naught to do with *us*."

"How can you say that? After all the secrets and lies, I could never trust you."

"Percy was part of a life that had naught to do with you." He took a step forward. "A life I'm leaving behind."

"Why bother? You will never change."

"I'm not saying I shall." He took another step forward. "You are in my blood, Mariana. That will never change. I'm done fighting it."

"I'm in your blood? How dare you speak those words to me? That has never been our problem. The problem is that I've never been in your heart."

Another step brought him within a few feet of her. She had only to reach out to bring her body into contact with his. But what would that accomplish?

"You want me, too."

So bold were his words. She could ignore or deny them, but neither would do. Only the truth would serve this night. "I've wanted you too much," she confessed.

His eyes searched hers. "Is it ever too much?"

"There is nothing substantial about you. Nothing I can hold onto. You always slip through my fingers."

She stood and made to step past him. She must leave. There was nothing more to say.

Her flight, however, was arrested when he said, "I love you."

Contained within his gaze was more emotion than she

would have thought possible: anger, fear, and love. Yes, love. How had she never noticed before? And now that she had?

It was too late. Sometimes love wasn't enough.

"I know," she said. "But here's what else I know about you: that other life, too, is in your blood, and I can't compete with it. I leave Paris at dawn."

"This isn't what you want."

"Perhaps not," she returned, "but it is what I need."

She turned and strode through the doorway without a single backward glance. She had some packing to complete and a restless night to suffer through. Then it was on to London . . . And on with her life. The same life she'd been leading these last ten years. And if a little voice protested that it wasn't possible? That Paris had changed her? She would pack that away as well.

What couldn't be isolated so easily was the wretched feeling that a bottomless void yawned at her feet and would consume her.

She'd survived it once.

Perhaps she would survive it again.

# Chapter 26

*Kettle of Fish: When a person has perplexed his affairs in general, or any particular business, he is said to have made a fine kettle of fish of it.*

*A Classical Dictionary of the Vulgar Tongue*
Francis Grose

*The Cotswolds*
*Two Days Later*

The carriage veered a sharp right, and Mariana's eyes startled open. She averted her gaze from Hortense, fast asleep on the seat across from her, and toward the view of an undulant green hillside racing alongside the carriage as it careened down Little Spruisty Folly's long, straight drive.

The familiarity of the scene released a measure of the tension that had been twisting her insides into knots for two days now. This patch of earth never failed to have that effect on her, even though this visit hadn't been part of the day's plan.

Just this morning, after a breakneck journey by land and by sea, Mariana had arrived in London with Hortense in tow. She'd immediately called upon the children's schools: first, the Westminster School to apprise Geoffrey of her return and deliver the box of French bon-bons. Then she was off to see Lavinia at the Progressive School for Young Ladies and the Education of Their Minds, where she was greeted at the front doorstep by Mrs. Bloomquist.

A minor rat problem—as if there was any such thing as a *minor* rat problem—had been discovered, and the students sent home a few days ago. The rat catchers and their terriers would have the run of the building for the duration of the week. Mariana thanked Mrs. Bloomquist for her dedication to the cause before making her way to the Duke of Arundel's mansion where Olivia had occupied a wing since her marriage.

Once there, she discovered that Olivia had decided to take advantage of the surprise holiday and whisk their daughters away to the Folly for an impromptu visit. Geoffrey had chosen to remain at Westminster and try out his bribe on the unsuspecting cook.

"Well, I'm off to the countryside, it would appear," Mariana had informed Hortense, unable to hide her annoyance at the inconvenience of it all. "You are free to stay behind in London, if you like."

"I was instructed not to leave your side until I receive explicit notice that all the loose ends of the French business are tied up."

Mariana wouldn't ask from whom this directive originated.

"Besides," Hortense continued, "I wouldn't mind seeing more of the country of my birth."

Mariana experienced a jolt of shock at the girl's revelation and immediately upbraided herself for it. Nothing should shock her anymore.

Now gazing out the window, she allowed some of the weight from the last few days to slide off her. She was arriving at the golden hour of dusk when the countryside, from gently rolling hills to the crowns of stately horse-chestnuts, burnished bronze in the warm glow of the setting sun. This was the most beautiful hour at the Folly, aside from dawn, of course. Where dawn bloomed with a dewy, yet crisp, clarity, dusk stole in with a still seductive softness irresistible to her.

Soothed by the subtle rocking motion of the carriage, she allowed her eyes to glaze over and her mind to drift back to the previous morning. She'd been on the road as soon as dawn had allowed enough light for travel, the previous night's sustaining, and protective, anger having left her numb, yet determined.

Once in Calais, she'd wasted no time locating Captain Nylander. True to his word, he was willing to make a quick detour and transport her back to England before making his way to more exotic locales.

*Nylander.* She'd been right not to involve him in her marriage woes. On the surface—his powerful, sun-kissed, tempting surface—he was exactly the sort of man a woman would use to forget another man.

But a closer study revealed vulnerability cloaked within his impenetrable reserve that most surely missed. She intuited that he'd been used by a good number of women in his life, and she wouldn't add herself to their number. He would want more of her than her body, and she couldn't offer him that. And why not?

Her eyes fluttered shut before flying open. Closed eyes only emboldened the memory of her and Nick's last time together. How had she allowed herself to fall in love with her husband . . . again? And now the inevitable emptiness was beginning to expand within her . . . again.

Nick's words would return to her in counterpoint: she was in his blood . . . he loved her. She could almost convince herself that the words were enough. But they weren't.

Nick was a man who bent circumstances and people to his whim and will. She refused to be bent any further. One more fold, and she would surely break.

Her fingertips brushed across her sternum where her beloved locket once lay. Now it was gone, forever. In all honesty, it was better this way. The locket had been yet another excuse to hold onto a past that held no future—a phantom lacking all substance. And yet some phantoms had felt so substantial, so real . . . The Woolly Mammoth. She mustn't allow herself to consider the Woolly Mammoth.

Nothing with Nick was real. The man told lies for a living. Take Percy, for example. Percy was alive. She wished she wasn't riding out to the Folly armed with that particular knowledge.

*Stay dead.*

Those had been her parting words to him. A few days ago, she'd meant them, but now she saw the matter differently. To keep quiet about Percy would betray all she and Olivia meant to one another. It would make her no better than Nick.

Olivia had come to her with the news of Nick's "affair" before it reached her ears any other way. She would do the same for Olivia. It was only a matter of time before the gossip rags caught wind of Percy. She only hoped she could find the right words. Whatever they might be.

The carriage hooked another right, offering the first full view of the Folly's mish-mash of a house that sprawled too haphazardly to be called beautiful. Yet now it felt somewhat stripped of its usual welcome warmth.

Uncle Bertie had been in some way involved with the French assassination plot. It was her prerogative to avoid the issue and pretend it never happened. After all, their only discussion about it had been veiled. But it wasn't her nature. When she next saw Uncle Bertie, which could be in minutes as the carriage was now slowing to a stop, she would have to confront the issue straightaway. She suspected him as guilty as Nick, perhaps more so, in the Percy business. But she would hear it from his lips before she jumped to any rash conclusions.

Hortense's coal black lashes fluttered open, revealing eyes the opaque and striking blue of a stone from the

Americas that she'd once beheld. Turquoise. How was it she hadn't noticed before now that the girl was quite a beauty?

"We've arrived," Mariana began. "How shall we—"

"I shall be your lady's maid until I hear otherwise," Hortense supplied.

The carriage ground to a stop, and a coachman handed Mariana down. She heard the crunch of Hortense's boot on gravel behind her.

"This place is much grander than I'd ever imagined."

Mariana faced the girl. "Have you spent much time imagining the Folly?"

Hortense shifted on her feet. "I've heard bits and pieces about Bertrand Montfort's Folly," she said, her gaze sliding away noncommittally.

Mariana couldn't recall ever having mentioned the place to Hortense in any detail, but once her feet crossed the house's threshold, the sound of girlish laughter drifting down a corridor entirely distracted her from the matter. She didn't want to continue with these spy intrigues; she wanted to feel the warm embrace of her sister and a pair of giggly girls.

She wanted soft and fuzzy love, not cold, hard reality. In short, she wanted a respite.

She assured the attending servants that she would prefer to announce herself before allowing her feet to cross the sun-bright foyer toward the inviting melodies of song, piano, and laughter. It was pure, unrestrained laughter—the sound of happiness and the joy of a family gathered round, enjoying a private joke. She wanted nothing more than to be nestled inside the center of that joke.

When she reached the drawing room, she hesitated in the relative dark of the corridor and observed the tableau spread before her. Lavinia and Lucy, giggling and singing ditties at the piano, were on one side of the room, blithely indifferent to Olivia on the other side of the room. She was crouched nearly into a ball on a footstool, her eyes lifted toward the raucous duo, even as her hand busily moved across the paper on her lap. Everyone in the family had long grown accustomed to Olivia whipping out her sketchbook when inspiration struck, a pastime she'd taken up after Percy's death.

The pleasant momentum of Mariana's thoughts screeched to a halt. *Percy's death.*

Percy wasn't dead. Percy was alive.

"Auntie Mari!" sounded Lucy's voice.

Mariana shook off the unwelcome thought of Percy and stepped out of the shadow, all three sets of smiling eyes upon her and making it easy to forget the unpleasantness of Paris.

Lavinia sprang off the piano bench and bounded across the room into her arms. "I'm so happy to see you, dearest," Mariana said into her daughter's sable hair that smelled of lily and horse.

"Me, too, Mamma," she replied, already shaking off her mother's embrace and scampering off to rejoin Lucy at the piano. "Did you hear our new song?"

Mariana thought back. Ten seconds could have been ten days ago. "Was it Herr Beethoven's Symphony Number 5?"

"Lulu is writing lyrics for it," Lavinia said, adoration for her slightly older cousin evident in her bright, shining eyes.

As if on cue, Lucy began banging at the piano, reducing the sublimity of Herr Beethoven's masterpiece to its most rudimentary notes. She cleared her throat before singing out:

*"Lavinia loves horses*
*Catherine the Great did, too*
*So much in fact*
*It made her husband blue*
*It's even said . . .*
*With horrible dread . . .*
*That she took . . . them . . . to—"*

"Lucy," Olivia cut in evenly.

The musical interlude came to an abrupt stop, and a deafening silence filled the void. Olivia understood how to use her quiet reserve to great effect.

"Yes, Mummy?" Lucy asked, eyes all wide innocence.

"Perhaps this piece has veered a bit off track?"

"Perhaps," Lucy replied, sounding not at all convinced.

Mariana caught Olivia's eye. She recognized a smile in there for their precocious daughters. Words had never been all that necessary between them. Except now . . .

Now she harbored a secret that would change, possibly destroy, the life Olivia had built for herself this last decade.

As she closed the short distance between them, it occurred to Mariana that for the first time in her life she had no idea what to say to her sister. She settled onto the dense Aubusson carpet beside Olivia, who was still watchfully perched on the low footstool, and glanced at the half-finished sketch.

"You've captured them down to their most frivolous essence," Mariana said, her eyes lifting toward the duo, who had moved on to Herr Mozart, judging by the rapid succession of notes sounding from the piano. "Have you and the girls had the house to yourselves?"

"Until this morning," Olivia replied, a distracted note in her voice as she continued watching the girls and scratching charcoal against paper. "Uncle and Aunt arrived just before tea, and now you're here a few hours later."

"And where is Aunt?" Mariana asked when she really wanted to know about Uncle.

How difficult it was to stop being a spy.

"Resting," Olivia replied. "The journey from Paris was *quite traumatic*." Neither Mariana nor Olivia could resist a wry smile. They knew their aunt well.

"And Uncle?" Mariana asked, trying to sound natural, which meant she surely didn't. Olivia wouldn't miss that, but she might keep it to herself. Her still waters ran deep.

"In his study," she replied.

A comfortable silence settled in as they watched the girls compose another set of bawdy lyrics. Herr Mozart would have been delighted. Herr Beethoven? Likely not.

Olivia's hand stilled, and her discerning gaze focused on Mariana. "You are altered from when I last saw you."

"Me?"—Mariana forced a laugh—"I never change. You know that."

"Do I?" Olivia's head tilted quizzically. "Sometimes I feel like there's an entire world inside you that I know nothing about."

"You would be the only person who sees that in me."

"Oh, I think there is one other person," Olivia said, discreetly returning her attention to the sketch.

She was, of course, speaking of Nick.

"You've always liked Nick," Mariana said, trying, and failing, to keep a crack out of her voice. It was the first time she'd spoken his name since she'd left Paris.

"For the most part," Olivia said on a nod. "I just wish he'd made you happier, but with that poisonous mother and father of his, I'm not sure he knew how."

A sudden charge of emotion clogged Mariana's throat. Olivia never wasted time with small talk. She cut straight to the quick.

Olivia continued in her soft, reedy voice, "You found him?"

"Oh, yes," Mariana croaked. She couldn't help a dry laugh. "Look at us. Two married spinsters."

Olivia's eyebrows knit together. "I'm a widow, Mariana."

"Of course," she said quickly, a needle of panic shooting through her.

"But I do see what you mean," Olivia continued.

"You do?"

"I've made the choice to be alone." A moment passed. "Like a spinster."

"Is that what you truly want?"

"Marriage isn't for me. I've made my peace with that."

"Is peace of mind enough for you?" Mariana's stomach twisted again into its familiar knots as she anticipated Olivia's reply.

Olivia, her blue eyes clear, bright, and razor sharp, faced her squarely. "Yes."

Mariana picked up on an unexpected hard edge in her sister's voice. She also couldn't help noting the blush pinking her sister's cheeks. Olivia's physical cues didn't match the content of her words. If she disregarded those words, Mariana would suspect Olivia didn't seem peaceful at all. Of course, Olivia rarely spoke of Percy. Mariana had always assumed it was because the past was too painful a place to revisit. But, just now, it seemed . . . different.

"I forgot the anniversary of Percy's death in July," Olivia said, a humorless huff of a laugh escaping her. "The Duke had to remind me."

Mariana detected a strand of guilt in Olivia's tone. A surge of anger and protectiveness swept through her at the very idea that Olivia would feel the slightest measure of guilt over a man like Percy.

"Can you believe it's been eleven years?" Olivia asked. "It feels like yesterday."

"Time can be a trickster," Mariana said to buy time, her mind racing.

Olivia deserved better than peace. She deserved better than to feel guilt over her conscienceless cad of a husband. She deserved the truth. She deserved . . .

Freedom.

Impulsively, Mariana snatched up Olivia's hand and rose, pulling her sister across the room and through the doorway. The girls at the piano didn't notice. Mariana guided them to the little window seat situated beneath the crook of the main staircase. Many an afternoon she and Olivia had spent here telling each other their deepest, darkest secrets. Tonight, Mariana had one last deep, dark secret to tell.

She looked into her sister's eyes. "There is more about Paris."

A knowing smile lit up Olivia's face. "Is it about Nick?" Olivia reached for Mariana's hands and squeezed. "I am so happy for you. I knew you and Nick would find your way to each other again."

Mariana's stomach simultaneously heaved and sank. "No, Olivia. Quite the opposite, actually." She inhaled a deep breath and took the plunge. "Percy is alive."

Olivia's wide, happy gaze transformed into one bewildered and incredulous. "Percy is alive," she repeated. "It seems I would have heard about this sooner."

"I'm not sure you would know him. He is a spy, and . . . altered."

"Alive . . . a spy . . . altered," Olivia repeated slowly. "You're certain it was he?"

Mariana nodded. "It was he."

Olivia's gaze fixed on the dusky, bucolic view outside the window. Reserved and watchful Olivia always took her time to process her feelings. Much the opposite of bold, brash Mariana.

"Did he happen to mention when he is coming home?"

Mariana hadn't imagined this conversation could get any more difficult, but it just had. "I don't think he has any intention of coming home." She hesitated, hoping to find any sequence of words that would comfort her sister. "I know you love—"

Olivia pinned Mariana with a piercing glare. "Love? What on earth does love have to do with Percy and me?" She shot to a stand and gazed down at a confused Mariana. "You will stay with the girls and bring them back to London in a few days?"

"You're up to London?"

Olivia nodded. "I must speak to the Duke."

"Be careful," Mariana said. "It will be the shock of the Duke's life to hear that his favorite son has risen from the dead."

Olivia leaned over and swiped a quick kiss onto Mariana's cheek before whispering into her ear. "You will stand with me? No matter what I choose to do?"

She shifted backward to better meet Olivia's gaze. "No matter what."

Olivia nodded once before swiveling and dashing down the corridor to say good-bye to Lucy. Her eyes fast on Olivia's receding back, Mariana knew that Olivia's course was set, and that she would share her decision when she was ready. Mariana experienced a rush of hope for her sister.

She allowed a few minutes to pass before she made her way back to the drawing room where Lucy and Lavinia were still busily composing lyrics to Herr Mozart, blessedly oblivious to recent familial developments. There would be time for that in the coming days, weeks, and months, she suspected.

As if drawn by a magnetic force, her feet carried her past the girls and through the room, nimbly navigating Aunt Dot's haphazard groupings of settees, tables, and randomly acquired bibelot from years of indiscriminate shopping excursions.

At last, Mariana found herself standing before the set of French doors overlooking the terrace, across a wide expanse of closely cropped grass, and on down to the copse of trees on the other side of the ha-ha.

Another moonlit night came to mind. A girl full of wild hopes, fears, and dreams she'd been that night. And now?

Now she wasn't as far removed from that girl as she liked to believe. Those wild hopes, fears, and dreams were like sticky burrs caught within her heart, tenacious little irritants that refused to let go and let be.

Now that she'd told Olivia the truth, she understood it was impossible to continue with the fiction that she'd left Paris behind. Paris had followed her.

Paris had reminded her of who she'd been all this time. She didn't want to be a married spinster. She knew that fact deep within her bones. And she could no longer deny it. Perhaps there was a man for her out there . . .

Her gaze caught a movement at the edge of the woods and narrowed. A responsive spark raced through her, lighting up dormant nerve endings as it went. Only a few weeks ago, she would have thought nothing of that shadow. Now she pressed her nose to the glass and tracked the shadow as it moved along the edge of the tree line. It could be a deer, a hare, an owl on his first flight of the evening . . . Her gut told her otherwise. She waited, her breath accelerating . . . And waited, her heart threatening to pound through her chest . . . She waited so long that she nearly gave up—patience had never been her signature virtue—when the shadow emerged from the copse, efficiently scaled the low ha-ha wall, and sprinted across the lawn toward the house.

Uncle Bertie's study lay at the end of that particular wing, and only one man moved like that particular shadow. Paris wasn't finished with her yet.

Instinctively, she turned the door handle and was halfway across its threshold before she remembered the girls. "I think I'll catch a breath of moonlight," she called over her shoulder.

Just as the door was closing behind her, she heard Lucy's voice sing out, "Lavinia, let's try Moonlight Sonata!"

The door snapped shut, muting the raucous sound of Lucy and Lavinia, and night quiet settled into the air around her. Her back pressed against a chilly pane of glass, and her heart raced to the speed of her mind. She couldn't be absolutely certain that the shadow had been *him*. There was but one way to find out.

She flattened her body against the house and began moving carefully in its shadow, her feet creeping along its length, her deepest dread the snap of a twig or the twist of an ankle. Although it felt like it took forever, she reached the nearest window of Uncle Bertie's study in a matter of seconds. Cautiously, she ducked and stopped, hoping to steady her breath.

On the surface, all she could hear was the symphony of night—crickets chirruping, frogs croaking, owls hooting. As her breath settled, she began to discern another sound, a sound soft and persistent. The muffled sound of deep, masculine voices at odds, but intent on privacy, drifted from the study.

A quick appraisal of the French doors to her right revealed them to be cracked open a sliver. From her crouched position, she waddled closer in small increments. With each inch, the soft murmur of the voices coalesced into syllables, then words.

She counted to three before venturing a peek through glass. It was as she suspected: Uncle Bertie and Nick. While instinct bade her rush in and confront the two men, good sense dictated she stay put. More was to be gained from listening. For now.

"Those men in your hotel suite were intended to scare you off, except—" This was Uncle's deep, mellifluous voice.

"They didn't," Nick interrupted. "I stayed and went underground, and you had to find a way to flush me out."

The deep notes of his voice emerged strong and assured, appealing to the wrong side of her. She had an incurable sickness for the man.

"I figured she would do the trick."

*She*? In a flash Mariana knew that she was *she*.

"You didn't count on her partnering with me," Nick stated flatly.

*Partnering?* The word sounded so very . . . equal.

Was that how Nick saw her? As his equal?

"I didn't think you would be foolish enough to involve her," came Uncle's response.

What was so foolish about involving her?

Before she could reconsider, or even consider, her intent, her palm pressed flat against the door, pushing it wide, and her feet boldly led her through its threshold.

Twin incredulous expressions greeted her, releasing another frisson of excitement inside her.

"I would appreciate it if you would stop talking about me as if I'm not here."

# Chapter 27

*Brim: (Abbreviation of Brimstone.) An abandoned woman; perhaps originally only a passionate or irascible woman, compared to brimstone for its inflammability.*

*A Classical Dictionary of the Vulgar Tongue*
Francis Grose

Nick must appear an utter simpleton, flat-footed and flummoxed, as Mariana sailed into the room like a wrathful fury, chest heaving, eyes flashing. But there was no help for it.

"I shan't be discussed like some pawn in your game of chess," she stated, coming to a decisive stop before him and Montfort. "I'm a woman of means, both worldly and intellectual, who makes her own decisions."

"My dear," Montfort began on a plaintive note.

Nick's ears perked up. He'd never heard that particular sound emit from the unflappable Bertrand Montfort. This night grew more interesting, and more confounding, by the moment.

"Do not *my dear* me, Uncle," she stated, effectively shushing the man.

Nick settled back, perching lightly against the solid oak table at his back. Mariana had seized total command of the room, and he was inclined to let her have it. Anything that upset Bertrand Montfort's equilibrium was welcome.

The fact of the matter was that he'd been unable to uncover a shred of physical evidence linking Montfort to the assassination plot. But he'd come here anyway with the intention of bluffing the man out and finding out his motive for initiating the entire business. In fact, he'd skipped London altogether for that very reason.

Well, there had been another reason: by avoiding London, he'd thought to avoid Mariana. Clearly, fate had other ideas.

"Let me see if I have this straight, Uncle," she said. "You sent cutthroats to—what?—murder Nick?"

"They were meant to warn him off the French king intrigue. Nothing more."

Nick couldn't help but enjoy watching Montfort squirm beneath Mariana's wrath and righteousness. Bertrand Montfort had never squirmed a day in his life. "I'm fairly certain," Nick cut in, "I mortally wounded one of them."

"They were ruffians," Montfort dismissed. "They deserved no better."

"They may have had families who depended on them," Mariana countered, her attention landing on Nick for a fleeting second before returning to Montfort.

But for Nick that split second of her attention felt like the warm glow of a springtime sun after an overlong winter. Forty-eight hours, give or take a few minutes, was entirely too long to have been without her.

"Ah, my dear," Montfort began, paternal condescension coating every syllable, "unfortunately that is not the world in which we live. Hard bargains are made, and hard bargains driven home. It's easy to forget such realities in our paradise of the Folly."

Mariana's eyes flashed fire. "Don't you dare patronize me," she said, her voice a lowered octave. "I'm coming to know about you, Uncle. The sweet uncle you've appeared to be is at disturbing odds with the ruthless operator revealed in Paris."

Montfort's gaze swung toward Nick. "Does she know about Bretagne?"

"I know about Percy," Mariana spoke up, clearly annoyed by the exclusion.

Still, Montfort continued to address Nick. "What does she know?"

Mariana shot Nick an irritated glance before pinning her uncle with an unflinching glare. "I know," she began, "he's been part of your spy network these last eleven years."

A short, surprised laugh sputtered out of Montfort. "*My* spy network? Percy Bretagne would gnaw off his own hand before he would work for me again . . . or fake his death yet again."

"Can you blame him?" Nick asked.

"Perhaps not," Montfort replied with an almost imperceptible shrug.

"What am I missing?" Mariana's eyes darted back and forth between the men.

Montfort shut his mouth and averted his gaze, leaving it to Nick to put this matter to bed once and for all. Nick cleared his throat. He should have told Mariana in Paris. "Although everyone thought him dead after the Battle of Maya"—He hesitated a moment—"Percy actually suffered from amnesia."

Mariana's brows knit together. "Memory loss? Olivia had him declared dead *in absentia*. Two witnesses testified to having dug his grave after the retreat."

"Your uncle"—Nick jutted his chin toward Montfort—"knew from the beginning that Percy was alive and began using him to gather intelligence without telling him who he really was." Mariana's expression darkened, a sure sign of the storm building inside her. "By the time I crossed paths with Percy in Spain, it had been a year since his *death*. I felt obliged to do something for him." Nick hesitated at the memory. He'd never encountered a man more in need of a lifeline. "He needed to know his past . . . who he was."

"You helped him recover his memory and get away from Uncle by"—Understanding dawned across her face—"faking his death."

Nick nodded once. The way she spoke the words, as if she'd switched angles and was now viewing him from a fresh perspective, made his insides go light.

"You gave him his life back."

And now he felt something more . . . something he'd thought long lost: hope.

"I wouldn't go that far," he said, attempting to rein in the feeling.

It didn't work.

It felt as though a tectonic shift had occurred between them, strangely connecting them through its trauma.

"What Percy chooses to do with his life is his decision, but you gave him the opportunity. And you never told anyone," she finished on a whisper.

Nick intuited what she left unsaid: you never told *me*. No matter how connected to him she might feel, his deception continued to form a barrier between them.

"I couldn't betray Percy's trust. But mostly"—Finally, he was free to tell her every last drop of the truth—"I couldn't betray his life. I didn't know—"

Her eyes brightened with epiphany. "What my uncle would do. Who knows what a man who would withhold an amnesiac's memory from him—an amnesiac who happened to be his nephew-in-law, by the way—is capable of?"

Nick nodded.

"You've been protecting Percy all along."

Nick remained silent, afraid to reply, afraid to move, afraid to break the gossamer spell that held their gazes locked. He detected nascent trust in there.

Montfort shifted on his feet, drawing Mariana's attention. "Uncle, do I even know you?" she spat. "You not only hid

Percy, but you used a sick man to do your dirty work. Are you incapable of empathy or remorse? You owe Percy."

"I owe Percy? What? An apology?" Montfort sputtered. "For turning a frivolous boy into a man? Percy Bretagne was champing at the bit to make something of himself. I presented him the opportunity he craved. He took it."

"He may be a *man*, but what of his humanity?" she countered.

"That is his concern," Montfort replied. "Every person on God's green earth has to figure out how to live his or her life. For some"—He held out his hands, palms facing the ceiling. He lifted one—"life clicks easily into place. For others"—He lifted the other—"life is the eternal puzzle."

Mariana took a step closer to Montfort. "You sent men to murder—"

"Not murder, my dear," Montfort interjected.

"—Nick," she pressed. "Why have you betrayed our family?"

"Betrayed our family?" asked Montfort, visibly bewildered. "My dearest Mariana, all I want is your happiness. You are like a daughter to me. This place"—He spread his arms wide—"will be yours one day. I would never betray you."

"And what of my husband?" she asked quietly. "A betrayal of him is a betrayal of me."

*My husband.* Those words filled a space within Nick that he hadn't realized was empty. The possessive *my*. And no longer *Nick*, but a husband. *Her* husband.

"Here is what will happen, Uncle. Now that you know Percy is alive, and now that Nick has foiled the assassination plot, you will let this entire matter pass."

"Of course, my dear," Montfort replied, recovering a dash of his usual sangfroid, "think no more of it."

"Furthermore"—She paused, allowing the weight of the

matter to sink in—"you will retire from Whitehall, thereby leaving your reputation and family intact."

Montfort's smug smile slipped a notch. Nick might have to accept that his wife had outmaneuvered them all. He'd never seen anyone put Bertrand Montfort in his place. Yet here was Mariana doing just that. Pride swelled within him. He may have lost her, but he'd once possessed this glorious woman.

"In exchange," she continued, "I shall remain a niece to you, and my children will stay part of your life." She inhaled deeply. "This isn't about you. This is about my children, Aunt Dot, and the unity of the family. I believe you love us, but that your love is sometimes misguided. Mayhap your retirement to country life will help you see that. Otherwise, you will lose family, standing, and reputation. I know the power and reach of a gossip rag."

Montfort darted a quick glance toward Nick before walking over to a sidebar stocked with crystal decanters of varying shapes and sizes. He very deliberately set out three stout tumblers and poured a few fingers of whiskey in each. "To my retirement?" he asked as he handed out the tumblers.

They raised their glasses in unison and gulped the fiery liquid down. Mariana didn't even sputter.

"You drive a hard bargain, my dear," Montfort said, his demeanor sheepish, but not cowed. He would recover from this night. Men like Bertrand Montfort always did.

There were others, however, who weren't so lucky.

"And what of Percy Bretagne?" Nick asked. He would have an accounting from Montfort before this night was through.

"What of him?" Montfort's eyes held a challenge within their depths. He flipped open the lid of a cigar box and silently offered one to Nick.

He shook his head, refusing to be distracted. "You won't pursue him now that his cover is blown?" He wanted an assurance stated explicitly. Mariana had only seen the tip of the iceberg where Montfort was concerned. His ruthlessness ran as dark and deep as the ocean itself.

"I rather expect it will be the other way around," Montfort replied, snipping off one end of his cigar before striking a match and gently puffing it alight. Cigar smoke reached out and permeated the air with its rich, earthy aroma.

Nick shifted impatiently on his feet. He wanted more from Montfort, whose hands invariably emerged from the messiest of situations spotless. A question plagued him. "Was the Foreign Office involved in the assassination plot?"

"You know the answer to that question."

"You directed a rogue operation to assassinate a future French king." Confirmation settled in Nick's gut. "Why?"

"For England's security, of course," Montfort replied. "I thought you of all people would understand that, even if you don't agree with my methods."

"How does plunging France into the throes of another revolution keep England secure?"

From the corner of his eye, Nick saw Mariana's head tilt in curiosity. She wanted to know the answer, too.

"Whitehall has been trying, and failing, to get a constitutional monarchy established in that self-important mess of a country for years." Montfort shuffled to the library side of the room and settled his massive girth onto a plush leather sofa, allowing an arm to rest comfortably along its spine of shiny brass tacks. Mariana didn't move to follow, so neither did Nick. He would stand with her.

"Get rid of Louis, Charles, and their cabal of Ultra-Royalists, and we have a shot at French stability," Montfort continued. "What's a few years of revolution in the grand scheme? Those nincompoops are going to incite another one at the rate they're going anyway. Reparations for dispossessed nobility?" He chortled drily. "That will never work. But get a man on the throne with the right ideas—

Louis-Philippe of the Orléans branch would like a shot at it—and an understanding of his obligations to those who put him on the throne, and then we've really gotten somewhere."

"Are you speaking of a puppet government?" Nick interjected. "Do you think it even a remote possibility that the French would allow you to influence policy?"

Montfort shrugged noncommittally. "A monarchy limited by a constitution and a parliament is the only long-term solution."

"What of the short-term effect of an assassination that would change the regime of a nation?"

"What of it?"

"Revolution."

"Haven't you been paying attention? There will be a revolt either way. This way, at least, England would have control over the outcome."

"You've completely overstepped the mark."

"The price for peace is often war," Montfort said with a finality that brooked no opposition.

Mariana stepped forward, her gaze locked fast onto her uncle. "Have you not considered your own great-nephew, Geoffrey? Did it not occur to you that he could become caught up in future conflicts that would have been a direct result of the plot?"

"Not our Geoffrey," Montfort replied with a dismissive flick of his wrist.

"Uncle," she pressed, "every family has a Geoffrey."

Montfort's response was a nonchalant sip of his whiskey, and it was all Nick could do to remain in place, to not stride across the room and knock that uncaring expression off his face. A specific sort of madness and an inflated sense of his own importance had overtaken a formerly good man. One had to experience a great deal of evil in the service of good in espionage. Over time, the two twisted together and, for some, became a Gordian knot, impossible to separate.

This was what happened to men who remained in the game too long. And, no doubt, Montfort had been in too long.

"I've reached the end of my involvement with the Foreign Office," Nick said. "I came here tonight to tell you that as well."

Although he felt the heat of Mariana's gaze on his cheek, he refused to meet it. Too many unspoken words simmered between them.

A pompous smile curved Montfort's mouth. "In all honesty, it's about time."

"Too late for fatherly concern now," Nick replied.

"Of course not. It's been obvious for some time that your stomach for the game on the ground has grown weak. A transition into strategic operations could be arranged."

Montfort rocked back and forth a few times before hoisting himself off the sofa. He made his ponderous way to the sidebar. "You may be right about retirement," he conceded. "No hard feelings?" His gaze darted between Nick and Mariana.

"I shall try not to take exception to the fact that you sent cutthroats to my hotel to *warn me off*," Nick replied.

"None of that, old boy," Montfort said on a step forward, landing a jocular slap to Nick's back. "Just a bit of a scare. No harm done."

Montfort grabbed a decanter and refilled all three glasses. He pivoted toward Nick. "Good bit of spy craft keeping Percy Bretagne a secret all those years." To Mariana, he said, "And you, my girl, I couldn't be prouder of you. You put me in my place tonight better than any grizzled, old professional"—He winked over at Nick—"could have. Well done, my dear." Montfort raised his glass. "To worthy adversaries and to England."

Nick and Mariana chose not to join.

Montfort absently set his glass down. "Nick, you will be staying the night, I presume."

"I . . ." Nick began. "I hadn't given it a thought."

"It's decided," Montfort called over his shoulder as he made his way toward his stately desk. "Your family are here, after all." He settled into his chair and leaned forward, his elbows planted on smooth, polished oak. It was clear that he'd regained control of the room. "Now, if you will pardon me, I have a resignation letter to compose."

Like that, Nick and Mariana were dismissed for the night like a pair of reprimanded children. His gaze slid toward her only to find her looking as incredulous as he felt. Montfort possessed an audacity that he could use to great effect when the moment required it. This was one such moment.

Tilted off-balance, Nick followed Mariana out of the room, her jasmine and neroli perfume trailing behind her, enveloping him in her scent. He inhaled.

The door clicked shut, and he found himself alone with her in the dimly lit corridor, its stillness and silence creating an unsettlingly intimate space. Separated by a few feet, they stood facing one another, awkward and tongue-tied.

"That ended—" she began on a sheepish wisp of a laugh that was gone barely before it was uttered.

"Unexpectedly?" he finished for her.

"Quite," she replied, her gaze focused on her feet.

A shyness pervaded and paralyzed the atmosphere. Not the sort of social paralysis that belonged to strangers who had never met, therefore had naught to say. Rather the opposite sort of paralysis that could suddenly strike two people who knew each other too well. They had nothing left to say . . . And everything left to say.

Where did one start when faced with the obvious? And it was obvious she felt it, too. For so long, they'd hidden behind carefully constructed defenses. Now those defenses had evaporated into the ether. And here they stood earthbound and stripped down, naked and exposed to one another.

"I'll be gone before first light," he said, understanding at once that his words were a test. Of whom, he wasn't certain.

Her gaze found him, and she blinked once . . . twice. She hadn't expected those words. Neither had he.

"You will say a good-night to Lavinia?" she asked, her previously steady and assured voice now thin and wavery.

The subject of their children had been a reliable and safe defensive position over the years. Now, it was back. He experienced a dull ache for what was lost.

"Of course," he said tightly. A bitter note wanted to sound.

Well, he wouldn't allow it. If she didn't respond with the imploring *stay* he longed to hear, he had no one to blame but himself.

"Nick?" came her voice.

His heart caught in his chest. "Yes?"

"Safe travels."

His heart released, and he nodded once. His body numb with despair—there was no less dramatic way of describing the feeling—he turned his back to her and strode down the hallway, his pace picking up with each step. It was the only option left to him. He must keep walking, placing one foot in front of the other.

Had he only imagined the force connecting them tonight? For a flicker of time in that room, she hadn't been irrevocably lost to him. He gave his head a shake to clear it.

Imaginings and wishes mattered not. They weren't tangible. He couldn't hold them in his hands, or envelop them within his arms. This position of having no control over the present or the future was a novel experience. But it was reality . . . his reality.

He'd played his hand.

And lost.

# Chapter 28

*Vagaries: Frolics, wild rambles.*

*A Classical Dictionary of the Vulgar Tongue*
Francis Grose

Nick cleared the ha-ha and stomped his way toward the copse of woods. It occurred to him that he was exhibiting all the symptoms of a lovesick wretch. He'd told himself he needed fresh air and blessed quiet to think, but the deeper into the woods he wandered, the worse he felt.

Simply put, he was heartbroken. He'd never experienced heartbreak before, at least, not that he was willing to admit to himself. The feeling was . . . singular. And, yes, wretched.

It was as if he'd been stripped of a vital organ, and all that was left in its absence was a hollow pit that ached and longed and could never be soothed or filled. Poetry didn't do the feeling justice, but he now understood the compulsion to try. Anything to relieve the anguish. For the poets, it was flowery words. For a man of action, it was a midnight ramble.

He should make his way back to the inn where his horse was stabled and ride like hell for London. His sanity likely depended on it. But, then again, he couldn't remember the last time he'd made a sane decision. Not since he'd laid eyes on Mariana in Paris, and certainly not in coming here tonight.

His feet carried him forward alongside thoughts that refused to be tethered to the back of his mind. An unconscious smile began to play about his lips. Mariana had handled Bertrand Montfort like a master, striding into that room and neutralizing her uncle within minutes. And Montfort . . .

Well, Nick could admit a grudging respect for the man. He'd chosen family over pride. Not many men were big enough to make that choice. Montfort had even voiced an admiration for his niece, a feeling to which Nick could well relate. Mariana was a rare woman.

A discordant thought wedged its way in. He'd waited too long to trust her—with his secrets, with his life, with his heart—and now time had run out. Some wounds ran too deep. Some heartbreaks were destined to forever be aching voids of the soul.

What mawkish rot.

He exhaled a rough breath and glanced around at the night wilderness rendered into various shades of gray by indifferent moonlight. Above, a soft breeze fluttered leaves cast dark slate against an indigo sky. Below, the undergrowth of shrubbery to either side of the path transformed into an indistinct morass by the deep ash darkness. A quiet world, both aurally and visually, surrounded him.

His eye happened upon a tiny grave marker to his left, and he stopped.

*Here lies Horace*
*A beagle after one's own bacon*

He wished he had a slice of ham with him to offer in remembrance. It didn't seem fitting that anyone should pass Horace's final resting place without a breakfast meat of one variety or another.

His feet resumed their ramble, his thoughts, too, resuming their newly established pattern of maudlin regret. Hopefully time would erase the maudlin part, but he suspected it had no fix for the regret.

His eye happened upon an object in the middle distance, momentarily diverting his morose state of mind. It was a slight, insignificant object. What lent it significance, however, was the simple fact that it glowed crisp and white against the dark and blurred world around it.

Curiosity piqued, he strode over and snatched it up. A line formed between his eyebrows as his mind registered the long, sinuous object in his hand: a diaphanous silk stocking the color of alabaster.

His head snapped up, his awareness of the surrounding wood suddenly razor sharp. Just ahead, at the bend in the path, he spotted another bright object. The stocking's mate. Within seconds, he held the matched pair, his feet continuing forward in a determined line.

Here was the thing about these stockings: they belonged to a lady. A servant frolicking with her lover didn't lose these stockings. If a servant had the good fortune to own a pair of stockings of this quality, she wouldn't forget them on a country path, no matter how diverting the tryst. A *lady* left these stockings.

If he didn't know better, he might think he was following a trail of crumbs. The crumbs in this case being a lady's undergarments. And not just any lady's undergarments, he knew deep in his bones.

Again, he scanned the area, but no more lady's finery jumped out at him. The path before him led to Duck Pond. He would know his way down this trail blindfolded. A hope threatened to blossom in his chest, a hope he must tamp down. He should know better by now. But the heart, it seemed, never learned.

After a few bends of the path, his eye snagged on another object, and his foot tripped on a root. In a single, efficient motion he righted himself and caught the object between forefinger and thumb. This item was smaller, yet more substantive. His heart kicked up a notch when the moon moved from behind a cloud and illuminated the bit of silk in his hand: a lady's garter—a lady's *fuchsia* garter.

A muted, rhythmic splashing caught his ear from just around the next curve of the path. It was coming from Duck Pond. His heart became a steady hammer in his chest. No longer could he deny this budding suspicion. Yet he couldn't quite allow himself to believe it either.

Slowly, almost reverently, he moved toward the noise. Almost as if he would spook her if he approached without proper intentions.

Proper intentions? What exactly would those be in this circumstance? He and Mariana didn't have a great record of abiding by *proper intentions*.

As he ascended the rise to the pond, he encountered more clothes—another garter, a dress, a shift, one boot, then the other. They lay haphazard as if they'd fallen off her body as she walked. Then he reached the top and all speculation, all thought, really, fell away at the sight before him: her naked form floating atop a black void of water, caressed by the mellow light of the moon's nocturnal rays. His breath suspended in his chest.

"I thought I might find you here," she called out.

Her words jolted a laugh from him, allowing his breath to release.

Playing along, he returned, "What a coincidence that you happened upon me."

Her serious gaze traveled across the water, dispelling the moment of levity. "I'm not sure I know you."

The directness of her words nearly leveled him, confirming what he already knew about his wife. She was formidable and brave. It was a rare strength to make one's self open and vulnerable. It was a strength he'd never possessed, but one he must summon if he was to slip inside this chance he was being offered. And he heard within her words a chance.

"Is that so very bad?" he asked, his body tense and hot with anticipation of her answer, as if his very life depended on it.

Perhaps it did.

~ ~ ~

"It might be very good," fell from her lips without thought. She was tired of thinking and overthinking. She was ready to succumb to a feeling, and she had a feeling about Nick.

"The man I thought you were made a lousy husband."

She began breaststroking toward the shore . . . toward *him* . . . luxuriating in the cool slide of water as it curved around her bare skin. Just before the water became too shallow to remain fully immersed, she halted her forward momentum and began to tread water. She had something to say to this man, and she preferred to say it from here with an insulating measure of distance between them.

"You couldn't tell me about Percy," she said. "I understand that now. You were protecting him from Uncle and . . . you were protecting me. You didn't want to come between me and a beloved family member. And"—She willed her voice not to crack with sudden emotion—"you've been that man all along."

She searched his face for a reaction, but he allowed her not the slightest glimpse into his thoughts. It was entirely possible that he'd only let her win at their card game in Paris. Unwelcome thought.

"Are you cold?"

Just as she began to shake her head, her body gave an involuntary shiver. "A blanket lies just to your right."

It didn't escape her notice that he'd evaded her words as if her praise had disconcerted him. If it was possible to fall more in love with her husband, she just did. This man was unaccustomed to recognition and thanks, his good works carried out alone and in the shadows, necessary and thankless.

Beneath her watchful gaze, he retrieved the blanket and spread it flat. Next, he shrugged off his overcoat and held it open before him. She glided forward. They both knew what was coming. She would step out of the water, naked.

Her feet found purchase on the bottom, and she began placing one foot in front of the other. Boldly, she rose out of the pond, like Botticelli's Venus. A frisson of excitement pulsed through her at the way his unblinking gaze drank her in.

Tempted by the warm, dry overcoat held out for her, she sidestepped it. Instead, she set foot on the dense, woolen blanket and laid herself flat and supine, face aimed at the stars. Maybe if she squinted hard enough, she could discern within the universe's depths a map to guide her through this night.

Nick hesitated no more than three heartbeats before joining her on the ground and silently stretching his long body alongside hers, their gazes now pointed in parallel at the night sky above. Awareness suffused the air.

Separated by a space no more substantial than an inch, a magnetic tension pulsed between them, daring them to succumb to the carnality achingly within reach. But, no, she would hold steady to the map she was improvising. She and he were on the border of a specific sort of territory . . . a territory too long unexplored. They must brave the edge.

"What I said in Paris was wrong." She inhaled and crept closer to the edge. "You are neither inhuman nor ruthless. All this time you were the man I spent an entire decade trying to forget how much I liked. And now I feel as if it might be safe to do so again. Why did you hide yourself, your true self, away from me all these years?" Her gaze steadily trained on the mute stars, she ventured further, "It wasn't due to your work with the Foreign Office."

A tense moment passed. Then another. And another. She thought he might not answer, but then he spoke. "From the first moment I saw you, I knew I wasn't worthy of you."

"Oh, Nick—"

He shook his head once, and she quieted. She must let him tell his story his way.

"I fled to the Continent in the name of Crown and Country, but mostly I fled you." He paused, and a nightingale trilled its lovely evening song. "This is the very spot where I first beheld you after that long year on the Continent."

"An experience seared into my memory, I can assure you."

"I wanted you to be nothing more than a too curious, too pretty girl—the sort of girl I'd met a thousand times over. I thought to shock you." She hazarded a stealthy sideways glance and detected an involuntary smile tipping up the side of his mouth. "I thought you would run for your life. Instead, you picked up my clothes, and I knew I had to have you." The smile fell from his lips. "It was instant."

Mariana rolled onto her side and propped herself up onto an elbow. She would see his face as he spoke the truth she yearned to hear.

"I wanted to understand this girl and her effect on me, as if it was quantifiable. Yet I knew on some elemental level that you were already mine and always would be"—His eyes found hers. He was at once so very close and so very far away—"You and I simply *were*. What we shared was inevitable . . . biological." He paused as if weighing how much to reveal. "*Elemental, inevitable, biological.* Those were the words I used to describe our bond. They were necessary words. Words intended to create distance. And never once did I allow myself to consider, much less admit, the one word that most accurately described my feeling."

Within his eyes she saw the ghosts from their past swirling. They were the same ghosts, she suspected, that had haunted her for the last decade.

Suddenly, he, too, rolled onto his side and propped himself up, his body a perfect mirror of hers with one exception: he remained fully clothed.

She sensed the breath hitch in his chest at the sight of her, his gaze unable to resist a roving scan of her naked form. A heady feeling of sensual power coursed through her, one she must suppress. She and he were on the verge of a truth that must reach the surface if there was to be a future for them.

"It was easy to tell myself," he continued at last, his voice a husky rasp, "that I had to keep my distance because of my connection to the Foreign Office. But the truth was I feared your effect on me. Our bond had come on so fast and so strong. It wasn't the sort of marriage I wanted. I wanted a Society match. It was my greatest fear that I would have a marriage like—"

"Your parents," she finished for him, feeling the confirmation of her words resonate deep within her gut.

"They began as a love match. And after the love curdled, they spent the majority of my childhood privately and publicly tearing one another apart. My understanding of love was that it inevitably collapsed, and that pure love eventually transformed into pure hate. From the very beginning, I knew our happy marriage was a mirage."

"Nick—" she began, but stopped herself. How she ached to ease his torment.

"Yet with each passing day my feeling for you increased."

"Only increasing your fear that we would repeat the mistakes of your father and mother," she ventured.

"You were my worst nightmare come to life."

Infused with a burst of nerves worthy of a green schoolgirl, she pushed herself up to a seated position, reached for the discarded overcoat, and draped it across her shoulders, reflexively inhaling the residue of his fading warmth.

He followed her up, his gaze never once releasing her. Again, they were mirrors of one another, yet he didn't seem nervous at all. Quite the opposite, in fact. It was this quality that had first drawn her in—his ability to remain ever calm and collected.

"I understood on a fundamental level that if I ever loved someone, I would have to let her go. I never had enough faith in myself, but mostly I never had enough faith in you. You are formidable, funny, intelligent, beautiful, loving, kind, brave . . . You are everything, Mariana. Even when my travels took me to distant lands and across oceans—"

"We still need to discuss the Mississippi riverboat," she inserted, unable to resist the pull toward humor, long dormant joy releasing within her and bubbling up. She wasn't nervous at all. In fact, she was ecstatically, effervescently happy.

"—You were *my* everything. I should have trusted you."

"No, Nick, you should have trusted *us*."

"Can you forgive me?" he asked, his gray gaze at once vulnerable and penetrating.

"I forgive you. After all"—Her buoyant heart threatened to lift out of her chest—"you did give me a Woolly Mammoth."

She tucked her hands into silk-lined pockets, and the slink of warm, supple metal wrapped around her fingers. Instantly, she knew what lay within her grasp. She pulled it from the pocket's depths.

"You've had it all this time?"

She held up the locket, its pendulous weight gently swaying from side to side, catching the transient shimmer of a moonbeam.

"Yes," he said without an ounce of apology.

"Why?"

"Because if I couldn't have you, I could, at least, have a piece of you. It was selfish, but I couldn't let it go. I couldn't let you go. Do you remember the words inscribed on the back?"

"*You are forever in my blood.*"

"A coward's words."

"I thought them lovely."

"You are forever in my blood, Mariana. You are forever in my heart."

He slid the chain from her slack fingers and leaned forward to reach around her neck. Her eyes fluttered shut, her other senses taking him in: the warm tickle of his fingertips as they worked on the latch; the catch of his breath in her ear; the release of his breath on her neck.

She could remain here, in this place and in this moment, forever. The weight of the locket settled onto her sternum, and she felt whole.

Of course, that feeling could also have something to do with the man whose arms encircled her neck. She sensed, rather than felt, his muscles tense as he began to shift backward. She couldn't allow that to happen; any amount of space between them was entirely unacceptable.

Her eyes flew open, and her hands shot up, grabbing his wrists, holding them suspended. Their noses nearly touching, eyes locked, breath mingling, she released her grasp and reached up to gently caress his face, hard angles unyielding beneath her touch.

Her fingertips began trailing across his face the way a blind person memorizing each individual detail of a lover might do. It wasn't enough to know him by sight. She would know him by touch.

"I am here, Nick, a flesh and blood woman, not a mirage. I'm not going anywhere."

When her fingers found his yielding lips, it was his turn

to wrap his fingers around her wrists.

"You never played predictably or safely," he said into the scant breadth of air separating their mouths. "I thought you were like me. But the truth is I overestimated myself. The truth is I was never as brave or as daring as you. I wasn't willing to brave the wilds of the heart."

He pressed first one palm, then her other, to his mouth, sending tiny shocks of pleasure through her.

"I love you."

All vestiges of the stubborn past fell away, leaving only her and him and but one response. The joy within her wouldn't be contained. "And I love you."

He closed the distance between them and touched his lips to hers. It was a tentative, almost reverent, kiss. It was the sort of first kiss young girls dreamt of, because they couldn't envision how much more a kiss could be.

Mariana didn't want a dreamy, girlish kiss. She wanted a kiss of flesh and blood and longing and need and raw, unfiltered desire.

She leaned into him and allowed the overcoat to fall off her shoulders. As the full length of her naked torso made contact against him, her hard nipples pressed into the fine lawn of his shirt.

She was a flesh and blood woman. She might be his wife, but she was his lover, too. This new marriage would begin as she meant it to go on.

Just as she moved to match action with intention, he moaned, grabbed her hips, and set her away from him. Her eyes flew open on a squeak of protest.

When he shot to his feet, it was next a gasp of shock that issued forth from the rounded "O" of her lips. Before she could formulate a thought, he was kicking off boots, pulling his shirt over his head, and discarding his trousers in an inelegant frenzy of movement uncharacteristic of the calm and collected Nick she knew. It was fascinating.

She reclined onto her elbows and took in the view of him standing utterly and completely naked, his body taut and magnificent. She didn't know whether to feel aghast or amused.

Quite unexpectedly, she felt aroused.

"You're wilder and braver than I ever had the courage to be," he began, his words nearly tumbling over each other in a rush. "I vow to always stand naked and unafraid before you."

"Oh dear, that might make for some uncomfortable dinner parties," she couldn't help quipping.

"Always, Mariana," he continued, his eyes burning bright with love. "You are forever in my blood. You are forever in my heart."

His vulnerable sincerity reached out and grabbed her heart. She suspected it would never let go. She rose to her feet and tipped her head back to meet his gaze. "We shall be wild and brave together."

This time when his lips claimed hers, the kiss was everything a kiss should be.

And more.

It was everything.